JESUS THE 15TH MESSIAH

JESUS THE 15TH MESSIAH

CHARLES SPELLMANN

To order additional copies of this book, contact:
Xlibris
1-888-795-4274
www.Xlibris.com
Orders@Xlibris.com
752507

CONTENTS

The Preparation ix

Chapter 1	Prologue 1: 5023 BC The Landing 1
Chapter 2	The Attack 5
Chapter 3	Prologue 2: 5023 BCE Assessing the Situation 8
Chapter 4	Gen Alerts Toler 11
Chapter 5	Prologue 3: 5024 BCE Time Structuring 20
Chapter 6	Departure for Earth 23
Chapter 7	Prologue 4: 5025 BCE Natives 38
Chapter 8	En Route on the Sprint 42
Chapter 9	Prologue 5: 5026 BCE Farmer Kine 46
Chapter 10	Pews 49
Chapter 11	Prologue 6: 5027 BCE The Sensitive 56
Chapter 12	Lybur and Sathel 60
Chapter 13	Temptations 65
Chapter 14	Prologue 7: BCE 5027 The Contest 76
Chapter 15	Derxter the Dreaded 79
Chapter 16	Prologue 8: 5027 BCE The Shadow 88
Chapter 17	Prologue 9: 5028 BCE A Celebration 91
Chapter 18	Jerusalem 96
Chapter 19	Masada 101
Chapter 20	Masada II 113
Chapter 21	Arie 118
Chapter 22	Prologue 10: 5027 BCE–0 Assimilation 123
Chapter 23	Prologue 11: 1963 BCE Nibon-Chetak 125
Chapter 24	The Light 131
Chapter 25	Pharisees 133
Chapter 26	Star Arrival 144
Chapter 27	Sarn's Past 146
Chapter 28	Sarn Meets Aleah 151
Chapter 29	Wagon 157
Chapter 30	Lish 167
Chapter 31	Healer 180
Chapter 32	Gaoll 184

Chapter 33   Lish II 189
Chapter 34   Ticol.. 193
Chapter 35   Derxter... 199
Chapter 36   Pigs 210
Chapter 37   Pigs II...215
Chapter 38   Thomas 228
Chapter 39   Derxter Again.. 237
Chapter 40   Sarn Returns.. 252
Chapter 41   To Gennesaret.. 254
Chapter 42   Derxter Recruits.. 257
Chapter 43   On the Run 261
Chapter 44   Last Leg 274
Chapter 45   Lish and Mary Magdalene 283
Chapter 46   Sarn Lost 295
Chapter 47   Find Aleah!... 305
Chapter 48   Look for Derxter 316
Chapter 49   The Decision.. 320
Chapter 50   Lish Looks... 327
Chapter 51   To the Cave 340
Chapter 52   Summing Up 350
Chapter 53   Home Again 358
Chapter 54   Final Scene 370

M-15

Charles M. Spellmann

The Preparation

Ahl leaned back in his chair and smiled wanly. It had been a hard time. Wizl smiled back in return. Yes, it had been a hard time. But often these decisions were difficult. So many people involved. For so many years. And the outcome was never for certain. But this was their job, and they did it the best they knew how.

"We've never been in that part of the universe before," said Wizl.

Ahl shrugged almost imperceptibly. "Maybe it was time."

Wizl said, "My instincts tell me it is the right place for the next placement, even though it does seem quite primitive by our standards."

"How many have we done now?"

Wizl looked at his desk and ran a finger down a list. "This will be the fifteenth placement."

"Hmm. Do you think it is worth it?" Ahl scratched his ear as if expecting an answer to appear.

"Of course. Think how things would be if there were no placements of messiahs. They might still make their lives miserable and even destroy their worlds, but there would be no hope."

Ahl reflected and said, "I suppose that is what our task is all about: setting up a hope for these poor creatures." He mused for a minute and said, "I still wonder if it is worth it. It seems the quality of these beings is so poor that ultimate success for them is hard to come by."

Wizl's eyes flashed. "But their lives are better, if only a little. Think how it would be if they did not have a messiah."

They sat in silence for a while. Ahl said, "Yes, I suppose you are right. What is the plan for this new project, Earth?"

"Oh, the usual. We need for the populace to come up to a certain standard of intelligence and have some achievements to show for themselves. Otherwise, they won't have any instinct as to what to do when the messiah does arrive."

"Yes. One thing we have learned is that a jump start is helpful. What do you have in mind?"

Wizl leaned forward and consulted his notes. "I was thinking about a five-thousand-year priming period."

"Hmm," said Ahl, "that should be enough time to be readied."

"Maybe. I have been thinking of fertilizing the populace with a fortuitous visit from an advanced planet, Bigor."

"Bigor," said Ahl. "Yes, I know that one. They were visited themselves at one time, were they not?"

Wizl nodded. "Turned out well. Of course, they won't know they have been selected to boost the advancement of Earth. These agents never realize they are being used for our purposes."

"Too bad. Sometimes I think the preparatory efforts should be stronger. That could lessen a good deal of the suffering the poor native wretches go through."

"But that is the whole point," Wizl said. "The suffering is necessary for them to grow strong, wrestle with difficulties, know themselves intimately, and hopefully someday become better people." He grimaced. "I often think we are giving humans a task too difficult to be realized."

Ahl looked down and nodded slowly. "But we see such heroic efforts as these creatures try to improve themselves."

"Not enough, usually," said Wizl.

"Are you ready to formulate the plan?"

"That is the part I enjoy the most," said Wizl. "Watching them trying to make sense of the plan is tedious and disappointing."

"And sometimes exciting and gratifying," said Ahl. "Let' do it."

Chapter 1

Prologue 1: 5023 BC
The Landing

The silver spacecraft swooped heavily from the fluffy bank of white clouds. Its sudden dramatic appearance was not as grand as a first visit to a virgin planet should be, but that couldn't be helped. The interstellar ship paused, altered course, paused again as if advertising its uncertainty, and resumed its slow circling descent.

Gliding to the southeast over barren lava beds, the ship headed for the mountains in the distance just before passing over the rugged peaks, the green of riverine vegetation, and oases passed beneath, fed from two giant rivers, which became one. The ship turned and aimed toward the union of the two rivers. More altitude was lost, and it became questionable that it would make it to the green valley.

The sound of metal skirting and groaning over sand, small trees, and a bed of lava rock was a noise never before heard on the planet. The *Star Finder*'s final landing occurred in that area where the mostly sterile lava field merged with the river valley; the encroachment of the valley was a fertile testimony to the healing powers of the flowing water and the passage of time.

The nose of the craft came to rest in the midst of a small group of trees surrounding a pond of water. An angry swirling of gray dust, which had protested the disturbance by chasing the ship to the oasis, settled among the trees as if nothing had happened. After a time the natural sounds, which had hushed for the grating landing, began again. The planet had paused momentarily for the arrival of the uninvited visitor and then went on about its business.

A door opened on one side of the *Star Finder*, and the head and shoulders of a man appeared. He was tall and straight and had the air of one who owned wherever he walked. His face was grim as he carefully surveyed his surroundings. Satisfied that there was no immediate danger, he exited the ship with a short jump to the ground. Other figures, more tentative than the first, followed until there were forty-six men and one woman silently assessing their surroundings. Their mood was somber, almost one of dejection, for they had not planned a stopover on this small planet.

Captain Aladarn spoke to his engineer, "Mr. Dopper, have you found the problem yet?"

"No, sir. I still cannot understand it. We were cutting along, everything normal, when that pulse of energy passed over us. Then barn! We couldn't control her."

The crew moved slowly around the area. There was none of the usual calling back and forth that spontaneously accompanied the exploration of new planets.

"And you say that control of the ship returned as we passed in the proximity of this planet?" The captain wanted to know exactly what had happened to his ship. Never had he lost and regained control of his ship in such a manner.

"Well, in a way of speaking. As you know, Captain, control of the ship was returned but not the power. I suppose we were lucky that this planet was here."

"And the reason for the power loss?"

The engineer looked at the ground. Dopper was a professional man who despised ignorance, especially when it was his own. "I don't know, sir."

Captain Aladarn was confounded by the mysterious happenings. A seasoned veteran of space travel, he had never heard of such a thing.

"Work on restoring the ship, Dopper. Meanwhile, we'll make the best of things around here."

The engineer was not sure he could repair the *Star Finder* but would do what he could. On the one hand, he was excited about the challenge of making a major repair. Most of his time was spent with maintenance items, and seldom was he called on to fully use his engineering skills. On the other hand, he was pessimistic about his chances of repairing the ship. If they had only landed in the grassy valley, the ship's body would not have torn up so badly. It was unfortunate they had not been able to glide that far, but then the *Star Finder* had not been designed to glide.

"Mr. Baken." Aladarn had spied the ship's communication officer.

"Yessir?" The tall thin man was an experienced spaceman and considered by his peers to be as good as there was. Baken was balding and had developed the habit of frequently rubbing his hand over his head as if wiping off excess water. The more upset he was, the more frequently he did this. Baken wiped his head three times while walking over to the captain. Beads of perspiration were visible on his forehead.

"What is your final report? Did we get a message out?"

"Sir, it's the strangest business I have ever been a part of. You told me to send out the distress signals, and I did. But they didn't go anywhere. At least I don't think they did. As best as I can tell, the messages were destroyed as they left the transmitters." Baken appeared apologetic. He was a proud officer who felt personally responsible for anything having to do with the ship's communication.

"Then I must conclude that no one knows where we are. Is that your assessment?"

"Yessir. That is my conclusion. After the radios would not work, we careened around for a good while before arriving here." He indicated the planet with a wave of one hand while wiping his head with the other. "And as far as anyone back on Bigor knows, we are not having problems and we are far from here." Baken wiped his balding head with both hands as if for emphasis. "Captain, I think we are in big trouble."

"You may be right, Baken, but please keep that to yourself. That's an order."

"Yessir." Baken doubted it would be much of a secret to anyone.

It was becoming chillingly clear to Aladam that he and his crew could be marooned on this strange and primitive planet for a very long time.

Chapter 2

THE ATTACK

Lost in deep thought, Toler at first didn't notice that he was being stalked.

What had he sensed?

Frozen in his tracks, Toler attuned his senses to the night. There was the incessant hum of power feeding the city and gently vibrating the pavement beneath his feet. The streetlight's pale-yellow rays were quickly absorbed by the fog, resulting in a luminous gray mist through which blind insects careened. The street was lost in the deep shadows of the night, punctuated only by the occasional gleam of something wet or metallic.

He was of average height and build with slightly large blue eyes and nondescript brown hair. Toler knew of no reason his presence should call attention to himself, yet he felt vulnerable in the yellowish light. All he wanted was to be left alone so he could continue on to Ahna's apartment.

No matter how hard he strained his senses, he could neither see nor hear anything that would explain his sense of foreboding. And yet he knew that something was there in the darkness watching, perhaps even stalking him.

There was a crunch of someone stepping on something.

Then the sound of another footstep, and silence again drowned out everything else. The darkness played with his sight, and he thought he could make out a shape; he looked harder, and the form dissolved. He found himself refocusing, creatively attempting to detect a shadow in the blackness.

"Who's there?" Toler called out self-consciously. There was no law against a bum hiding in the shadows and watching people as they made their way home at night.

He shrugged and resumed walking, imitating a casual saunter while his body remained tense like a coiled spring.

So attuned was he to the shadows behind and to the side that he did not notice the soft muffled ka-thumping of paws on the pavement directly ahead. Toler didn't have time to throw up an arm before he was knocked backward by the leaping creature. His head snapped back against the curb, and consciousness was lost in a foggy swirl of darkness.

He was wakened by a throbbing pain, which rhythmically shot through the middle of his brain and exited through the back of his head. He imagined that his brain tissue was oozing into a neat pool of gray globules.

A rough hand grabbed his head while another pulled open an eyelid.

"Hey, you! Wake up! Wake up!" The voice was foreign, possibly from one of the planets on the Western Fringe, but Toler didn't care at that particular moment where the man had come from.

"Wake up or I will have Artha eat your belly! You hear me?" Artha recognized her name, rumbled deep in her throat, and sidled closer to Toler. Toler could make out the vague form of the beast sitting close to his leg. It placed a large paw on Toler's stomach, spread its long claws, and slowly flexed its toes, leaving four thin crimson lines on his white skin.

Two yellow eyes sat atop a reddish head. A mouth slowly opened, revealing double rows of razor-sharp teeth; hot foul-smelling breath rolled down a rough tongue and into Toler's face. The creature was purposely intimidating him.

"You see, we're not kidding. Artha would love to eat your innards. I've seen her do it before. How she likes to crush human guts with her big jaws!" The man chortled while the animal made grumbling sounds.

"I . . . I'm listening," said Toler. His stomach quaked, lurched, and sought an escape from the hot paw.

"Then here's the message and hear it well! Do not take the M-15 assignment! If you do, we will know, and you will die. And Artha will dine!" The man laughed while Artha, caught up in the excitement, flexed her paw again, sending the claws beneath the skin surface. Toler didn't dare move for fear that the beast would be further agitated and with a simple twist of the paw disembowel him.

Toler was still cringing and holding his breath when he discovered he was alone.

Chapter 3

PROLOGUE 2: 5023 BCE
ASSESSING THE SITUATION

"Captain Aladam!" Evaze called out to the preoccupied captain.

"Hello there, Doctor. Didn't hear you come up."

She stood beside him, and they surveyed the men moving about. In spite of her sense of foreboding about their landing, there was also some persistent, though perhaps irrational, feeling of excitement. Always one for adventure, she had spent her earlier years traveling about the galaxy, helping to colonize new planets. After a few years she became bored with the constant travel and sought a husband. Unfortunately she married the wrong man, a wife abuser, and she shortly divorced the man. Severely burned by that relationship, she returned to space. She was unable to contract on a colonization flight but was able to sign on a routine mapping venture. No stopovers on planets were planned, and for that reason, she almost rejected the offer but felt the need to get away.

"Well, Evaze, what do you think about the situation?" When out of hearing of the crew, he called her by her first name, even though she had not brought herself to the point of reciprocating the informality.

"I can think of a lot of places I'd rather be. That was a rather forlorn bit of country we came down on. Lucky we made it this far." She gestured toward the trees of the valley. "Why didn't we land in the valley? It would have been easier on the ship."

Her tone was not sarcastic or critical, merely inquiring. She respected Aladam enough to know that there had been good reason for landing wherever they came down.

"This, Evaze, was the best we could do. I tried to land in the valley, but the ship didn't make it. I suppose I made an error in glide speed." He admitted guilt to the misplaced landing but did not really believe it was his fault. He had made a long low approach toward the river valley, and the ship, against his will, had prematurely come down on the lava bed as if it had been determined to land there no matter what he wanted. He tensed as he recalled battling the controls and losing. It could have been a mechanical fault but did not feel like one.

"There are some large oceans on this planet, and we didn't have the luxury of scouting the entire globe. The *Star Finder* was not built to glide." He shrugged. "All things considered, I'm thankful we're in one piece."

"How long do you think it will take for help to come?" she asked.

Aladam stared at the mountain range in the distance. It was a light-purple color with snow on the top. He did not feel ready to thrust his conclusions onto his crew, but he trusted Evaze to handle the news better than the others.

"We did not get a message off. The radios wouldn't work. Or the signals were intercepted. We don't know for sure what happened."

Evaze was silent for a while. The implications were clear enough. A part of her was immensely saddened not only for herself but for her fellow crew members. Another part of Evaze—the tough, adaptable colonist—took charge. She gazed at the captain and said, "It is going to be an interesting challenge."

Aladam appreciated this woman more than ever. He forced a smile.

At Aladam's insistence, Dopper continued to work on the ship, even though he had made it clear to the captain that such efforts were hopeless. The crew was notified that they should make themselves comfortable on the planet as they could expect to be there for a while. When asked how long, Aladam was evasive. Evaze, perhaps more easily than the men, set about to make the best of their stay. It was natural that she and the captain, both in parenting positions—his one of authority and hers one of caretaking—should spend considerable time together. This was considered by the crew to be inevitable and desirable: Aladam and Evaze were both greatly respected, and the arrangement dealt effectively with the question of how forty-seven men would handle their feelings about the one available woman.

With the passing of time, the crew sensed that their stay on the planet would likely be much longer than anyone bargained for. The odds of another ship from home happening to find them on this obscure planet belonging to a small star in a foreign galaxy were too small to calculate. The area had not even been mapped; that had been their job.

The months passed, and in spite of everything, the crew adjusted surprisingly well. Aladam kept all of them busy, and that, together with exploration of the new world, gave them little time to worry about their plight

One night Captain Aladam woke up in a sweat, his hands trembling in fear. He lay still and let his mind play back the dream he had just had. He and his crew were the pawns in a grand game of the universe, and there was nothing they could do but play it out. He lay awake the rest of the night, limp, feeling sad, and helpless. No matter how he stretched his imagination, he was unable to fathom the identity of the game player.

Chapter 4

GEN ALERTS TOLER

"What happened to you?"

Ahna, eyes wide with alarm, reached for Toler as he stumbled through the doorway, grimacing in pain. Without waiting for an answer, she helped him to a couch and pulled his bloody shirt back to reveal the claw marks. Her face showed shock and then knitted in concentration as she examined the wound. Within a short period of time, she had cleaned and bandaged the lacerations. When she was finished, she sat back and regarded Toler.

"The wounds aren't deep, but they must hurt a lot. I don't think you need stitches. If you want, I'll take you to the hospital, but the bleeding has stopped now." She sighed.

"What happened?" Toler could see her mental gears change, leaving the mind-set of the competent nurse to that of the concerned girlfriend.

He told her what had happened. "I don't know how he knew I was supposed to go on the M-15 project. Guess he is working for someone in the government."

"You'd better call Sathel and cancel out. I don't want you dead. Didn't you say that animal eats people?"

"The man said the beast likes bellies. And I believe him."

The phone rang. "If you'll answer that, I'll get you something to eat." Ahna left for the kitchen.

"Hello," said Toler into the phone.

"Toler? This is Gen, and I've got to talk to you."

"What? Gen? What's going on?"

"Tonight! In thirty minutes."

"Huh? But—"

"Don't argue. Meet me at Dak's." The phone went dead.

A thin, wiry man with a large angular nose, Gen was head of the Information Bureau in the Space Office and one of the few people important to Toler. It was his job to supervise the gathering of news from around the galaxy and organize it for distribution to civilian news agencies.

The capitol of Xerxes Galaxy was the planet Bigor, a rather large body as planets are measured, located near the center of the star cluster. Every inhabited planet in the galaxy, even most of the newly colonized ones, maintained an emissary on Bigor. Like any other galaxy, most decisions were political to some extent, and it was prudent to have one's own interests represented where those decisions were made.

Toler lay back on the couch and tried to collect his thoughts. If Gen insisted on a meeting, then it must be important. His friend would not lightly ask for such a sudden parley at this time of night, especially knowing that he had interrupted Toler's evening with Ahna.

"Who was it?" Ahna asked, bringing a tray of food and a bottle of wine.

"Gen. He insists on seeing me. Now."

She raised her brow in a question mark. "Does it have to do with what happened to you tonight?"

Toler shrugged and stiffly pulled himself up. "I'll tell you later. I don't have time to eat, but I'll take a glass of that wine."

Alma had prepared a variety of meats and cheeses served with a bottle of wine brought from Euba, a planet colony known for its diverse and fine wines.

Ahna was an employee of Xerxes University. By avocation she was Toler's close companion and lover and by training an anthropologist whose work took her to newly discovered ruins on various planets. She loved her work but admitted to Toler that the travel was often a terrible bore. However, given a choice of that or being confined to a job back on Bigor, she chose the former.

Of average height, with short brownish hair and blue eyes, Ahna usually had a twinkle in her eyes to complement her easy smile. For her, the only serious thing about life was the current dig. Everything else was fair game to be made light of, including Toler, who, fortunately, was not bothered by her teasing. The two of them laughed a lot and spent much time with their heads together discussing a wide range of topics.

Ahna was in her middle thirties, and her parents had given up on her ever marrying, settling down, and presenting them with grandchildren. Although they had always encouraged her to think for herself and do what was important to her, that didn't seem like such good advice anymore. So they called Ahna their "professional" daughter and tried to be pleased—or at least noncritical—about her uncustomary employment.

While they were inseparable when schedules allowed, Toler and Ahna had discussed marriage only briefly; and when Toler backed away, she did not bring it up again. They valued their relationship as it was, and when in port at the same time, where one was, the other could be found. Toler had argued that marriage would not change anything about the amount of time they spent together or enrich the quality of their relationship. Since neither wanted children, a legal binding was irrelevant, he pointed out, and she said nothing more.

"I'm thankful you have a tolerance for disruptions."

"Who said I did?" she retorted in mock anger.

He kissed her on the cheek and left, feeling a sense of genuine gladness for having two friends like Gen and Ahna.

Jo Dak was a tall thick man known best for his burly strength and his body hair. It was said that so much hair covered his body because of an accelerated and necessary evolution of body chemistry on Alker. Within a few short generations, the inhabitants of that cold little planet developed the hair covering as protection against the extreme cold. Why anyone would choose to live on the frigid planet was hard to understand, but the colony had thrived for more than a hundred years.

Twenty-two years ago Jo Dak made the migration from Alker, spent two weeks looking around the city, and then plunked down enough cash to pay for the bar. The seller's mouth fell open when the sack of bills was dumped on his desk. Maybe that was the way things were done on those frontier planets, he thought, and giggled to himself as he pocketed the pile of crisp currency.

No one knew where Jo Dak obtained the large amount of cash, and not many cared. It was not usually a good idea to ask too many personal questions of travelers from other places, particularly those from the outlying planets. Those folks were still adjusting to the hard life of a frontier where rules were made up as needed. Unaccustomed to being told what to do, they were quite touchy about meddlers. Quick violence was often a necessary tool of their existence, and they didn't always appreciate the way things were handled in the civilized cities of the home planet.

Jo Dak had become well-known in the port city, and his bar was a favorite for visitors from the colonies. It was a place where one could discreetly inquire about matters better off not discussed in the light of day. At any given time of day or night, one could find a collection of strange persons meeting over drinks in the dim corners of the bar. Other people, like Gen and Toler, were drawn to Dak's for the confidential atmosphere and the variety of its customers, which provided a most interesting ambiance. Besides that, Gen often picked up news from the colonies, bits and pieces of information often made the basis for later news stories. It was not unusual for Gen to make a news coup by haunting Dak's bar.

Gen was easy to find, sitting in the shadowed booth he and Toler often occupied.

"Coffee," Toler said to the waiter as he passed the bar. "A big one. Black."

Toler slid into the booth beside a grim Gen.

"Are things really that bad, or do I not know despair when I see it?"

Gen said nothing and waited for the coffee to arrive and Toler to take a sip of the hot brew.

"Well?" Toler said, looking at his friend.

Gen leaned forward on the table. "Tell me about your mission to Earth."

"How did you know about that? You rascal, you're not supposed to know about that project. It's classified." Toler sounded more exasperated than he really was. He rather enjoyed Gen's ability to ferret out secret information and frustrate government officials. Toler glanced around the room and spoke in a low voice, "I'm scheduled to leave tomorrow." He glanced furtively around the room. "If I go."

"What do you know about the mission? M-15 is its name, isn't it? What is its purpose?"

Toler studied his cup of coffee. "This is a scientific-cultural mission, orders say. Should be routine, probably boring. These sorts of trips usually are. We'll bring back the data and give it to some egghead in a laboratory. He'll study the results and go gaga over them. Maybe he'll write up a short article, which will be published in an obscure academic journal. No one will read it, but everyone will be happier."

"Think carefully," Gen said. "Is there any reason why this mission would be of importance to Internal Control?"

Toler tried not to appear startled. He sipped his coffee. "Nope. Not that I can see. I have been on missions where security was a concern. IC sent along an escort ship or lent us a few strong bodies to make sure we didn't get in over our heads." Toler shook his head. "The mission files give no reason to expect any problems. No, Gen, IC has no reason to be interested in our mission."

"What would you say if I told you IC has stamped this mission as top priority?"

"Earlier today I would have said you were mistaken because I would have known about it if that was the case." Toler found himself looking around the room, watching for the form of a hungry beast in the shadows.

"Toler, IC has already sent a party to Earth. They'll be there before you land. Hell, they're already there!"

Toler raised his brow in surprise. "That's strange. I wonder why they didn't tell me so we could coordinate the missions."

"I was hoping you'd know the answer to that one. I don't know what's up," said Gen, "but this trip is very important to someone high up in IC. What else do you know about M-15?"

Toler groped for an explanation. He had made a cursory reading of the mission files but found the information to be boring. "Some man was supposedly planted on Earth about thirty years ago. It's one of those PEIs, as they are called, preternatural extraneous intervention, and our mission is to confirm that the fellow was in fact planted." Toler shrugged. "If it was called preternatural intervention—extraneous, it would be a PIE in the sky." He smiled at his attempt at humor, and Gen rolled his eyes and groaned.

"We're to document any leadership ability, unusual events, and make an estimate of the agent's influence on the populace. Lots of it will have to be speculation, guesswork. How do you measure a man's influence on people by just watching? You can't give tests or even film the people because you have to be absolutely incognito. But that's what they want, and the experts will find a way to give it to them."

"Anything else?"

Toler furrowed his brow. "Not that I can think of."

"Who are you taking with you? Experts, you said?"

"I suppose so. That information was not available when I picked up my mission details. Whoever Sathel has picked for the mission will meet me at the ship tomorrow. I don't even know how many are going!"

"I am interested in finding out the identity of your passengers," said Gen. "My sources cannot locate anything about them. Most puzzling."

"Yes, it has been handled strangely. Generally, long before now I have a list of the crew with a complete rundown on each, and they're calling me weeks ahead of time, asking questions and bothering me with details."

"Most unusual."

"If I find out tomorrow before I leave, I'll let you know." Toler sipped his coffee. "So what else is there? You wouldn't have insisted on meeting me tonight just to ask these questions."

"You are right, my friend. You see, IC's mission to Earth is to sabotage the PEI, to make sure it fails."

Toler studied Gen's face, blank surprise showing on his own. He slowly mouthed his thoughts. "But if M-15 is top priority with IC, that means—"

"That if you get in the way," Gen continued, "you and your party will be eliminated." Gen sipped his coffee. "That is why, Toler, I had to see you. Your life may be in danger."

Both men were still, lost in thought, pondering answers to barely formulated questions. The cuts on Toler's stomach burned. Three short men bustled by their table, lost in their own conversation, sounding much like a hive of bees as they whispered furiously among themselves.

"Gen, my life is already in danger." He brought his friend up-to-date on the attack and threat by the man and his large animal. Shaking his head, Toler groaned. "Explain that to me!"

"It's nothing personal against you, I'm sure. It's just that they won't let anyone interfere with their plans," Gen said.

"Not personal? Let them start sending giant carnivorous animals after you, my brave and daring philosophical friend, and then tell me if you take it personally."

"Point made," said Gen. "What did the man look like? Any identifying marks?"

"None. Just an ordinary, seedy-looking middle-aged fellow who might have fallen off any starship from one of the outer planets. With his pet. Never saw an animal like that before."

"Guys like that are everywhere here in Bigor. I'll keep an eye open for someone of that description, but he was probably just hired to do what he did and doesn't know any more than what he told you."

A hand fell on Toler's shoulder, and he startled. "It's just me. I'm sorry I startled you." Ahna sat down beside him and nodded a greeting to Gen. "The more I thought about what happened tonight, the more worried I became. Why can't I be in on this too? I already am, you know."

Toler glanced around the dimly lit room. It seemed that there were more people than before. "Am I just paranoid, or are a lot of these people watching us?"

"As a matter of fact," said Gen quietly, "I was just thinking the same thing."

"I don't want to alarm you unnecessarily," said Ahna, "but when I arrived, there was some man outside. He had a large animal with him. They didn't look very friendly."

"Did they notice you?" asked Toler urgently.

"No, I don't think so. They were standing in the shadows to the side, like they were waiting for someone."

"Yeah! Let's go somewhere else. Let's go out the back. How about the SpaceCafe?"

SpaceCafe had been opened over twenty years ago by a family who arrived from another planet and didn't have sufficient funds to leave the terminal. After years of saving so they could come to Bigor, the family of two parents and seven children found they did not have enough money to even get into town after they landed. Being resourceful people, they made camp in an empty lot adjacent to the spaceport, prepared and sold what food they had brought with them, and made enough money to buy some more. The wife's reputation as a cook spread quickly, and pilots stopped by their "camp" to buy meals. Space food was decidedly unappetizing, and the pilots were more than glad to buy several meals from the woman to take with them on their missions.

When their ships returned, pilots and crew found it convenient to stop for a bite to eat. It just so happened that the main eating establishments were on the other side of the terminal where the tremendous flow of passengers could be accommodated. No one had ever thought that there would be a market for flight personnel, and so there was no other restaurant on this side of the giant terminal. Besides that, pilots and their crews enjoyed doing anything unconventional.

Soon the family rented a storefront and hung out a sign. The woman had brought several unusual recipes from her home country, all of which utilized a garlic-like bulb. Everyone found these dishes to be delicious, and it was not long before the family had several buy-out offers. The husband was a good businessman, astute enough at least to know that he had hold of something good, and the rest was history.

Within a few minutes the three had settled at a table in SpaceCafe.

"I apologize for the lack of atmosphere," Toler kidded Gen, "but at least we won't have to worry about who is at the next table."

Toler waved at the waitress and asked who was on cook duty.

"Farz is. Farz is the cook tonight. You want something from the kitchen?"

"Yeah, tell Farz it's Toler and some friends. Fix us one of those plates of Doiboin appetizers."

The three were soon lost in a conversation about M-15 and IC's interest. Toler repeated to Ahna about IC's intent to exterminate anyone who stood in their way.

"That's not only probably illegal," she said, "it's wrong. It's dangerous!" She was so upset that she had trouble collecting her thoughts. "That's just like the government!" she finally managed to say, slamming her hand down on the table. Heads at the next table turned. She usually dismissed as exaggerated Toler's and Gen's cynicism about government but occasionally became even angrier than they did.

"How much does Sathel know about IC's intentions?" Toler asked Gen.

"He knows enough but can't prove anything and, what's worse, can't do anything about it without disturbing life on that planet—what's its name?"

"Earth. He could send a contingent of special troops with you, but that would be fairly disruptive to the natives."

"What upsets me right now is that Sathel knew my life was in danger and didn't tell me." Toler shook his head. "Either the head of the galaxy is faced with such big problems that he believes I am expendable for some greater good, or else there is something going on I just don't understand."

"You can't go," Ahna said simply. "They'll kill you if you do."

"Only if they can catch me before blastoff tomorrow. But I'm not sure if I want to go now. I've got to talk to Sathel."

"A caution," said Gen. "If you talk to Sathel, believe that his line is bugged and that whoever threatened to kill you will know your decision."

They sat in thoughtful silence for a while. "So, Ahna, do you have any ideas about how come this trip is of interest to IC?" Gen asked.

Ahna furrowed her brow in thought. She was a very intelligent, professionally trained woman who fulfilled some of her deepest needs by digging up the remains of ancient civilizations. Finding artifacts and deducing how they fit into the lives of a people, discovering how old objects served as the glue of a culture's day-to-day life, and learning the symbols of its age-old myths, that was where Ahna was at her best. But this business of modern-day politics was of little interest to her and an arena she considered stupid.

"Who is head of IC these days?" Toler asked.

"A man named Lybur," Gen answered. "You really do lose contact with what goes on here, don't you? Lybur has been at the helm for about four years now, long enough to put his programs into effect and become fairly well entrenched."

"What kind of a man is he?" asked Ahna.

"Not a lot is known about Lybur's history," Gen continued. "He came up the hard way. Spent several of his early years on a frontier planet. Had a rough time of it but survived. Came to Bigor, went to work for the government, and worked his way up. Lybur is a secretive duck, paranoid, convinced that there is someone behind every door plotting to get him if he relaxes."

"Maybe that's the key," Ahna said. "If he is paranoid, maybe he feels threatened by someone and is trying to defend himself."

"Come on, everybody," said Toler. "Who on Earth could be threatening him? Earth is a simple, backward relatively new planet off in the backwaters of the universe. Lybur is head of IC, one of the highest offices—and probably the second most powerful position—in the government of Xerxes Galaxy, which is probably the most advanced civilization around these parts."

"You may or may not know this," said Gen. "After Lybur came to power, Xerxes troops massacred the entire population of an outpost on some new planet. The people there were not properly compliant or something. That's one I'm still trying to plumb. Anyway, the troops went berserk and shot everyone. There was an investigation, of course, and the field commander was convicted and punished, but Lybur was cleared. Some thought Lybur should have been held responsible. Me, for one."

Toler and Ahna were silent, thoughtful. "No, I had not heard of that," said Toler. "Why would troops go berserk and shoot people? I didn't think we did massacres."

"What's the point, Gen? What does that massacre have to do with the present situation?" asked Ahna.

"Just to point out that Lybur has previously been involved in some questionable and violent incidents. Frankly I think the man is a little crazy."

The three of them sipped coffee and thought of questions for which they knew there was no available answer.

"It seems to me," mused Gen, "that the whole thing has to do with the—what did you call it?—PEI or something like that?"

"Preternatural extraneous intervention," Toler offered.

"PEIs are supposed to result in peace and quiet and all those good things. These agents are against war and violence. If the PEI succeeded on Earth, I cannot imagine how that would affect Lybur's position in Xerxes."

"The only thing I can come up with is this," said Ahna. "If Lybur can discredit a PEI on Earth, then does that discredit PEIs on other planets? That sounds far out, but think about it."

"I'm trying and not doing too well," said Toler. "Maybe Lybur believes his job will be in jeopardy if a PEI brings peacefulness."

"If PEIs can be cast in a bad light, how would that matter back home?" continued Ahna.

"Maybe I see a thread," said Gen. "Take the Hoxd Galaxy, for example. They've had a PEI or two, haven't they?"

"One, I think," said Toler. "But he was a dandy—seemed to affect the whole galaxy. Things haven't been the same in Hoxd since."

Gen rose from his chair. "You best go home and sleep lest you crash your ship tomorrow."

Ahna said, "Why don't you just ask Sathel what is going on? You have a right to know."

"Sathel can't stop IC," said Gen. "But I do believe he has an obligation to alert you and your passengers about the dangers. You should be prepared. I am frankly surprised—and greatly disappointed—that you have not already been briefed."

"Or else the mission cancelled," said Ahna. "You've contracted with the government many times, but I don't recall them ever letting you go on a mission blindly."

Toler was thoughtful. "You're right. I'll call Sathel first thing in the morning. I couldn't get through to him tonight."

Gen nodded, and Ahna patted his hand. "Do you still want to know who my passengers are?"

"Yes. Please let me know before you leave." Gen waved good night and left his two friends.

Chapter 5

Prologue 3: 5024 BCE
Time Structuring

Sheniile enjoyed eating more than most anything he could think of. His big belly and his exceptional height made for a rather formidable appearance, but his fellow crewmen knew him as a jovial, kidding fellow, whose gentle nature was admired by all. They had also come to realize that his size belied his agility. In fact, while crawling down catwalks and up and down ladders in the bowels of the ship, he was almost graceful in his movements. Shemile enjoyed his work and was sensitive to the men with whom he worked. On this day he was aware that Ernal had something on his mind.

"What's up, Ernal?" Shemile asked offhandedly, glancing up from his full plate of food.

Ernal smiled and shook his head as if he was full of something that wasn't quite ready to be told but was too good to be kept to himself.

"What's the news from the South Quad?" Shemile asked. The area surrounding the *Star Finder* had been divided into quadrants, and crew members had been assigned to the areas.

Such organization was not only practical, but it gave the men a sense of owning and regulating the planet.

"Oh, you could say things are interesting in the South Quad," Ernal replied between bites, still smiling.

"Is that so?" said Argon from down the table. "I'd sure trade you for what we've got going in the East. It is sooo boring. Dulldom itself."

"So? What's going on in the South?" Shemile pressed, throwing a quiet smile toward his friend.

Ernal glanced around the dining hall as if making certain no one was listening and lowered his voice conspiratorially, "Those groups of natives have been watching us while we are on patrol. They've been real curious, even almost look over our shoulders trying to see us run our tests."

"As if they'd know what you were doing if you told them." Argon laughed. "These natives are curious but so ignorant."

"Believe it or not," Ernal said and laid his spoon down, "one of these natives is a female. I started noticing her a couple of weeks ago. Not bad looking, by local standards, anyway. Not bad by Bigor standards either come to think of."

"At this point in time and space, all females look good!"

"Uh-huh," Argon moaned. "Here it comes. Ernal is in love with a native wench!"

Ernal pulled himself up straight. "Maybe you prefer boys, Argon, but there are some of us who have sufficient instinctual integrity to be interested in those of the opposite sex."

"Instinctual integrity? Where did you read that, Ernal?"

Shemile reflected aloud, "Let's see. It has been almost a year that we have been here. I suppose almost any female will look good before long. If you find an extra one, Ernal, let me know and we'll double date."

Argon's face had turned red. "You dummy! Of course I like women, but you know it is against policy to fraternize with the natives. Aladam would have me put away for a year if he caught me fooling around with a native female."

"I don't think so," said Ernal. "It seems that the captain is looking the other way when it comes to fraternization."

"You may be right," Shemile said. "Come to think of it, it does seem that discipline has been loose. You don't hear of anyone being called up for disciplinary reasons. And there have been situations when that could have been done."

"I'll tell you what it is," Argon said, his face still red. "Aladam knows we're not ever leaving this place, and he's afraid to hold the reins too tightly, afraid he can't control the men. Not with him having the only woman."

"Or else," mused Shemile with a wry smile, "he is giving us freedom to settle in with the natives and live happily ever after."

The men sat in silence, each lost in his own thoughts of Bigor and the families they had left behind. Loneliness was a regular visitor to the crew of the *Star Finder*.

"Well, I've got work to do," said Argon and left the table.

"Yeah, me too." Ernal pulled back and gathered his plate and utensils together for deposit in the kitchen.

Shemile sat silently as one by one the crewmen left the table and wandered away, each choosing to be alone with his loneliness. After a while Shemile was the only one still sitting at the table, and his food was cold and half eaten. He jerked at the realization that a tear had formed in his eye. He self-consciously brushed it away, quickly glanced around to make sure no one had seen, and left the table.

It would be a quiet evening aboard the *Star Finder*.

Chapter 6

Departure for Earth

Toler called Sathel's office at midmorning. Although not available right away, Sathel returned Toler's call within the hour. Toler was to the point and asked what Internal Control had to do with his mission.

"You have a good source of information," said Sathel. "Believe it or not, I had planned to contact you before you left. Of course I would never send you—or anyone else—on a mission without the fullest preparation possible!"

"I have had no preparation at all for this mission." Toler's voice barely controlled his anger. "Besides that, somebody threatened my life over M-15 last night. This morning."

There was a silence while Sathel processed the last information. "Tell me what happened."

Toler told Sathel about the events of a few hours ago. "What is going on? Why haven't I been better prepared?"

"I'm sorry about your scare. I don't know anything about it, but you can rest assured I will check into it. If you wish to back out of the mission, I will respect that under the circumstances. Are you all right?"

"For now. Will you keep an eye on Ahna? They could try to use her against me if I don't cancel."

"Of course. I'll have her watched until you return. And listen, Toler, you have been prepared as well as was possible under the conditions," Sathel said in a firm voice. "These are most unusual circumstances, and on your return I hope to share them with you. Take me seriously when I say that you are the only man I would trust for this job."

Toler had been doing contract jobs for Sathel for many years and knew that his work was valued. Nevertheless, it was good to hear an occasional word of appreciation. "Thank you, sir. Another question: I'm told IC is already on Earth."

There was a pause. Then Sathel said, "That is my latest information too. In fact, I haven't been able to confirm that as of now, and that's why I'm late contacting you."

"Do you still want the mission?" asked Toler.

"More than ever. The opportunity to study a PEI is a once-in-a-lifetime experience. Neither of us will ever get such a chance again!"

"I understand that," said Toler grimly, "but I don't want to get killed over it."

"The key is this," said Sathel. "IC doesn't think I'll send anyone, and even if they did, there is now no way to get word to their agents. So just stay incognito while on Earth and you'll be all right."

"You don't want me to interfere with their interference," said Toler.

"That's right," said Sathel, "unless in your judgment you need to. I trust your judgment." The implications of Sathel's statement were not clear, but Toler didn't have the energy to ask for clarification. He was sure he wouldn't understand it anyway. Under what conditions could a contracted ship captain interfere in the course of history on a primitive planet?

"One thing bothers me a lot," said Toler. "And that's what this is all about. It's more than IC not wanting you to observe a PEI. That's no big deal!"

"IC wants to obliterate the PEI regardless of me. They threatened you—and me, I might add—because they don't want any witnesses to what they are doing. If you don't go to Earth, IC won't bother us anymore."

"Why does IC want to get rid of the PEI on Earth?"

"Let's be accurate about this. It's not the Office of Internal Control that is behind it. It's Lybur, who just happens to be an official of the galaxy. But your question is legitimate."

"Listen, I don't know if I can get this over to you in a few words, but when you get back, we'll go into more detail. Essentially the PEI is a movement of sorts, and I expect it to gain some impetus as it develops on Earth. Lybur represents another movement, a rather strong force, which is devoted to eliminating PEIs wherever they can find them."

"Are these political movements?"

"They end up political in many ways inevitably. They are often cast in religious molds, but at core they are movements that ultimately control people. That is the overriding issue: control."

Toler paused, tried to digest what he had heard, and filed it away; he needed now to clarify more pressing and practical issues than the control of whole populations. "What about my crew? I usually know by now who is going with me."

"Yes, I know, and again I apologize. Just one is all you'll need. More than that and it would be hard to stay undercover. I'm counting on the two of you observing enough to make a full report."

"We will report what we see."

"If you're uncomfortable, you can cancel out. No hard feelings."

"I don't like it, but I'll go," said Toler. "Thanks for the information. Oh, by the way, how long is the mission expected to last? I didn't find that information in the file."

"It's not there because there is no way to know. I suspect you'll be there several months, maybe longer."

Toler was shocked. He had never been on a mission that required longer than three months, and that was only once. For long-term projects, he usually deposited the professionals on the planet and returned later to pick them up.

"Did I understand you correctly? Several months or longer? I don't know if I can be gone that long. My other contract suppliers will find someone else to do their work. When I come back, I'll have to start over. Do you know how long it has taken me to establish?"

"Hold on, Toler," Sathel interrupted. "You weren't told before because I didn't want you making extra arrangements. That would have alerted someone to the project. As it is, IC does not know for sure if anyone is going for me. By the time anyone asks questions about where you've gone, it'll be too late for them to do anything different." Sathel paused. Toler waited. "As to your concern about your business, relax. I'll make sure you get all the work you can handle when you get back. Besides that, for this job the rate is doubled plus expenses, plus bonus, plus hardship pay for being gone so long."

Toler mentally calculated the hefty fee while Sathel waited. "All right, I'll do it. On one condition. That you let Ahna and Gen know that I'll be gone for that long. I likely won't have time to speak with them before blastoff."

"Done!"

And that had been the sum of Toler's conversation with Sathel.

The *Sprint* was a small ship designed to carry as many as eight passengers and their baggage and equipment. It could be outfitted for long journeys if necessary but primarily was used for charters and ferrying people back and forth between planets. It was an older craft, well taken care of, and the only thing of any real value to Toler. He had almost paid it off and was looking forward to the day when it would have no debt.

The sole crew member was waiting when the captain arrived at the hangar.

Toler walked to the pad where the *Sprint* was parked and noticed a gangling figure waiting for him. The boy, one hand stuffed awkwardly in his pocket and the other holding a duffel bag, nervously ambled over to him.

"Hello. I'm Sarn." The boy was self-conscious, and Toler looked at him questioningly.

"What can I do for you?" Toler was in no mood to be friendly.

"I'm supposed to ship out with you. On the *Sprint*. Here." He fumbled for the OBA card and handed it to Toler. "You are Captain Toler?"

Toler carefully looked at the card and then at Sarn. He wasn't too impressed with what he saw. "Are you Sarn?"

Sarn nodded. "I wasn't told my crew would be a kid!" Toler added gruffly.

"I'm eighteen," Sarn blurted out. "And I work hard."

Toler looked the boy over and shook his head. "Follow me."

Sarn picked up his bag, stumbled, and almost fell over a step. The boy stood around looking useless while the captain did his preflight checks.

"Give me a hand," Toler commanded, indicating the top of the wing. To Toler's satisfaction, Sarn didn't hesitate to climb the ladder and make a visual check of the wings. The boy helped eagerly when he knew what to do. Other than Toler's commands and Sarn's "yessirs," nothing else was said between them during the rest of the preflight and takeoff.

Once they had cleared the airways of Bigor, Toler shifted the craft into hyperspace drive.

"You can unbuckle now." Toler kept an eye on Sarn, his one passenger and crew member, totally inexperienced and young enough to be his son. Toler shook his head in disgust.

After he had taken Ahna home, it had been no problem to hide out for a few hours while waiting for the time of departure. Once he had slowly passed his apartment and caught a glimpse of a man and animal in the shadows. He didn't go back by the apartment after that. He consoled himself with Sathel's statement that once Toler was gone, there was no way IC could do anything—short of sending another force to Earth to track him down and destroy the mission. That seemed unlikely since there was already a force there with that very purpose.

But Toler still fumed about the way he had been treated by Sathel. It should have been handled better!

"Can we move around?" asked Sarn, breaking Toler out of his reverie.

"Sure. Make yourself comfortable."

Sarn stretched his long slender eighteen-year old body and uncoiled himself from the chair. Tall and boyishly handsome, Sarn had perpetually rumpled blond hair and a fair complexion. Possessing the long and supple muscles of a swimmer, he walked with an easy grace, which sometimes alternated with adolescent clumsiness. Sarn had a quick smile, even teeth, and an unassuming air about him.

Sarn had proven to be handy when helping Toler ready the *Sprint*. He was an able learner, possessed a quick mind, and was willing to work hard without complaining. If the boy tended to be shy, maybe a little reclusive, that was a plus.

Nothing was more irritating to Toler than to have a chatterbox passenger wanting to talk his ear off.

Toler knew little about the boy's background even after he read Sathel's brief identity report. It gave the usual vital statistics and two references from past teachers. The information had apparently been taken from the local hiring agency as it did not seem complete or especially relevant to anything in particular. It was essentially the same information he would get when taking aboard a cabin boy. The only possible relevancy was contained in one of the letters of reference from Sarn's former philosophy teacher, T. Jonti, who mentioned in the middle of a favorable report that "this serious young man, in the two years I have known him, has exhibited a sharp interest in the phenomenon of religion."

"Captain Toler, I just want to thank you again for letting me take this trip with you," said Sarn, again interrupting the captain's thoughts.

"Oh well, you know how the government is. It's much easier not to plan too well." Sarn's face fell. Toler realized that he wasn't being fair to the boy but didn't feel like apologizing. He was still too piqued over how the mission had been put together. "The more the government plans, the bigger the problems created," he said, ignoring Sarn's hurt expression.

There was an awkward silence before Toler asked, "Besides, Sarn, you already had some interest in religion, didn't you?"

Sarn blushed. "Yes—I mean no. That's all right, isn't it? Is our mission about religion?"

"Is there something wrong with having an interest in religion?"

Sarn turned even redder, shook his head, and mumbled, "No. Maybe. I guess it depends on who you talk with."

"If you have a problem with religion, you'd better get over it soon. From what I've read in the preparatory report, the trip may be more religion than the average person can stomach."

It was hard for Toler to believe that such an inept person would be assigned to what was supposed to be a mission of some importance. The boy came across innocently enough as if he had just happened to be standing in the right place when it was decided that a crewman was needed. In spite of having no training or experience. In spite of being so green. Toler half expected to see grass growing out of Sarn's ears.

Before launching, Toler called Gen's office but could not reach his friend. He left Sarn's name with Gen's secretary and added, "Tell Gen he's just a kid!"

"Pardon me, Captain, I did not catch that last part you said."

"Let me understand something, Sarn." Toler ignored Sarn's question and turned to face him. He was suddenly feeling paranoid about his unknown crewman. "I need to be perfectly clear on this. How much do you know about the mission?"

Sarn looked puzzled. "Nothing. I told you already. Nothing, really."

"How was it that you were chosen for the trip?"

"I don't know."

"Isn't it strange that you would be chosen for an expedition to outer space and yet not be told how you were so qualified that you were chosen over many others?" Toler was familiar with the many young people on the OBA steps jostling for a place in space.

"Yes, sir. I mean no, sir. I don't know how they choose anyone. Have I done something wrong?"

The boy slumped in his seat and turned his head away to hide his gathering tears. He had been so excited about making the trip, and so far he had been the butt of the captain's sarcasm and mistrust. It would have been better if he had not been chosen, he thought. Sarn looked straight ahead as he spoke, trying to ignore the burning lump in his throat.

"They didn't tell me much of anything. I don't know where we are going. Or why. Or when we'll get back. They gave me a chance to make the trip, and I took it."

"All right." Toler decided he believed the boy. "Now settle down and don't take it so personally when I ask you questions."

"Yes, sir."

"Go read the preparatory report. It should give you an understanding of what it is we are about. As much as I have, anyway."

The days passed without incident. Although in reality there was no such thing as day and night on a spaceship in the middle of the universe, a clock schedule was observed in order to preserve time structure; otherwise, people became disorganized and inefficient. In spite of everything, Toler found that he liked Sarn. He seemed respectful and reasonably bright.

The boy spent a good deal of time in the ship library. Expedition ships such as the *Sprint*" carried extensive libraries on microchips. It was possible to quickly locate as much information as needed—usually much more than usable. The ability to appropriate information many times had made the difference between survival and death in new and hostile environments.

After reading the file, Sarn found his original enthusiasm about the trip rekindled. He forgot that his feelings had been hurt several times by the captain, and he turned his attention to understanding the project.

The mission had been codenamed Star Light and was described in a file by the same name.

The title page read: "Star Light: An Investigation into the Appearance of an Isolated Star-like Phenomenon Located at the Planet Earth."

At the bottom of the page was the inscription: "Reference Hoxd Incarnation Project."

Sarn had read about expeditions sent to explore newly discovered stars or other celestial bodies. He had never talked to anyone who had actually made such a trip, but he had heard that the missions were incredibly boring. He hoped the Star Light mission would be at least interesting.

Events had moved quickly since he had been suddenly hired on the *Sprint* a few days ago. There had been no time to reflect on how he had been so fortunate to get the job. He had registered at the Outward Bound Agency, referred to simply as the OBA by most people. A privately owned company with close government associations, its purpose was to maintain a pool of space personnel who could be available on a moment's notice. Most of those chosen were skilled or professional. There were occasionally slots for nonskilled persons, but Sarn had always been skipped over because of his age and his lack of experience.

He had spent much time on the front steps of the OBA with others his own age, lamenting the poor prospects of ever being able to take a mission. Some young people, those with more resources, went into training and eventually were hired on as apprentices. Others, such as Sarn or his roommate, Tull, did not have the funds for training. They, along with many others, hung around the OBA hoping for a chance to sign on a ship. Chances were very small, and in a year or two most of them went on to something more productive than waiting on the OBA steps. They were replaced by an endless supply of young romantics, all dreaming of space travel.

Sarn would have gone into training but did not have the funds. Although his parents were both professionals with access to adequate resources, they had chosen not to send their son to school. This was a painful subject for Sarn, one he preferred not to think of.

On the day he had been hired, Sarn had registered first thing in the morning as he had done for several months. He sat on the OBA steps and bantered with several of the other boys.

That morning he had been thinking of how he came to be on the steps of OBA. It was not because his parents had wanted him to be there. Actually he had received little encouragement from his parents when he had left home several months before.

Hah! That was an understatement.

Sarn had never understood the way his parents treated him. Sometimes he was certain they had him confused with someone else; and one day they would realize their error, apologize, hold him tight, and everything would be all right.

The end had come rather suddenly. His father came to his room as Sarn was dressing.

"Sarn, your mother and I have come to a most regrettable but inevitable conclusion. We believe that it is time for you to be on your own and discover your own course in life. As you know, we have diligently attempted to help you make a satisfactory adjustment but have failed. We believe there is nothing more to be served by your continued residence in the home."

Sarn sank to his bed, mouth open, unable to believe what he was hearing. He knew he made his parents uncomfortable, but he never thought he would be evicted.

"Therefore, Sarn, we would like for you to go out to meet the world, find out what you need to know, and develop what talents you may find in yourself." His father laid some money on the bed. "This should be enough to get you started." He rose to leave.

"Oh, there is no hurry about it. You'll need a few days to get your things together and make your plans. Shall we say five days?"

Sarn sat on his bed, stupefied. After a while he made a decision: he would leave immediately. He let his eyes rove over his room: the desk where he had spent many evenings studying, the two shelves of books he prized so much because he had bought them himself, the abstract posters that upset his mother so much "because they just didn't mean anything!" and the box of valuables he had collected over the years including a small book, home published on Seket, a newly colonized planet, and a dried giant locust from another newly settled planet.

He got a few of his things together, including the money he had saved, and walked downstairs. His father's money was left on the bed. He wanted nothing from them. They looked up as he came into the front room with his bag as if he was a stranger passing through. He told them he was leaving, and they did not seem surprised or upset. His father nodded, and his mother clucked something about being careful of strangers. Sarn had never felt so frustrated as he did at that moment. He loved them, for he had been with them all his life. They were supposed to love him too, or at least care about his welfare, for they had birthed and reared him. In spite of their differences with him and in spite of the disappointment he had been to them, they were still supposed to love him. He was their flesh and blood.

They were supposed to love him!

But there was no show of emotion as he passed through the room. The thought flashed through his mind that he should explain he was leaving then and not later and that they might never see him again. But he knew they knew. And deep down he knew they didn't love him, and that was what was so frustrating: they were supposed to love him, and they didn't.

He paused at the door and turned toward them, hoping they would say something. The little boy inside Sarn cried out for a reprieve, and his parents regarded him with disinterest.

Walking away from his home with a single bag of his belongings was the saddest Sarn had ever felt. If they had called after him to return home, he would have turned and ran back to them. He didn't understand why, but Sarn was convinced that there was no way he could please them, even though he had genuinely tried for as long as he could remember.

For the rest of that day and into the night, Sarn roamed the streets, feeling lost and bereft, occasionally crying. He walked until he was exhausted. Sometime early the next morning he found an opening under a house, crawled into the space, curled up, and slept.

The sun had been up for some time when Sarn awoke. He lay under the house for a while, listening to occasional footsteps above him or catching glimpses of movements on the street.

He had an impulse to return home and ask his parents if they could try again but dismissed it. Maybe his father was right about Sarn being a "softie" who needed to grow up. If so, now was the time to do it.

Sarn rolled out from under the house and began walking again. By noon he had made his way to the Departure Area, a huge complex of hangars, launching pads, terminals, shipping depots, and structures of related use. Over the top of the buildings, he could occasionally see the tip of a ship pointed toward the sky. There was a great deal of activity in the area, and Sarn found himself in the midst of a crowd thronging the sidewalk. People of varied descriptions passed him, all part of the space travel industry, the most extensive and important complex of activities in the galaxy. The economies of the planets had become extremely interdependent, and it was no longer possible to think in terms of what was good for only one planet.

Sarn was hungry but too tired to figure out where he could get something to eat. He sank down on against the pillar, which was part of a huge commercial building. He knew he shouldn't sit here at a business site but didn't care. The pillar was cool to his back, and his eyelids drooped. He was almost asleep when someone sat down next to him.

"Hi." The voice belonged to a young man not too much older than Sarn. He reached into a sack and pulled forth what appeared to be a sandwich. He broke it in half and offered one part to Sarn.

"Thanks." Sarn didn't pause as he gratefully accepted the food and promptly disposed of it.

"You were hungry. My name is Tull. What's yours?"

"Sarn." He watched his benefactor eat his part of the sandwich. Tull was not as tall as Sarn but was wider in the shoulders. His long black hair and dark complexion contrasted with Sarn's light coloring. Tull's mouth curved downward as if he was chronically sad, but his eyes twinkled and hinted of fun and secrets. Sarn liked him immediately.

"You're new around here," Tull said. "Are you registered at OBA?"

Sarn looked at him blankly before it occurred to him where he was. He shook his head. "No, I'm not." Everyone knew about the Outward Bound Agency from the time they were old enough to dream about space travel.

Tull looked at Sarn incredulously. "You're not registered with OBA? All right, my friend, what are you doing here?" he inquired in a direct but friendly manner.

Sarn shrugged. "Passing through, I guess."

Tull glanced at his bag. "Traveling light."

"I can move faster that way. Get there quicker—when I find out where I'm going."

Tull's face lit up. "Why don't you stay with me? My roommate left, and I need somebody to help with the rent. It's not much of a place, but it's good enough for us." Tull's reference to *us* brought a warm feeling of relief to Sarn. It was nice to belong somewhere.

Tull's apartment was high above the street at the end of a hall in an old hotel. At one time it had been a large bathroom.

There were two beds, a table with two chairs, an ancient refrigerator, and an endless variety of nails protruding from the walls for the purpose of hanging things on.

"It's not much, as I said, but it's a good-enough place to hang your hat at night. For the price, especially." His eyes twinkled.

Tull apparently wanted a roommate not only to share with expenses but also to listen to him. He talked until late the night, and Sarn was asleep long before Tull gave up his monologue and turned out the light.

Sarn learned that Tull was a "space freak," one of those people who still believed, even after passing adolescence, that the most wonderful thing in the whole universe was space travel. Not having any formal training and in most cases very little experience, space freaks waited for their chance to work on a freighter. The pay was poor, but it was one possible way to get into space.

The next day Sarn found a part-time job in front of the main municipal terminal. While taxis waited for customers to come out of the terminal building, their drivers would pay to have their cabs cleaned. Sarn worked hard, wiping off the cabs, cleaning the windows, and running small errands for the drivers who did not want to leave their stations.

Every night Sarn listened to Tull relate stories of space travel and adventure he had heard from the other boys. The verity of the stories was questionable but irrelevant, for they were entertaining and sparked excitement in those who listened. It was in that way that Sarn became a space freak.

Sarn had been about ready to leave the OBA for the day, having decided that the chances of being selected were slim and none, when the door of the OBA opened and the face of the OBA official appeared. The boys had named him Squeaks because he wore a pair of squeaky shoes. He didn't wear those shoes every day and, in fact, may not have still had them. But it was enough that one day, once upon a time, he had worn loudly squeaking shoes. Besides, they did not know what else to call the man.

"Sarn," Squeaks called out. "Is there a Sarn present?"

So surprised was Sarn that he felt paralyzed to respond. He could not utter a word but did manage to raise his hand.

"Take this if you are available," said Squeaks.

Sarn was handed a card with a time and dock number and the ship's name, *Sprint*. Under that was Toler, the name of the captain. The others crowded around Sarn.

"That's a small ship. I've seen it before."

"Never heard of the captain. Don't think he runs the big ones."

"Probably a garbage run." Garbage run was the name given to a short jump from one planet to another and return. Such trips didn't amount to much in terms of time and experience. Their purpose could be anything from delivery of passengers to a package pickup. In spite of the pejorative references, any of the boys would have given an arm and a leg for an assignment to one.

"How did you get it? You haven't been around here as long as some of us."

Sarn did not know how he was chosen, but he walked around on a cloud for the rest of the day. Tull congratulated him and seemed genuinely happy, although by all rights he was more deserving. After all, it was he who had converted Sarn to the dream of space travel.

"Should I keep your bed empty for you?"

Sarn shrugged. "I have no idea how long I'll be gone." He read the call sheet again, but there was nothing entered in the space describing the duration of the trip. "Here's money for the rest of the month. After that, if someone good comes along, move him in."

"All right! That's fair enough." Tull placed his hands on Sarn's shoulders. "Good luck to you, Sarn."

"Have you finished the report?" Toler asked as they sat down for a meal.

Sarn eyed the meat—artificial meat, actually, which was more nutritious and easier to store than the real stuff but did not taste as good. Government-issued food was the same throughout the universe: good enough to eat and bad enough to please no one.

"No, sir. It's a long report. And if you'll excuse my saying so, it is not very clear to me."

"What do you understand so far?"

"That we are to investigate a small planet that once had something to do with a small wandering star. Earth is the name of the planet." He paused. "Reading between the lines, it sounds almost as if the star may have something to do with a god—or the power." Sarn raised his eyebrows in question.

Toler nodded. "I don't know about that, but as you know from the report, Sathel finds this expedition to be of the greatest importance."

"That's one thing I don't understand, sir. Why is the head of the Xerxes Galaxy interested in a star on the other side of the universe?" asked Sarn.

"Sathel believes a conflict is going to take place on Earth. He wants us to witness it. So we can let him know how it comes out, I guess." Toler shrugged. He had not thought much about it since he had talked to Sathel.

How well had the expedition been planned? There had been no news released on the project, even though there had been thirty years in which to prepare. Not even Gen had heard anything about such a pending project. It was as if one day Sathel woke up, realized thirty years had passed, and ordered a scientific expedition launched within the week with a boy off the street to handle the technological details. That was poor planning on somebody's part!

"Why," continued Sarn, "would this star— a small one, according to the report—hovering over an unheard-of planet in a faraway minor solar system be worth this trip?"

Toler leaned forward. "Sathel expects something important to happen on Earth as a result of the star's appearance some thirty years ago. As I read the report, we can expect some special person, an incarnation of a god or an embodiment of the power, to appear. Lybur's men are purportedly planning to launch a covert sabotage of this messiah."

"Yes, I remember reading that in the report. Sathel expects the incarnation because that is what happened in fourteen other cases of star visitations."

Toler nodded. "A star appeared, and an unusual and powerful person soon after left his—or 'her' in two cases—mark on the race." He shrugged. "Or so they say. A star like that appeared above Bigor several years ago, and nothing happened. I was on a mission when it happened, but from what I've heard, no one could explain it."

"Do you suppose there is a supreme god like what they call the power?"

Toler looked carefully at Sarn and shrugged. He was not particularly interested in religion and was very uncomfortable with religious fanatics. Sarn, however, did not seem to have graduated into that category just yet.

"I think I'll study some more," he said. His interest had picked up a great deal in the past few minutes. Star Light promised not to be boring after all.

The file became more fascinating as Sarn continued. All it needed was a war and they could make a video production of it. And from what Toler said, there might even be one.

Sarn continued reading, "The mission shall reach Earth thirty years after the star visitation. It has been reliably calculated from previous instances that the messiah does not launch his career until thirty years after the appearance of the star. This timetable will allow the investigators to be in place when the messiah first establishes himself as an intervention. His style of impacting on the populace will be duly noted and recorded for further study. See file for more details."

Sarn happily surmised that he was an "investigator" as well as a crewman. That certainly was more appealing than to be the lowest of crew helpers.

Sarn pressed the reference key. He wanted more details about how the messiah usually impacted on the populace. Would he and Toler be impacted along with the natives, whatever that meant?

The screen went blank and then filled itself with a title *How to Launch a Messiah*, authored by Dorf Hextor. The book had been written seventy years ago based on research carried out by Hextor at the direction of the Ministry of Science.

That was interesting. Sarn did not know that the government, particularly the Ministry of Science, had any concern with religion. Both his parents worked in that ministry, and they certainly never let on that such was the case. Sarn was quite sure that they did not have any interest in religion except to stamp it out wherever they could find it.

Except for a few isolated communities, usually on the outlying planets, there was no religion in the Xerxes Galaxy as far as Sarn knew.

The subtitle was *The Appearance and Spread of Religion in Hoxd Galaxy.*

Hoxd Galaxy was a neighbor to the Xerxes Galaxy and had lived under a strong religious influence for several centuries. Sarn knew that much. On more than one occasion, he had heard the Hoxd religious phenomenon mentioned in derision by his parents; it was their favorite example of how supposedly intelligent people could be stupid.

Hextor's book brought together much material, gathered mostly through anthropological and observational studies, and sprinkled liberally with his own speculative conclusions. It had been a fun and exciting book to write and was a favorite text of many teachers. Students typically found the subject of religion primitive and boring possibly because it was irrelevant to anything they had experienced in their own lives, but Hextor's studies brought a fresh and fascinating viewpoint to the subject.

Sarn read on:

To successfully launch a messiah, the following elements are highly desirable and usually present in the cases researched thus far:

1. The humble beginning. It is more credible for the messiah person to work up than down. Those who have less will have more need and thus be more receptive to a leader who can promise them something. The messiah can also say to the have-nots, "I have been where you are. I know what it is like." This allows for the natives to more easily identify with the messiah.

2. Proper timing. The messiah must not make his move until he is a mature adult; otherwise, he may be dismissed as a child prodigy who is too young to know what he is talking about. Yet he must be young enough to withstand a strenuous schedule.

3. Relevance to basic needs of natives. Whatever the people's basic needs are, the messiah must address them. In most of the instances thus far studied, the messiah spoke to the needs for food, social acceptance, and love (defined as a specific personal caring for others). Personal change of the individual as a means of better achieving these needs is strongly advocated.

4. A new slant. The messiah must have a new and refreshing way of looking at the world. A catchy phraseology may be helpful, but it seems that best results are achieved when the same tired old problems (see 3) are addressed within a new framework. His slant must be unique enough to call attention to himself but familiar enough to appeal to the average native. For example, nonviolence has been consistently touted by the messiahs.

5. Dramatic ending. There must be an exciting confrontation with the forces of the status quo. Best results are achieved if the messiah is severely mistreated yet holds true to his teachings, e.g., nonviolence.

6. Magic. Magic is nearly always used during the teaching phase of his life but sparingly. The use of a large dose of magic at the end may establish the victory of the messiah in spite of his apparent and expected defeat. In most cases researched so far, resurrection from death after being killed was done with quite effective results.

Sarn stopped reading. *Resurrection from the dead? Come on,* he thought, *nobody can do that yet.* He knew one thing for sure: he wanted to be there when it happened.

7. New values. The messiah must disparage material wealth and emphasize spiritual riches. This is essential as it makes successful discipleship a possibility for everyone. In the more effective messiah launchings studied, enough natives were able to achieve a sufficient degree of success with this mind-set to make the idea more credible to larger numbers of people.

8. Self-assurance. The messiah figure must have a solid self-identity, i.e., must, in fact, believe he is an incarnation of a god. Such a belief lends itself nicely to self-confidence and singleness of purpose.

Sarn sat motionless. *This is incredible,* he thought. *What kind of a god would play such games? What was the purpose of going around stirring people up, getting messiahs killed so that he could do magic tricks?*

As far as Sarn knew, there had never been a messiah in Xerxes Galaxy. Maybe the power thought they didn't need one. Or maybe they were too advanced to need a messiah. Or maybe one was in the making; Sarn had once read about the unexplained star above Bigor but had forgotten all about it until Toler mentioned it. One thing he knew for sure was that his parents would never go for anything like that. Another possibility was that all this stuff in Hextor's book was based on coincidence and fancy while in reality there was no supreme power. That's what his parents would say.

However, it turns out, Sarn thought, somebody will be a fool.

Chapter 7

PROLOGUE 4: 5025 BCE
NATIVES

Eventually personal contact with the planet's human race became common. For the crewmen this was both a reason for gladness and disappointment. The female companionship was welcome; but as a whole the natives were poorly advanced: they were dull, superstitious, and prone to violence.

"Never have I seen a people behave so violently so easily," Aladam said to Evaze.

"I must admit they are easily provoked and often irrational."

"And often not even provoked. There seems to be a mean streak in them. The animals are more peaceful than the humans."

Aladam remembered the uneasy feeling he had the first day he stood outside the ship and surveyed the planet.

"What is it?" asked Evaze, noting the faraway look on Aladam's face.

"Have you ever felt uncomfortable about this place? Maybe *uncomfortable* is not the right word. Right after we arrived, I had a feeling of, well, foreboding may be close. Do you know what I mean?"

She nodded. "It's hard to put into words. I've been on many different worlds, some more primitive than this, and I don't recall ever coming across a human race that seemed to be feeding off of something . . . bad."

Evaze and Aladam discovered that they enjoyed each other a great deal and spent most of their free time together. Within a few months Evaze had moved into Aladam's quarters, and they no longer made any pretense that their relationship was only a professional one.

On the positive side of the ledger, the natives were human and seemed to welcome the crew of the spaceship as if they were gods. Fraternization with the natives was not discouraged by the captain, even though official policy was quite clear on that matter. If Aladam could have seen the end of their stay on the planet, he would, of course, have enforced the policy as he had done many times before.

The crew took an interest in the local inhabitants at first out of curiosity, then as a diversion, and finally out of sheer loneliness. By the end of the first year, it was common for the crewmen to pair with chosen females, and inevitably there were children of these matches. The offspring were not as intelligent as their fathers but certainly much advanced over the level of their mothers. The captain was aware that this practice would affect the development of the human species on the planet, but he elected that option as the lesser of two evils. Besides that, fraternization was inevitable over the long haul, and he had rather flow with the tide than be overrun by it.

"What am I supposed to do?" he asked Evaze. "Tell the men they can't mix with the natives? Lie to them about our chances of leaving? We're not going anywhere, and if they can find some kind of happiness with the natives, I'm sure not going to stand in their way! Interplanetary rules be damned!"

As time passed, the crew members were accepted into the lives of the natives, and eventually all of them moved from the ship and into the village. They were, however, required to report for duty on a regular basis. Aladain would not give up all semblance of an organized crew, if not for their morale, then at least for his own.

Aladam fretted over the lack of purposeful activity available on the planet. Crew members thrived on having important jobs to do—else, they would not have signed on a starship—and now there was no activity to engage them.

"There is just not enough for them to do. Some of them had rather lain around the local village and let the natives wait on them hand and foot. They are getting fat, and worse, their brains are growing stale." He sighed in exasperation.

"They need a challenge. Why should they keep their minds sharp if there is no challenge? These men responded to a career in space because they like to be tested," said Evaze.

"Daring is the other side of dared," Aladam said. "What do you have in mind, my dear?"

Evaze wrinkled her brow in thought. "How about contests? Pit the men against one another. Something like that."

"Hmm. Now what kind of contests could we have? Clean rooms? Prettiest girl?"

Evaze ignored Aladam's attempt at humor. "How about something more utilitarian? For example, divide the men into teams with the contest being the building of an efficient sewer system for the village."

"If we are going to interfere with the natural development of this planet, let's do it in a big way. How about if the contest is to see who can develop laser guns

39

for their respective villages? Then they can blow one another up. From what I've seen, they'd enjoy a more efficient way to disfigure one another."

"Now, Aladain, aren't you being too harsh?" she asked this in mockery because it was usually she who commented on the violent nature of the natives, especially after a wounded native had been brought to her for repair.

"Maybe. Maybe not. But I do like your idea. Let's play with it some more."

In the end, Aladam divided the crew into four teams, assigned a quadrant of territory to each team, and then invited the crew members to give their input as to what would be a worthwhile contest.

The suggestions ranged from good to very poor. The worst was a contest to see which team could impregnate the most females in a quadrant. The best, and the one Aladam chose, suggested that each team, in collaboration with the natives, undertake a project that would be both esthetically pleasing and useful.

There were four shuttle crafts aboard the *Star Finder*, and each team was given one of the ships. The time limit of a year was placed on the contest, which gave plenty of time for the men to survey the continent and even the far parts of the planet. After all, theoretically each team had a full one-fourth of the entire world to deal with.

The men were glad for something to do. Expeditions were sent to various places for investigation with ensuing debate over prospective projects. Feelings of rivalry ran high.

"It appears that the contest idea is working out well," Evaze remarked.

"Yes, beyond my greatest hopes. The men were terribly bored."

"By the way, what is the prize? What does the winning team get?"

Aladam shrugged. "I don't know, and I'm not sure if anyone really cares. Not one person has asked me what the prize is. It's irrelevant."

"You can bet that one day they will ask. I suggest that you be ready when that day comes."

"I'll work on it."

Before they could arrive at a prize, a group of the crew approached Aladam and Evaze with an idea. They seemed urgent about it as if they had a bee stuck in their caps and needed to unload it.

"Sir, we've been thinking about how no one knows where we are and all that. What if we include in the contest a construction on landmasses so great in size that passing ships in space might pick them out?"

The captain cocked his head quizzically, not sure what the crew had in mind.

"What if someone on a passing ship happened to focus on this planet? What would they see? Nothing to catch their attention. But what if we made giant designs in the ground, squares and circles and such, connected by lines? When somebody saw those on this primitive planet, they would perhaps see them as messages, calls for help."

Aladam and Evaze looked at each other. "I like that," Aladam said.

And so the crew of the ship set out around the planet Earth, using their shuttle craft and tools to form huge designs on the ground. The designs could not be recognized from the ground itself, for they were too large, but from space they were striking in their design and clarity.

Chapter 8

EN ROUTE ON THE SPRINT

Sarn learned to speak two languages.

Through the use of tapes and learning aids used during sleep and considerable conversational practice with the language computer, Sarn was able to master the rudiments of the Hebrew language, which would be the primary tongue spoken on Earth. He also gained some ability with Greek, which had been introduced into the area when that part of the world was under the control of that nation. Greek was still spoken by nearly everyone in the geographic area and provided a common language for people from neighboring countries. Sarn would not be as fluent as Toler, but he could pass for a newcomer who had not yet had time to learn the language very well, which was precisely the case.

Toler insisted that they speak only in Hebrew or Greek for the duration of the voyage.

"Captain Toler, how is it that you know the languages so well? You must speak as well as a native."

"Yes, as nearly as possible considering that I have never heard the natives speak it. With all the codifiers and decodifiers developed by the language professionals, just about anyone can be trained fairly quickly to speak a language quite effectively."

"That is amazing!" said Sarn. "I didn't know that was possible."

"Look how much you've learned already. The language people have learned a great deal from field studies on the newly developing planets. Put that together with the new breed of language computers and there is nothing they can't do. They've developed a mathematical basis for language development. I can't talk their language, but they can sure teach me a language."

"But how did you learn languages from a planet as obscure as Earth?"

"Sathel began my instruction several years ago. At the time I did not know why or even what it was. He contacted me and asked if I would be interested in learning languages in preparation for a possible future government job. He explained that one day there might be an opportunity for me to use it as part of a government contract in the mill. They offered to pay me well to go to school, so I said why not? I have a talent for languages, anyway, the tests say. I suppose they had that on record somewhere, and that was how come they chose me. Or that's what they told me the reason was. It might have been something entirely different." Early in the journey, Toler had quit trying to hide his disdain of government.

"And Star Light was the mission in the mill," added Sarn.

"Sure looks like it."

"Captain, I have a question. Years ago Sathel assigned you to study these Earth languages. He knew then what he planned to do. But the Hebrews are only one of many peoples on this planet, and they are not even the most advanced. It's a barren, sparsely populated, backward land of goats and shepherds. So how did Sathel know that a messiah would appear among them? Did he guess?"

"You make it sound like a terrible place to visit," said Toler, who almost grinned. He rubbed his chin. "That is a good question. And yes, I have the answer for you." He pushed away from the table and settled back in his chair.

"Sathel found two clues, and on that basis he did make a guess. You're perfectly correct about that. An educated guess, and we'll find out after we arrive just how educated his guess was."

"I really do hope he was a good guesser. I'd hate to be at the wrong place!"

"First, a perusal of the available literature on Earth—what there was—revealed age-old predictions of a great rescue of the race by a special person. Which group made the predictions?"

"The Hebrews, of course," said Sarn.

"Of course," said Toler. "For hundreds, even thousands of years, they have been writing of it—previews of coming attractions. If a messiah doesn't come to them, it'll be the biggest cheat in history."

"I'll bet they'll be upset if he doesn't come! And what is the second clue?"

"Second, the bright star, for which this whole mission is named, stationed itself over this part of the planet. It focused a strong beam of light as if calling attention to something sort of like a celestial finger pointing."

"Those clues would be even more significant if they had been found before," observed Sarn.

"You mean in those other places in the universe where a messiah appeared'?"

"Yes. Don't you think so?"

"Yes. The research shows that every messiah who was introduced to a race of people was preceded by careful preparation," said Toler.

"The soil must be cultivated if the seed is to take root, my grandmother used to say," said Sarn.

"My, you are full of literary expression today," Toler groaned. "Try to restrain yourself or I may throw up."

Sarn grinned; he enjoyed bantering with the captain. Toler had begun treating him like an equal, something the boy had not experienced before. His parents had been uncomfortable with him, and his teachers had treated him like a student.

"Now, take it another way," Toler went on. "Was a people ever prepared for a messiah and the messiah never came?"

"I don't know."

"I don't either. I read somewhere in one of the file footnotes that there are currently at least two waiting planets. How long do you wait for a messiah before you give up and go to bed?"

Sarn looked down at his plate and put a crumb in his mouth. "How do we know all this? I mean, how did Sathel find out about the early Hebrew predictions?"

"Spies," Toler said. "Spies."

"Sathel must have a very efficient network."

"Yes, I suppose he does. The head of the galaxy probably can't do without one. And I'll bet he isn't the only one with spies."

"Sometimes the whole project scares me. At other times it's exciting."

Toler looked at Sarn for a moment. "Think of it this way: we are Sathel's spies, although officially we are on a scientific mission. We know there will be other spies present on Earth, and we know they are there for political reasons."

"You're sure they're there to stop the Messiah?"

"That's what Sathel said. And my good friend Gen."

"Isn't that against the rules of the universe? I mean, no one has the right to interfere in the events of another planet, do they?"

Toler looked grim. "Most galaxies have a code of ethics, which spells that out fairly explicitly. Xerxes certainly does. Lybur is playing a high stakes game. If caught, he would be in trouble with the Galactic Council. Those guys don't fool around."

"I cannot imagine what might be gained by stopping a messiah," mused Sarn. "How does one stop a messiah? Do you buy him off? Offer to take him to a better planet? Set him up in an expensive palace with servants to cater to his every whim?"

"I suspect you have to kill them."

Sarn nodded. "I thought you would say that."

The two sat lost in their own thoughts. Sarn finally broke the silence.

"Well, at least we are forewarned. Do you think the other spies know about us?" The thought of being ambushed on a strange planet was chilling.

JESUS THE 15TH MESSIAH

"We do not think so. The other spies are already in place on Earth and cannot be contacted from Bigor. Lybur, or whoever is in charge, cannot send notice of our arrival. So it appears that the element of surprise is ours."

"How will we recognize them? Surely they are as well prepared as we are."

Toler shrugged. "That I don't know. Not yet."

"And if we find them, are we supposed to stop them?" Sarn's expression suggested incredulity that he and Toler would be expected to stop any organized sabotage.

"No. Our orders are to observe. After all"—Toler winked—"if someone or something can arrange to place messiahs around the universe, then its success or failure certainly doesn't depend on us."

"I guess that makes sense," Sarn said.

"We'll be all right as long as we are not recognized. If they know we are from Bigor, you can bet they'll come after us. No witnesses will be allowed to return home."

"Is that what Sathel said?"

"Nope. That's what Toler said," said Toler. "I feel safer when I'm paranoid."

Chapter 9

Prologue 5: 5026 BCE
Farmer Kine

By vocation Kine was a technician in the control room of the *Star Finder*. At this time, however, he, like the others, was a retired spaceman and not by his own choice.

He had moved to the village when the crew had done so, perhaps more reluctantly than most, because Kine was a shy man. Of medium height and build, he had a receding hairline, which made his nose more pronounced than it objectively was; the effect was a hawkish appearance.

He lived by himself in a small hut he found deserted. It had required some repair before it was livable, and although not handy with construction, Kine had welcomed the project as something to occupy his time.

Although never one of the favorite crew members on the *Star Finder*, Kine had been accepted by everyone as an easygoing and reliable fellow who took care of his job.

While most of the crew enjoyed a leisurely existence in the village, which they had named Adun, Kine spent his time reading. One of the books he brought from the library of the *Star Finder* was a volume on horticulture.

Agriculture was poorly developed on Earth, and most of the natives were content to be gatherers. It became Kine's goal to introduce the concept of crops and harvests to a people who gathered what grains and vegetables they ate from wherever they found them growing in the fertile valley.

It was with much care and planning that Kine planted his first crop: a small plot of wheat. The natives watched curiously as he tilled the land and planted the seed, which he had gathered from wild wheat.

There was one native, a woman, who helped Kine carry water for the garden. Soon they became close, and it was not long before she moved in with Kine. She did not speak, which was fine with him, and seemed content to be his ever-present helpmate.

Early each morning Kine could be found working his garden. Usually he was the only person up and around at that time, at least among crew members. So it was a surprise one morning as he tended his young stalks of wheat to hear his name called.

"Kine, so it is true. You do get up this early to play in your garden. Well, isn't that something!"

Kine looked up to see Obul silhouetted against the rising sun. A perpetual scowl twisted the face of the dark brawny man. Obul was—had been—chief technician in the engine room of the *Star Finder* and had perhaps more years of space experience than anyone aboard the ship. Obul had a heavy way of kidding others and often abused the more sensitive of his fellows. Kine had never cared for Obul and avoided him whenever possible.

"It is good to see the crew taking hold here in Adun. You are tending the soil and guess what I am doing these days."

Kine looked at him blankly.

"What I am investing in, my friend, is sheep. I plan to selectively breed these little fellows into real prizewinners, acquire pasture land, and establish myself. Anyone who wants sheep will have to come to me. Sounds good, huh?"

Kine shrugged and turned his attention back to his wheat. He had nothing to say to Obul and preferred not to be drawn into conversation with him.

"You'll be the chief farmer, and I'll be the big rancher. Together we can rule Adun. We'll have all the resources that count for anything." Obul snorted a laugh and turned on his heel.

Kine had not thought of gaining power through the development and refinement of agricultural techniques. For him, the project was primarily an interesting way to structure time and one that would likely be helpful to everyone. He enjoyed growing wheat and looked forward to improving the strains each year. If the natives wanted him to share his information as well as his wheat, he would gladly do so. He had no inclination to hoard either.

Kine had wisely planted a small garden, which he could easily handle by himself. The unexpected help from the woman made things even easier, and before long his crop showed good growth. Natives made daily visits to check on the progress of the wheat. They were duly impressed with the man, Kine, one of the "sons of Aladam."

And so the spring of the third year was a contented one for Kine and his woman, for the early signs pointed to a fine crop and a most worthwhile harvest. It would not have been excessive to say that the meaning of life itself for Kine was wrapped up in his work as a farmer. More than once he wondered to himself how he had ever gone into space rather than farm. Oh well, better late than never.

Chapter 10

PEWS

The dusty street was pale yellow in the afternoon sun. A thin faded ocher dog turned around twice and assumed his place in the shadow of the wall. Through a window came echoes of a mother fussing at her son. The soft and deep voice of a workman drifted down an alleyway. It was a typical hot afternoon in Nazareth, a nondescript town on the edge of the desert. Its neighbors considered the place especially worthless. "What good could come out of Nazareth?" it was asked.

On this particular day a short stout man was standing outside his shop, arms crossed, listening intently to a visitor. Recessed under craggy brows, his brown eyes glinted alertly as the other man talked. His black beard was amply flecked with gray, and wrinkles made his square face appear distinguished rather than old.

"And you say you want twenty benches for the synagogue?"

"Yes, Joseph," said the other man in his high-pitched voice and sliced the air with his hands as he described the details of the furniture. "Of course, we cannot pay much, but it is for the glory of Yahweh, and he will bless you and your house."

Abdah was of medium height, thin, slightly stooped, and sported a large hooked nose, which together with his receding chin gave him the appearance of a predatory bird. His black eyes protruded rather unnaturally, and Joseph thought the man looked perpetually startled. His thin brows displayed a gymnastic ability to move on his forehead as if they had a life of their own. As a result, he was never without an expression on his thin and angular face.

"Now Abdah, my friend," Joseph's deep voice rolled out of his thick throat, "I know that you are of an honest disposition and would never take advantage of anyone." Joseph placed his hand on Abdah's shoulder and patted him. "Now would you, my friend?"

Abdah swallowed. "Oh no, never. The payment I promise you is what has been authorized by the council, and that is all the congregation can afford."

Joseph was a craftsman with wood. If a customer could show him what was needed, he could fashion a chair or yoke or table with no trouble and everyone was happy. Never accused of being artistic, Joseph was known for his simple but sturdy and lasting work. And no one had ever mistaken him for a bargainer. He hated that part of his work more than anything. He was vaguely aware that this weakness of his had something to do with his lack of assertiveness and his need to be liked by others, but knowing that and doing something about it were two different things.

"If only everyone was honest and told things like they really are," he complained to Mary, his wife of thirty years, "then I could pay attention to the job I am asked to do and not worry about being taken advantage of. But it is not enough that I am a skilled carpenter who can turn wood into useful items. I have to be a dealer who can outtalk the people who want my works."

"It would be nice if the world was like that, I agree," said Mary. "But if you are going to sell your wares, then you must set a price at what they are worth. Is that so hard?"

"Yes, for me it is. I cannot charge the same for everything I do. Some things take a long time and much work, but they will not bring much. Other things turn out quickly and bring much better money."

"Then spend your time making the quick things that sell for more. Is that so hard to figure out?"

Joseph was quite good at forming visual images of what was to be crafted and then following his mental plan to its completion. But when it came to joining words together into effective sentences, he was clumsy.

Mary was the opposite and could not understand how a man so talented as Joseph was with his hands could find it so difficult to say what was on his mind. Early in their relationship she found him an easy person to manipulate with words. If she could entice him into a verbal exchange, then she most likely would get her way. If he clammed up and refused to discuss a topic, then she knew she had probably lost.

Joseph was now frustrated. His wife had posed the problem in such a seemingly logical manner that he felt like a fool for not being able to give a reasonable answer. He knew that the issue was not so simple, and yet the needed words eluded him.

"Not everyone wants something made that is quick and expensive, but never mind that. What I was really saying was that very often a customer expects to talk down my price. And if I don't come down, then he is indignant and walks off."

"So what is so hard about that? You put your price high to begin with so you can lower it and end up with a fair price." With raised eyebrows, Mary looked at her husband. "So what is the big problem?"

"Now you can see what the problem is if you have eyes to see. The problem is I am an honest man and I don't like this game of trying to outguess the other fellow. What if I gave a very high price and the customer took it because he thought it was wrong to question a man's work? Then he would be cheated." He waited for her "so what is" reply.

"So what is wrong with making money? You make more with one customer and not so much with another. Don't we have to eat too?"

"And I have to live with myself." Joseph was more frustrated now than when he first broached the subject with Mary. He turned and walked back to the shop, leaving his wife with her work. For her, life was simple. Why was he cursed with making simple things so difficult?

Joseph looked at Abdah and did not believe what the man was saying. No doubt Abdah was authorized by his congregation to spend a larger sum than the figure he quoted and hoped to pocket the difference. Surely there was a way to argue the man up to something reasonable, but a man should not have to do that. Joseph thought it was not that. Joseph did not mind giving a better price to a congregation or that the difference in question was large, for it was not that great. The issue, which stuck in Joseph's throat and tempted him to run the man off, was simply the principle of the matter. Abdah squinted at the carpenter and tried to read his thoughts. "Well, Joseph, what do you say? If you do not want the work, I can find someone else who would welcome the job."

A younger man came to the shop door, a hammer hanging from one hand. He wiped his brow. His dark-brown hair was long, pulled back, and tied behind his head. His shirt was open in front, and sawdust was clinging to his sweaty chest. He was a powerfully built man although in a different way than his father. Whereas Joseph was squat and thick, Jesus was taller and broader of shoulder. Both were muscular with thick forearms developed from the labor of plying tools on wood.

"Jesus," said Joseph, "what do you think?"

Jesus stood squarely before the two men and regarded them with a steady gaze. His face was handsome in a rough sort of way, but it was his eyes that caught people's attention.

His mother thought he was a picture of gentle strength, and she imagined that everyone who met her son could not help but be as impressed as she was. As for Jesus, he found it easier to ignore his mother's doting than to deal with it in any other way. It seemed the more he ignored her, the more she carried on about him.

"If it would please my father to perform this gift for God, then do so. The satisfaction that would come from that labor of love is sufficient unto itself."

Joseph frowned. He pulled Jesus off to one side where he would not be overheard by Abdah. "But what if Abdah here is pocketing some of the money and paying us less than has been authorized?"

"You may deal directly with the church council if you choose, and then you do not have to worry about this middleman. But in any case, your reward will be yours and Abdah's will be his."

Abdah shifted his feet uncomfortably and then his eyes. He did not like to be talked about when he was trying to pull a fast one. Joseph walked back to him.

"Tell the council that it is a bargain. I will live with my end of the agreement, knowing that I have been honorable—more than honorable. It is up to you, Abdah, to live with your end of the bargain."

Aabdah bowed, muttered thanks, and scurried away. Joseph wondered why messengers scurried. Were they chosen to be messengers because of that quality? Or did they develop a scurry as a necessary part of the job?

"Thank you for your thoughts, Jesus. I can live with that if I am happy with my bargain, then why should I worry about what others get from their bargains? We will have our hands full with the twenty benches without worrying about that man Abdah."

Jesus spoke softly, "Father, I will not be here to help you with the benches. It is very near the time when I shall be leaving."

Joseph stared at his son. Only the tightening of his jaw muscles signaled his tension. He had known that someday his son would leave, but he was not prepared for it to happen.

He had hoped that Jewish family tradition and the established business would keep Jesus there, working in a father-son combination. That was a common arrangement and made a lot of sense. Two men working together could produce more efficiently than one. For several years, however, Joseph had known deep down that his son would someday leave. He had not thought much about what Jesus would leave to do or where he would go. He just knew that he would leave one day and there would be nothing he could do to change his son's mind.

The two men faced each other for a long moment. Much passed between them in that gaze, for over the years they had shared much together as father and son and as two men. There was no need for words. Joseph nodded and walked into the shop. Jesus followed him.

"Did you tell your mother?"

"Yes."

Joseph returned to the chair he had been making, a heavy one made of oak. It had been ordered by a very obese man who was tired of chairs giving way under his bulk. He had finally decided to have his own custom-made chair. Jesus held the chair firmly while Joseph pulled the adze across the arm. By the end of the day, the chair was finished.

That evening, after a meal of roast goat, cheese, and wine, Jesus walked to the center of town. Evening strolls were a common practice and made up a good deal of the town's social life, particularly for the young people. Jesus paused in

the center of the well curb, he watched the young
people walking together in the shadows, giggling and talking in whispers. A few
older children were engaged in an exciting game of chase. The adults, if they
walked, would choose a later time when it was cooler. In the distance he could
see the hills surrounding Nazareth on the south, and to the west he could see the
sheen of the setting sun dancing on the Mediterranean. As he watched, the sun
fell beyond the edge of the horizon, leaving a rosy glow in the western sky.

The moon was almost full that night, and the streets were bathed in a pale-
yellow light. Small figures scurried in and out of the shadows next to the buildings.
Jesus reflected on how many times he had played in the same alleyways and streets
when he was growing up. He had been fast of foot, and the chase had been a sheer
childhood delight. It seemed that children had always enjoyed the chase. Was that
part of their nature? It seemed so. Why would they be like that? His father had
once remarked about kittens playing with their mother's tail and explained that
the mother's nature was to provide training for her offspring's pouncing. What
was it that children were training for when they chased one another?

"Hello."

The softly-spoken greeting jarred him from his reverie. He turned to find his
friend Sara behind him.

"You're jumpy tonight, Jesus. What's on your mind?"

"Oh, nothing special. Just remembering how it was when I was a kid playing
those same games. Did you play chase when you were small?"

Sara was a few years younger than Jesus and had always looked up to him
as a childhood hero. As they had matured, a bond was established between them.
They enjoyed talking about matters most of the others found boring, and many
an hour had been spent together discussing their dreams and what life meant to
them. Over the years it had been assumed by more than one that the pair would
someday marry, but they never had. It had not seriously occurred to either, for
their relationship was not one of romance but of compatibility of mind.

"Not very much. I was too slow and got caught too easily. It wasn't much fun
after a while. You did, though. I remember watching you and the other older kids
play. You were fast, and I always cheered for you."

"Those were the good old days," Jesus reflected.

Sara sat down beside Jesus, and they leaned back to peer into the clear
black sky.

"Did you tell your parents?"

"Yes. Father took it like I thought he would. Stoical. Mother was not too
happy. In fact, she became hysterical. Finally I had to just walk away." Jesus shook
his head as if trying to shed the image of his mother excitedly berating him for
even thinking about leaving home.

"Sounds rough but that's what you expected."

"I sometimes have second thoughts about going, Sara. What would happen if I decided not to go? I could go on about my business with father, live at home, and have an easy life. So why am I planning on leaving a good life to go on the road? Preaching is such a thankless job!"

Sara smiled and shrugged her shoulders. "Who am I to say? I have already told you that I don't understand it."

"I have explained to you."

"I didn't understand. Tell me again. Maybe it will make sense this time."

Jesus took a deep breath and stared down the darkened street. "All right, I'll tell you again, my friend with the short memory. It's very simple. I have always had an interest in religion and the law."

"Yes, and you have understood it better than most."

"And recently I have felt, well, *called* is the word that comes to mind. I have felt called to go teach what I know about the law. The calling comes from God himself? I . . . I cannot ignore it. It is too strong."

"But to go on the road? Come on, Jesus, that is a way taken by those who are either mad or can't make a living any other way."

"Sara, if you will arrange for the people to come to me here in Nazareth and listen to what I have to say, then I will remain. I wish it would be that easy."

Sara's eyes were playful as she asked, "You're not just thinking about the applause you'll get from standing in front of a crowd and saying wise things, are you?"

Jesus shook his head slowly and firmly. "No, it does not seem to me like an exciting or fun way to live. I had much rather be in the workshop building a chest than laying myself open before people. At least the wood will go together the way I shape it. People are not so cooperative. At the end of a day I can hold my chest, stroke it, behold its beauty and strength, and go to bed satisfied that I have done something worthwhile for that day. But with teaching or preaching? Hah! I go to bed and don't know if I have done any good at all."

Sara chuckled. "People can be rotten."

"And yet we are people," Jesus said. "We may say those other people are rotten, and yet they no doubt say the very same thing about us."

"I was joking. Of course, people—all of us—are just hard to deal with most of the time. But I am sure you will change all of that because of your superior techniques of speaking to the crowds."

"You!" Jesus grabbed at the laughing Sara and shook her in mock anger. He laughed a little but could not locate the humor as easily as did Sara. He looked at her a long time in the dim light.

"I wish you were able to come with me, Sara. I will miss our discussions and your sometimes too-candid opinions."

JESUS THE 15TH MESSIAH

"And I will miss you too, Jesus," she replied. "But you must do what you must." She stood up and forced a smile.

"Don't worry, I will keep tabs on you. No doubt you'll be in all the news, the hot topic on everyone's tongue."

Jesus stood and gazed upward at the starry sky. "I hope to see you often, Sara."

"Do you know when you will leave?"

"Tomorrow."

She moved toward him, put her arms around him, and squeezed. He hugged her in return, and they stood joined together for a few moments before Sara pulled away. She looked up at him, smiled, and turned to leave. Jesus watched her until she had disappeared down a side street. Then he made his way home.

Tomorrow would be a big day.

Chapter 11

Prologue 6: 5027 BCE
The Sensitive

Uber was an engineer by training and a sensitive by birth. Tall and slender, with a balding head, perpetually pursed lips, and large gray eyes, he had the stereotypical appearance of a scientist. Anyone who had ever known him considered Uber peculiar and a bit different from the others, and they were right. Uber knew that he was not like his peers and had often been painfully reminded of his lack of social finesse. He was a loner but was not often lonesome, for Uber enjoyed his solitude.

On this particular day he was sitting in a window seat of a shuttle craft hovering above a crowd of working men. Directly below him was the beginning of a rather large structure. From his vantage point a thousand feet above, it appeared that a giant had laid the foundation for a square building using huge stone blocks. When the blocks were lifted into place, the shape of the edifice would form a pyramid. The building site was covered by hundreds of workers, who appeared from the craft as a swarming bed of ants. The construction was part of a team effort but one that held little interest for the engineer. *Just one more construction project to keep the crew busy and the captain happy,* Uber thought.

He grimaced and felt nauseous. Something was wrong, had been wrong all along, and he could feel it more strongly than ever before. Uber was a man who, by professional training, valued reason and objective data. Yet he found himself the victim of emotions; he could not shut out the dark, probing vibrations that came from everywhere. He cursed the genetic quirk that had made him a sensitive. Uber had thought many times that ignorance was bliss, and he wished that he was not aware of the black force, which drifted in and out of his consciousness. Whatever it was, his discomfort was growing stronger, and he occasionally experienced bouts of fear bordering on panic.

The pilot turned and noticed Uber's expression.

"If you'd just relax and let yourself enjoy these contests, maybe you wouldn't be so grumpy."

A voice from the ground radio asked the pilot to lower its cargo into place. Below, dangling by cables, was a twenty-ton stone block. It had been cut by laser beam from a quarry some distance away, brought to the site by shuttle craft, and would be lowered gently and precisely into place. The pilot prided himself on his good "eye," his ability to make accurate visual judgments when depositing his load.

With hand signals, the natives assisted in the proper placement of the block. Once the stone had been loosed from the cables, it was against the game rules for the ship to move it again, although it could be repositioned by hand. It was therefore in the interest of the natives to have the block placed correctly the first time.

Uber ignored the familiar scene below. He sat huddled against the wall, a grimace covering his face. Against his will, he shuddered.

"What's the matter with you? Sick? Tired of the game?"

The pilot misunderstood his mood, for Uber had nothing against the contest and, in fact, sometimes found it mildly interesting. No, the contest had nothing to do with Uber's feelings.

Uber was preoccupied with something else.

Wavy circles closed in on his mind like reverse ripples of water reacting to a thrown stone. A picture formed in his mind, an old one that first showed up in black and white and then slowly added color. Initially he felt dissociated from the actors in the picture but gradually felt himself pulled into the action.

"That boy knows this was going to happen?" A middle-aged man, short and bald, turned his heavy-jowled face toward a little boy and blinked scorn toward him. The little boy became Uber in time to feel the percussions of the disdain and recoil in shame.

"Yes. Uh-hmm. That's the one." The woman looked straight at the boy, her face showing no hesitation in confirming the man's suspicion.

The man kept his gaze on the boy as if memorizing every line of his face. Then he slowly nodded, apparently indicating that he had the identity of the child filed away in his brain.

The boy stared back, wishing he could look away and disappear, but caught in some kind of frozen suspension where all he could do was stare and feel like his eyeballs were about to pop out of his head.

"It beats all I ever seen," the woman continued.

"When did it start?" The man had turned his attention back to the woman. The boy thought that it was the best time to get away, now that they were not looking at him; but before he could move, the woman looked again, pegging him to his seat.

"He said something about two weeks ago. Maybe ten days." She shrugged. "Nobody paid any attention to him. He's a kid."

"Yep." The man glanced at Uber again. "Who did he tell?"

"His grandmother. Said he didn't know who else to tell. Naturally she didn't believe him."

"Hell! Who would? That kind of thing doesn't happen every day."

"You got that right! Anyway, you have to give the kid credit. He did try to warn her."

The man turned around, leaned against the wall, and stared into the sky as if looking for answers to this peculiar situation. "Yes," he said, starting slowly, "but whoever would have expected the old man to die like that?" He shook his head. "It's not every day that a man gets run over by a wheelchair. His own damned wheelchair!"

"It was a real freak thing. That's what the doctor said."

The little boy began trembling as he recalled the feelings of foreboding, which left him frightened and shaking. One afternoon an image formed in his mind, demanding all his attention: a picture of his grandfather falling out of his wheelchair. The chair rolled up over him, its large wheel resting against the windpipe of the old man. Because he was stunned by his fall, the old man could not move, and it was not long before he had suffocated. Later the doctor would say that it was highly unlikely that such a thing would happen again in a hundred years.

But when Uber felt/saw the image of impending doom, he knew that it would happen, and soon. Not knowing what else to do, he went to his grandmother and told her what he had seen in his mind picture. Being a common woman, she had no way of knowing that her grandson was a sensitive and dismissed him offhandedly. When he persisted with his story, she sent him to his room. The look on the child's face was urgent, terrified, but it did not register as within the realm of possibility.

The grandmother mentioned Uber's story to a friend, and two weeks later the accident occurred. The friend was only too glad to be able to bring it up to family members, and no one knew how to react. There was some anger, as in why didn't the boy warn someone—never mind that he tried. There was guilt by grandmother for not listening to his warning. Most of the family felt defensive for the widow, and this somehow irrationally included putting some kind of blame on the boy.

Uber did not understand what had happened, only that he had done the only thing he knew: warn Grandmother. That was his first experience as a sensitive, and it taught him well to keep his mouth shut.

Now he was on a strange planet ruled by dark and evil forces. Something bad was going to happen to the crew—or part of it—and he knew by experience that the details would come later. Meanwhile he could enjoy nothing, for he was like a radio antenna overcome by interference. His reception was jammed by unwelcome signals.

And he didn't know what to do about it.

Chapter 12

LYBUR AND SATHEL

Sathel stared calmly at Lybur's barrel chest and waited for the general to finish his diatribe. He was fascinated by the regular rising and falling of the man's chest as if Lybur had learned to rant and rave without disruption of his physiological processes. The rhythm of the general's medal-covered chest was almost hypnotic, and Sathel wondered if one could really trust the anger of a man whose breathing was uninterrupted by his apparent emotional catharsis. It didn't matter because Sathel didn't trust the head of IC anyway.

Surely, Sathel thought, there must be a better way of conducting business with this loathsome man. Their meetings were infrequent and yet so predictable that a casual observer would be convinced they were following a script. Lybur inevitably lost his patience with Sathel.

The two men did not like each other; each embodied everything the other loathed. It was Lybur's nature to loudly express his frustration; Sathel's easygoing nature condemned him to suffer the general's performance.

Still talking, Lybur strode to Sathel's desk and slammed down his glass. Sathel cringed inwardly and craned his neck to see if a scar had been left on the desk.

Lybur wagged his finger in Sathel's face as he continued his harangue.

Sathel could not stand to have someone wag a finger in his face. Abruptly rising, he turned his back on Lybur and walked slowly to the window where he stared across the lake. Where were the ducks? There used to be so many kinds. Those from Atheus were the best, so many colors.

"And I hope you'll have the good sense for once in your life to stop this ridiculous mission!" Lybur said in his precise and loud authoritarian voice. So caught up in the telling of what was on his mind, he was oblivious as to whether he had been heard.

Sathel idly wondered if the other people in Lybur's life also tuned him out. Waiting for one's tormentor to run down worked better, Sathel thought, than a shouting match no one won. Besides, that was not Sathel's style; he was a peaceful man with a gentle spirit who found an advantage in letting the other person do most of the talking.

"Leave things alone! We in Xerxes Galaxy are doing fine. There is no use in tampering with what we don't understand." Lybur's furrowed forehead seemed very heavy above his bushy brow. Sathel wondered if all the blood in the general had run to that one spot on his forehead and was about to burst forth. He tried to imagine what he would do in such a situation. Would a towel sop up the blood before it could stain the carpet? Would the brain tissue be too chunky for a towel? Sathel shook his head to clear it of irrelevant thoughts.

Sathel spoke as Lybur made an infrequent pause, "Why, Lybur, is it so important to you that I stop my investigation of the star?"

"Why? Because there are better things to do with one's time than chase superstition and myth halfway across the universe! After all, you, dear Sathel, are the leader of the people of the entire Xerxes Galaxy. How many billions of people depend on your leadership? And you would squander your time on silly whims!"

"But what is the real reason, Lybur?" Sathel asked. "Do not give me platitudes. We both know you don't care that much about the niceties of leadership. What is the payoff for you?"

Lybur did not like being pinned down. His face reddened, and his mouth formed a word without making a sound. "Have you not been listening to me all this time?" he finally uttered.

"You're terribly upset that I may be investigating the star phenomenon," said Sathel. "And that just does not make sense."

Sathel was quite irritated that anyone, especially Lybur, had found out about his project, Star Light. How long had the investigation of the star phenomenon been Sathel's favorite project? It had been many years since he first began reading about the strange stars appearing around the universe. Or was it one traveling star?

What had started as an adolescent curiosity had become an adult hobby and eventually grown into a serious scientific exploration. Sathel firmly believed that information from the study would someday be useful and worth the expense, although he knew that his primary motivation was simply curiosity. And there was a thrill in finding out something new. How many times in this day and age did a man get a chance to find out something new? It seemed like everything else was already known.

His interest in the project had grown into a near obsession, and all his free time was spent thinking about the star phenomenon. If he could have just kept the whole thing a secret, he wouldn't have this complication with Lybur.

But that wasn't true either. Lybur had been making plans with regard to the star phenomenon independently of whatever Sathel was doing. It seemed coincidental that they both should be interested in something apparently so trivial and esoteric as an alleged itinerant religious star. The whole thing became absurd when one considered that there had not been a star in the Xerxes Galaxy for hundreds of years, and the full meaning of that visitation had not been entirely clear. It still wasn't. Nevertheless, once Lybur turned his energies to the star, then it became Sathel's business and his problem.

And what a scheme Lybur had hatched! Whereas Sathel's mission was simply a covert observational visit, Lybur intended to directly interfere in the affairs of the Earth people. Not only was this unethical, as agreed upon by the Federation of Universal Galactic Governments, but it was purposefully destructive in its intent.

"I will stop your mission to Earth," Sathel spoke quietly and decisively. He had dealt face-to-face with powerful men many times and was not intimidated by the general.

"No, Sathel, you will not. It is already in place, and I could not call it off if I wanted to. My men are on Earth at this very moment, and I have no contact with them," he spoke triumphantly. "And even if I could call it off, I wouldn't because you would not dare expose my plans."

"And how come?" Sathel asked, although he thought he already knew the answer. "How is it that I would not expose your plans?"

"Because I would then expose your little game. There are people in power who would be disturbed that the head of their galaxy is spending his time and government money playing in the affairs of primitive, demented religious peoples. You would be a laughing stock, Sathel, and then they would kick you out!"

Lybur was exaggerating, most likely, but it would be an unpleasant bit of publicity. "You would use blackmail, wouldn't you?"

"Whatever it takes, Sathel. That is the difference between you and me. You dote on your high principles, and that immobilizes you. I am able to cut through the irrelevancies and do what needs to be done. That is why I am a successful man. You are where you are because you charm people. I am where I am because of what I get done. I would not change places with you for anything!"

"And it is men like me who try to keep your kind from blasting us all to bits. I think it is time you left." Sathel held his hands together behind his back to keep them from trembling. Lybur had yanked his chain, and he was very angry.

Lybur put on his twisted smile and stopped at the door. "Sathel, my mission is already in progress and there is no way to stop it. Yours has not yet begun, and it would only hopelessly complicate things if you went ahead. Drop the idea or else."

Sathel had turned away. He hated threats from thugs and had long ago found that ignoring was the best method of handling them.

Why Lybur had sent a force to Earth with the intention of interfering in its internal business, Sathel had no idea. What he did conclude in that moment was that Lybur, head general of Internal Control, was a dangerous man who should not be underestimated.

Sathel had not revealed that his own mission was also in progress. It was not too late to cancel the mission, but he did not want to do that. He needed to find out what Lybur did on Earth. If Lybur's men did, in fact, interfere with the Earth people, Sathel's party would provide eyewitness accounts, which could provide the downfall of the general.

Sathel stood before his window and watched the lake. A pair of ducks had appeared and left a fine wake line as they glided across the surface. *Such a simple life they lead,* Sathel thought. While they paddle leisurely around the l*ake and wait for their daily feeding, I must wrestle with issues that affect the whole galaxy.*

Lybur stomped back to the IC building. Face and neck bright red, he closed himself in his office. Consumed with his hatred of Sathel, he was determined to stop Sathel from sending his expedition to Earth. He buzzed the outer office.

"Send Vazo in to see me. Now!"

Vazo was a tall frail-looking man who reminded Lybur of a single tree about to fall in the wind. He did not like the man but respected his ability to get a job done discreetly.

Vazo's large sleepy-looking eyes gazed over a long hooked nose. His small mouth was open, lips pursed, waiting for the input of a question so he could say something. He stood before Lybur's desk and waited.

"Has Sathel put together his expedition to the planet Earth?"

Vazo replied in his emotionless voice that he was not sure how far along Sathel's preparations were. "We know that he picked out a man named Toler to head the expedition and from the amount of supplies probably one other man. But we do not know his identity." Vazo let a sly smile play on his lips. "We used some persuasion with Toler. I doubt that he will be further interested in taking the job."

Lybur grunted. He didn't care to know the details. He just wanted to know if it worked. "Would you know if such an expedition left Bigor?"

"Most likely. We have a person close to Sathel who keeps us abreast of most developments. There is a problem, however. Sathel does not always go through channels to get things done. Sometimes no one knows what he is up to until it is an accomplished fact."

"Damn him! He cannot be trusted!" uttered Lybur. "Alert your contacts. I want to know if the fool launches an expedition."

Vazo turned to go. He had given what information he had, and now he had been commanded to obtain more. He would do that to the best of his ability, using cajolery, bribes, or torture. It did not matter to him. Vazo was not sadistic; he was pragmatic. He would do whatever was required to get the job done.

"Oh, and what do you know about this—did you say his name was Toler? The fellow chosen for Sathel's expedition—the one you 'persuaded' not to take the job?"

"Not much is known about him," said Vazo in his monophonic voice. "He is something of a loner who does not care for politics. He has a girlfriend with whom he spends a great deal of time. He is a friend to the head of governmental information. Gen, I believe is his name. He minds his own business and keeps a low profile."

"Make sure you get to him. I don't want any surprises."

Vazo nodded. He had been given one more assignment, which he would carry out in an efficient and productive manner, although he was almost sure the pilot had declined the trip after his encounter with the beast.

Lybur's hatred for Sathel was so strong that his head felt like it would explode. He closed his fist around a cup and squeezed until his knuckles were white.

Vazo had never known Lybur to be so possessed by anything as he was about the traveling star phenomenon. Not usually bothered by what others thought or did, Vazo nonetheless felt decidedly uncomfortable around the general.

With a crash, the glass broke. Lybur looked at his hand, not comprehending. Bright red appeared where the glass had cut. Vazo handed him his handkerchief. Lybur blankly stared at the cloth and then wrapped it around his hand. When he looked up to dismiss Vazo, the man had already gone.

Lybur walked around the desk, his hand wrapped. He stopped before a mirror and focused on his image. What he saw caused his eyes to widen and his face to pale. Lybur shook his head and quickly moved on to the bath where he would take care of his hand. He was unnerved by what he thought he had seen in his reflection.

It defied reason that his face could have been covered by hair, his nostrils flared wide, and something like horns projecting from his head. It had happened again. He would have to go back to Dr. Matril. A stronger medicine was what he needed.

Lybur shook his head again. It made no sense. He put his hands over his head but could feel no horns; he brought his hands over his face, but his nostrils were not flared or his face covered by hair. It was like that every time. What he saw wasn't true. But he didn't like it. It scared him.

It had started before his appointment to the head of Internal Control. At first he did not notice it. Then he found himself lying often and easily usually about unimportant matters. Sometimes he was appalled at how deceitful he had become. And it kept getting worse. And now these hallucinations.

Chapter 13

TEMPTATIONS

Obviously fatigued, the man designated as the fifteenth messiah walked wearily up the trail; he had been fasting for some days, and his strength was lagging, sapped also by the emotional burden he carried on his shoulders. His face was ordinary and haggard, but from behind his beard, there radiated an ambiance of warmth and quiet strength. Although average in most ways, this man was remembered by those who met him. Kind was an apt description but did not go far enough. Rugged had to be included. His hands were large, calloused from years of tool handling, and yet his touch was deft and sure, that of the craftsman as well as the laborer.

He did not often climb the mountains, but this was a special occasion. If asked why he was making the trek up the rocky path on a late afternoon, he probably could not have put the reason into words. If asked who or what he hoped to meet on the mountain, he may have said he was not sure.

But if you inquired as to who he was, he would have replied without self-conscious hesitation that he was Jesus the Messiah, the chosen one sent from God.

As Jesus rounded a bend in the path, he came across a group of goatherds. Tending goats was a lonely business and anytime the men could justify getting together, they did so. Besides the social aspect, it was important to trade information on market prices, grazing conditions, and news of the world any of them might have come across.

On this day there were five goatherds squatting around a small cook fire, deep in conversation as they ate, bones making smacking noises as they were plucked from hungry mouths.

Five pairs of wary eyes watched the newcomer. Jesus paused and returned their gaze. Because he was weary, a tone of impatience crept into his voice.

"Greetings," he said.

Finding him a curious person, they continued to look him over. Finally one of them, Baleoff, spoke, "Sit and share our meat and bread."

"But don't eat his cheese, for you may choke. His goats are all sick," bantered one of his comrades. The men laughed and kidded among themselves, a sign that they were accepting of the stranger.

"My, but you look grim," one said to Jesus. "Have you come up here to fast and heap ashes on your head?" The men laughed loudly, for the idea of wearing sackcloth and ashes, an affected way of showing sadness and self-suffering, seemed both ingenious and a waste of time. They often made fun of those who practiced such as a way of appearing holy.

Jesus did not share their levity. His mind was elsewhere.

He waited for the lighthearted conversation to die down.

"Have you . . . have you felt anything unusual up here on the mountain?" Jesus asked.

"Just a chill wind up my legs at night," one joked.

"And the rocks under my spine when I'm sleeping. Except that is usual, not unusual."

Baleoff, unlike his friends, gazed solemnly at Jesus.

"Unusual? How do you mean?" he asked.

Jesus locked eyes with the goatherd. It was as if they were now in communication about something the others could never hope to grasp.

"Something evil." Jesus shrugged. He was not sure how to explain what it was he felt.

Baleoff studied Jesus's face and then spoke, "Yes, I know." He gestured behind him toward the trail that wound up the mountain. "I can feel it too." His tone was matter of fact yet edged with a sense of apprehension.

"It calls me," Jesus said, "and I must face it."

Baleoff flipped a bone into the fire without looking. The flames leaped for an instant, the heat making a sharp contrast with the coolish air, which swirled around the men's feet.

"What will you do when you confront this . . . this force?"

"I do not know." Jesus turned toward the mountain, eyes searching for some movement farther up on the rocky ground. "But I will know when the time comes."

The other men had stopped their talking, blankly looked at one another, and waited. The manner of the two speakers was unsettling and caused chills to run up their spines. One of the men huddled nearer the fire, and another glanced over his shoulder into the late-afternoon shadows.

"I must be going," Jesus said.

"Peace be with you," Baleoff said.

Jesus murmured words of parting to the others and departed.

"Who was that?"

66

Baleoff stared after the disappearing figure. "I don't know. I forgot to ask his name." Baleoff shuddered, and his friends exchanged glances. They did not like it when Baleoff was like this, for sometimes he could feel things that the rest of them could not. He said no more, and the other men shrugged and resumed their conversation where it had left off less than five minutes before. Baleoff, lost in thought, gazed at the empty trail until he felt his body shudder; then he rose and walked into the shadows so his friends would not see him shaking.

Jesus continued up the mountain until he came to a place that seemed right. After building a small fire, he sat on a stone and gazed into the clear sky. Perhaps he was meditating. Or praying. Or even in a trance. Maybe all of the above. Soon the tensions left his tired body, and he relaxed, the furrows fading from his face.

Jesus appeared younger than his thirty years, although he was wise far beyond his years; he had not underestimated the importance of the imminent confrontation on the mountain.

As a youth Jesus had been different from most of his peers. He had an unusual aptitude for the religious laws, and at the same time he had the capacity to laugh loudly at the common absurdities of life. At other times he displayed a capacity to be quite serious about matters, and his mother early noted his uncanny ability to perceive strangeness in a situation that was not readily apparent to others.

His parents had never known just how to take him during his growing-up years. There was the usual parental pride when Jesus excelled at anything and the equally usual dismay when they could not understand their son. At times they felt very close to him; at other times Jesus seemed totally alien. In many ways he was a typical adolescent who often differed in opinion from his elders, especially his parents.

Fortunately both Mary and Joseph recalled the specialness of the events surrounding his birth and were able to explain away his strangeness by invoking those memories.

"I wish he was normal!" Joseph moaned

"Normal? What is normal? Does your son not work as hard as any boy his age or man his size for that matter?"

Joseph spread his hands in a gesture of futility.

"Yes, Mary, he is a good worker. But he is also different."

"So what is so bad about different? You want him to walk lockstep with every other addlebrained boy?" Mary retorted in defense of her son.

And at other times it was Mary complaining and Joseph on the defensive. If one became exasperated with Jesus, the other felt compelled to take his side, an unspoken strategy that kept the family equilibrium rocking along on a stable basis.

"Why are you sad?" Joseph asked.

"Oh, you know how a mother is. I worry about our oldest son." Mary sniffled and wiped away a tear.

"So what is it you worry about this time? That he won't ever take an interest in the girls?"

"But, Joseph, the other boys his age—they like the girls."

"You should be thankful! I am thankful! There will be plenty of time for that. Besides—"

"Besides what?"

"Besides, if he is happy living without a girl, then maybe he is among the blessed." The last was spoken halfway through the doorway; Joseph knew that he had just uttered an exit line.

"But where will we get grandchildren?" Mary wailed after him.

"We have other sons, you know," Joseph muttered as he stalked away.

Jesus knew that his parents worried about him but figured there was nothing he could say that would change things. Besides, he had other matters on his mind that needed sorting through.

The birth of Jesus had been unusual by any definition of the term. Not only was it the subject of visitation from kings and shepherds, but the event caused quite an uproar with King Herod. Because of the immediate danger from the king, an irrationally paranoid person who was deeply threatened by the birth of a "new king," Jesus's parents acted quickly to hide him. After their move to Nazareth, they assumed a low profile.

Actually Jesus knew little about the events surrounding his birth. He had overheard allusions made by Mary and Joseph as they talked together late at night but never enough information so he could understand the import of what had transpired. Something had happened when he was born, something only his parents knew about and would not reveal. Whatever it was, it had badly frightened them and influenced their perception of their son. The way they hushed their conversation when he suddenly entered a room made him uneasy, yet he did not ask about the strained silences.

His earliest trips to the Temple with his parents were fascinating excursions. More than the intrigue with ritual and polemics, Jesus sensed that the Temple held answers for his questions of how people could best relate to one another. Or rather, he decided one day as he sat in the temple this was where people attempted to find the answers that would explain life's important matters, most notably how one went about the business of relating to his God and to his brother and sister. Jesus was not too old before he realized that some of what he found in organized religion was courageous, sensible, and pragmatic. There were doctrines that pointed the way to better living and theology, which made sense of the unknowable.

But Jesus was often dismayed by what he considered the stupidity of what he learned at the temple: pettiness, political obligation to the privileged and wealthy, and a slavery of strict obedience to a vast multitude of laws, many so trivial as to be laughable. Jesus thought that the value of a person was often sacrificed on the altar of "rightness by rules."

On one occasion he had an insight into what was being taught in the temple.

"May I speak, Rabbi?" The small hand had been raised for some time without acknowledgment.

The teacher slowly turned his gaze toward the boy's voice. Jesus thought that there was a hardness in the face and a coolness in the voice that should not have been present in a man who purported to be invested in the welfare of his fellow human beings.

"I have heard the discussion and ask to make a point, please." Jesus had stood, ready to make his comment. The rabbi was about to ask Jesus to sit down and behave like any other twelve-year-old child when he noticed that the other men in the room were giving Jesus their full attention. Some were curious and others bemused; there were few who appeared to disapprove. The rabbi nodded assent.

"I know I'm not old enough to understand about these matters as well as my elders," he said sincerely, "but I do have a question about the Law." Jesus turned as he spoke, casually making eye contact with the men, demonstrating a natural talent as a speaker.

"Is it possible that the Law can become too heavy?"

"How do you mean?" someone asked. "Is it not the Law that, when faithfully followed, allows people to more fully obey God and thus find contentment?"

"I was thinking," Jesus said as he turned his attention to the bearded man, "about working with my father in the carpentry shop. My father knows all the rules about how to use tools to build things. He teaches me the rules. I know how to build a stool the right way, and I'm glad I know those rules." He paused to choose his words. "But my father lets me not follow the rules sometimes."

"And what kind of stool do you produce then?"

"Sometimes not very good, I'm afraid," Jesus replied with a shy, winsome smile. "But when I have an idea about how a new kind of design might be better, I get excited and cannot wait to go to work. So I may bend some rules about building a stool and ignore others. Most of the time, I must admit, I end up following the rules if I want a useable stool."

A large gray-headed man chuckled deeply. "My boy, we too have been through that phase of life where we had to try our own way, only to discover that the age-tested ways were more efficient and humane after all." His eyes glittered with both amusement and appreciation that this youngster would have such an insight. "Can you see that?"

"Yessir, I see that, but—"

"But what? Go ahead and make your point," the rabbi found himself saying. He was encouraging this boy whom he had wanted to shut up only a few minutes before. Did Jesus remind the rabbi of a time in his own life years ago when he wrestled with the same questions only never had the courage to express them?

"The wasted wood, the extra time it takes me to try out my ideas, I think there is good that comes from that."

"Such as?" a voice challenged.

"I enjoy seeing my father laugh," he said with a twinkle in his eye. The men laughed with Jesus, imagining the strange styles of stool the boy had probably made. "And I try out my own ideas. That is good because when my ideas don't work, then I find out for myself that the rules are good and trustworthy. And when my idea does work better than the old way, I am proud, and I enjoy the work even more."

"But why waste your time? The wise man learns from what others have already learned. Trust your father. Is he not an expert in his trade?"

"Father is very good at what he does, and I do trust him. I also trust myself when I have an idea," Jesus said.

"You trust yourself to make a mess nine of ten times, it sounds to me." The large man laughed, obviously enjoying the debate.

Jesus was thoughtful. "Yes, that is true, I suppose. But is it not worth it? I put more of myself into the work. I do it because I like to do it. Isn't that worth something?"

A tall thin man stood. He appeared to have just enjoyed an insight of his own and wanted to share it. Standing with hands on hips, the angular man moved his slender body back and forth as he spoke, "Excuse me, my brethren, but I see where this boy is going. Or coming from. A friend of mine is an artist. At first he learned the rules of painting, such as, well, I don't know what they are myself. His paintings were technically correct, his teacher told him, but there was something lacking. It was only after he got past the rules and began painting beyond the 'right way' that a part of him became a part of his work." The man smiled as he made his point. "So now he is an artist whereas before he was a technician."

Another man stood, whiskers like bristles. "Are you proposing that we teach our children the rules of the Torah so that they can be technicians for God and then tell them they can forget the teachings because it is time to become an artist for God?" He snorted. "I'd rather live with a group of technicians than a bunch of artists. At least technicians are predictable, and you can depend on them when you have to. Let a few artists get into positions of power, and you will see what chaos is really like!"

There was a chorus of shouts, some agreeing, others disagreeing, most wanting the floor to make their own statement. Jesus did not have an opportunity to say much more on that day, but he listened raptly to all that was said using it as grist in his own theological mill.

There was so much to learn, he decided, that it was no wonder these men were still struggling with their own belief systems about the meaning of self and God.

Sitting before his fire, Jesus thought on those moments from his past as if seeking to define who he was. Occasionally he tensed as he felt the dark force rippling across the mountainside. It brushed against him like a cold wind that slaps one's naked skin and leaves goose bumps, reminding Jesus that it was still there. The presence was chilling and caused him to shudder and move closer to the fire. Once he heard an eerie laughter like dry bones rattling in a cave, and he felt his skin crawl up his belly. He may have finally slept sitting up, but he was not sure. After a long time he lay down, curled his body around the small fire, and slept fitfully.

The morning came early and cool on the mountaintop. Jesus woke and listened for the sounds of birds; but there were no bird songs, only the quiet of the cold ashes. The thick gray air shut out the sun and lay around him like a heavy blanket.

This was the day of the confrontation! Jesus's brown eyes scanned the rocks and bushes around him, and it came to him for the first time that the meeting had been foreordained. And the outcome? Was that already set too? If so, did it matter what he did now? To let himself be beaten by his unnamed adversary was unthinkable; his was a competitive spirit, and his body was charged with adrenaline. The theology, philosophy, rationalization, and storylines would come later.

Jesus rose and stretched. A glance at the sparse amount of food he had brought convinced him that he was not hungry. After so many days of eating so little, his appetite was almost nonexistent.

Looking around, he found a stone outcropping, and it was there he perched so that he could see the valley below stretching to the horizon.

The sun had begun its ascent toward midmorning when Jesus first became aware of the return of the dark presence. His skin crawled as if a long-legged spider had done a light tap dance across the back of his neck. Jesus's stomach tensed in a knot, and the first feelings of nausea began. The dark force was heavy in the air. The sky, which had been clearing now, became a dank, thick, and palpable gray.

Involuntarily Jesus turned sharply. There was the blur of a squat ugliness lurching out of sight among the rocks and then nothing but the jerky swaying of a bush where something had been. Jesus tensed, leaning slightly forward on the balls of his feet, and smothered the tendency to call out for the presence to identify itself. A part of him, for he was man as well as God, longed for some structure to impose itself on the situation. Jesus waited for the visitor to make the first move; after all, it was his show.

Jesus turned his gaze out toward the valley below but saw nothing, for his full attention was riveted on the area immediately behind him. Occasionally

Jesus heard the rattle of small rocks disturbed by scurrying feet, punctuated by the guttural grunts of a beast making its way closer to the outcropping on which he sat.

Jesus felt the hair on his neck rise. Fear tried to force itself into his insides; it was as if someone was working a bellows attached to his stomach, attempting to infuse him with a frenzied terror, which would propel him racing hysterically down the slope and away from this place. His ears strained to locate the movement behind him. Somehow he knew that his fear fueled the force, which stole closer to him, and he resolved to control his anxiety. He closed his eyes, face uplifted to the sky, and breathed deeply and slowly. Jesus repeated this several times and visibly relaxed, his face seeming more tranquil and his body more centered upon the stone seat. He became less aware of the intimidating presence, which now seemed to be everywhere like smoke wafting slowly through the air. And yet that wasn't true, for he was even more aware of the presence; the difference was that now he did not feel so vulnerable.

"Jesus!" a strong commanding thought voice boomed and rolled down the mountainside and across the valley. There was no masking what it was or who its owner was; this was the essence of evil, the embodiment of all that was bad. An image of a horned face with long yellow teeth flashing from a grinning mouth formed in Jesus's mind. Jesus fought his revulsion and breathed deeply again, feeling himself relax, creating a little more distance between himself and the presence.

Jesus said nothing and waited.

"Jesus!" the voice said again more loudly. "So you call yourself the Son of God. Well, now isn't that just a trifle grandiose?" There was derisive laughter, full and laced with sarcasm. "Come now, Jesus, how could you, a frail human, be a Son of God? Isn't that just a little preposterous?"

Jesus made no sign that he had heard.

There was an impatient, menacing movement among the bushes just behind Jesus, perhaps engineered to startle and frighten him.

"If you are the Son of God, you should be able to pass a simple test or two. Aren't gods and their progeny possessing of at least a little magic?

"And to make it more satisfying for you, Jesus, I shall offer you a prize if you pass the tests." The laughter rolled from the thick throat

"Let us begin."

Jesus continued to sit still on the rock. He didn't know what else to do besides to stay calm and wait.

There was a movement directly behind him. The hair on his neck rose, and his back arched. Now there was the sound of deep rasping breathing as the creature stole even closer. Then smacking of lips and a groaning whine.

"Jesus, Jesus, I'm here with you, with you, with you!" the voice chanted from behind. "Look at me. See me, see me!"

Jesus took a deep breath and slowly exhaled it. Something touched his shoulder, and he felt his skin trying to roll up and escape. A cold hand with long rough fingers now spread on the side of his neck. The smell of the creature was almost overpowering, and Jesus fought an urge to retch. Another deep breath, slowly exhale.

"So you are the Son of God?" The voice had taken on a syrupy, sarcastic tone that spoke in cadence with the hand moving on Jesus's neck and shoulder. Its foul breath seemed to beat on the side of his face like a dry hot wind from the desert. "No doubt you have been fasting before coming here, and you are hungry. Are you not?"

Jesus said nothing. Deep breath, slowly exhale, ignore the smell and touch and sounds.

"If you are the Son of God, then you must prove it to me. You see these stones scattered on the hillside? Of course you do. They are everywhere. All you have to do is command that the stones be made into bread. Then not only will you have proven your identity, but you will have something to eat."

Jesus became aware of a strength entering his being. Whatever doubt he had about being able to stand his ground against the creature was gone. He took another deep breath and said, "It has been written that man doesn't live by bread alone but by every word that comes from the mouth of God."

Did the hand flinch? Was there a gasp from the creature hanging over his back? Jesus's nausea subsided, and he felt stronger. A smile touched the corner of his mouth, for he had weathered the temptation of the creature.

Suddenly he was no longer on the hillside sitting on a rock outcropping. Within the blink of an eye, the setting had changed. Now he was seated on a pinnacle of the temple in Jerusalem. The creature was behind him, an arm draped over Jesus's shoulder, its coarse hair scratching his neck. Jesus turned his head and scanned the city and beyond. It was an impressive sight.

The hoarse whisper beat into his ears. "If you are the Son of God, then you could throw yourself down from the pinnacle. Didn't your people write that your God would send angels to catch you? Why, I would wager that the angels would not allow you to suffer even one bruise." The creature put his head on the other side of Jesus and whispered into his other ear, "Come on, come on, come on, jump, Jesus, jump! Jesus, jump!"

Jesus felt himself tottering on the pinnacle but was steadied by the return of the God spirit. Again he felt strong and powerful enough to overcome any obstacle.

"It is written," Jesus said, "thou shalt not tempt the Lord your God. Would you have me tempt him?"

"Oh yes, I would I would. Let's tempt him if you are, in fact, the Son of God. If you are, that is."

Then the pinnacle and the city of Jerusalem were not there. Jesus was back on a mountain, only it wasn't the one on which he started. This one reared itself into the sky so that one could see for many miles in every direction. The air was thin and light blue, and a stiff chilled wind blew. Jesus found himself sitting on a rock in the middle of the mountaintop, with the creature still behind him. Now both hands were on his shoulders, and as he spoke, Jesus could feel its roughness as it rubbed against him.

"Look all around you. It is beautiful, is it not? You are looking at the kingdoms of the world, a sight not many ever see. Now, if you are the Son of God—and I doubt that you are—I will give you these kingdoms—all of them, in all their glory—if—and here's the test, Jesus—if you will fall down and worship me."

Again the spirit filled Jesus, and without pausing he replied, "Get away from me, fool! It is written that man shall worship God only. Him only shall be served. You are wasting your time!"

Jesus became aware that he was now standing and facing the creature that had stood behind him. He was surprised at how small it seemed, how powerless it appeared.

"Go away! Leave me alone!"

The creature turned and scurried away, disappearing into the underbrush. Jesus was left alone on the mountaintop, and now it wasn't the mountaintop any longer. He was back on the hillside, sitting on the rock ledge.

Jesus thought he heard a bird singing, but he was too tired to listen. He leaned back against the side of the hill, nestled his head on his arm, and slept. While he rested, he dreamed that angels came and rubbed ointment on his body, bathed him, and perfumed his clothes. It was a beautiful dream; and when he awoke, the sun was coming up, and he felt rested and refreshed.

Jesus lay on the ground with eyes half open and unseeing, drinking in the sounds of the earth. He had been exhausted after the ordeal with the creature. He marveled at how tempting the offers had been even though they had been so theatrical in presentation. Jesus wondered if he was actually capable of performing the tricks outlined by the creature.

Jesus dozed in the morning sunlight. There was still a circumambient stench hanging on to the mountainside, but the voice and the maniacal laughter were gone. Jesus recalled how the creature had become increasingly angry and frustrated when he would not play his game with him and how the force of his rage had physically caused Jesus to recoil. Never had he experienced anything close to the anger that had been unleashed against him, and never had he seen a force so thoroughly whipped as was the creature when it skulked away.

It was late afternoon when Jesus woke to a ravenous hunger. Somehow he was not surprised to find food beside him. He ate heartily and discovered he was sleepy again. He leaned against the rock and succumbed to his fatigue. The next day would be soon enough to return to the valley.

His last thought as he fell asleep was *What else do you have planned for me, God?*

Chapter 14

Prologue 7: BCE 5027
The Contest

The rules of Captain Aladam's game were simple. Each team had the task of constructing a project to be judged on the basis of originality and its utility for the natives, in that order. Each team could construct as many projects as they wanted but could make only one their official entry. It was a difficult task in itself to find out what sort of unique structure would be of use to the primitive natives, for they had never thought in such terms and, besides that, had limited verbal skills. Usually the decision was made by the team without consultation with the supposed benefactors of the contest. After all, what did they know?

"How are the contests going?" Evaze asked.

"The men have invested themselves in the contests. I am pleased on that point."

"Good. How are the teams selecting which natives they will help? I've been curious about that."

Each team could choose anyone within their quadrant even if on the other side of the planet. After all, if restricted to the landmass on which they were established, two of the quadrants would have a decided advantage over the others because of the geography. The land immediately to the south and west was desert.

Aladam smiled ruefully. "It has turned out sort of backward. In the beginning the conventional wisdom was for a team to choose the more highly developed peoples in their quadrants. The idea was that the smarter natives would have a better idea of what would benefit their people. And furthermore, the reasoning went, they would be more capable of helping to carry out a project."

"And they didn't?" Evaze raised her brow in surprise.

"The more advanced peoples on this planet seem to be uniformly agreed on what should be built."

"I'm not sure I'm ready for this," she said.

"The leaders insist that the teams build fancy tombs for them."

Evaze looked perplexed, smiled, and said, "How strange. Why would they do a thing like that?"

"It's a status symbol, I suppose. The bigger the structure, the greater the leader. Or I guess that is what the leader hopes they will say about him after he is dead. I suppose that before he dies, he can order them to believe that. Why, I don't know, since he'll not be around to enjoy the plaudits."

"That is the height of self-indulgence! These natives are unlike any I have come across," Evaze said thoughtfully.

"Oh, one other thing I heard the men talking about. One of the leaders wanted a tomb for his burial, and he planned to seal into the vault with his body no less than one hundred of his best warriors."

"While they were still alive?" Aladam nodded.

Evaze frowned. "That's awful! What is it about these people that they are so filled with pride and destruction?"

"I don't know, Evaze, but I find that I like them less and less."

One of the teams opted for originality at the expense of utility; they constructed a huge statue of a thur, a catlike animal native to Bigor. Its face was similar to that of a human, but prominent bone protrusions came down on each side of the head and covered the ears. The monument was so impressive that the rulers of the area began fashioning head gear to match the shape of a thur's head.

Life on the planet was not boring if one had the energy to involve himself in an activity. There was sufficient technical expertise among the crew and tools from the ship to make most any project feasible. The shuttle craft allowed travel to any part of the globe, and several very beautiful geographic areas were discovered. Meanwhile, the contests provided an ongoing camaraderie, which made for fun and excitement.

Uber tried to involve himself in the activities. He knew that for his own good he should be a part of the activities, but his attention was constantly invaded by a morose sense of foreboding. He was unable to adequately describe his feelings other than the fact they were disturbing and frightening.

Having noticed his own discomfort immediately upon their arrival on the planet, Uber had considered telling the captain. But he was not sure what he would say other than "Captain, I feel there is something evil on this planet. Can't we go somewhere else to be shipwrecked?" What could Aladam do even if he believed his crewman?

Uber felt trapped in a no-win situation. To tell someone would invite ridicule, and to not tell anyone meant suffering alone. Either way there was no way to change anything. The foul waves of evil beat upon him unmercifully, with the only consolation being that some days were less frightful than others.

One morning after breakfast, Uber walked to the edge of Adun and gazed across the plain toward the mountains in the distance. For anyone else, the scene would have been beautiful, but for Uber it was just something to do as he tried to distract himself from his feelings. In the distance he could make out a few villages and even the forms of people moving about. He wondered how long the people had lived in those locations like the one village to the west. The inhabitants were largely gatherers of food and hunters; they had not yet learned to cultivate the ground and enrich the place where they resided. It would be up to Kine and others to pave the way.

Uber thought back to other places where he had stood at a distance and observed the natives. He never sought to make meaningful contact with them, only to search the places of discard in their midst: the garbage dumps, campfires, and ruins of temples. It was in places like these that the artifacts were to be found. He had great interest in the bits of buried history although he could recall little of it after leaving a planet. He nevertheless enjoyed the process of seeking and finding hidden information.

That's how he spent his free time on whatever planet he was assigned, poking around campsites and villages, looking for clues to what had been.

Because of space limitations, he could not carry many of his prizes with him on the ship, but he photographed and catalogued his findings on microfilm. After all, Uber enjoyed the search more than the actual find. The conclusions were not nearly as important as the satisfaction gained from the search and discovery. This solitary hobby was the only thing approaching satisfaction for the lonely and tortured man.

Chapter 15

DERXTER THE DREADED

Derxter squinted and shaded his eyes with one hand. The heat of the noonday sun caused sweat to run down his brow, and he wiped it away impatiently. Although he would have been more comfortable in the shade, he could see better from his vantage point. Derxter could be amazingly single-minded in purpose, which accounted in some measure for his success as a secret agent.

His companion, Squirb, a short squat man who was clearly restless and at that moment not so impressed with Derxter's powers of concentration, spoke, "Don't you think we should be in the shade? I mean, not only shall we likely be hit with sunstrokes, but these crude natives will surely think us mad for electing to expose ourselves this way. Really!"

"Shut up!" Derxter hissed. "If you are so hot, crawl under a stone!"

Squirb pulled his cloak about him and haughtily flounced around the corner of the building where he found shade. He raised a clenched fist and shook it in Derxter's direction. "One day," he muttered.

Derxter gazed toward the river and tried to make out the shapes of people. Surely they would be coming soon, he thought. If, in fact, Jesus had sought baptism from the man, John, then there was an excellent chance that John, not Jesus, was the messiah. If that was the case, then Derxter's attentions should be placed on John.

When first given his orders to become part of the Star Light operation, Derxter had been disappointed. By nature and training, Derxter enjoyed the spilling of blood but also thrived on the challenge of a difficult and intriguing assignment. He had demonstrated his uncanny abilities several times, winning the admiration and trust of Lybur.

"Star Light?" Derxter had said.

"Yes," said Lybur. "Is anything wrong?"

"I just thought I might be needed in other places."

"Such as?"

"Oh, some place where there might lurk more danger, more opportunity, shall we say, for cunning, carnage, and cruelty."

Lybur smiled. Half the time he did not know if Derxter was serious or being facetious. He found that he liked the man even if he would never completely trust him.

"You shall have that, my eager soldier. Read your instructions."

Derxter had returned to his quarters and read the orders. He was not disappointed.

When Derxter was a child, his father bludgeoned his mother to death in a fit of rage and fled with his son to one of the outlying planets. Growing up in a frontier colony was quite difficult for the youngster but excellent training in survival. Fortunately for Derxter, he was intelligent and physically well developed for his age. Unfortunately for him, his father had frequent rages, which caused the boy to avoid him as much as possible.

Driven into the streets, Derxter found himself part of the rough and dangerous crowd so common on an outlying planet.

He became an astute observer and eventually an effective and quite deadly fighter. Derxter killed his first man, a street drunk who tried to molest him, when he was eleven years of age. Death was common, and street derelicts had no value; therefore, no one thought much about it. His reaction to watching the man writhe on the street bleeding to death from a slit throat was one of excitement. After that, Derxter looked for opportunities to inflict pain on others and, if possible, murder them. This not only gave him vent for his repressed rage but ensured his survival. Such early training and experience enhanced his current worth as a hired agent for clandestine operations.

Although he was not a witness to the death of his mother, there was never any doubt in Derxter's mind about who murdered her. At that time he was simply too young to do anything but flee with his father. Before he grew old enough to confront the man, his father was killed in a street fight.

After that, Derxter found he could survive better by his wits and the shrewd use of force than through the hard mining work available on the planet. It did not take long to establish himself as prominent among the criminal element; and he became successful with the black market, extortion, and assassination. He figured that he had inherited the best from both his parents: his mother's charm and wit and his father's cold cruelty and absolute lack of any semblance of a conscience.

Derxter moved up so quickly that his base of power soon threatened other criminal ringleaders. He became paranoid and doubled his bodyguard, not without good reason. He spent more time looking over his shoulder than developing his illegal enterprises. This dulled his enjoyment as Derxter was a man who craved excitement and pleasure, and it was merely tedious to spend his time guarding his flank. It was at that time that Derxter was recruited by Lybur.

Long ago Lybur discovered that the best recruits for the ranks of his henchmen came from the colonies. Life there was hard, and those who survived were usually the toughest anywhere.

Derxter considered Lybur's offer and accepted the same day. Knowing that he would never return to the colony, he turned what assets he could into cash and walked away, coldly closing the door on his former life; he would never think of it again. He could do that, for life in the colonies taught emotional detachment and expediency.

Although he preferred to work alone, Derxter was assigned a companion for Star Light. When he first met Squirb, Derxter laughed out loud. Then he became angry. The little plump man seemed obscenely incompetent and grated on his nerves when he talked. Nevertheless, Lybur insisted that Derxter be accompanied by Squirb. The Star Light mission was a potential political bomb, and it was Lybur's intention that Squirb's presence would encourage Derxter to use discretion.

Their training program was intense and prepared them for entry into an alien, primitive civilization on an obscure faraway planet. Their job was to blend into the population until a certain man announced that he was a messiah. When located, he was to be closely observed. If at all possible, the natives were to be turned against the Messiah and incited to put him to death. If this did not work, then Derxter himself had license to kill the Messiah. In either event, the Messiah was to be terminated before Derxter left the planet.

Derxter had carried out enough similar missions to know that there would be bloodletting; he would make certain of that.

Derxter wiped his brow just as he heard a shout. Someone was running down the street calling out in an excited voice, "He did it! He did it!"

"Who did what?" Derxter snarled under his breath. People were incredibly stupid! They all should be put out of their misery. He and Squirb had been living among the Hebrews for several months waiting for a messiah to come forth, and Derxter had come to hate the people. "They are sweaty and smelly and stupid!" he told Squirb.

"John baptized Jesus!" People gathered around the winded man and pressed for details.

"It was like a bird, a dove, that came out of nowhere and lit on him. And a voice, it was surely the voice of God himself. It said he was pleased with his son." After his run, the clamoring crowd was too much for the man, and he fainted from excitement and heat exhaustion.

Derxter made the instant and wrong conclusion that John the Baptist was the man he was after. Nothing else made sense. Surely a man who considered himself a messiah would not ask a lesser being to perform a holy ritual on him. No, the Messiah would be the one with the power and status to baptize others. And didn't the man say something about a dove landing on his shoulder? Derxter beckoned Squirb to follow, and the two made their way to their small rented room. There they plotted the demise of the messiah, John the Baptist.

Salome bowed properly to her stepfather, King Herod. She breathed heavily from the exertion of the dance but held her poise.

"My dear, your performance was exquisite, most satisfying." He smiled and turned to the court, a signal for the spectators to clap in agreement.

"And now, in return for this most enjoyable entertainment, I shall honor a wish. Anything you desire shall be yours this night. Nothing shall be spared, for you have made my birthday party a delightful occasion." There was applause from the crowd.

Salome, though beautiful in body, was not overwhelmed with intelligence. In addition, she had been most dependent on her mother, Herodias, all her life. Her mental deficiency had been well hidden by her beauty and Herodias's protective manipulations.

"Father, let me speak with Mother about this," she asked her stepfather.

"Very well," said Herod.

Before Salome had reached her mother's side, Herodias knew what it was Salome would ask for. Herodias was an ambitious woman who had defied the law by leaving Phillip and marrying Herod. People looked the other way, not daring to question anything Herod's royal family did. All but John the Baptist, who made no secret of his displeasure with the match. That had been enough to land John in jail where he would likely stay until he made a public apology.

But that afternoon a peculiar thing had happened. A stranger appeared in Herodias's quarters. He made no threats but gave Herodias information that brought her blood to a boil. The stranger said John would not only refuse to apologize but that he would make public other facts, scandalous stories of Herodias's past, tales that would, true or not, shame her greatly and embarrass the king.

Herodias's tendency toward ruthlessness made her decision a quick one.

Salome approached Herod at the great table after conferring with Herodias.

"Ah yes, my dear, have you decided?" Herod smiled, for he was happy this evening and was about to be generous with this lovely stepdaughter. "What is your wish?"

"The head of John the Baptist on a platter." Salome glanced at her mother. Herodias nodded, indicating that her daughter had done well.

Herod was not so happy now, for he had no desire to harm the wilderness preacher. But he had made an offer before witnesses, to his own family. To back down would be to lose face.

He turned to the guard and gave the command for John's head to be presented on a platter to Salome. Herod did not try to smile.

The palace servants carried many stories from the royal chambers, and it did not take long for the news of John's death to reach the streets. Derxter and Squirb walked around the marketplace early the next morning and listened to the gossip. Squirb was openly delighted upon hearing the news.

"We did it! Can we go home now?"

"Yes, that was too easy, almost. We will wait awhile. Perhaps another messiah will come along. It is too far to be running back and forth from Bigor to Earth just to kill men who call themselves messiahs."

"But who would know?" whined Squirb. "We could truthfully tell Lybur that we had the Messiah killed. Would it be our fault if another came out of nowhere?"

Derxter raised his hand as if to strike his short companion. "We will do it my way."

Squirb cringed from the threatening gesture. There were times when Squirb hated the man, but he needed Derxter as long as they were on Earth; Squirb had no illusions about his ability to function well on his own in an alien culture.

It was the next day before they heard the news that Jesus was allegedly the messiah. Derxter cursed and broke a chair against the wall while Squirb tried to appear invisible until Derxter's rage passed.

"And what do we do next? Is it time for us to kill him?" asked Squirb when the worst of Derxter's anger was spent.

"No, I do not think that it is time for that."

"But," argued the short fat man, "it would be so simple. And quick. And then we could leave this place."

Derxter cast a disgusted look at his helper. "We will do it right, fat man. We will see what we can do about getting the Messiah killed by the natives, just as John was." He shook his head. "Squirb, you are stupid. When you are in our business, you must do things right. Those who hire us are not forgiving people and do not allow second chances. Just as I do not."

Squirb lowered his gaze, embarrassed and resentful. "Yes, I suppose you are right."

"Tomorrow we will find this man Jesus and follow him. Anyone who calls himself a messiah will offend someone." Derxter put his large hand on Squirb's shoulder. "And we might hasten the enemy-making by planting some disinformation."

Squirb put on a smile and nodded dutifully.

The next morning found Derxter and Squirb on the road to Cana in Galilee, where Jesus was reported to be preaching. It was late afternoon before they came around a bend in the road and saw the people seated on a hillside. Seated on a rock ledge slightly above them was a man talking to the crowd. It was not a large crowd as Derxter had expected; but then again, when one was starting out in the messiah business, one had to be patient.

A man squatted in the shade of a rock ledge, and Derxter asked him who the speaker was.

"Oh, that is a man named Jesus," the fellow said. "I just got here myself, but I heard that he is good to listen to." He moved over. "Would you like some of my shade?"

"Yes," said Squirb at the same time that Derxter grabbed him by the elbow and firmly directed him closer to the crowd.

"No, we will go closer so that we don't miss anything." The man in the shade nodded and turned his attention once more to the speaker.

Derxter found a seat under a tree and turned his attention to Jesus. Squirb managed to crowd into the same shade, most of it made by Derxter's bulk. Squirb had no interest in theology and paid no attention to what was being said. Derxter, on the other hand, had long ago learned that it was important to know one's enemy in order to defeat him. If it required sitting on a rock trying to keep from overheating and listening to a bearded preacher talk about theology and tell simple stories, then so be it. Derxter was a professional.

As the afternoon wore on, the audience began to drift away. Several people bid Jesus good-bye and left while others moved closer to him. Many stood and stretched, Jesus included.

"There were not as many here today as I had hoped," one of the men, a tall muscular, fellow said.

"Do not worry. They will come when they know who I am."

The man looked at Jesus with some puzzlement. "And who are you exactly, I mean?"

It was at that moment a man came up the side of the hill toward the small group. He was stooped, walked with a limp, and one hand was twisted back and hidden in his cloak. Derxter's first impression was of an assassination attempt, and he automatically tensed. It would be an unusual treat to be part of the audience of such a murder rather than the perpetrator, as he usually was.

"Jesus! Jesus!" the man hoarsely called as he lurched up the rocky pathway.

As he came closer, it became evident that the man was suffering from a disease in its advanced stages. His face was red with swelling, and the lesions on his face and neck were discolored and running. The watchers recoiled as he drew near.

Upon reaching Jesus, the man fell to his knees.

"If you want to," he uttered in a gravelly voice, "you can make me clean."

Jesus was fatigued from his long day of teaching, but at the sight of the wretched man at his feet, renewed energy seemed to course through his body. The lines on his face softened, and his eyes were as deep still pools as they fastened on the sick man. One of his hands went out and touched the man's shoulder. His sleeve was pulled up to reveal more sores.

"The man is eaten up with something," Squirb whispered to Derxter. "There is nothing to be done." Derxter's hand automatically touched the handle of the laser gun under his robe. The wretch should be put out of his misery!

"I do want to," Jesus said softly. His body seemed to grow large, perhaps by the intake of a deep breath, and a power seemed to flow from the Messiah down his arm and into the body of the man.

"Be clean!" said Jesus.

The man's head lifted, and his eyes rolled back into his head. He collapsed on the ground and quivered, face buried in the earth. Derxter concluded that the man was undergoing a seizure and wondered what Jesus would do when the man stopped his convulsions and still had the skin disease.

Suddenly the shuddering stopped. The man pushed himself to all fours and raised his head. Jesus pulled back his robe to reveal the man's face. There was no sign of disease. There were gasps from the crowd. Derxter stared hard at the fallen man. How could that be?

The man felt his face, and realization slowly caused a smile to cover his face. Jesus reached out, firmly grasped the man's shoulder, and said sternly, "Listen, don't tell anyone about this. But go straight to the priest and let him examine you. Then in order to prove to everyone that you are cured, offer the sacrifice that Moses ordered."

Still smiling, the man looked up at Jesus. He threw up his arms, leaped into the air, and let out a whoop. Grabbing Jesus in a bear hug, he picked him up off the ground, kissed him on the cheek, and exclaimed, "Thank you!"

Then he turned and ran—more like danced—down the slope and toward the village.

Jesus was left with his hand up and mouth open, ready to again admonish the man to not spread the news of his cure, but he was too late. Derxter thought to himself that not even a real messiah could expect someone to keep his mouth shut after being cured of something as ugly as the skin disease he had just seen.

One of Jesus's followers, the large muscular one, excitedly asked if he should go after the healed man. "I can catch him if you don't want him going into the village.

"No, Peter, we cannot keep as prisoners everyone we help." His eyes seemed to twinkle.

Peter smiled, relaxed, and said, "No, I guess that doesn't make much sense. Cure people and then keep them prisoner." He shook his head and walked away.

Squirb stepped forward as Jesus turned to leave. "Excuse me, sir, but that was quite a—what do you call it?—miracle you performed. Would you mind telling me how you did that?"

Jesus stopped and regarded the short man only an instant before Squirb was yanked away by Derxter. "Excuse my friend," he said to the Messiah. "He is not very smart, and he might need to be cured someday."

When they were out of earshot, Derxter pushed Squirb against a tree, his massive hand choking him. Squirb perspired freely, made a few choking whimpering noises, but could form no words. Derxter had killed several people before in this very fashion. There was a certain fascination in watching the life slowly drain from a man, and it was exaggerated by his closeness to the victim. Eyes bulging, Squirb was close to losing consciousness when Derxter suddenly released him, letting his squat body slide to the ground where he lay gasping and wheezing for breath.

"Don't ever do anything stupid like that again or I'll kill you!"

Squirb lay on the ground for a while gasping for breath. After a while he was able to stand, and he followed Derxter down the road. He made no attempt to catch up to the big man but followed behind a good hundred yards. Although shaken by his brush with death, Squirb was filled more with hatred than fear.

Behind them, on the hillside, James turned to John with a perplexed expression. "What do you suppose it is with those two? They are unlike anyone I have ever seen."

"They are strange. If they show up again, I think we should keep an eye on them," said John. "Do you think we should tell Jesus about them?"

"No, he has enough on his mind. We will keep our eyes open."

The sun set before they arrived at Cana. Derxter stopped and made a camp off the main road. After a while Squirb shuffled into the camp area and slumped to the ground some distance from where Derxter sat.

"Tomorrow they will go into Cana. We will follow them for a while." Derxter had already put out of his mind the incident with Jesus and Squirb. He did not allow his mind to be cluttered with grudges or apologies or sympathies. It was more productive to deal with the present in terms of efficiency and expediency.

Squirb was wakened the next morning by the toe of Derxter's sandal. "Wake up. It is time to go."

The two men walked to the road, and it was a short wait before they spotted a group of men ambling in their direction. Jesus was talking, and the others listened intently.

"He never stops. He must have a lot to tell," observed Derxter. Squirb said nothing, and Derxter ignored him.

The messiah and his group gave scant notice of the pair beside the road, although James and John exchanged glances. Derxter and Squirb fell in behind the band, trying to be as unobtrusive as possible. Squirb was still too upset to hear what was being said, and Derxter had great difficulty focusing on the Messiah's dialogue with his followers. It seemed that most of the talk had to do with codes of ethics regarding one's behavior, a lot of "shoulds" and "should nots," which had little meaning to the professional agent. For him life was simple: you did what needed to be done and what you could get away with at any given time. You did not bother yourself with "niceness." And if you were going to survive, you always put yourself first. Plain and simple. Anything else was foolish and probably dangerous. It could get you killed. His frame of reference was so different from what he heard these people talking about as to be nonsensical. After a while he stopped trying to keep up with their conversation.

Before they reached Cana, several young people had come to meet them. They were excited and danced around in front of the group.

"Are you going to heal someone today?"

"Show us another miracle!"

"Heal my grandmother. She is very ill."

When they reached the village, they encountered a large crowd. One of the villagers came forward.

"I am the village elder. We have heard of your cure of the diseased man Odom. Thank you for that, for Odom is the nephew of my brother. He would not go home because of his condition, but now Odom is with his family."

Jesus stepped forward. "We wish only to find supplies and take some time for teachings. If you have a place where I could sit while talking, perhaps there are those who would care to hear."

The crowd heard most of what Jesus said and surged forward. They were expecting more miracles and pressed to gain the best seats. They did not care where he taught as long as they could see what he did. The elder was pushed up against Jesus and his men.

"Tell them to go back home. When it is time to teach, I will send out word. Then they can come."

The elder was pressed against Jesus and could not even turn around. Being of slight build, he had no interest in trying to fight the tide. "You tell them, Messiah!"

The messianic group began to fall back and finally turned and left the village. The crowd followed for a while but soon became convinced that no miracles were forthcoming and drifted back toward Cana.

"There is a good place to stop," said Mark and gestured toward a grassy area under a few trees. The group made its way to the place and regrouped.

"Master, if you perform miracles, we may not be able to enter the villages anymore. It may be safer for all if we stayed out in the countryside." Jesus nodded.

Derxter fingered his laser gun under his cloak. He was thinking of how dramatic it would be to gun down a few of the pushy villagers. How simple it would be to outshine this messiah! He smiled. *My, my, Derxter, now aren't you theatrical?* he said to himself.

Chapter 16

PROLOGUE 8: 5027 BCE
THE SHADOW

One morning in the fall of the year, Uber went on one of his expeditions. He chose a village about two hours' walking time. It was far enough to give him some exercise and large enough to have a well-established garbage dump, which would keep him occupied for the remainder of the day. He carried a bag and a stick with which to poke the ground and possibly discover an artifact.

It was a clear, beautiful morning, and the air had a clean and fresh taste to it. Uber felt good and walked with a bounce. He was looking forward to this outing.

Uber slowly circled the village while its inhabitants warily eyed him, wondering what this stranger from the *Star Finder* was about. He crossed a ridge, and from that vantage point spotted the dump. To get there, he would have to either enter the village and follow a main street out the west side or continue circling the village until he reached the other side. Although it was rougher, Uber chose the latter route. He was not comfortable around the natives unless he was on official business. On his own errand, as he was that morning, he was afraid his intentions could be misunderstood if he appeared too intrusive.

Over the next ridge Uber faced a ravine he would have to cross. The other side was a steep and difficult climb, but down the center of the ravine was a well-worn path. After studying the opposing ridge, he decided to follow the path, which would presumably provide a route to the dump.

Uber wound his way through the twisting ravine and within a short distance was walking in deep shadows. Ahead, where the ravine turned back, he could see a part of the mouth of a cave with markings on the wall. Had he stumbled onto the village tombs? Short of breath, Uber stopped, suddenly aware that his heart was beating faster than it should have, his palms sweating, and his stomach twisting into knots. He became aware that he had sensed danger!

He breathed deeply and tried to relax. His efforts were wasted as he suddenly heard the sound of footsteps around the bend. Someone heavy, from the sound of it, Uber thought nervously. The ravine twisted back out of sight, and several cave openings on the opposite bank stared back at Uber. He took one step forward and peered around the bend.

A wave of dark energy swept against Uber, almost toppling him. As he stumbled to regain his balance, he caught a fleeting glimpse of a dark shape looming in the shadows; before he could focus, it had disappeared into one of the caves.

Had he seen something? He was not sure. What he was certain of was his terror. His skin was covered with goose bumps, and the hair on his neck stood out straight. A roaring sound filled his ears, and his vision dimmed. His legs felt immobilized as if encased in solid rock. Time had no meaning, and all he could think of was vomiting. Somehow he turned and stumbled from the ravine, filled with fear that the thing was following him. He dared not look back until he was safely out of the ravine, and then looking back on where he had been, he saw nothing.

Uber made his way home; there he sat trembling in a corner for a long time. It wasn't until the next day that he felt sane again.

I didn't even see or hear anything for sure! he moaned to himself. *I just felt it.*

And so, while the crew engaged in contests, played with the natives, and cheered one another as best they could, Uber remained aloof, buffeted by the unseen and dark forces whose nature he could only guess.

Once Captain Aladam came upon Uber when he was sitting on a ledge overlooking Adun. Aladam put his hand on the man's shoulder.

"Mind if I join you?"

Uber was startled. He had been staring at the ground, heavy in thought for some time. Either the dark—he could feel it more clearly these days—was either making its presence more strongly felt, or else Uber was becoming more attuned. In either case, it was now more difficult than ever to focus his attention on routine tasks.

"Uh, yessir, sit down." Uber moved over so that the flat rock could be shared as a bench.

"I'll get to the point, Uber. I've noticed—and the crew is equally concerned—that you are preoccupied, more like depressed, really."

The engineer glanced at Aladam and then back to the ground. He had wanted this chance to talk to the captain but now was leery of revealing his turmoil. But one thing he knew for certain, and that was he could not keep the matter to himself any longer.

"Captain, I'm a sensitive. You probably know that from my records. Ever since we've been here, I've felt a force, a darkness." He glanced up at the captain and felt himself on the verge of tears. "Something terrible."

"Hmm. What is it like?" Aladam asked awkwardly.

"It's bad! I don't like it!" Uber was startled by the amount of emotion that had crept into his words. He shook his head and almost whimpered, tears welling in his eyes. "It won't let me alone!"

Aladam was not sure what to say and was embarrassed at the man's show of emotion. He had once known but had forgotten that Uber was a sensitive. But he did not know much about dark forces and was not sure what questions to ask of his troubled crew member.

"See the doctor for a sedative, Uber. You need rest." He rose, touched Uber on the back, and felt genuine sympathy. Aladam not only felt a deep responsibility for the welfare of his crew but had developed a genuine fondness for them. *I would battle Uber's demons for him if I could,* he thought as he left the torn man holding his head in his hands.

Chapter 17

Prologue 9: 5028 BCE
A Celebration

It was at the end of the fifth summer that the crew had its first celebration.

"We've been here almost five full years, and I think the men have done remarkably well. Why don't we have a party?"

"Wonderful idea! Why don't we make it a time of sharing? The men could tell about their accomplishments. Some of them are very proud of what they've done here."

"Sounds like tall tale time," said Evaze.

"You can count on that. Some of these guys must lay awake nights thinking up stories to tell."

"It may be more entertaining to listen to the stories than to hear what they actually did."

"I have no doubt about that," agreed Aladam.

And so the first annual Adun celebration was planned.

Roots was the ship cook or had been for many years prior to the present situation. Although a chronic complainer, the large man enjoyed his work immensely. The size of his stomach was ample evidence of his liking for his own preparations. His frequent declaration as he served up his meals was "Allow me to introduce you to a culinary delight that may culminate in bouts of gustatorial ecstasy." Even though the men would not admit it, they liked Roots's cooking and there were seldom leftovers.

When Aladam approached Roots about a banquet, the cook was almost beside himself with excitement. He had not cooked for the crew in a long time and found it unsatisfying to prepare for only a few people.

"I'll take care of it, Captain," the burly man said.

"I know I don't have to say this, Roots, but make it something special."

Roots raised his brows and gasped in mock amazement. Aladain, always slow with the subtleties of human communication, reacted apologetically. "That's probably too much to ask of you. Why don't we make it something simple?"

"Dear, Captain," Roots said, "I was only hiding my amazement that you even thought you had to ask. Of course it will be special!"

"Oh, I'm glad that's settled." Aladam turned to leave and had a second thought.

"If this is personal, you don't have to respond. Uh, I have always wondered what your real name is."

"Roots," the cook said.

"I know that's what we call you. They were calling you Roots when I was assigned to the *Star Finder*. But what is your real name?"

"Roots." The cook stared blankly at the captain as if he was prepared to repeat his name all day if necessary.

Aladam waited a moment, thinking perhaps Roots would continue and offer an explanation of his name. When the cook said nothing, the captain said, "Oh, I see. I had always thought that you had perhaps gained the name because you cooked lots of roots. You know, when you hit a new planet, you send someone to locate the local roots so you can invent some new dish indigenous to that planet." Aladam shrugged and said, "I just wondered."

"Now, Captain, you have made me curious. How is my name given in the records?"

"Roots. I think it's Roots. I always meant to check but never thought of it when I was in records. You know how that goes."

"My name has always been Roots, Captain Aladam," the man said politely.

"Oh. Well, if you need anything, just let me know." Aladam left, feeling rather foolish.

The day of the celebration came and with it an atmosphere of festivities. Everyone was excited.

"We should have done this long ago, Evaze," Aladam said.

She smiled. "I don't remember ever seeing the men so animated. And some of them are even bathing for the first time in who knows when."

"It appears that several of the natives will be present. Besides their mates, I mean there has been a lot of interest on the part of the locals."

"My, but they are a curious bunch!" Evaze said.

"Yes, and I like that aspect of their character. But on the whole there is something about them I don't trust. They are so concerned with what is theirs and how they can get more. Greedy is the word." Aladam was clearly exasperated when talking about the natives. "I have heard them say things that were hurtful to their own spouse or child. To me they are a cruel people."

"You may be right, Aladam. I have not paid so much attention to them. It does not seem that the men have taken to them in a big way."

"Only to the women, and you can chalk that up to biology. What concerns me, Evaze, is that these people don't corrupt the crew."

"Aladam, what do you think I should wear tonight? She was not really counting on any valid opinion from her mate but was changing the subject. She did not like to see him upset himself over something about which he could do nothing. The two of them had been over the subject before, and she saw no advantage to plowing the ground again.

"Why don't you wear—oh, it doesn't matter, Evaze. You always look outstanding whatever you wear."

"Just as you say. It will be such a fine time tonight, won't it? Let me show you what I have picked out for you to wear."

The festival was held in Adun. Interstellar ships obviously did not come equipped with ballrooms, and there was no one room onboard large enough to accommodate a large gathering. Most of the men were surprised at how easily they had grown accustomed to the outdoors after years in a spaceship and rarely, if ever, returned to the *Star Finder*.

The natives were very cooperative in helping to prepare for the festivities. Several lambs and pigs had been slaughtered and cooked over a slow fire. Other dishes, mostly native, had been put together on a long table. But most of the crew had eyes for the table set up by Roots. They may not have missed the confines of the spaceship, but they certainly missed the culinary delights created by its resident chef.

The crew and their women sat in a large circle. Other natives sat behind them or made their way around the area, busying themselves with freshening the food or serving the crewmen. The evening was spiced by the serving of fine liquor from the ship's store. It had been the gift of a king on the planet Edor, located somewhere far away; and like many of the items presented to the captain and his crew, it had been stored away and forgotten. Occasionally these gifts were rediscovered—some several times—and often were jettisoned in space. Although they carried much significance for the givers, they were often worthless to the receivers and, worse, took up valuable space.

As the meal wore down and conversation lagged, Aladam made his opening comments, "It is with much pleasure that I welcome you to the first festival of Adun located here in the beautiful fruit grove." Aladam had rehearsed the first sentence after agonizing on how to start off his speech. He hated to make speeches.

"Life has not always been easy for us here for obvious reasons. We don't need to go into on this occasion, but I am proud, as your captain, to be a part of this group. You have made a fine adjustment to life in Adun and have related well with the natives." He had wanted badly to add "In spite of their ugly nature" but decided that would not be the diplomatic thing to say.

"And now let me invite you each to take a turn sharing your experiences with the rest of us. Perhaps you have a favorite moment you haven't told. Of course, we expect the truth and only the truth, and I would never suspect that you would exaggerate . . ." He was drowned out by hoots and laughter as the men joined in the spirit of the evening.

Shemile stood and immediately drew hisses and boos. He moved to the center of the circle, bowed, and signaled the group to quiet. "My friends of the *Star Finder*, we have come together on a fine occasion. When the good captain said we could tell on one another—"

"He didn't say tell on one another, you dope!" someone called out.

"Now, how did you know I was going to tell about you, Ernal?" Shemile said with a straight face.

There was much laughter and noise to drown out the protestations of Ernal, who was red-faced and obviously embarrassed about some as of yet untold incident.

"No, I'll let someone else tell about you, Ernal, because I have a tale about Clotiele that has to be told."

And the evening went like that, with much kidding, fun, and laughter. Aladam took Evaze's hand in his, smiled at her, and said, "This is a good time!"

Toward the end of the festival, Obul took his turn at the center of the circle.

"My fellow crew members, as you know, I have taken an interest in livestock." He swayed as he talked, and it became evident that Obul had been drinking more than he could comfortably handle. Alcohol abuse was rare on Bigor and unheard of among members of a starship crew. Laughter died as Obul continued, "I'm getting more and more of these animals 'cause I found out I'm a good trader. Can't sell the animals, but I can trade them."

"Sit down, Obul," someone said. "You're boozed!"

"Nope I'm not in . . . in . . . intoxicated. What I really wanted to tell you was about the funny thing that happened late today just before I came to the fes . . . festival." A smile twisted his face. "I was driving my stock to the watering hole—everybody knows where that is—when we came across this garden. It was a beautiful garden, I must say." He chuckled and then coughed. "My animals just ran right through it before I could do anything. It was so funny." He began laughing, doubled over, and continued until tears were streaming down his cheeks. Embarrassed, the crowd became quiet, which only made the raucous and inappropriate laughter of Obul seem even louder and more vulgar.

All eyes turned to Kine who had stood when Obul mentioned a garden. No one had to ask whose garden Obul had marched his herd across, for it was no secret that Obul had no use for Kine and his crops. The crowd visibly recoiled, for the thought of anyone doing such a thing was revolting.

But no one could know how wounded and enraged Kine was, for no one knew how much work the man had put into his garden. No one could understand the anguish Kine felt as he visualized his torn and trampled plants. Without a word, he turned and strode from the camp, his woman scurrying to catch up with him. The festival was effectively ended, and people gathered their things and left, with Obul still standing in the circle, laughing and recounting the stomping of the wheat.

The next day Obul was found dead of a knife wound. Aladam was heartsick and knew he had to be decisive. He was almost certain that Kine had committed the murder and could sympathize with him after Obul's crude and cruel behavior. But murder—that was unthinkable, and it had to be dealt with.

Aladam found Kine kneeling in his garden, motionless, staring at the wreck of what had been his pride and joy. The captain stood watching the man, pondering how one of his crewmen, a citizen of Bigor, could come to this. It did not make sense that a man who loved digging in the soil and watching plants grow and thrive would be capable of taking a life.

"Kine, we found Obul's body. If you deny responsibility for the murder, speak up. Otherwise, it is my duty to pass sentence."

Kine continued staring into the ground. Aladam waited, and no response was forthcoming.

"Kine, you are banished from Adun. Take your things and go." Aladam felt despair as he uttered the words yet knew that if this kind of behavior was now a possibility among the crew, then strong sanctions needed to be taken to discourage other such acts.

The last anyone saw of Kine was of him and his woman, Syri, belongings on their backs, walking westward from Adun and into the desert.

Chapter 18

JERUSALEM

In the days that followed, Sarn and Toler walked the streets of Jerusalem gathering what information they could about the so-called messiah. Most people had not yet heard of him.

Itinerant preachers were not uncommon, and the average person didn't pay too much attention to them. Their grand claims never materialized; and their discourses were predictable, often boring, and frequently strained the listeners' limits of credulity. The better ones were entertaining and provided a brief respite from one's worries, but that was all that could be said for them. Besides, most of them said things contradictory to the Jewish faith and were better not heard by those faithful to the One God. It was too bad, the old-timers often said, that another prophet didn't come along. Now those old-time prophets were real preachers, and God spoke through them loudly and clearly!

Several gods were worshipped in the land as there were any place in the world. Baal had been worshipped for hundreds of years and was still considered by many to be a necessary party to any successful undertaking. The Greek influence had left behind the worship of Zeus, and other groups had their own favorites. From time to time the reigning emperor decreed that he himself was the greatest god, and by law everyone in occupied land must worship him. The ruling monarch typically erected statues of himself in public places, and soldiers enforced the ritualistic worship of his godship, blatant narcissism made worse by extreme arrogance.

The Hebrews had worshipped only one god for many hundreds of years and called him Yahweh. Sometimes their people worshipped other deities as secondary gods, usually "just to be on the safe side." But the Jews, by their own law, could not tolerate graven images of a god and thus refused these statues when they could. After all, their god— the one true God, the Holy of Holies—was too great to be contained in any physical manifestation.

"I think his name is Jesus," the woman said as she washed her clothes. "I have not seen him myself, but I know someone who heard the man speak not long ago. It was nice, really, the way he spoke, or so my friend said."

In another market a young man reported having seen the Messiah, "He was not as excitable as the other preachers I have heard. He spoke in a quiet, calm way. I think he was a laborer before he decided to preach. His name is Jesus."

The other information Sarn and Toler gathered was essentially the same. The Messiah was named Jesus, and he came from a common family and had worked as a carpenter. He spoke in a kind, quiet voice and was more of a teacher than a preacher. He moved around the countryside, mostly in Galilee, sometimes sleeping in the open, accepting food from whoever offered it, and stopping to speak to almost everyone. It was said that his main base of operations was in Capernaum on the northern shore of the Sea of Galilee. There he frequented the home of a friend and often used it as a base for his teaching operations.

"Hextor was right on another point," said Toler.

"Yes, Jesus came from the lower class—better to go up than down or something like that," said Sarn. "Do you think we might become messiahs if we keep living like this?"

The two of them had been spending their nights in stables, on the open ground, or wherever they could find some amount of comfort. They bought their food where they found it and ate in the marketplace or on the curbside. Toler reasoned that they would be more likely to gain the information they sought from the poor side of life.

"I liked it better when we were eavesdropping around the Temple," said Toler one night as he huddled on the ground and tried to go to sleep. "I don't think I was cut out to be a poor person."

"I suspect we'll pass for poor folks easier than we will for religious sages."

"Could be," said Toler. "If I was in charge of messiah deployment, I think I would create a model that appealed to those on top, those with warm, soft beds and great food. Then when guys like us went out to scout their progress, they would at least be comfortable."

"If you were down and out—like we are—and some person claiming to be a god made a habit of helping your kind, don't you think you'd be talking about it?"

"Maybe," said Toler, "unless I figured it was just another false hope. Once poor, always poor." He turned over, feeling for a spot on the ground without lumps. "I'd be suspicious of anyone who wanted to help me. What's in it for them? I'd ask. Why would anyone care? A god should be currying favor with the rich class. They are the ones who can give money to build big temples. If I was a god, I'd much prefer to have the admiration of the rich than the poor."

"Oh?"

"Sure," continued Toler, "a god has to consider human nature. Maybe the rich are not interested in gods. For what do they need a god? They have everything they need. If I was a god, I'd consider where the market was, and it seems to be that the market lies with poor folks. I suppose there would be what one could call a god market."

"God market?" asked Sarn, frowning.

"Sure, who wants a god? If you are poor, then you want a god who tells you that you are worth something. If he manages to feed you, that's a bonus."

"I think it's the other way around," said Sarn. "They want to be fed first."

"If you are rich, then you might enjoy having a god who agreed with everything you wanted to do, but you might not even want that. You already know that you're worth a lot, and you don't need a god for that. And," he added, "they're well fed too."

Sarn let Toler's words hang in the air for a while.

"I don't think I agree with everything you said," said Sarn, surprised to hear his voice contradicting the captain.

Toler turned his head toward the young man, somewhat surprised himself.

"There has got to be more to it than just a trade in favors," said Sarn. "That just doesn't sound convincing to me. I don't care how poor I was. I wouldn't worship a god just to feel important or to get food. And if I was a god, I wouldn't want poor and worthless persons being my people because I didn't have anything to offer the rich. If it was like that, I'd say the god ought to find a better line of work."

Toler stared up into the clear night sky. The stars twinkled back at him. If only he could see far enough, he thought, he could see Bigor. And even Ahna. He wondered what she was doing at that moment while he was lying in a field arguing about gods and poor people.

"Sarn, if a power did exist and it lived on both Bigor and Earth, I have to be honest I'd have trouble accepting that. Give me some reasonable explanation, one I can understand, and I may change my mind."

"Why?"

"They're so different. Bigor and Earth, I mean. Look at these natives. They use theology to fill in the gaps. When they don't understand something, they explain it with a god."

"What's wrong with that? It's better than just leaving big blanks. People want to believe something."

"They could wait until good answers are found. Isn't that what we do?"

"I was taught that too," replied Sarn. "Just be patient and someday we'll know everything. Do you really believe that?"

Toler reflected on the question. "Not entirely. There have been times when, just when I thought I understood something well, the same questions were asked in a different way, and we had to start all over again."

"There is more to having a god than just filling in the gaps."

"Hmmm." Toler couldn't imagine what it could be, but he was too tired to ask. Maybe he would remember to ask Sarn next time the topic came up.

The next day found them again moving from village to town, seeking information about the Messiah.

"This guy needs a promotional campaign," Toler said after the third day. "He's moving too slowly for a god. He needs to impact. At this rate we could be here for years!"

Sarn nodded. He too had expected things to move faster.

"What does the manual say?" asked Toler. "By now what should a god be doing? A magic trick per day? Genuine, crowd-pleasing homilies and souvenirs for the kids?"

The pair roamed the streets of Jerusalem, making mental notes of what they heard about the alleged messiah. They stayed in crowds when possible and always kept a keen eye for any sightings of Derxter, Lybur's agent. On the fourth day Toler announced a change in strategy.

"Today we head for the outcountry. It seems that our friend doesn't intend to come to the big city, and I'm afraid our enemies may already be with him."

Sarn furrowed his brow. "What would keep Dexter from walking up to the Messiah and blasting him into dust and anyone else who got in his way?"

"That would be extremely risky for Lybur," said Toler. "I'm sure he would rather have the locals perform the deed."

"According to Hextor, messiahs get themselves killed anyway! All Lybur has to do is wait until Jesus gets himself killed."

"Good point. Maybe Lybur's timetable is different from that of the Messiah. Maybe he thinks this messiah will be different from the others and not be killed. Or maybe he wants to keep the Messiah from resurrecting."

"At the rate this guy is moving, it may be years before anyone notices him, much less gets offended," quipped Sarn. "But then what do I know about messiah timetables?"

The day was early, and they figured to make the next village before dark. Before they had reached the northeastern edge of the city, they came across a beggar. Reaching out his hand, the dirty man in ragged clothes pleaded for a gift.

"Give me but a penny and I'll take it to Jesus and he will multiply it many times over. I'll bring you your share, and we'll both have more. Oh, please . . ."

Toler stopped, placed a coin in the man's hand, but held on to it.

"Tell me about Jesus. Where is he to be found?"

The beggar tried to pull the coin from Toler's grasp. "To the north. He is in Galilee."

"Where is Galilee?" Toler demanded, holding on to his coin.

"It is to the north, around the Sea of Galilee. Follow the Jordan River." The man whisked the coin from Toler and scurried away to beg again.

"How did he know where the Messiah is?" asked Sarn. "He doesn't look like he gets out of the local gutters."

"Beggars make it a point to know where the miracle workers are."

From Jerusalem they trekked eastward to Jericho, a very old town that had been leveled so many times its inhabitants had lost count. Each time the city had been rebuilt, the new walls were placed on top of the previous structures so that over the centuries the ground had actually been built up more than a hundred feet over its original elevation.

The road to Jericho passed over and through the rounded hills. At one point they first heard and then saw spring water unexpectedly babbling down the opposite slope of a canyon. Farther down the road they were afforded a better view of the canyon and could see an aqueduct winding its way toward Jericho. Later they were to find out that the aqueduct provided an abundance of water for the desert city, turning it into a lush oasis and a beautiful and fruitful garden. The aqueduct had been designed and built by Herod the Great, the late and still-hated Roman king.

Several times they passed tribes of Bedouins, the nomadic Arab and his family, who lived in crude tents in the hills tending his sheep and goats. They were a simple people who stayed away from the cities as much as possible, for they were far more comfortable in the open country. For thousands of years, the great armies of Babylon, Greece, Egypt, and Rome had marched back and forth over the land, fighting one another and usually conscripting what Jews they could find in the cities and towns. When that happened, the Bedouins melted back into the fringes of the desert and usually escaped the fate of their city neighbors, the Jews. Similarly, when the road through the land was alive and active with trade among those great powers of Europe, Asia, and Africa, the Bedouins ignored the new ideas and extravagant goods and retired to their own counsel in the hills.

Chapter 19

MASADA

The rocky and barren area between Jericho and Jerusalem was thinly covered by sparse grass lying low to escape the occasional nuzzling of goats and sheep. It was therefore a welcome surprise to top the hill and discover the green lush farms surrounding Jericho. Because it was late summer, there were ample supplies of fresh produce for sale in the old city. Dates, apricots, pomegranates, along with cheese, bread, and wine, made a most enjoyable and filling meal. The variety of food was not as great as in Jerusalem, but what there was appeared fresh and appetizing. Purchasing enough food to last for several days, Toler and Sarn set their sights on Galilee to the north.

Sarn admired the countryside. "When we first landed in the desert area outside of Jerusalem, I had no idea that there would be any fertile areas like this one."

"It is beautiful, isn't it? I don't recall ever visiting a country where there was more variability of geography in such a small area." Toler gestured toward the squat rock buildings around them. "Jericho probably has a long history behind it. A site like this would be a natural place for a town."

They stopped at a well on the north side of Jericho and drank their fill. Toler leaned against a date tree and contentedly rubbed his back against the rough bark. Thoughts of an afternoon nap intruded, making the hot and dusty road seem even more aversive than it already was.

"That's not a good posture to take, considering what's showing," said Sarn.

Startled, Toler became aware that in his effort to relax and let cool air under his tunic, he had unwittingly revealed the laser gun strapped to his side. He quickly pulled the robe shut and glanced around. He shook his head in disgust at his carelessness.

"Advertising laser guns on the primitive planet Earth—now that's a smart thing to do!"

"I don't think anyone saw the gun. Want me to carry it?"

Toler cast him a sarcastic look. "Hah! You're not any more used to carrying a gun than I am."

"Excuse me, please." A voice startled them.

The speaker was a short dark-complexioned man of about thirty-five years of age. His large brown eyes sparkled from under his head covering. A thin smile gave an upward lilt to his black mustache and lifted his short beard forward as if it was trying to touch his sharp nose. The slight tilt of his head to one side announced his friendliness, much as a puppy might regard his master while waiting to be addressed. Attired in a red-and-blue shawl and a yellow robe, the fellow had an attractive flashiness about him.

"I am sorry. I did not mean to startle you. Please pardon me." His smile broadened to reveal gleaming white teeth. "My name is Arie, and I am a guide. Those who are passing through the countryside often need the services of one who is familiar with the land." With a bow and a grand sweep of one hand, he continued, "And I, Arie, am here to serve you."

Sarn and Toler exchanged glances. Toler stepped forward and spoke to the little man, who was at least a foot shorter, "Thank you for your offer, but we know our way."

"You know the way to the north to Galilee. That is no problem for anyone to find as long as they can walk beside a river." Arie turned and faced toward the south, to the Salt Sea and the palace at Masada. "Masada, my friends, I wager you have not seen."

Sarn was surprised and almost startled by the little man's knowledge of their destination. Toler figured it was no great feat for the guide to know they were headed toward the north since they had just bought food and were about to leave the northern edge of Jericho in a northerly direction. But he was intrigued about the Salt Sea and the palace at Masada.

"You have seen the palace on Masada?" Toler asked Arie.

"Does the sky have stars? Is a donkey stubborn?"

"Is that the one Herod built?" asked Sarn.

"Of course," said Arie in his smooth voice. "When Herod was appointed king of this region, he built three palaces. Masada was his winter quarters, a beautiful place set on a mountain, its courtyards always in warm sunlight. And totally impregnable."

"Why would he build such a palace?" asked Sarn. "He was king. He had Rome behind him. Who was going to bother him?"

"Herod was no dummy," and Arie glanced around and lowered his voice. "Crazy but no fool. He thought that a day might come when he fell out of favor with Rome, or there might be an uprising from the Jews."

"He had to be crazy to do some of the things he did," said Toler.

"Like those years when he crucified hundreds of Jews at a time?" Arie nodded slowly. "Yes, I think that was crazy."

"Was there anything to the story that he had all recently born infants killed because he had heard that a king had been born?" Sarn shook his head. "That seems a little preposterous."

"He was a preposterous man! A dangerous man!" Arie's voice had taken on an intensity that revealed his strong feelings toward the late king. He shrugged. "I do not know if he had the babies killed. That is the story, and it could be true. Without question his soldiers have done worse than that. That is why they are good soldiers. They do what they are told even by demented leaders."

He straightened himself, put on his smile again, and beamed at the two men. "But I digress with a history lecture! The palace on Masada is a wonderful sight, and from it one can see all of the Salt Sea stretching to the north and south."

The noon sunlight danced on his teeth as he made his pitch of intrigue and beauty in Masada.

"To be honest, a side trip would be a nice diversion. It might be good to get away for a while and let something develop. What do you think?"

Sarn considered the image of a mysterious palace on a fortress hill overlooking a dead sea. "Let's go," he said.

"Who lives there now?" Toler asked Arie. "We don't want any trouble with the Romans."

"No one is there now. Occasionally a traveler will stop off to see Herod's palace, but that does not happen often. Family members sometimes took vacations there, but rarely did Herod go. Now that he is gone, no one from the royal family goes there. His sons do not. They have their own favorite retreats. They think Masada is too far away." Arie threw his toothy grin at them as if to dismiss their doubts. "It would be just us."

"How soon can you take us?"

Arie's smile broadened. "Right now as soon as we discuss the little matter of a fee."

"The matter of a little fee?" Toler asked.

Arie chuckled, and within a short time a guide fee had been agreed upon.

"Is this how you get your business?" asked Sarn. "I mean do you just wander around looking for strangers who might want a side trip?"

Arie smiled. "Sometimes. I am self-employed and ready to find a fare anywhere. If a potentate from another country needs expert guidance to the Sea of Galilee, then who am I to refuse him? If farming experts from Rome want to be shown where the best olive groves are, then I take them. I am not too proud or narrow to handle most any job."

Toler felt a kinship with the little man. He too knew the tough world of the single entrepreneur.

After two hours the three came to the northern shore of the Salt Sea, or Lake Asphaltites. The light-blue water contrasted sharply against the yellow mountains to the east. Arie led them down a trail to a beach.

"We will take a swim," he announced. "It will cool us off."

All three removed their robes and shawls but kept their tunics on. The native men were very modest about revealing their bodies and would not allow themselves to be seen naked. Sarn was the first to jump into the lake, and Toler and Arie waded in behind him.

"This feels great!" said Sarn, and then his face screwed into a terrible spitting mask. "This is the saltiest water I have ever tasted! Ugh!" Toler raked his wet finger across his tongue and made a face. It was unbearably salty.

Meanwhile, Arie was floating with ease on his back. Fascinated, Sarn and Toler immediately imitated the guide and found they could not sink below the surface. Lying back, arms and legs out of the water, like pieces of driftwood, Sarn and Toler, to their delight, found they could not sink. Sarn took a deep breath and dove below the surface—almost. He came up sputtering and wiping his face.

"I don't think I could swim under the water if I wanted to!"

It did not take long for them to be refreshed and resume their trek south. They had not gone very far when they came across a small town between the lake and the mountains to the west.

Two men came from the settlement to meet them; Arie greeted them in his friendly manner and made small talk. He casually explained that he was taking the two foreigners to the south to En-gedi, which was north of Masada by several hours.

"And what, my friend, might be your purpose be in going to En-gedi?"

Without faltering, Arie said, "These men are looking for a dye and have heard that in the rocks near En-gedi is a deep red, which would be beautiful in robes." His own clothing contrasted wildly with the drab and colorless clothes of the men. "Do you think I would look good in a red robe?" Arie flounced his robe for the men, who were uncomfortable with his ostentatious display.

"You are welcome to spend the night in Qumran," said the other man, ignoring Arie's question. "You could leave early in the morning."

"Thank you, my friend, but it is more than a day's journey when you consider that we may be digging in the hills as we go. We had best go now."

While Arie talked with the two men, Sarn and Toler watched the people moving about the town, all seemingly with a purpose. To the west were mountains, and numerous caves dotted the heights. Paths leading up to the caves served notice that they were used frequently for storage and retreat. The water supply to the town was a series of ditches, which cleverly gathered the runoff from the mountains and directed it into the underground cisterns in the town itself. Qumran was located in a dry and hot area, but because the builders of the town had planned well, the people were still able to have water for the ritual bath, an important part of their religious practice. Soon Arie waved them on, and the three passed the town of Qumran.

"That seemed like a strange town," said Sarn.

"It is indeed," said Arie. "Those are dedicated people. They call themselves Essenes and choose to live out here by themselves where they won't be corrupted by the world. At first they started their colony without women. They planned to really keep things pure. But the consequences of a community without women were too dire to bear."

"And not very helpful to the future of their group," added Sarn.

Arie nodded. "They finally agreed to have a limited number of women come live with them, and now they have children too."

"Their plain clothing—is that because of their religion?"

"Yes. Everyone must work, and everyone must be totally dedicated to God. Bright colors only serve to distract them from their quest to be pure."

"Why did you not tell them we were going to Masada?" Toler asked. "Why did you lie to them?"

"Lie? No, a mere creative distraction. What business is it of theirs if we visit Masada? What if we told them we go there, and tomorrow a squadron of Roman soldiers happens by and finds out? Maybe the soldiers are just looking for something to do, so they follow us. No, my friends, when you live in occupied country, you learn to mind your own business and keep matters to yourself."

Toler pointed to a larger cave off to their right. "What are they doing?"

"That is their library," said Arie. "They study and write a good deal, these Essenes, and the cave is a good place to keep their books. They are a studious group. Some of them live in the caves."

"You sound well informed about them."

"I have been by here before, and they talk with me."

"Do you suppose the Messiah has been here?" asked Sarn.

"Who? The Messiah?"

"You know, Jesus, the man they call the Messiah."

"Oh. Jesus. Yes, I have heard of him. And yes, I think he has been to Qumran and even studied with them for a while. But he didn't stay too long. It was too confining for him, and I think they were ready for him to leave too. It was not his style to seclude himself."

"On the way back," said Sarn, "I would like to stop and visit with the Essenes. They sound most interesting."

Arie looked suspicious. "This messiah—you have an interest in him?"

"Some."

"What is your interest in this messiah if I may be so bold as to ask?"

"Nothing special. We heard he did magic tricks, and that caught our curiosity. You don't see good magic tricks every day, you know."

Arie nodded but seemed unsatisfied. "Yes, I heard that too."

Sarn noticed Arie's discomfort and asked, "What else have you heard about Jesus?"

A cloud of worry crossed the guide's face, and it seemed he clamped his jaws shut before answering. "I heard he has made some important people very angry and that his life is in danger. I would not want to be around him very much. It is best to be careful with whom you are seen."

Toler wanted to ask more questions, for he believed that Arie was not telling everything he knew, but thought it best not to seem so interested in Jesus. There would be other times when they could ask Arie about the Messiah.

The night was spent under an overhang where the mountain sprawled to within fifty yards of the sea. A fire felt good as the men shared their food under the stars. Toler tried to initiate a conversation about Jesus, but Arie was evasive and talked of other things.

"The Romans are a contradiction!" Arie said. "They are brilliant in some ways. Never has the world seen such successful armies and military tactics. And their building—Herod was a genius. Of course, he had plenty of slaves, but he had the genius to make use of them. So Herod built for the Jews, and then he brutalized them."

"Like you said, he was crazy," said Sarn.

"I know. But in some ways he was competent. Those who are now running the empire from Rome are stupid."

"Is it better to be occupied by craziness or stupidity?" pondered Sarn.

"I'll take stupidity," said Toler. "It's not so apt to be cruel. At least not intentionally."

"I like neither. Why can't the world's greatest power rule without either craziness or stupidity?"

No one had an answer for that question, and soon they had stretched out and drifted off to sleep.

The men were on their way before first light the next morning. On their right the red-and-brown cliffs crouched in hazy shadows, patiently waiting to leap on center stage when the sun rose higher, when the dark umber smears would become bright-red-and-gold rocky crags.

Arie had insisted they bring extra water, which was a good thing because they saw no fresh water before coming to Masada at the end of the day.

"It hardly rains around here," said Arie. "But when it does, the runoff from the mountains comes roaring down these wadis and into the lake. If you happen to be in the way, it'll take you with it."

Coursing through the mountains were canyons and gulleys, called wadis, which led to the lake. No one had any idea that the bottom of the Salt Sea was a fissure with a depth of over 1,200 feet, which helped to account for its low elevation and consequent inability to drain off its contents. Water from rain and the Jordan River fed the Salt Sea, deposited minerals, and evaporated. The surface area covered by the Salt Sea varied so that the famous old cities of the plain, Sodom and Gomorrah, were believed to be covered by the southern part of the lake, where they had been built hundreds of years before.

"It looks like a good lake to sail on," observed Sarn. "You could have a good race from one end to the other."

"No boats on the lake," said Arie. "There are no fish, so there are no boats." He shrugged. "Races? There are no boats kept on the lake, so how could they race? Besides, the sea requires only a little time before it encrusts everything with its salt."

The shadows of the mountains lay across the lake like a blue-gray mantle, slowly reaching out to the opposite shore. Whereas the day had started with the bright sun colors on the mountains to their right, by the end of the day it was the turn of the slopes on the opposite shore to light up briefly with their own flares of color.

"There it is," announced Arie.

Ahead of them, gracing the top of a mountain, was a walled city. Winding upward on the eastern slope was a path, which presumably led to the only gate. On the northern edge of the butte was one of Herod's palaces, a circular multistoried affair that stood on a step of the mountain and connected to the main fortress.

"There are two palaces here. The one you see there, it was his favorite. He had the northern light, a beautiful view of the sea, and could watch the horizon for enemies."

Resting on a flat mountain, the walled city made an imposing sight. It did not take any imagination to see that it was impregnable. The only path was a circuitous affair, which snaked up to the wall, openly exposing anyone who would be foolhardy enough to launch an attack.

"Can we get up there before dark?" Toler asked.

"Maybe. But even if it is dark, we can make our way to the top. I know just the place where we can bed down."

It was dark by the time they entered the doorway of Masada and stood in the open courtyard. The wind blew their hair and brought a welcome coolness, which was refreshing after their day-long trek on the valley floor. Arie led them through a building, down steps, and into a large room that had windows opening to the south. There was enough light from the stars and moon to illuminate several comfortable beds arranged around the room.

"These are the guests' quarters, and we are the guests. Pick a bed and make yourself comfortable."

Sometime during the night Toler had a dream. Giant frogs hopped after him, long trains of drool flying about like wild ropes as they twisted their heads this way and that. Their eyes were deep velvet and green, and their mouths were rows of sharp sawteeth. In one instant Toler was sure he could outrun them, and in the next moment they loomed over him as if he were a wingless gnat, almost not worthy of the effort necessary to eat him. No matter how fast he ran, they were all around; and he had the pitiful, hopeless feeling that it did not matter what he did. It was out of his hands.

One of the frogs with velvet and green eyes must have caught him because something was shaking his body. Soon he would be crushed by the mighty jaws. If only there was something he could do about it.

"Wake up! Wake up!" Arie's urgent voice splayed his ear from close by.

Toler tried to focus and finally recognized the little man beside his bed as Arie. Over Arie's shoulder was the shape of another man. It was Sarn. Toler felt so relieved that he had been rescued from the frogs. Arie and Sarn would enjoy hearing about the dream.

"Come on, Toler! Wake up!" Sarn's voice verged on panic.

Toler sat up, trying to focus his ears and eyes on something—anything that might explain the fear so obvious in the guide's face. In the background there was a sound, a regular cadence, but he could not make it out.

"What? What is it?"

"Come! We must hide!" Arie pulled Toler to his feet with surprising ease. A glance told Toler that Sarn had already gathered up his belongings for him. With Arie holding on to Toler's arm, the three of them stumbled through the door and into the moonlit courtyard between the buildings. They hurried down a street until they came to its end, and Arie ducked and led them through a low doorway. He shut the door behind them, and in the darkness their breathing was loud and labored.

"Be still and wait! I think we are safe here for the time."

"Who is after us?" Toler asked.

"We don't know. They might not even be after us."

"All we know," said Sarn, "is that they're soldiers of some kind."

"Then it would be Romans, right?" asked Toler.

"Maybe, but then again it might be a troop of Egyptians scouting the country. They would like to take home some slaves, believe me!"

Toler felt the pit of his stomach twist. That's all they needed: become slaves.

"How did you spot them?"

"Sarn went to the window in the middle of the night—to relieve himself, I suppose—and heard them below on the pathway. He woke me, but we could not make out how many there are."

"I thought you said no one would be here," said Toler, knowing that recriminations were useless at this point but hoping that Arie might explain further how things went awry.

Arie shrugged in the darkness. "So I was wrong."

There was a long silence as each man nursed his own thoughts. Finally Toler spoke, "Where are we? I can't see a thing."

"This is one of the food storerooms. The last time I looked, there was plenty of food stored here in Masada."

"Maybe the soldiers are stopping in for a bite to eat," said Toler, "and they'll be knocking on our door just anytime now. That was thoughtful of you to hide us in the pantry."

"I think this storeroom is empty. Besides, do you think they'll come looking for food tonight? There is no way for them to see what is here. No, they will wait until the morning to do whatever they plan." Arie paused. "This, my friends, is just a temporary place for us to hide. Let them settle down, and then we'll quietly leave."

Over an hour passed before Arie slowly opened the door to the storeroom. He listened and could hear no one.

"I will scout around. Wait for me here," he whispered.

Arie melted into the darkness, and Toler took his place at the door. Time passed, and nothing happened. After a while the sound of Sarn's snoring was audible. Toler shook his head to keep himself alert.

Finally there was the sound of footsteps in the street. Toler's eyes flew open, and he became aware of daylight outlining the pantry door. Had he slept? Where was Arie? In the dim light from the cracked doorway, he could make out the slumped, still-sleeping figure of Sarn. Toler kicked him twice and then shushed him before he could make a sound. The steps stopped a few yards down the narrow street, and there was the sound of a doorway being opened. After a moment of silence, a voice called down the street.

"There is food here! Come help me carry it!" The language was Roman.

Toler looked to the rear of the long narrow room in which they were hiding but could make out little. There were baskets and shelves and pots, but he could not tell if there was food.

"What's back there?" he whispered.

Sarn slowly made his way to the back of the room. It was over a hundred feet long and about ten feet wide, one of several storerooms that could hold enough food for a large number of people for a long period of time. Toler could hear Sarn touching things and moving pots while at the same time the sounds of men in the next room came clearly to them.

"Take those baskets of wheat. What is that? Is that bread? No, no. Take that pot." The leader gave directions to whoever had come to help him, and they went about the business of gathering up foodstuffs.

Sarn reappeared out of the darkness. "I can't find any food. I think our room is empty. Where is Arie?"

"I don't know. I haven't seen him since he left to scout last night."

"What are we going to do?" Sarn was apprehensive.

"Is there a place to hide back there? If they come looking in here . . ."

"There are some big pots and baskets back there," Sarn said. "We could hide behind them."

They had barely settled behind the empty containers when the door suddenly swung open, and a figure stood silhouetted in the doorway.

"Look in here." He stood back, and two other men made their way into the storeroom. They felt their way in the dark along the dusky rows of pots and baskets but did not bother to go all the way to the end of the room.

"Nothing here."

"All right, come on. We'll try the next one."

The men left, half shutting the door behind them.

Sarn and Toler breathed a sigh of relief and waited. After a while no one came back and there were no sounds from the street.

"What now?" asked Sarn.

"I wonder what happened to Arie."

"Maybe he saw a chance and ran." Sarn shrugged. "I liked the guy, but maybe he just got scared. I guess when you've personally known people in slavery, it is more real than when you've just read about it."

"If they tried to take us into slavery, I think I'd use this." Toler laid his hand across his hip where the laser gun had been carried under his robe. Instead of finishing his sentence, Toler's face turned ashen. He quickly checked his other hip and then began frantically searching on the ground.

"What is it?" asked Sarn, although he thought he already knew.

"The laser gun. It's gone. Help me look for it. I must have dropped it on the ground last night."

Sarn dropped to his knees and assisted Toler in searching for the weapon. It was no use; it wasn't in the room.

"Maybe it's in the room where we bedded down last night," offered Sarn. "We left in a hurry when we heard the soldiers coming."

Toler reflected on the events of the preceding night. "You may be right. I don't recall actually touching it after we left the bedroom."

"When we get the chance, let's go back and look."

Toler grimly nodded. He didn't even want to think about what might happen if a native, especially the soldiers, found the weapon.

Making his way to the half-opened door, Toler cautiously peered out. Directly across the narrow street was a wall, and to the left he could see down the street and into the open area between buildings. The door opened inward, and he could not see to the right without sticking his head out of the building, something he was reluctant to do. There were no sounds from that direction, and most likely the soldiers were to the left in the open area or in the surrounding buildings.

"I can't see or hear anyone."

"Maybe they got their food and left," Sarn said.

Toler grunted. "Maybe, but how will we know if we don't look?"

"I could scout around," offered Sarn.

Toler shook his head. "You don't know the place. It would be too risky. Let's wait awhile and see what happens."

They settled into the back corners and made themselves as comfortable as possible. As the day wore on, it became hotter, and Toler had second thoughts about waiting to scout the area.

"If they're still here, they'll be out of the sun. If we're careful—and lucky— we might get away with it."

"I'm ready," said Sarn.

There was still no sign of life around the storeroom. Toler opened the door wider and peered around the corner to the right. The street opened into several more storerooms before stopping against a wall. There was no one to be seen in either direction.

"Let me go," urged Sarn. "I'm quicker than you."

Toler snorted but stood aside and let Sarn pass. "Stay in the shadows."

Sarn moved against the building and quietly stole down the storeroom street. At its end, he looked around the open area and saw no one. The open windows of the buildings stared blankly, unwilling to share their secrets. The sun beat down on the pavement, and a small swirl of dust curled up and disappeared. A lone bird soared overhead and made a plaintive cry.

Standing still in the shadows, Sarn watched and waited, but there was no other movement or sound. Although tempted to investigate further on his own, he returned to the storeroom and reported to Toler, "I didn't see anyone. I think they've gone."

Within a short time Sarn and Toler had explored several buildings and found no trace of anyone. They made their way to the palace on the south end of the mountain and immediately found someone. In the foyer, where guests waited to see the king, a dead soldier sat on the marble bench, head thrown back. His throat was ripped open, and the crimson blood contrasted dramatically with the white stone. His hands lay palms upward on his thighs as if he had been killed before he could fight or flee.

"The blood is still wet," Sarn said. "He wasn't killed by a laser gun, was he?"

Having already looked closely at the body—the same thought had occurred to him—Toler shook his head.

They resumed their search into the palace. The top floor was a masterpiece of ceramic tile; the floors and walls were covered with colorful designs. Stout ornate furniture was arranged around the rooms with countless pillows of all sizes and hues surrounding the couches, chairs, and tables. The atmosphere of the palace was luxury, and yet everything was functional and comfortable. Sarn stopped and stared at the beauty of Herod's palace while Toler explored downstairs.

"Sarn."

Sarn quickly descended the inlaid stairs to the lower level. Toler stood in a large room, mouth open, eyes wide, as he surveyed the bodies of more soldiers on the floor before him. The multicolored tile floor was almost covered solidly with the red of Roman blood.

"I count five," Toler said hollowly. "I don't know what happened, but it wasn't long ago."

Sarn felt the skin on his neck crawl and repressed the urge to wildly look behind him. He felt himself becoming ill at the sight of the carnage, and he turned away. Before he could make it up the stairs, he vomited. He was aware of Toler passing him on the stairs and after he regained his bearings followed the captain. Toler was at the eastern wall looking out across the plains.

"What are you looking for?" Sarn asked, still trying to calm his stomach.

"Look!" In the direction Toler pointed, to the east, was the Dead Sea; and just this side of it, almost to the bottom of the steep path, was a band of horsemen dressed in black.

The lead rider seemed unnaturally large. Upon reaching the plain, they headed to the north along the sea.

Chapter 20

MASADA II

Toler and Sarn watched the black-clad horsemen until they were satisfied the riders were well on their way. Breathing a sigh of relief, they sat on the portico and looked at each other.

"We had a close call and didn't know how close," said Sarn. "Those guys must be mean."

"Hah! That's an understatement. I didn't hear anything last night. Those guys were efficient killers."

"Did you get a look at the leader? He was a big man."

Toler nodded.

"It would be coincidental coming across Derxter out here."

"Too much so."

"When were the soldiers killed? It had to be after some of them came looking for food."

"Unless," pondered Sarn, "the guys in black were the ones who came for food."

One last look over the wall showed the horsemen as a small black splotch headed north on the road by the sea. Toler led the way back to the southern palace where they descended the stairs to the lower area. A strong smell of death was heavy in the hot still air.

Sarn shook his head. "Sorry I got sick. It wasn't just the smell. It was more than that. There is something evil about what happened down there. It makes my skin crawl. It hit me like an ocean wave when I first went down there."

He gazed across the sea. "Is this something like Derxter would do?"

Toler nodded. "I've never seen him in action, but what I've heard about him would make this a small altercation." He was silent for a while. "I suppose we should bury the bodies or do something with them. Do you think you're up to that?"

The rest of the day was spent dragging the bodies to the open area between the palaces and covering them with rocks taken from a wall bordering the courtyard. The sun was settling on the horizon when they placed the last rock.

It did not take long for the evening air to cool, but rather than build a fire, the two went into the northern palace on the opposite side of the town from the massacre and found comfortable beds and warm covers in one of the royal bedrooms. Both were too tired to worry about any more nighttime visitors and slept soundly.

The next morning was spent looking over the mountaintop city of Masada. It was a comfortable and beautiful place, capable of sustaining a large number of people for a long time. Besides the food storehouses, there were areas set aside for growing crops, and inside the mountain itself were cisterns cut into the solid rock and filled with water.

"Arie said they cut the rock out of the mountain itself to use for building the town. That left those big caverns for storing water."

"Did he say how they got water to the cisterns?" asked Toler, who had not listened to Arie's stories as well as the fascinated Sarn.

"Nothing easy. All day long, every day it was the job of the women to take the mules down to the water supply, fill jugs, and bring the filled jugs to the cistern. In that way they kept the cisterns filled."

"Where did they get the water? It looks dry out there." Toler gestured toward the desert and the mountains to the west. "And they sure didn't get water from the salty sea."

"If you look closely, you can see an aqueduct coming from the mountainside down to the base of Masada. The runoff from rain collects there in a lower cistern, and the mules bring it up to the higher cisterns where the city can have easy access. Another of Herod's examples of genius."

"As long as the cisterns were kept full, you could stand off a siege indefinitely," mused Toler. "Has anyone ever attacked Masada?"

"No," said Sarn. "Arie said it was unlikely that would ever happen because no one is ever here. I wonder what was behind whatever went on yesterday."

Sarn shrugged. "Did you see the hot baths? If we had some cheap labor to fill the tubs and start the fire, we could have a real heated spa." One of the buildings was a gym and included a large room with a false floor, under which steam was made to create a sauna.

"That might be good in the winter, but I'm not in the mood for a hot steam bath right now."

After filling their water jugs and replenishing their food supply, Sarn and Toler made their way to the gate. By early afternoon they were well on their way to the north.

Toler looked one last time at the city. The laser gun had not been found anywhere in the city of Masada. "I wonder if we'll ever see Arie again. I have a few questions for him."

His questions had to wait only until the next day.

By the middle of the afternoon of the second day after leaving Masada, Toler and Sarn came to Qumran. They were spotted by lookouts high in the caves, and several men were waiting for them at the southern gate.

One of them was the man who had talked with Arie when they had passed through. He eyed the pair suspiciously before offering a greeting.

"Welcome again to our village. We see that you are still among the living."

"Thank you," said Toler. "And it appears that you too are still living." The last statement came across with some flippancy, but Toler did not care. Not only was he hot and tired from walking all day, but the vacation to the south had gone badly: the precious laser gun had been lost, his guide had suspiciously disappeared, he and Sarn had almost been killed by someone who could break bones like twigs, and they had spent half a day lugging heavy rocks to bury dead people. That didn't even include the possibility that Derxter had been at Masada and was likely responsible for the murders.

"My name is Abram, and I represent the people of Qumran." He looked at their empty hands. "I see you did not find much of the dye you looked for."

"No, we did not." The air was pregnant with all that was not being said, and Toler hoped Abram would soon get to the point.

After an awkward silence, Abram said, "Your guide is here."

"Arie?" Sarn exclaimed.

"May we see him?" asked Toler.

"First, may we ask you what happened?" said Abram.

"Happened? What do you mean?" fenced Toler.

Abram worked his jaw, debating with himself about how to proceed further. "Look, we know you went to Masada and that Roman soldiers were killed while you supposedly were present. When word gets back to Rome, drastic action may be taken to punish whoever was guilt and maybe others as well."

"What did Arie tell you?" asked Toler. "What is your story? We must know."

Abram was clearly concerned about retribution from the Romans. That seemed strange, on the one hand, for a spiritual group that was supposedly apart from the pettiness of politics. On the other hand, such a withdrawn and eccentric group could make a handy scapegoat for an angry potentate.

"Can we get out of the sun?" Toler asked. He could see no reason not to tell Abram what had happened, and besides that, it seemed clear that they would not be welcome in Qumran until the Essenes were satisfied about what happened on Masada.

Abram led them to a printing room, a long rectangular enclosure with equally long narrow tables used for laying out scrolls for transcription. At one end were several plain benches and chairs, and there Sarn and Toler sat with Abram and his men.

Toler related how they had gone to Masada to see Herod's palaces and how the soldiers had arrived during the night causing them to hide in the pantry. Arie left before dawn to scout and was not seen again. By the time Sarn and Toler left the storeroom later in the day, the soldiers were dead and a band of horsemen clothed in black were leaving Masada and headed toward the north.

"Who were the horsemen in black?" Abram asked.

Toler spread his hands and shrugged. "Could have been Bedouins or Egyptians or someone else. We did not see them from up close."

"If they kept their heading," observed Sarn, "they should have passed here."

"They did in the night, and we did not see them clearly. It does not sound like Bedouins. They are not well organized and not usually warlike. The Bedouins are desert people who like to be left alone."

"What did Arie say? As you can surmise, we are quite curious about what happened to him."

Abram nodded. "Come. Let's ask him."

The men followed Abram through the narrow streets to another building. Inside, they found Arie, head bandaged, lying on a bed. He opened one eye and squinted at his visitors.

"Arie!" Sarn said and rushed to the little guide. "What happened to you?"

Arie opened his mouth to speak but made only a whisper. Sarn put his ear close to Arie's mouth, but he made no further attempt to speak.

Toler had spotted Arie's soiled clothing and casually picked it up as if to look for bloodstains. It was not difficult to ascertain that there was no laser gun hidden in its folds. Abram glanced absently at Toler.

"He is weak. We thought he would die before he could tell us what happened. All he could say was that he found the soldiers just after they were slaughtered."

"What? Did you say the soldiers were killed before Arie left us to scout?"

"That's what he said, and so far his story does not contradict your own version."

"What else did he say? How did he get here?" asked Sarn.

"He said little more than that, except that the horsemen brought him as far as Qumran. We heard them gallop by last night but did not see Arie until we found him this morning at the gate. He had crawled there during the night. His head was bloody, and we think maybe they threw him from a horse and he hit his head against a rock." Abram shrugged. "If he recovers, we will find out more about these horsemen in black and the mysterious killer of Roman soldiers."

Arie's eyes were closed, and his breathing suggested that he had drifted back into unconsciousness. Abram led the men from the room.

"His recovery will be a slow one," Abram said. "There is no reason for you to wait here."

"You want us to leave," Toler said matter-of-factly.

"Yes, that is putting it bluntly. We don't know just who the horsemen are, but if they have alerted the authorities about finding the soldiers dead, you may be prime suspects. We don't want to be accused of harboring fugitives. Not political fugitives, anyway. As soon as Arie is able to travel—if he lives—we will put him on his way."

"We must talk with him! Will you direct him to where we will be waiting for him?"

Abram nodded. "Yes, I will do that."

"If you will allow us to fill our water bags, we will be on our way," said Toler.

After they had filled their water bags and he had walked them to the gate, Abram said simply, "I am sorry for our inhospitality and thank you for understanding."

Toler and Sarn rode northward. That and succeeding nights were spent at Jericho.

"We were here a few days ago preparing to go north. We should have stayed with our plans," said Toler.

"I'm glad we saw Masada and the Salt Sea. I'm even glad we met Arie, and I hope we meet him again. And in a crazy way I'm not sorry we had the adventure on Masada."

"Youth has an insatiable thirst for excitement!" Toler said in mock disgust. "If we hadn't lost the laser gun, I'd agree with you. That really worries me."

"Do you know what I want to know more than anything right now? I want to know who killed the soldiers."

Toler grunted. "And who those men in black were. But most of all, I want to know who has the laser gun." He grunted. "I can't wait to talk to that little guide!"

The captain and his crew member lay awake for a long time, each wondering about the events of the past few days. Before they would again turn their attention to pleasant thoughts of the Galilee, several days would be spent waiting for their mysterious guide.

Chapter 21

ARIE

Jericho was a reasonably hospitable place to spend a few days, and Toler decided they would make the best of it. It lay on a relatively flat piece of land in the river valley, nestled among trees and crops. To the west was the rugged hilly country that led to Jerusalem, and to the east was the river plain, which stretched to the red and gray hills a few miles away. Northward lay the path of the Jordan River, flanked by lush farms as far as the eye could see. The traveler could follow the river upstream and know that in three days he would find the blue waters of the Sea of Galilee waiting for him. To the south was the Dead Sea and beyond that deserts too desolate to be regularly traveled. Perched on the northwest corner of the salty body of water was the religious village of Qumran, and within its walls rested the tourist guide Arie, who was now in great demand.

"Your wounds are healed, Arie, and it is time you met with our council. We still require to know what happened on Masada," Abram spoke in his authoritarian monotone while Arie lay inert on his bed. Although the guide appeared to all intents and purposes to be unconscious, Abram believed him to be awake. Abram did not make an issue of Arie's reluctance to talk; he simply stated how things would be.

"Within the hour we will meet you here for a conference. That will give you sufficient time to ready yourself." The elder turned and left the chamber.

One hour later Abram and four of his council members entered the sick room and found it empty. One of their guests was just about to discover his horse had been stolen.

Later the same day in Jericho, Toler inspected the dates on a cart and debated whether to purchase them. Bored, Toler attempted to make the transaction as interesting as possible.

Watching him closely, the farmer waited for the foreigner to make his decision. Never had he seen anyone hold dates up to the light. Grapes maybe but not dates. He started to say something to Toler that might help expedite his choice, and it was at that precise moment that the lone horseman appeared from around the corner of the marketplace and galloped full speed through the square. People jumped out of the way to avoid being trampled and cursed the inconsiderate rider. Toler stepped to the other side of the wagon just as the little man on the sweaty brown animal passed. The farmer shook his head in disgust at the disruption.

"Toler!" Sarn stared after the horseman sprinting away from the edge of town. "Did you recognize that man?"

Toler stared hard, but it was too late. "No. Didn't get a good look. The fool almost ran me down."

Sarn caught his breath. "It was Arie! Our guide!"

The rest of the day was spent trying to locate horses in order to pursue Arie. Toler was convinced that the little guide was the key to locating the lost laser gun and placed repossession of the weapon as top priority. But there were no horses to be had. The animals had little utility in a farming village, for oxen were more efficient and had more uses.

Toler kicked at the ground in obvious dismay. Sarn stared to the north, the direction in which Arie had fled. Perhaps they would find him in Galilee.

The rest of the day was spent following the Jordan River northward. That evening they camped near a festive gathering where people of all ages sat around a fire eating, talking, and laughing loudly.

"Looks like a family get together," said Toler.

A feeling of homesickness surrounded Toler. Not that he ever did much with family members, but he and Gen and Ahna had taken picnics on several occasions. He suddenly had an impulse to walk over and sit in the circle of revelers, to become a part. He turned his gaze to the horizon where the sun's golden rays slowly shrank, becoming sunrise for someone else.

Toler's lifestyle had always been a busy one, and very seldom did he stop to smell the flowers and reflect on what his life was amounting to. When those rare moments arrived, they came without announcement or fanfare. It was like looking up and seeing that someone had come unobserved into the room and stood over you, and now that you were aware of their presence, you didn't want them there.

Toler pulled himself up with a start. *What am I doing?* He put the memories from his mind, ushering the unwelcome stranger from the room. Yet he continued to feel lonesome for Ahna's touch. And maybe something else he couldn't identify.

The next morning, while Toler was washing up at the river's edge, one of the men from the family reunion came up beside him.

"Nice day," said Toler.

"Now it is, but it will be a scorcher before it's over," the man said good-naturedly.

"You had a good time last night."

"Yes. I hope we were not too loud." The man's smile was easy and disarming. "We had not seen one another in a long time, and it was good to revisit old times."

Toler smiled and nodded understandingly. "We are looking for a little man on a brown horse who may have passed here."

The man's brow furrowed in thought. "Maybe I saw someone like that yesterday. I thought he pushed his horse too much. He went on north."

At least Toler knew they were still on the right trail.

"By the way, do you know of the messiah named Jesus? We have heard he is a good teacher, and we would like to hear him."

"Oh yes, I have. As a matter of fact, several of us were discussing the man last evening. I believe he is still at Gadara. But he may have moved on by now. The farther north you go, the more you will hear of his movements. He seems to be quite popular."

"That is good," said Toler. "What is the latest news of Jesus?"

"The usual teaching. Oh, I hear that he is attracting larger crowds and that he is now forming a close group of followers, sort of an inner circle. You know how it is when you become popular. You have to set up an organization." The man chuckled and ambled back to his group.

"Hey," the man turned and called back to Toler, "maybe you can become a member of his council." He grinned, waved, and was gone.

The road to Gadara was hot and dusty, and their feet were sore. Sarn thought it would be smart to buy a donkey to ride. They located a man wanting to sell his animal, and Sarn dickered with the native for a while.

"Before you strike a deal, I suggest you find out if this is really what you want to do," said Toler. "I'm curious to see if you can ride it."

Sarn mumbled something and climbed onto the donkey's back. While Sarn sat awkwardly, the animal stood still for about two seconds, then sat down on his haunches, and brayed triumphantly. Sarn wrapped his arms around the animal's neck to avoid sliding ignominiously off onto the ground.

"How long will you stay there?" inquired his grinning partner. "Actually I am not too impressed with the animal's speed."

Sarn felt conspicuously silly hanging on to the animal's neck and let himself slide off. The donkey seemed to smile smugly at Sarn.

"We'd just have to worry about feeding him. Let's walk," said Sarn and turned on his heel.

Bigor had few animals, and those were kept in public parks. Sarn had never ridden on an animal in his life and, in fact, had touched very few. He suddenly felt very culturally deprived in comparison to the primitive natives who grew up with donkeys and goats instead of computers and high tech.

"Toler," Sarn mused as they walked the road to Gadara, "when you compare our race with these natives, we are so advanced it is simply amazing!"

"Except they can ride donkeys and we can't. Or at least you can't. I haven't tried yet."

"That's another thought I had. We are advanced compared with them, and yet I feel like I've missed something they have. I've never learned to contend with a stubborn donkey, and I've never dug in the dirt to try to get something to grow so I could eat it. Those are basic things, tied to survival, and I don't know how to do them!"

"Sarn, listen to me. If you ever join an expedition to colonize a new planet, you'll have more than a chance to do all the things you are complaining about missing. And I'm not so sure you'd like it.

"On the other hand," Toler continued, "you are capable of running machines and calculators and firing lasers, which can be tied to survival too, only at a higher level. When we are hurtling through space in the *Sprint*. Our survival depends very much on our technical knowledge. We Just don't get our hands dirty while using it."

Sarn thought about it for a while. "In a way that is correct, but I think you are missing my point. When I sit in front of a console on the *Sprint* and punch in numbers, that computer represents a hundred computer geniuses and several giant companies and thousands of hours of engineering. All I have to do is master a keyboard."

"I think I see your point, but I wouldn't worry too much about it," said Toler. "Someday you can have a backyard garden, and you'll feel all better."

"Toler, these people know animals, birth them, rear them, butcher some, tan hides, make clothes. Maybe they sleep with them sometimes."

Toler opened his mouth to suggest that someday Sarn could buy his very own donkey and rear it in his garden but decided that Sarn would not appreciate the humor.

"And other things too, I've noticed. This morning we bought some bread from the old woman. I could see her daughter through the doorway. She was a plain woman, kneading dough. As she worked with that dough, she sang to herself, and her face was radiant."

Toler said nothing, looked at Sarn, and made a gesture as if asking for the point of all that was said.

"I guess what I'm saying is that these people literally touch the basic parts of life. For these natives"—Sarn waved his hand toward the town they had just left—"everything is hands on. I don't remember much being that way when I growing up." He clamped his jaws shut, a sign of having finished his statement.

Toler said nothing, and they walked in silence for a while. Finally Sarn could stand it no longer.

"Well, what do you think about what I said?"

"My reply is 'So what?'"

"You didn't understand me," protested Sarn.

"Oh yes, I did, my sentimental young friend. And I ask you, are you any less well-off for not having wet flour under your nails or the splattering of the blood of a fat sheep on your bare feet? Are you adjusting well to weekly bathing? Smell yourself, my romantic, and know that you are experiencing the base parts of your own being!"

Toler stopped to laugh at his monologue. Sarn glanced at Toler but did not share his sense of humor.

"I may not fully understand what I'm trying to say," Sarn said, "but one thing I am certain of, and that is that you don't!"

Toler grimaced. He didn't know why he had made fun of Sarn, and he felt ashamed of himself. He resolved to say nothing more for a while.

He glanced at Sarn as they walked down the center of the rough road. The young man stared ahead, jaw jutting forward as if he was determined to hold his course to matter what forces might try to push him awry.

"Stay with your guns, boy!" Toler said under his breath.

Chapter 22

PROLOGUE 10: 5027 BCE–0
ASSIMILATION

The crew of the uninvited spaceship *Star Finder* lived for a long time on the planet Earth. Their lifespan was far superior to that of the natives, and they had many children by several wives. Long after their deaths, they were still talked about and became the substance of legends. Until the end, the crew remained in a state of expectancy, waiting for rescue from the skies, and so the natives of that part of the planet also developed a hope for a rescue sent from above and a belief that they were a special people.

As for Uber, he became even more tortured and spent much of his time in deep depression. He never mingled with the natives and spent hardly any time with the crew. Uber was found dead in his room one day, an apparent suicide victim by sedative overdose.

His last conversation had been with Aladam, and the last thing he had said was "We have landed on a planet overcome by an evil force. Was it that force that brought us here?" His tortured eyes looked into the captain's face, begging for an answer.

Aladam said nothing, for he did not know what to say. He watched with sad eyes as his crewman, head down, walked away.

Aladam sighed as he sat up late into the night. Evaze sought to provide comfort, and he spoke of Uber's fear, "Are we part of something—a plan or conspiracy? Was our landing no accident?"

Evaze shrugged. "We've made the best of it."

Aladam nodded. "I know. If we could live another thousand years, we might find out what it is all about. If there is a scheme of things, then we must have played a role of some kind."

"Maybe it was to improve the genetic stock of the natives."

"Maybe. And perhaps someday we will be legends, which reminds me. We've got to get rid of the *Star Finder*. We've intruded enough into the development of this planet without leaving a lot of clutter."

"I had thought of that too," she said. "What do you plan to do with it?"

"Maybe we'll lift it with the four shuttle craft and drop it into the sea. Then we could fly the shuttle craft into the river. No one in the future will have to wonder about those things."

"The men don't fly the shuttle craft much anymore, do they?"

"No. They're happier on the ground now. Never thought I'd see that happen." He looked at Evaze. "It's happened to us too, don't you think?"

She tilted her head, thought a moment, and said, "I suppose so." Nestling against him, she murmured contentedly, "I love you, Captain Aladam, and I am thankful for our lives together here."

Captain Aladam held his wife, ship physician Evaze, and wondered if, in fact, they were unwilling actors in some scheme of things.

Chapter 23

PROLOGUE 11: 1963 BCE
NIBON-CHETAK

The story of Nibon-Chetak is but a split second in the overall scheme of things in the universe. Nibon-Chetak is related to nothing else in this story of Messiah 15; and yet, as is Messiah 15, Nibon-Chetak is related to everything.

Nibon-Chetak literally means "the reframer."

Nibon-Chetak was a woman born on the planet Arn and destined by legend and other forces to become a teacher and eventual martyr. The gist of her teachings was that the experience of evil could often be drained of its power by reframing it into good.

Her birth was not an easy one. Only her mother and an old woman were present, and fortunately the latter had some knowledge of difficult birthings. Nibon-Chetak was turned wrong and could not be thrust from the body of her mother. Realizing the gravity of the situation, the old woman wrestled with the unborn infant until it was turned enough to be born. In the process, Nibon-Chetak's arm was broken and she turned black from lack of oxygen. Somehow she survived the ordeal of her own birth, and the traumatic experience became the first of many for the child. From the first day of life, Nibon-Chetak had to fight to stay alive, and she grew up struggling. Perhaps the early hardships tempered her, for she always knew how to keep on keeping on and not give up.

It was storied that her father (if he really was her biological father) often came home in a fit of despair. A chronic depressive, the man would not tolerate noise including any sound of merriment or sign of happy spirits.

One day the father trudged home to find Nibon-Chetak, then four years of age, caught up in song, a tune about good and light. A child singing at the top of her lungs while standing on a chair probably would have been hard for anyone to tolerate for very long. On this particular day, the story goes, the man took one look at singing child and then knocked her from the chair. Before he could turn around, the scrawny child had clambered back up on the chair and was again singing as loudly as she could about goodness and light.

Smack! And again she went down in a tumbled heap. And again she resumed her singing even before she had climbed all the way to the chair's top.

Four times the man sent the child to the floor. Four times she rose, her voice louder than before. After the fourth attempt to shut the child up, the man felt a stab of guilt flash through the gloom of his depression and rage; and he turned on his heel and left, leaving behind a red-faced, teary-eyed little girl standing on a chair singing as loudly as she could about goodness and light.

When her time had come to deliver child, Nibon-Chetak's mother left the house. She was afraid to have the child at home because of the mercurial moods of her husband. The mother did not get very far before the baby demanded to be born. Subsequently Nobon-Chetak was born in a dry creek bed just outside a small village. Besides the old woman, her birth was noted by a clan of cave dwarves who passed the next day and found the mother huddled under a bluff, holding a bundle to her breast.

The leader of the clan, a swarthy hairy man with large black eyes, stopped before the mother and her baby. He looked them over, his eyes intense with feeling. The mother's fawn-like eyes reflected the apprehension she felt as she waited for him to show his intentions.

"It was you that the starlight pointed to last night," he said. It was a statement of simple fact, not question. "The one you hold, he is holy."

The woman nodded almost imperceptibly. She knew the lore of which the cave dwarf spoke: "He will be hailed as the one sent to change our destiny."

The man's eyes dropped as his voice faltered. "Take good care of him—for all of us.

The mother spoke softly, almost a whisper, "It is a girl."

The leader's eyes widened in surprise. "Then it will be even more difficult." He turned and walked away. His followers passed the woman and her child, each offering a slight bow of deference and respect.

Nibon-Chetak grew up much like the other children of the village. The things of life were scarce, but by hard work the family survived in spite of her father's depression. From a young age Nibon-Chetak demonstrated a prodigious aptitude for the laws and codes of behavior generated by thousands of years of tribal traditions. The moral prescriptions handed down over the years were based on uncounted generations of practical wisdom acquired through the vicissitudes of daily living. The ways of these simple people had historically been essentially good and honest. No one wanted to hurt another tribal member, and there was no effort at deceit; the people were transparent in that respect.

"My father feels bad a lot of the time," Nibon-Chetak confided to her teacher. The child had earned the respect of her teachers because of her quick mind and sharp wit. Yet there was a melancholy about her at times that concerned others, especially Apster, her favorite teacher.

"I know you are worried about him," Apster said.

"Yes, I can't help it. I want him to be happy like the rest of us try to be. Why is it so hard for him to feel good?"

"There are many of us who are not content," Apster said. "Not like we once were."

The child looked questioningly at her teacher. "What do you mean?"

Apster settled into her chair. It seemed like a good time for a history lesson.

"Make yourself comfortable, Nibon-Chetak, and I will tell you something about our history."

The child sat down and leaned forward, eager to gain a better understanding of her people.

"Once our people were happy all the time, it seemed like. It was unusual for a crossword to be spoken. People looked for the good in one another. When they saw a fault, they ignored it or tried to help the other overcome it. Life was very pleasant."

"Were you a little girl then?"

"No, that was before my time. My mother and father would talk about it when I was growing up. They had grown up during the contented times and often discussed how things had changed. Fortunately my parents talked about it when I had questions, and now I can pass on to you what I learned from them."

Apster had a faraway look in her eyes as she recalled her parents. Her mother had died at a young age, disillusioned and angry at how life had cheated her. As an adult, she had never been happy for any length of time and blamed this on her husband. Apster's father had done his best to make his wife happy; and when he could not, he became depressed himself, feeling like he had failed. Both yearned for the times gone by when life had been good.

"The change in our people began during the year of the Great Earthquake."

"Did you see it?"

"No. There are not many people alive today who were born when the Great Earthquake occurred. I suppose everyone has his own version of what happened. My parents told me about it, and I have passed it to my own children, and they in turn will tell theirs."

"My parents have not told me about the Great Earthquake."

This was not a complaint but just a statement of how things were. Nibon-Chetak's parents did not take time to talk with their children. It seemed to the child that her parents expended all their energy just trying to survive.

"That year was a bad one. The usual hot season turned into a severe drought. Food became scarce, and people were hungry. It became even more necessary than usual for everyone to work together and share what they had. By the end of that season, there was little to harvest. Understandably everyone was quite concerned about the gathering of food to support them through the harsh winter. They met many times to discuss how that could best be done. Just when the leaders of the tribes believed matters were well in hand, the quake happened."

Apster paused, seeming to pull herself together.

"Never before had anyone felt such a trembling of the ground. One wise man said that Arn was ill, invaded by a demon, which was taken literally by some and figuratively by others."

Nibon-Chetak let herself be drawn into the story as Apster involved herself more intently into the telling.

"Whatever caused it, the effect was the same." The child solemnly nodded her head.

"The trembling began before dawn one day, causing some excitement among the children but no real concern among the adults. Most people had experienced small tremors before, but these continued far longer than they should have.

"By noon the tremors had become harder and walls were shaking. As the afternoon wore on and the trembling grew even worse, people left their homes. They would not enter any building for fear it might collapse on them."

Nibon-Chetak was transfixed by the story. Like all children she loved a good tale told by an able storyteller, and Apster was that.

"By late afternoon people squatted in groups and waited, sometimes talking, more often just silently waiting for things to get better or worse. The men gathered all the food onto open ground where there was no danger of a building falling on it.

"Darkness came, and the tremors worsened. Fear had taken a stronghold over most of the people, for there was no place to hide, no place of safety."

"That would be terrible, not to have some place where you could feel safe," said Nibon-Chetak breathlessly.

Apster continued, "At midnight there was an orange glow to the north, followed by a great increase in the severity of the ground tremors. Immediately following that, the ground split open, causing great bottomless crevasses into which many fell, never to be seen again. And the ground opened under the food that had been brought together in a huge stack, and most of it was lost."

"Oh no!" the child said in a low voice. "That is so terrible!"

"Some say that there was the loud sound of a cackle with the orange glow as if someone or something had been glad for the calamity and was laughing. And then it was all over."

Nibon-Chetak's face was serious as she replayed the tale in her mind. Anger became evident as she said, "Someone awful was behind the earthquake. I just know it! Someone evil and powerful and mean."

Apster gazed intently at the child who spoke as if she knew something others might not. Many times Apster had been impressed by the girl's wisdom. It was not uncommon for the teacher to have a precocious student, but Nibon-Chetak was more than bright. It seemed that she knew things she had no way of knowing. Or maybe it was more accurate to say that the child could draw conclusions about events that were beyond her years.

"In response to these terrible happenings, people turned to their religious faith. It was their belief in Darhn-Shen, the life force of all beings, and the ritual retelling of how their forefathers had triumphed over hardships that sustained them through these hardest times."

"Sometimes," commented Nibon-Chetak, "I think that people turn to Darhn-Shen only when they are in trouble, and I don't think that is right."

Apster nodded and continued, "The wisest of the leaders was a man named Von-Rea. He was an old man who lived by himself most of the time. The people called him a proclaimer. He went before the people and told them things he thought they needed to know. Sometimes he said things that made them angry. At other times he said things that gave people hope."

"I'll bet they came out to hear him more when they were in trouble."

"You are likely right. Von-Rea told the people that their lives would be much better when a messenger of the life force would appear and explain the meaning of life."

"Do you think people would understand the meaning of life even if you told it to them?" There was a hint of cynicism in the child's voice.

"Other proclaimers followed Von-Rea after he died. They were unhappy because the people were not getting along with one another."

"You mean since the earthquake?"

"Yes, since the earthquake, people had not gotten along like they had before. It was as if the earthquake marked a turning point. The proclaimers preached that relationships among the people of Arn would be quite different after the messenger brought clarity to people's thinking."

Nibon-Chetak thought about that. "I like that idea, that problems are caused by the way people think. If that is true, then people can make things better because they can decide to think good things."

Apster nodded slowly. The child was bright.

Thirty years passed after the star's appearance and the meeting of the dwarves with the new mother in the creek bed. Nibon-Chetak had grown into an attractive and intelligent woman. One day she approached her mother.

"It is time for me to go."

Startled, her mother stared at her daughter. "But where will you go?" her worried mother asked.

"Do not worry." Nibon-Chetak gathered a few things together and left the village. She walked for four days to the foot of Mount Carbith, the highest mountain in the land. She climbed the peak and remained there for many days.

After she returned, gaunt, hungry, but keen of mind, Nibon-Chetak stood in the village square and proclaimed the message sent from the life power, Darhn-Shen. Many people came to hear the transforming news. It was all about how one has the power to change evil into good by the control of one's thoughts. Life's problems were usually caused by inaccurate thinking, thought combinations that led to habitual and destructive behavioral patterns. Negative thinking needs to be replaced by cognitions with more positive possibilities.

"Problems," she proclaimed, "can become opportunities. Enemies can become allies. Weaknesses may be our strengths. Those who have not can have. There is no need to covet our neighbor's goods when we can decide to celebrate what we already have. It is a waste of time to go looking for the life power when it is already present in you."

She said many other things and acquired a large following. Not everyone understood all that she said, but everyone liked the way she said things. They felt more hopeful after hearing her, for she told them that they were in charge of their destiny. They were not victims of some evil force.

Eventually she said too much too quickly for some people, those who were in control of the status quo. For them Nibon-Chetak was a threat, for she said things that challenged the exiting order.

So they arranged for Nibon-Chetak to be killed. Some said an evil force caused it to happen, but it could not be proved.

The teachings of Nibon-Chetak lived on after her death and resurrection, told by eyewitnesses to those who would listen and then retold endless times, until they were recorded on parchment for posterity.

And the fame and influence of Nibon-Chetak grew, and the people of Arn were never the same again.

Chapter 24

THE LIGHT

Far away in space, somewhere on the other side of the universe, distant from the boundaries of galaxies, in the mist of nothingness, there was a faint stirring. In the emptiness of the stygian vastness, the movement went unnoticed, undetected by even the most precise radar available anywhere.

A pale globe of pulsating light appeared, its silvery glow somehow out of all proportion to its dimensions. Size was impossible to estimate in the depths of space. It could have been as small as a drop of water or as large as a sun. Here, in the middle of nowhere and everywhere, far removed from anyone and anything, size was totally inconsequential. Large or small in comparison to what? There were no comparisons to be made and no one to care one way or another.

The globe patiently waited, softly throbbing, its light pulsing outward in gentle waves to be eventually lost in the darkness. Time passed. How much time was uncertain and irrelevant to its purposes. It could have been seconds or centuries.

Another globe appeared. It was suddenly there, spontaneously existing, giving forth a pale-greenish light, which contrasted pleasingly with the silvery-white globe. They waited, bathing each other with undulating rays, maintaining a prescribed distance, enjoying complementary pulsations. Was there contact? That seemed a more logical conclusion than to believe that these spheres had chanced upon one another by accident. But then what did logic have to do with any of this?

Perhaps they had been placed there by some mysterious power that had drawn the shape and color of globes out of nothingness for its own pleasure and bidding.

A third actor appeared onstage, blue in color. There was no competition between the triad but only ultimate compatibility.

They locked in tandem, although an observer could not have known if they had always been thusly aligned or if they had just become that way. Lazily at first they began moving around one another. Their course described a circle and gained speed until they became as one ring of light. Then there was a sudden burst of colored incandescence, and the globes melted into one body.

It was unlike anything else in the universe. There was about the body a rare beauty of blended hues combined with a sense of unlimited energy and infinite intelligence. There were no words in any part of the universe that could adequately describe the presence as it hung poised, gracefully balanced and full of power.

It was now ready to fulfill its purpose.

As if on some predetermined schedule, it began moving through space, faster and faster, heading toward some prearranged destination; and then it was gone, disappearing into the distance of nothingness. Again there was only empty space, cold and soundless. The rendezvous had been completed and unrecorded as if it had never happened.

Chapter 25

Pharisees

The old woman picked at her nose. "Yes, he's going to be at the council meeting. That's what I heard."

"When?" asked Toler.

"Tomorrow." She focused on something at the end of her finger. "At noon."

"Thank you." To Sarn, he said, "Let's go back to Jerusalem. Maybe we can catch up with him."

Sarn and Toler had been circuiting several small towns north of Jerusalem but found themselves a day or so behind the Messiah at each stop they made. By luck they had come across a washer woman at a creek who insisted that the Messiah would be in Jerusalem the next day and would likely appear before a routine meeting of the Council of Elders.

They arrived in Jerusalem just before dark.

Although exhausted by the long day's walk, they were ecstatic about the possibility of seeing the Messiah. Perhaps even more exciting was the possible confrontation between the Messiah and the Pharisees.

Toler and Sarn slept soundly in a stable near a marketplace and were woken early by the sounds of the early risers gathered around the neighborhood well.

Sarn yawned. "These stables aren't half bad sleeping."

"Some are and some aren't," Toler replied, rubbing his eyes. "If I recall correctly, we've been in some which we haven't wanted to revisit."

"Yes, and the one that stands out in my mind was the place where the donkey kicked me." Sarn grimaced at the recollection. "You didn't have to bring up the bad times just because I mentioned a good one."

"It gives balance. Whenever things are going very well, it helps me keep perspective if I remember that there have been bad times too, and no doubt times would again be bad at some future time."

"Why balance out the good? It can be pretty good in itself."

"Oh, I do it the other way too. When I'm up against bad times, I recall the good times and remind myself that the bad won't be permanent."

Sarn shook his head. "Maybe you have a habit of finding ways to avoid feeling good when times are good."

"Nope. The real reason is to avoid feeling overly bad when times are bad."

"It may be," Sarn offered, "that keeping your perspective has robbed you of some really nice highs."

Toler shrugged. "Granted. It has also saved me of some pretty rotten lows."

Sarn sighed. "Last night was still a good night's sleep."

After paying the owner of the stable a small sum, they wandered into the street, which by then was filling with people. Breakfast was eaten while standing around the town cistern as it often proved a useful place to hear gossip and news.

Toler munched an apricot as he watched the people in the square. He always found natives interesting, especially the young ones, and remarkably similar no matter which planet he visited. The children played with one another, followed dogs, hung on to their mothers, or cried while lost. These scenes could be found back home on Bigor, as well as on the outer planets where colonists were just beginning to make a dent in the wilderness.

"These kids are like the kids back home," Sarn interrupted his thoughts with a statement sounding like he had been reading Toler's mind.

"Yeah, and like the kids everywhere else," said Toler. "It's like we all came out of the same mold."

The two stalked toward the Temple, their thoughts focused on the upcoming meeting of Jesus with the Council of Elders.

From what they had heard so far, everyone expected the confrontation to be interesting. It was widely known that Jesus was not well accepted by the religious establishment. He had appeared from nowhere and presented teachings not in strict keeping with those of the council. That in itself was not so unusual; it was commonplace for strange and misguided self-proclaimed messiahs to make their brief splash on public attention. Some were motivated by political considerations, others by religious causes, and some for personal reasons. What was discomfiting to the elders was the unexpected popularity of Jesus. He had already established a following and drew large crowds when he taught. Besides that, he was terribly informal for a religious leader. Perhaps worst of all, as far as professional decorum went, Jesus was not careful about the kind of people with whom he spent his time. Respectable religious leaders simply did not mix with just anybody!

"It sounds like at least part of the council is disgusted with Jesus because he acts like he knows their laws as well as they do," Sarn said.

Toler nodded. "I think what really scares them is his power over people. He has some kind of uncanny influence over those closest to him. That, and the fact that he just did not go away after a day or week."

"The guy is gaining momentum. The council probably wants to know what his goals are. Do you know what the Messiah wants, Toler?"

"I doubt that the council is threatened by the possibility of him taking their jobs. His style is that of a freelancer and he'd probably be awfully bored and constrained in the trappings of some office. The council has built up a whole system of tradition and bureaucracy, and they are going to be around a long time after Jesus has gone."

"Good point," said Sarn. "These Pharisees and Sadducees are the backbone of the religious system, aren't they?"

"It seems that way. There appears to be little glory and applause for them, but their work is part of the societal bedrock, the glue that holds everything together. In their hands is the identity of this people. These guys know they'll be around and employed long after the flashy amateur preachers come and go."

"That makes sense to me," said Sarn. "But what does the Messiah want?"

Toler shrugged. "I don't know. Something about getting people to change the way they look at things. I guess it's supposed to make them happier."

Sarn looked around and seemed puzzled. "Do you know where we are?" The streets were often twisting and ill planned, and his directional sense was not strong in any case.

"Just follow me. I'm not lost yet."

"So what is it that the council objects to? Why don't they just wait this guy out?"

"For one thing, they have to be feeling increasingly less popular than Jesus. That must be quite important."

"Hah! And not only with them," said Sarn. "I've known a few people like that myself."

"And you are still a mere child," Toler said. "Wait until you are older, and then you'll really see some hurt feelings when people believe they are ignored."

"Are there other reasons they don't like Jesus?"

"The council is afraid of Rome. What if Jesus's following grows too large? More attention would be drawn to it."

"I can understand that," said Sarn. "The Romans don't want any trouble from the natives of the pacified area and will do whatever is necessary to discourage any uprisings. For this reason alone, the Pharisees will want to minimize any movement that might invite a crackdown by the Romans. And in so doing, they are performing their function of providing security and stability to their people."

"I'll bet it's a thankless job," said Sarn.

"No doubt. In every primitive culture I've been around, someone has played this role. They stabilize the society, and what do they get in return? Derision. Criticism. Hatred. But in the long run, it's those bureaucrats that make sure the thread of civilized stability continues from one generation to the next."

"But couldn't they also keep new ideas from expression? That could cause stagnation, couldn't it?" Sarn respected his mentor who had been around far more than himself. Toler, he had discovered, was an astute observer of the human scene—wherever he found it.

"I suppose the people in power could cause stagnation. But what happens most of the time is that the new ideas, if they are worthwhile, will eventually earn their place. And what usually evolves is a combination of the new and the old. New ideas are good, but don't forget that the old ideas were once new, and they survived only because they worked."

"Yeah, well, I can see both sides," Sarn said. "But I guess I'm sympathetic to the camp with the new and better ideas. If there's a better idea, let's use it!"

"I once apprenticed with a wise old captain," said Toler. "He observed that young people, if they had any heart, would want every change that sounded halfway good. Twenty years later the same people, if they had any brains, were very cautious about making any changes."

"It still seems a waste not to implement changes for the better when they're available," said Sarn.

"And maybe," reflected Toler, "that's why messiahs launch their careers when they're thirty years old. They're in between impetuous youth and conservative middle age."

"Could be," said Sarn. He was not old enough to appreciate Toler's line of speculation.

"In any case," said Toler, "it looks to me like Jesus will eventually go too far and the Romans will take care of him."

"Then Lybur's men will have made a wasted trip."

"On the other hand, if the Romans don't move fast enough to suit Lybur's timetable, Derxter may decide to make a move. He'd like that!"

A group of Roman soldiers passed them, dressed in military garb, short swords at their sides, carrying spears. They marched four abreast, gazing straight ahead, exuding an air of supreme confidence.

"Those guys are rather formidable," said Sarn.

"They're good. They're been in control of a good part of the world for over two hundred years. That's better than most of the past conquerors could do."

"This messiah business must be very important to Lybur," Sarn remarked after the troop of Roman soldiers had turned the corner, "for him to send his own executioners."

"It looks that way. This Jesus may have a way with the people, but he just does not understand politics, and like it nor not, that is what makes the world go round."

Sarn nodded. He felt sympathy for the Messiah. Jesus was in some ways naive, a simple person who persisted in calling attention to himself.

"It makes you wonder," said Sarn. "If Jesus is naive, bordering on dumb, about political conditions, then is the power also naive or whoever is behind this?"

"Maybe," said Toler, "the power is not totally omnipotent. On the other hand, maybe we are too close to the situation to appreciate the larger perspective. Do you remember reading about how the other messiahs operated? In that context, Jesus is not so different from the others."

Sarn shrugged and looked at Toler.

"It seems that whoever is behind the messiah business either is a slow learner or else knows something we don't know."

"I'm going to bet on the latter being true," Sarn said. "Maybe the Messiah will be better remembered if he is murdered."

"Yes, especially if he comes back from the dead," added Toler.

"That I would like to see. What a story that would make back home!"

"I hate to remind you of disappointing news, Sarn, but most likely we will not be discussing any of this back home. Confidential, you know."

The Temple was not difficult to find once they were in the neighborhood. It was a large imposing structure, and it was impossible not to be impressed by it. The crowd thickened as they drew closer to the courtyard.

Sarn and Toler made their way to the gate. When it was opened, they passed unnoticed onto the porch and beyond that the inner courtyard where women were not allowed to be. Non-Jewish persons were not allowed there either but because of the large crowd they were able to pass unnoticed.

"Wow! Look at this place!" Sarn stared at the huge building towering above them.

Toler grabbed Sarn's elbow and squeezed it. "Act normal!" he hissed under his breath.

The meeting was to take place at one side of the courtyard, and the elders took their positions in a circle with onlookers gathering behind them. There was excitement in the air as the people milled around, waiting for the meeting to start. Most of the elders had arrived, and those who had not seated themselves in the circle were standing in small cliques of intense discussion.

Toler spoke to Sarn, "Stay here. I'll scout around and make sure we're not surprised by Derxter."

"You'll miss the confrontation?"

"No, I'll be sure to catch that part. I'll meet you here afterward."

Toler disappeared into the crowd, and Sarn leaned against a column, already a little bored. Finally one of the elders, a stately old man, moved around to the small groups and quietly let them know it was time to begin. He took his place at the head of the circle and began the opening prayers. The ensuing ritual was less than entertaining, and Sarn soon lost interest.

A stirring at the gate caught his attention. People were milling around trying to see over the onlookers in the rear. The sound of voices became audible. The crowd parted, and a bearded man of medium height and strong build appeared, assertive in posture. Sarn could not make out the Messiah's features because the sunlight was behind the man and framed him with an iridescent glow. Sarn was certain that this was Jesus!

Jesus waited until the prayers had been recited. He was a visitor, a guest, and it was not his place to intrude on the council. He stood behind the circle with the other onlookers and waited.

Abdul was the head of the Council of Elders. A short thick powerful man with white beard and balding head, he possessed a stentorian voice, which easily carried throughout the courtyard. His permanently furrowed brow and hawk nose gave him an aggressive and stern appearance. After the prayers he began the business meeting.

"Brethren," he began, "we have heard of a new preacher who calls himself Jesus. What he has said to his hearers has usually been true to the scriptures, and we welcome such instruction, for it makes our people stronger in the law. However, some of his proclamations have raised questions in our minds. But then perhaps we have not always received a true accounting of what has been said. So we have invited this teacher to come and sit with us." Abdul turned toward Jesus and with courtesy and grace addressed him, "Will you join us?"

Jesus entered the circle of elders and seated himself on one of the benches. His even gaze moved around the circle, assessing each of the Pharisees in turn, sometimes offering a small smile, sometimes a gentle nod of greeting. Neither did he clearly appear intimidated nor did he seem intent upon intimidating the council.

One of the elders, a lawyer by vocation, stood and said, "Abdul, I ask your permission to be first in asking our guest a question."

Abdul nodded assent.

"Jesus, I have a question for you. It may seem trivial, but then it is one that occasionally comes up when we are dealing with our people."

Abdul broke in, smiling apologetically. "Jesus, forgive our enthusiasm, but this unintroduced man is named Bulla."

"Forgive me, Jesus. Yes, I am Bulla, and I seek your wisdom on a point of the law."

Sarn studied the tall lean lawyer with the bushy brows and felt uneasy about the man's intentions. A smile played around the corners of the lawyer's mouth, and the darting of his eyes hinted at a hidden agenda. Bulla reminded Sarn of a skilled hunter trying get his prey to come a little closer.

"What is your question, Bulla?" Jesus asked.

"My question, Jesus, is, what is the greatest commandment of all?"

Bulla's manner suggested that Jesus's answer would be a stepping stone for his next question. Sarn did not know the answer to the question, but he could follow the steps in the gamesmanship of the lawyer.

"What is written in the scriptures?" Jesus asked in answer.

This was not what the lawyer had anticipated. He was being referred back to the scriptures like a schoolboy being asked to recite what he already knew well.

"The scriptures teach us to love God first and to love our neighbor as ourselves." Bulla's face was flushed.

"That is good, Bulla. I hope that answers your question."

Bulla appeared momentarily disoriented. He had not been prepared for the discussion to be made so simple.

"But, Jesus, here is one of those questions that plays havoc with us as we endeavor to instruct our people in right living: who exactly is our neighbor?"

Bulla was poised, waiting to spring into an intricate and complex debate about a definition of neighbor, already savoring the accolades that would come after he had demonstrated his knowledge of the law and considerable skills of argument.

But again he was caught off guard. Instead of giving a direct answer, Jesus told a story.

Sarn found himself caught up in the story of a Samaritan who helped a man who was robbed and beaten and left for dead. Samaritans were looked down upon by most Jews, and that gave the story a twist with a not-so-subtle meaning. The point was underlined when the Samaritan saved the injured man's life only after respected Jews, including a rabbi, passed him by without helping. Jesus was a natural storyteller and held the complete attention of his audience. When the story was done, Jesus squarely faced Bulla.

"Now who was the neighbor to the man who had fallen among thieves?"

Bulla could only give the obvious answer, again feeling much like a schoolboy. "Why, the Samaritan was the neighbor."

"You are right. Go and do likewise."

The elders murmured to one another over the unexpected turn of events. Jesus had clearly emerged the winner, and there was obvious appreciation for his clever yet straightforward approach. Bulla, mouth partly open, stared blankly at Jesus. Jesus had countered a tedious exercise in the definition of terms into a simple operational prescription of life: your neighbor is whoever needs you.

This seemed to blunt whatever confrontation the council may have prepared for Jesus. From there the council meeting became a lively discussion of theology, human nature, and homiletics. Sarn noted without surprise that the elders spent more time listening than talking and that most of them appeared to be listening with respect. *Score one for the Messiah,* thought Sarn.

After Jesus left, the old men of the temple sat on their benches and continued talking. Some were clearly impressed while others were disgruntled by what had happened without being sure of how they could have handled things any differently. Finally one of the elders raised his hand for attention and addressed his fellow Pharisees.

"He makes it too simple, I tell you; pleasing God is no simple matter."

There was a murmur of assent. Sarn, standing in the shadows, was so caught up in the drama that he was startled by hearing his own voice addressing the council.

"But why can't it be simple?" he asked as he stepped forward. "Isn't religion as simple or complex as a person wants it to be?"

As one, all heads turned toward Sarn, craning to see who had questioned them. Abdul stood and faced Sarn, surveying the young visitor, sizing up this one who had the courage or audacity to challenge the council.

"Come. Come into the light where my tired old eyes might see you better. Who is it that who would make religious faith a simple matter?" Abdul's voice was gentle and commanding at the same time. He was both a warm, caring person and an assertive individual who backed down from no one. This combination of personal assets had won for him admiration and respect from many but had also gained him enemies. Among the latter were those who thought his willingness to consider the opinions of others a glaring weakness in his leadership ability. Nevertheless, he had so far held on to the role of council president.

Red-faced, Sarn felt like kicking himself. *What am I doing? Toler will kill me when he finds out! Now just turn and walk out, stupid! Nobody will bother you, and maybe, if you're really lucky, no one will even recognize you if they see you again.*

But it was too late. Abdul was extending his hand to Sarn, an invitation to come forward and speak his piece.

Sarn discovered his feet were moving toward the wizened priest. *If I'm going to do this, I might as well give it my best shot,* he said to himself.

"My, you're a young lad," mused Abdul. "And you have this interest in theology, do you? That is excellent. Perhaps one day you will be a Pharisee." The twinkle in Abdul's eyes suggested that his was a humorous comment. Scattered chuckles came from the council.

"So what's your name and where are you from?" Sarn's dry mouth managed to form an answer.

"Sarn. My name is Sarn. And I come from far away to the east."

"And what is the name of the country from where you come?" gently probed Abdul.

140

"Uh, you probably haven't heard of it. It is a great distance from here."

"You could try us. Perhaps one of us will have heard of it." Abdul's twinkle was still present.

"Xerxes," said Sarn. No one would recognize the name of his galaxy.

Abdul raised his eyebrows. "Xerxes," he repeated and turned to the council members. "Has anyone heard of this land of Xerxes?"

The men shook their heads, some impatient to get on with the religious debate. After their encounter with Jesus, they felt the need to gain a victory of some kind.

Abdul turned back to Sarn. "It appears that no one has heard of your homeland. But that is of little consequence. We welcome you to our land."

"Thank you, sir," Sarn replied.

"Now, my boy, don't be nervous. I want to hear more of this notion of yours. You said something about religion being simple or complex, depending on what a person desires. Is that what you said?"

Sarn nodded.

"Are you by any chance a follower of the man Jesus who was just here?"

Sarn shook his head.

"You see, my young friend"—he gestured toward his colleagues—"we are all, shall we say, religious professionals. We have been trained in religious law and tradition for many years. It is our duty to interpret the holy word to the people. They are ignorant, and how else would they know what is right and wrong?"

Sarn started to speak, but Abdul continued, "Perhaps in your land the priests do not instruct the people in rightness and wrongness. That would be wonderful if it was possible to not have that onerous chore. But here, unfortunately, the common man does not understand what pleases God. He is lost. He agonizes over what to do. He sweats over questions of morality. And when he comes to a conclusion, to his dismay he finds that it differs from that of his neighbor. And his brother. Even his wife. So what is he to do? How are these people to know what is right when each of them has a different opinion?"

Abdul was a natural teacher and enjoyed pontificating before an audience. He turned to the council, palms upward, emphasizing his rhetorical question.

"Yes, what would the people do to solve these kinds of questions? Some of them are simple, it is true, but some are quite difficult." Abdul paused, turned back to Sarn.

"I will tell you what the people are to do about finding answers to their many questions of life. They are to do what they have done for hundreds of years. They turn to those trained in the laws of God. And that, my young friend, is who we are." A gesture indicated the council whose members were nodding.

Sarn swallowed. Abdul had expressed his position so clearly and eloquently that Sarn had difficulty recalling what he had intended to say. All eyes were upon him as they waited for his reply.

"I really shouldn't be here, and I'm sorry I interrupted your meeting," Sarn stammered, hoping that Abdul would summarily dismiss him and his agony would be over before Toler returned. Indeed, Toler might be in the audience at that very moment, counting the ways in which he might punish Sarn.

"But we are glad you are here. It is a good thing when our minds are stretched by new ideas from afar. Even ideas from the land of Xerxes." Abdul's smile was disarming and served to relax Sarn.

"I know how important religion is to your people . . . and you too," Sarn began, noting the guarded expressions surrounding him. "I understand that because religion is such an essential part of your frameworking."

"Please explain that, if you will, Sarn," asked Abdul.

"Frameworking?" It occurred to Sarn that these people had probably never heard the word used with the meaning he attached to it. "That means we are all struggling to make sense of life, and as we do so, we erect a mental framework. After we have a framework set up, we hope that everything else in life will fit in, fill the gaps between the main beams of our beliefs." He turned, panning the faces of the council members, wondering if he was being understood.

"Go on," said Abdul. He had never heard it put that way before, and he was curious about where Sarn would take his line of reasoning.

"Religion is useful for building a framework when you don't have enough facts to build one."

One of the elders interrupted. Carzo stood and spoke in his deep bass voice, "Are you saying that religion is not a fact? That suggests that we use religions to build this framework only until we can replace religious beliefs with 'real' facts."

Sarn opened his mouth to reply affirmatively for the elder had clearly deduced where Sarn's argument was headed. He paused, choosing his words carefully.

"What I am saying," Sarn continued, determined not to alienate these people any more than they already were, "is that one of the important uses of religious belief is to help people understand."

Carzo considered that, nodded, and sat down. Although he, along with most of his fellow priests, believed that the primary purpose of religion was the control and proper management of the people's behavior, he would accept the idea that theology helped people to understand. Not that it was important for people to understand. It was not. What was important was that people followed the teachings of the law.

Sarn's comments were based on what he had been taught while growing up on Bigor, plus what he had read about religion and its role in the evolution of societies.

He had covered everything in the *Sprint*'s library, all of which was written from an anthropological/sociological viewpoint.

Sarn was poised to explain to the council that after all the facts were in, when all the information about life was available, when science had established a comprehensive explanation of mankind's experience, then there simply would be no need for religion to fill in the gaps of mental frameworking. That, after all, was what an educated and advanced person from Bigor would say. Toler would say that.

But Sarn wasn't sure he believed it.

The people of Earth were primitive and relied heavily on superstition, magic, and religion to bring order out of chaos. And to some degree it worked. There was more social order because of religious prescriptions. His own people on Bigor, Sarn reflected, didn't have all the answers but had enough so that there was no need for religion to explain things. Ultimately science would explain everything, even though it could be a long time in coming. Gaining knowledge was like peeling an onion. You took one layer off, and there was another waiting to be removed. And when you had taken all the layers away, what did you have left? Certainly not an onion. Just more questions about how the onion came to be. Maybe there was no end to it, Sarn wondered. And if not, why wasn't there?

Part of Sarn did not want all the answers to be known; some sense of mystery needed to be preserved. Maybe that was the little boy within him who had so enjoyed playing the game of "what if."

The council was waiting.

"Is that all you have to say to us?" Abdul asked.

Sarn wrestled with himself. He wanted to continue the discussion and challenge the council with his thoughts. But what good would that do? Would he change any minds? No, they would just burrow deeper into their existing beliefs. Would his opinions help them in any way? No, and he wasn't even sure what he believed. And even if they were open to an unbiased consideration of what he had to say, how would that change anything? These people were locked into the business of getting through life as best they could, and their framework had done a pretty good job of helping them maintain some equilibrium. And yet the man Jesus, the Messiah, was sure throwing a few rocks into the machinery.

"Thank you, Sarn, for sharing your thoughts with us," Abdul was politely saying. The council had adjourned and was moving off into different directions. The abrupt ending of the meeting was most fortuitous for Sarn as a hand on his shoulder turned him around.

"What's been happening?" asked Toler. "Oh, nothing," said Sarn.

Chapter 26

STAR ARRIVAL

Habib Yassar reared his head back and stretched his young body. He yawned as he gazed into the clear night sky sprinkled with flickering stars. Watching the flock was no fun thing to do, but somebody had to do it. Habib just wished it wasn't him.

There was a slight chill in the air, and the night sounds had already begun. The contented herd of sheep settled in for the night, satisfied to risk their safety with the fourteen-year-old boy. His dog, Haggar, head on paws, looked up at his master, ever alert to do Habib's bidding. Nothing was more important than to please Habib.

"I wish you could talk," the boy said to his dog. But at least you are a good listener."

Resting against his staff, Habib stared absently at the horizon. The boy did not immediately react to the appearance of a point of light, but after a moment he became aware of the intrusion into his line of vision. He had seen many falling stars, but this light was on a straight line with the top of the hills to the east and did not appear to be falling.

The pinpoint grew larger, wavered just a bit, and it was then that Habib took a real interest. Eyes narrowed, he watched intently as the speck became a pea and then a grape. Was it moving toward him or just growing in size? The boy was hypnotized by the strange sight of a star seemingly racing toward him from the edge of the world.

The sound of bleating sheep roused him from his trance.

Haggar whimpered and paced toward the sheep and back. Muttering to himself, Habib grasped his staff with both hands, straining his senses. *Stars don't make sounds,* he told himself. *They don't scare your sheep either. Or shepherd boys.*

Time stopped for Habib; he would forever remember that moment when the inky sky loomed blacker than usual, forming a backdrop for the dramatic onrush of an alien light.

There should be some sound, he thought again.

And then it was upon him. The star's acceleration was quite impressive and beyond amazement for the young boy. No longer the size of a grape, the luminous sphere suddenly filled one quarter of the sky. Its brilliance cast an eerie light across the hillside and for a moment starkly illuminated every rock and bush.

Then it was gone.

Habib screamed, turned his head, but no, it had not passed him. He could see no fast-moving light disappearing in the distance. Where was it? He looked up and there it was, rapidly diminishing in size as it sped on the vertical until it suddenly stopped.

Habib blinked. Yes, it had stopped and was just a little larger than the other stars. Had he really seen what his eyes had told him was a star, moving across the eastern sky at a speed faster than anything Habib had ever imagined possible?

The sheep were louder now. Haggar raked Habib's leg with a paw, as if pleading for an explanation. Habib strode among his charges, soothing them with his reassuring voice. Occasionally he looked up; yes, the new star was still in its place. Had others seen the star? Habib dared not leave the sheep, though he longed to go into town and find out what others knew of the strange happening.

An hour later Habib thought the star had grown brighter but was not certain; two hours later he knew that it had. After another hour Habib and his sheep dog stared transfixed at the star's tail, which had connected with the ground.

Before the sun peeked over the mountains to herald another day, the new star had established itself in the eastern sky as a signal, a beacon, whose beam of pale light bathed in its glow the little Judean town of Bethlehem, on the planet Earth.

Chapter 27

SARN'S PAST

Is there really a power somewhere in the universe?

Sarn had not wondered that question in a long time, probably since he was a kid. He and his friends had played "What if there really was?" with whatever was of current interest being placed in the blank space. The question was an inkblot onto which each child could project his own creative fantasies without regard to how irrational or silly they might sound.

Occasionally the blank was filled in with power or God, which usually led to animated discussions among the youngsters. To believe in a great overseeing presence behind the whole of creation was an exciting proposition, for it offered the possibility of all manner of mysterious godly interventions in the affairs of mankind.

And if the power could place itself in the middle of things and do whatever it wanted, then it became necessary to somehow enlist the power on one's side.

"If I do this, the power will like me better and help me out when I get in trouble with the bad guys. But if I do that, the power will be unhappy and help the bad guys against me." Such thinking led to all kinds of attempts at cosmic mind reading, ethereal blackmail, and celestial influencing. And when it was all over, when the kid talk of "what if?" had grown boring for that afternoon, the kids had no better idea than when they started of what such a god would be like or what he might want from his creation.

Tobi, the chubby member of the group, favored filling in the blank with "three wishes" or even five wishes on those days when he was especially hungry. His wishes generally had to do with gathering about him the ultimate comforts and pleasures of life, mostly food.

"I'll go first," he would say and quickly ask the question. "What if each of us had three wishes?" Without waiting for someone else to answer the question, he would begin, "For my first wish, I would want a giant freezer in my house where I would have a large container of every kind of ice cream in the galaxy. And each container would never run out."

"That's two wishes," Yashki would say.

"No, that's only one: large containers with every kind of ice cream and they would never run out."

"Oh no. First you said large containers of ice cream in a freezer. Then you said, 'They would never run out.' That was second. That's two wishes."

"That's not fair. I was just so excited I made it sound like two different things, but it was really just one. Anybody would know that!"

When it was Yashki's turn, he invariably inspired imaginings of faraway planets with strange and threatening creatures, all of which had to be mastered in some way in order to survive. He possessed a plethora of survival strategies, and Sarn thought that Yashki must lay awake at night thinking up dangerous scenarios and daring ways to escape them.

Sometimes Sarn was impressed with Yashki's creativity, but more often he just wanted the game to be over. Yashki would become so caught up in his imagination that it seemed he would go on forever.

"What if we landed on a jungle planet and when we got out of our ship, a large rock—I mean a really big one—fell off a cliff and wrecked it? And then these giant monsters started coming out of the ground? Big green ones with these long tentacles, and the tentacles had claws on the ends that were hooked and sharp as razors. What would you guys do?" More often than not they stared blankly at him, which was his signal to begin, "What I'd do would be to . . ."

Sarn enjoyed this game most of the time and found that the topics he enjoyed most had to do with the power. There was a magical aspect to this as gods could do anything they felt like, and it was fun to imagine a being with unlimited power. What usually appealed to Sarn was the idea of having someone in charge of things. An ultimate caretaker who really cared. A super parent who could make sure you were looked after and maybe even comforted you when things did not go well.

Religion was not mentioned in Sam's home. The whole subject of gods was irrelevant to the thinking of his parents. Koshil was a scientist by training and an accountant by nature. Everything had its place and could be put in that place or transferred to another either by logic or policy.

"The universe can be represented by mathematical equations, and when all those formulas are known and computed, then we will know all there is to be known. Why, given an exact knowledge of the genetic makeup of a mother and father, we can predict with a high degree of probability just what the offspring will be like."

When Kosh-il used that illustration to state his confidence in man's ultimate cognitive abilities, Sarn felt uneasy.

With a father as intelligent and analytical as Kosh-il and a mother who was head mathematician at the Institute of Science, Sarn wondered if his birth had somehow been a cruel betrayal of their scientific purity, a master stroke of espionage by family enemies. Sam's parents were so certain of everything, and Sarn was so unsure of so many things.

Sarn did not want his parents to ever know about his conversations with Tobi and Yashki and the other boys who walked slowly from school and wrestled with the "great questions."

Sarn not only had doubts about the big issues of life but also wondered about the small matters: Why was it important to know everything? Why did he sometimes want to question his father's pure scientific position and even secretly hope that Kosh-il would be wrong? Surely, he thought, something terrible would happen to him for harboring such disloyal and scandalous ideas!

Sarn often wondered if Tobi and Yashki held similar doubts. If they did, they didn't let on. All three boys avoided personal responsibility for their conversations and instead spoke in terms of "what if" and "I heard somebody say." None of them quoted their parents, Sarn noticed, but he wasn't sure what that meant. Maybe he made his parents too important and the other kids just didn't pay much attention to their own even to the point of forgetting about them until they saw them again each day. When Sarn thought about that possibility, he wished he could be like that. Thinking about his parents was a burden he didn't like to bear.

One day Sarn realized that the subject of religion was brought up often, and most of the time it was himself that did it. If Tobi liked to talk about food scenarios and Yashki preferred adventures in dangerous places, then it had to be admitted that Sarn liked to imagine "What if there was a real power?"

When this became clear to him, Sarn was embarrassed. He was sure that the others had noticed this too, but were too polite to say anything about it. For some time after that, he declined to take an active part in discussions about gods, much less be the one to bring up the topics.

Sam's number one nagging question—the one he bothered himself most with—became "What is wrong with me so that I want to talk about theology so much?" At times his answer to that query was that he was a primitive pervert and an abomination to his parents. Not that he put it into those words, but that was how he felt. Sarn never went further with his personal analysis, partly because he did not know how and partly because he didn't want to face the possible answers. He might be worse off than he thought.

It seemed that the more he tried not to talk about gods, the more he wanted to. Being so conflicted was just about more than the boy could handle, and so, when he was fifteen years old, he settled the issue with a momentous decision. He decided to put the subject of theology out of his mind forever. It was possible that he would have eventually done it anyway, but overhearing his parents talking with one of his instructors made the choice an imperative.

"The man would have been a good cadet except for that," Aris said to Sam's parents.

"Yes, he has many qualifications suitable for the fleet," Kosh-il said. He shook his head and made his "It's a shame what people will do when they don't think things through clearly like I do" frown. "But in a pinch, a softie is not the kind of person needed to make decisions."

Sarn knew what a softie was. It was one of Kosh-il's favorite words.

"A softie? That's short for *softheaded*."

"Which is short for *softheaded fool*!" his mother injected.

It was easy for Sarn to conclude that he never wanted to be a softie.

Aris was not one of Sam's favorite instructors. In fact, it could be said that he was Sam's least favorite. The subject matter in the class was interesting, for Sarn did possess an abiding and typical interest in space travel. Aris taught space physics, an introductory course that covered everything from the basic mechanics of spaceships. He lectured in a hypercorrect, condescending tone, which his students either deplored or found amusing. Sam thought it deplorable because it reminded him of his father.

"I must say the fellow has some good qualities," continued Aris. "I do believe he has an affinity for space. I checked his transcript, and he made excellent marks while in school."

Sarn did not find the conversation particularly interesting at this point and was about to move on out of earshot when his father spoke.

"How did you find out he is of a religious bent?" Kosh-il asked.

"Now that I think back, I can remember that faraway look in his eyes. I had assumed he was dreaming of traveling to faraway worlds. But, well, he asked questions having to do with the meaning and purpose of life." Aris said the last words in a tone of exaggerated gravity that clearly expressed his opinion about such silliness. "And he couched his questions in such a way so that it was clear to me he was seeking supernatural answers."

"That's too bad," said Kosh-il, "but I'm sure they will find a place for him somewhere."

"I suppose," said Aris, "but I don't think they have religious orders, do they?"

Kosh-il laughed at Aris's joke. Doree, Sam's mother, a voracious reader, said half seriously, "Only in the Hoxd Galaxy. He might do well there. Imagine, a galaxy peopled by softies. It's almost more than I can bear to think about."

Kosh-il and Aris chuckled at the image of billions of softies milling around together, shoulder to shoulder.

Sarn's father then made one of those rare statements that imprinted itself into Sam's young mind.

"You know why that is, don't you? Life in a primitive galaxy like Hoxd is difficult at best and usually dangerous. Under those conditions, everybody seeks a cognitive framework that will help them understand the world in terms that allow a negotiated survival. A religious component is needed in primitive places to counteract fear and to fill in the gaps of knowledge." He paused for effect and then concluded, "What that sums to is, if you're ignorant, you need religion."

"Or stupid," added Doree.

"My, that was well stated," said Aris. "May I quote you in my class sometime?"

"Of course."

His father's discourse explained something to Sarn. He had already decided on his own that theology was a way of putting together an understanding of what he knew and felt about life. But now he discovered that he had been engaging in a primitive and distasteful exercise, which was loathsome to his parents. Furthermore, he found that he was a softie who would surely be uncovered and deemed unfit for space travel. Sarn's only sane choice at that moment was to give up his what-if games and become serious about life. Later he was to think of that day as the turning point in his life, the day he grew up. He was lucky, he thought, that he had overheard his father's remarks and put the god foolishness behind him before he was found out.

The next day after classes Tobi said to his friends, "Let's sit on the hill and talk." He was referring to the hill of green grass on the edge of the city, a place the boys considered made especially for the discussion of "the big questions." Yashki was agreeable, but Sarn made an excuse and found his way home alone, feeling like he had lost a part of himself and did not yet know whether to feel good or bad about it.

And now, Sarn thought, here he was in the middle of a theological mission with no way to avoid being interested.

Interested? More than that. There was no way to avoid being a part of it!

What am I supposed to do now? he asked himself.

Just do my job, he answered, *and the rest will take care of itself.*

Chapter 28

SARN MEETS ALEAH

The sounds of people chattering, donkeys braying, and dogs barking beat against the door of Sarn's consciousness. Sequentially relaxing each individual limb of his body, he sought to hypnotize himself back into sleep, but it didn't work. He slowly opened his eyes and surrendered to the new day. Glancing to the side, he noted that Toler's blanket was unoccupied.

Sitting up on his blanket, Sarn felt his body come alive as he stretched his arms and yawned. The air was cool with a promise of warmth to come. Before him was a large boulder and to the left a row of bushes, the arrangement providing some semblance of privacy. On the other side of the bushes was the lake, and Sarn was afforded a pristine view of the gray-blue water spreading into the distance where it was stopped by the far hills.

The Sea of Galilee was one of the most beautiful sights Sarn had ever seen. It stretched the length of the fissure that swept from the north all the way south into the next continent. Toler had mentioned that this was the longest valley on the planet.

The town of Gennesaret rested on the northwest shore of the lake. Behind the town a fertile valley wandered away into the hills. Well-tended fields were visible as far as the eye could see, but much of the town's activity centered around fishing. Sam's camp was just outside town, and as people passed on the nearby road, they often waved in greeting. Several horses drank their fill of water while a group of squatting men ate their breakfast. Soon they would be on their way. Sarn had watched similar scenes before, and it seemed as if a group of men was always going somewhere in this land. Someday he would ask somebody where everyone was going. He stretched his arms again and yawned.

On the lake several brightly colored fishing boats were hard at work, pulling their nets through the water while dutiful reflections playfully mimicked their every movement. Sam watched in fascination as the ballet of ships bobbed and pirouetted in rhythm to the wind.

Gennesaret was one of the scenic towns dotting the coast of the Sea of Galilee. Capernaum, a few miles to the north, was another, and it was there Jesus spent his time when not on the road. It was reported that the Messiah stayed at the house of Peter's mother-in-law when he was in town.

Toler decided that they should circulate throughout the countryside rather than hang around the Messiah's headquarters. "We'll get a better idea of the impact he's having on the population. Besides, can you imagine how boring it would be to hang around any one of these little towns for any length of time?"

After fetching a bit of soap from his bag, Sarn sauntered to the lake's edge and looked for a suitable place to wash up. To the left a point of land jutted into the lake with its trees overhanging the water. The bushy growth around the trees left an open space, almost cave-like, facing the lake. Sarn was attracted to the place and walked down the bank until he came opposite the short peninsula. It was evident that he was not the first person to go there; a well-worn path testified to the popularity of the place.

He followed the trail, more like a tunnel through the bushes, until he came to the water's edge. Disrobing, he waded in and splashed the water over his body until he felt clean and refreshed.

The water's surface was smooth as glass in the early morning, and Sarn swam away from shore for a while. He had never been in a natural lake and found it exhilarating.

A movement onshore caused him to pull up. So unexpected was the intrusion that he had trouble focusing on what he had seen. A girl's face, framed by leafy boughs, peered at him, and the two stared at each other in surprise. Sarn slid deeper into the water until it lapped under his nose.

"Hello," Sarn finally said, sputtering water and feeling foolish.

The girl's face disappeared behind the bush and reappeared by the water's edge, now attached to a body. She wore the usual linen tunic gathered at the waist by a sash and a shawl over her head.

"Hello yourself!" she called out. Her teeth flashed white as she smiled.

"Who are you? I didn't see you when I came in," he managed to say as the water tickled his bottom lip.

"I am Aleah, and I was not here when you arrived. What is your name?"

"I am called Sarn," he replied.

She stood tall on the bank, arms crossed, looking down on the blushing boy.

"Please don't drown, Sarn," she said teasingly. "I will turn away when you are ready to come out."

Sarn's face turned redder as he realized that he was swallowing water.

"Oh. I'm all right. Guess I'll come out now." Sarn stood up straight, shoulders out of the water.

Aleah walked to a large tree and turned her head. Sarn took the cue, hastily sloshed to shore, and retrieved his clothing.

"All right, I'm dressed," he announced.

Aleah turned and approached Sarn, looking him over with curious eyes. He blushed and quickly looked down at himself. The girl laughed.

"Where are you from?" Aleah asked. "I have not seen you around before. You are not from here. You are different."

"Well, no, you see, my friend and I—his name is Toler—are passing through. I needed to bathe, and then you came. I'm all clean now." Sarn spread his arms as if proving that he was clean, then clamped his mouth shut, and folded his arms over his chest.

Aleah smiled, amused at this self-conscious person. "Are you always so nervous?" she asked.

"No—yes. Well, some of the time," Sarn stammered. "Mostly with girls, to tell the truth." He shrugged. "And you're a girl, so I guess that's why I'm nervous."

"But where are you from, and to where do you travel?"

Sarn and Toler had carefully decided how to safely answer such queries.

"We come from east of here. Far away. And we are looking for possible markets of trade. If we find something that might be of value back home, then we will take samples with us for our master to see. And if he likes them, he will send us back to trade his perfumes, the finest anywhere." This was the first time Sarn had explained his origins and purpose to a native, and he watched her face carefully.

"No, I did not think you were from around here. Your appearance and accent are strange to me." Her smile returned. "But welcome to our village."

Aleah was seventeen years of age and a very pretty girl with big eyes and long brown hair. She had blossomed in the past year and was not yet aware of how attractive she was to men. A late bloomer, in many ways she was still a playful child who liked to laugh and play tag. She knew no strangers, looked for and expected only the best in others, and usually was not disappointed. Within the past few months, her mother, Darene, had begun to notice how men looked at her daughter and knew that it would not be long before someone took her as a bride. Darene knew that if the family had property or title, Aleah would have already been taken. But there was little since her husband's death, and Aleah was therefore no prize for a man who was counting on a dowry.

"Do you come here often?" Sarn asked, walking beside Aleah.

"Almost every day," she said, tossing her hair over her shoulder. "I like to watch the fishing boats." Her white teeth glistened in the morning light, and her eyes twinkled like sun reflections in a rippling pool. Aleah's arm swung against

Sarn as they made their way through the brush, and once she bent over to pass in front of him while he held back a limb, and he smelled her hair as it spilled from her shawl.

Sarn lost track of what she was talking about and did not notice that they were walking toward the village. He knew only one thing: he was in love with this beautiful girl and must be with her.

"Sarn! Sarn!" The trance was broken by Toler's voice.

"Where are you going?" Toler caught up to them, panting. He had come back to camp in time to spot Sarn and Aleah walking toward Gennesaret.

"Oh, uh, this is Aleah, and, Aleah, this is Toler. He's my partner I was telling you about."

"Hello, Toler," said Aleah. "Would you like to go with us?"

Toler looked from Sarn to Aleah and back to Sarn. It didn't take a genius to figure out what was going on. His first concern was to ensure the secrecy of their identity. As long as they were asking impersonal questions of people on the street, they were not likely to arouse interest in who they were. But getting to know someone and relate on a personal level, and the risks multiplied exponentially. And who knows what stupid statements the boy might make while under the influence of his glandular disturbance!

"It's nice to meet you, Aleah. Thank you for your invitation, but Sarn and I have so much to do."

"Would you have time to come to the house and just have a cake with me? Mother, maybe Uncle, might be there. Uncle Lish would be very interested to meet buyers from the east."

She showered them with her winsome smile while her eyes danced from one to the other. Toler thought she was the most natural seductress he had ever met.

"No, but thank you anyway." He firmly took Sam's elbow and led him away.

"Maybe I'll see you again sometime," Sarn called to her over his shoulder.

"All right." She laughed, turned, and was gone.

"I've never met a girl like that!" said Sam. "Didn't you think she was great? And I think she likes me!"

"Yes, she is quite attractive. Now if you'll beam yourself back to reality, we need to have a long talk about fraternization with the natives!"

At that time neither Toler nor Sarn could fully appreciate how fortuitous for them and tragic for her their acquaintance with Aleah would later be. As a matter of fact, Sarn would not see her again for several weeks, and it would be even longer before Toler once more met up with her.

During that span of time, Toler and Sarn traveled around the countryside. Their assignment was to gauge the effectiveness of the Messiah, and it proved more fruitful in the long run to watch and listen than to ask direct questions. Some of the time was spent traveling with Jesus's entourage, but mostly they drifted among the villages and towns, meeting folks and listening to what was important to the common people. Occasionally they went to Jerusalem and spent their time around the Temple listening to the public utterings of the religious establishment.

Their findings were not surprising. The poor people were attracted to the Messiah, often in large crowds. The established leaders were usually annoyed at his success and sometimes threatened by what they perceived as an attack on the status quo. The prevailing justification for alarm was the premise that should the occupying Romans consider the movement a menace to pacification, they would come down hard on everyone. It was not that the Jews liked the Romans, for they did not. But the gentle preacher hardly seemed an appropriate focal point for a rebellion, and until the time was right for such a movement against the occupying forces, it was better for the Romans to believe everything was all right.

The work was mostly unrewarding for the two men as it involved a great deal of walking across a hot arid country, a meager selection of food, poor or no nightly accommodations, and the constant tension of remaining incognito among a primitive people. These inconveniences were balanced by the lush gardens, orchards with ample supplies of fresh produce, and friendly people whom they found in other parts of the land. The country was one of stark contrasts.

"Do you know what the worst part of this mission is for me?" Sarn once asked Toler as they were commiserating about things in general. "It's not knowing when it's going to be over."

Toler nodded. It was true! He listened sympathetically as Sarn vented his frustrations.

"We could be here for years! Not knowing how many more nights we've got to spend in a manger is what gets me."

"Can a messiah who stays around for a long time be good?"

Sarn looked at Toler quizzically. "You're saying that a good messiah gets himself killed quickly?"

"Is he doing his job if no one wants to get rid of him?"

"My idea of a good messiah is a guy who drops in, tells people how to do better, maybe even shows them how, and then leaves." Sarn paused. "By that definition, I suppose it follows that the longer he stays around, the more effective he will be. He can teach them more."

"It doesn't seem to work that way," said Toler. "Not from what I've seen. And I suppose it's that way any place a messiah goes."

Sarn thought hard. "I think I see what you mean. We've heard Jesus tell people to sell what they have and give the money to the poor. Not many people have done that. In fact, I've not heard of anyone going that far."

"The one I like is when he tells the Pharisees to quit worrying so much about rules and instead attend to the spirit of things. If they did that, they'd have to give up a lot of rules they've invested hundreds of hours writing and memorizing! Not to mention status and position!"

"He has real nerve," said Sam, "to ask people to do these things. No wonder they get rid of messiahs!"

"And he is aware, I believe, that his requirements are difficult for people to satisfy."

"Then why does he keep on with it? There must be easier lines of work." Sarn answered his own question, "He's not your regular man. He was placed here by the power, right?"

"That's what I hear," said Toler. "But I wouldn't blame him if he was a reluctant messiah."

"You don't really believe in a supreme being, do you?" asked Sam.

Toler shrugged. "I suppose not. But please understand, I'd like to. I really would. I just haven't seen any good reason to, that's all."

Sam's expression turned to incredulity. "The Messiah isn't enough for you?"

"I like him, but no, he is not enough for me to think there is a power."

Sarn turned away and stared across the Sea of Galilee. Toler shrugged and walked away. After a while Sarn caught up with him, and they resumed their mission.

Chapter 29

WAGON

Capernaum hugged the Sea of Galilee a few miles northeast of Gennesaret. Like the other coastal villages, its economy depended heavily on fishing. Jesus stayed in the house belonging to one of the fishermen's mother-in-law; it would later be said that this was the first theological school north of Jerusalem.

During the two weeks Sarn and Toler visited Capernaum, they heard the Messiah preach from the mountainside just west of town, a favorite place of his. Jesus started speaking early, soon after sunrise, and quit by midmorning when the heat became obtrusive.

"I am amazed at these people! They are common and uneducated, but look how they hunger for what the Messiah says!" Sarn was disappointed when the crowd broke up after three hours.

Toler stood, stretched leisurely, and shrugged. "The acoustics are good. This little valley is a natural amphitheater. I estimate there were fifteen thousand people here this morning, and that's probably more than the entire population of Capernaum."

"He puts an interesting twist on the old teachings. Did you like what he said?"

"It was all right. I was so busy trying to estimate the crowd that I didn't hear much."

While the Messiah was in Capernaum, the disciples, most of whom lived there, stole as much time from their families and fishing as they could in order to listen to the man they had come to call Master.

Ten of the disciples had grown up in the little town and were respected citizens. When they first cast down their nets and followed the Messiah, there was much talk against their action. Pressure was brought to bear on the men to return home and take care of their families but to no avail. When it became apparent that the disciples would be coming home occasionally, sometimes to stay for a while, the people were less dissatisfied. As the Messiah's reputation grew, especially after he worked a few miracles, it became a cause of great satisfaction to have one's family member named among the close followers.

At the end of two weeks the Messiah and his band departed west for Cana. Toler thought it would be a good time to leave the messianic band and explore farther east, and he and Sarn trekked to Sogane and Gamala. Those towns were not a part of the Jewish nation and had their own sets of gods and customs. Whatever else he was, Jesus was a good Jew and related most easily with his own people.

The terrain was rough and travel was difficult the farther east they went, so it was a relief to them both when they turned back to the west and came to Bethsaida on the northern tip of the Sea of Galilee. Sarn suggested they travel to Damascus using the main trade route to the northeast. Well traveled by the merchants of Persia and Babylon, it was a favored way of bringing their goods to Acco for shipment to Rome or Egypt. After considerable discussion, it was decided that it would be more worthwhile to visit Cana so that they could follow up on the Messiah's recent visit there.

"It's not too far from Cana to Sepphoris. I hear that's one of the larger cities. Nothing near as large as Jerusalem, but about sixty thousand. I'd like to see it."

Sarn nodded. "I'd really like to see Acco. I've heard it's a bustling seaport. People from everywhere come through there."

"That's the port where the Romans come and go. It would be interesting to see their ships."

"Why do you suppose the Messiah doesn't set up his base in Acco? With all the traffic from so many countries, that would be ideal for the export of his teachings." Sam scratched his head. "It seems a shame for him to confine himself to Galilee. Except for occasional trips to Jerusalem, I'll bet he seldom travels more than twenty-five miles from Capernaum."

"Maybe you could hire on as his agent," quipped Toler.

"No, I don't mean to be presumptuous. There's probably a good reason for staying among his own people, but I just don't understand it."

"Messiahs have their own peculiar rules," said Toler.

Almost three months after their encounter with Aleah, they stopped over in Gennesaret.

"Don't look now," murmured Toler, "but I believe those are our friends from back home." Sarn noted the direction in which Toler had been looking and casually glanced up. Looming against a shop front across the market square, Derxter talked to two men. Beside Derxter was his assistant, Squirb, shifting uncomfortably from one foot to another. Derxter's deep voice rose in anger. Someone glanced in Derxter's direction but paid no further attention. It was common for people to shout at one another in the market as they haggled over goods.

One of the natives shrugged and started to walk away. Derxter's hand shot out, grabbed him by the neck, and yanked the startled man up against his barrel chest. He said something into the frightened man's ear. Reaching under his cloak, the terrified man produced a rolled-up parchment. Derxter immediately grabbed it and pushed the man aside. The two natives scuttled away, stopping at the corner to hurl a few choice insults.

What happened next was totally unexpected. Derxter and Squirb turned and strode away in the opposite direction from the men. Derxter stuffed the parchment under his robe at about the same time that a man leading his donkey collided with Derxter. With a loud swear, Derxter pushed the surprised man, tumbling him into the side of his animal, and passed on. It was then that Toler and Sarn saw something fall from under Derxter's tunic. Either Derxter had missed the pocket or else the scroll had been jarred loose by the collision.

The man with the donkey, a thin middle-aged fellow who was eager to go home to his wife, was bent double attempting to catch his breath after being thrown against the bony donkey. The parchment landed in front of him. He looked at it, stared after Derxter and Squirb, and made to pick it up.

"Move!" said Toler. "Get it before he does." Toler's instant decision was that possession of the parchment might give them some edge in dealing with Derxter.

Sarn sprinted across the square and reached the slow-moving man just as he picked up the parchment. Sarn snatched it from the hand of the unsuspecting fellow, who was just beginning to catch his breath, and ran.

"Robber! Thief!" The wildly indignant man shook his fists in the air; if he had been more able, he would have jumped up and down. Not only had he been rudely shoved aside, smashed against the hard side of his ass, but his one consolation, the important-looking scroll, had been whisked from his possession before he could even relish even a temporary ownership. It was too much!

Looking over his shoulder, Sarn saw that the fellow was not giving chase but was content to yell obscenities. He headed for an alleyway where he planned to wait for Toler to catch up to him.

"Hey, you! Stop!" Derxter's voice rolled over the crowd in the marketplace. Fear grabbed Sarn, and he ran.

Directly ahead the wall of a building blocked the alleyway, and narrow passageways led off to the right and left.

A quick glance told him that the passage on the left narrowed before it veered out of sight. The right turn appeared to dead end at the doorway of a building. A figure in the doorway signaled to him, and Sarn leaped to the right; jumped around a gray-headed woman, knocking her basket of fruit to the ground; and ran for the shadowy doorway, which was now empty. Behind him sounded the grunts and oaths of his two very angry pursuers.

"There he is!" shouted Squirb.

"Catch him, you fool!" boomed Derxter.

Sarn burst through the doorway into a dimly lit room and could see nobody.

"This way," someone whispered. It was a woman's voice and sounded vaguely familiar.

Sarn moved quickly toward the voice and could then see the blackness of another doorway. Arms outstretched, he felt his way through the opening and felt a hand take his and pull urgently.

"This way!" the voice repeated. Sarn was led through a darkened room into still another space. Pausing before a low closet, his guide opened the loose-fitting door, pulled Sam in, and shut the door behind them.

"Thanks!" Sarn whispered between gasps. "You're welcome," she said.

Sarn was certain that his labored breathing was loud enough to be heard throughout the building. He could imagine Derxter homing in on the sounds of panting and stalking directly to their hiding place; without fanfare he would drag forth the wheezing boy and proceed to punish him severely.

A hand clutched his knee in warning. Her breathing had stopped. Sarn held his breath and listened. A sound of voices, running, stumbling came from somewhere; it sounded far away, yet it was difficult to tell. Then the noise moved in the other direction and became fainter.

"Who are you?" Sarn whispered.

"I am Aleah. The girl you met at the lake. Remember?"

"Of course!" Sarn could imagine her big brown eyes gazing at him in the darkness. "I thought I recognized your voice. You may have saved my life, you know."

"Oh? Is it that serious? I thought maybe you had insulted the man or stolen something from him, and he would give you a few licks if he caught you. But . . . you sound quite serious. And afraid."

"Shhh!" Sarn touched her lips. There was the unmistakable sound of footsteps in the adjoining room where Derxter's voice reverberated. "Search everywhere! He couldn't have gone far."

Sam's heart stopped. Derxter was searching each room, and it would be only a matter of a few minutes before the pair would be discovered. He leaned forward and peeked through the crack in the door. He had come from the doorway to the right, and Derxter was in the next room; as soon as he searched that one, he would be in the room in which the closet was located. The closet was about to become a trap!

Sam's only escape was the door to the left.

"You stay here." Sarn pressed the scroll into Aleah's hand. "Bring this with you to the lake in the morning."

Sarn climbed out of the closet as quietly as he could and closed the door behind him. Sarn located a table and pushed it over with a loud crash.

"What's that?" Squirb's voice was high pitched from the next room.

"This way!" Derxter shouted, and suddenly he was in the doorway almost before Sarn could leap for his exit. Derxter grabbed for him and missed.

Sarn came upon a window, a small opening no more than two feet square and about five feet off the ground. Without pause Sarn thrust his head and one arm through the opening while the sound of running feet thundered down the hallway. He struggled to pull his other arm out into the bright sunlight. Sudden pain clouded his face as his legs were firmly grasped and violently twisted. He brought his other arm through the window and kicked, but the grasp by the burly Derxter was too much. Sarn was being inexorably pulled back through the window.

Frantically he looked for help. Running toward him, face contorted in anguish, was Toler. He leaped for Sam's extended hand, but it was too late; the boy was whipped back through the window and into the waiting arms of Derxter and Squirb.

When Sarn had snatched the scroll from the man with the donkey, Toler found himself laughing at the spectacle. It would not have been more comical had it been staged. Still chuckling, he walked toward the alleyway down which Sarn had fled. Since the old man was not pursuing Sam, there seemed little reason to hurry.

But there had been an angry roar behind Toler. Derxter had heard the man with the donkey cursing, turned out of curiosity, and spotted someone running through the crowd holding a scroll in his hand. Derxter felt his robe. Horrified, he discovered the empty pocket.

"Come back, thief!" he bellowed and pursued the fleeing figure, knocking people from his path as if they were straw baskets. Squirb ran after Derxter as fast as his short legs would carry him.

Toler had an impulse to stick his leg out and trip Derxter but figured the boy would easily outrun them. He followed the chase close enough to see Derxter and Squirb enter the door in pursuit. Toler immediately made his way toward the other end of the building where he would wait for Sarn to emerge. On his way he spotted a figure struggling to pull himself through a window; by the time he recognized Sarn and ran over to help, the boy had been pulled back into the building. He wasn't sure what he should do at that point, but he knew he must maintain contact with Sarn. Toler made his way back to the doorway where the chase had originally entered the building.

Where was Derxter? And Sam? With a start of apprehension, Toler hurried to the doorway of the aged building and entered the darkness.

Toler ran through the building as quickly as he could while still searching each room and closet. Thirty minutes later he emerged on the other side of the building, blinded by sunlight, sweaty and tired. He had found no one.

Aleah placed the scroll in her inner pocket as soon as Sam exited the closet and shut the door behind him. Peeking through a crack, she saw Sarn leave through the doorway to the left with Derxter and Squirb hot on his heels. Aleah clambered from the closet and ran from the room, not stopping until she was outside. Holding her hand over the bulge of the scroll, she paused long enough to take a deep breath. Entering the next building, she made her way to another street, and by the time Toler began looking for Sarn in the building, Aleah was gone.

Huge arms wrapped around Sam's legs, and the sound of heavy breathing echoed loudly as he was drawn back through the window. He desperately reached out his hand to Toler, but the tug on his lower body was too strong. As he popped back into the building, another set of arms wrapped around his upper body.

"Quick! Take him through that door!" Derxter ordered. The two men, carrying Sarn like a log, made their way through two rooms, found an outside door, and exited.

"Where are we? This is not a street I know," Squimb said, blinking in the sunlight.

"Keep moving. We may be followed." Derxter had no fear of confronting the natives. He was certainly powerful enough to deal with the strongest of the locals. Besides his own brute strength and well-trained fighting skills, he carried a laser gun under his cloak. What he didn't want was a scene. Derxter had been strictly warned by Lybur that he should not call attention to himself. "We will shape history without making any footnotes in the history books," Lybur had said.

The short narrow street into which they stumbled was empty of people. A yellow dog growled as they passed. Across the street was an opening, its door ajar on its hinges. Derxter carried Sarn to the empty room, Squirb being yanked right along.

Sarn was unceremoniously dumped on the hard stone floor. Derxter stood above him, hands on hips, and glowered at his captive.

"You are a sneaky thief! Where is the parchment you grabbed from the old man in the market?"

Sarn did not look at Derxter. He managed a shrug.

"Pig!" Derxter grabbed Sam's cloak and tore it open. A quick search located nothing but Sam's personal kit.

"Where is it?" Derxter spat at him. Sarn shrugged.

"Speak up! Where is it?" Derxter's fury glistened on his face.

Sarn shook his head and shrugged.

"He's a mute," said Squirb. "Just a poor, mute street thief. He doesn't even know what he had."

Derxter yanked Sarn to a standing position and pressed him against the wall. With one finger pushing at the boy's chest, he said, "You are going to show us where you placed the parchment. If you don't, I shall dismember you! Slowly!"

Sarn had no doubt that Derxter would do exactly as he threatened, but he really did not know where the scroll was. And if the parchment was valuable, the girl might not show up at the lake tomorrow, and the chances of finding her again would be quite slim.

"Show us!" Derxter pushed Sarn ahead while tightly clutching his cloak. Sarn moved as if to let the robe slide off his arms. Derxter read Sam's intentions and tightly held the boy's left arm.

They crossed the street and reentered the building through the side door. Pushed ahead into the dimly lit room, Sarn acted on an inspiration born of sheer desperation.

"Stop! In the name of the law, stop!" Sarn shouted in his most authoritarian voice, hoping that his words would seem to be coming from across the room. Derxter could see nothing in the dark, and Sarn felt the giant freeze, uncertain.

Something had to happen quickly, or nothing would happen at all.

"Seize them, guards!" Sarn shouted into the darkness.

Just then there was the rattle of furniture on the far side of the room. A chair fell over. Someone grunted and bumped into the table. Derxter reflexively took one hand free to reach for his laser gun. As soon as Sarn felt the grip on his arm released, he sprang forward, trailing his arms, allowing the robe, which was still held by Derxter, to slide from his body. Adrenaline catapulted him across the room, crashing into a body.

Sarn found himself lying on top of an old man, the terrified face a few inches from his own. The old fellow's rasping breath reeked of sour wine, and he wondered what he had done to deserve this. He had been sitting in the corner with his drink, minding his own business, when two men had hurriedly passed through carrying a body. He had barely resettled when the door opened, and someone ordered guards to seize him. It was more than the man could handle, and he had tried to get away, falling over a chair and table in the dimly lit room.

"Catch the pig!" Derxter roared.

"Where is he?" Squirb's voice came from the still-open door.

Sarn rolled off the bony old man and came up off the floor running. Derxter reached out to grab him and stumbled over the drunk man on the floor. His wide eyes bugged like fried eggs when Derxter's great weight fell across him. He began retching, emptying himself of wine, bile, and what little food he had eaten that day.

"Where is he?" Squirb repeated and then tripped and fell across the two bodies. Derxter crawled from under his henchman, found his feet, and left Squirb to roll in the old man's fetid vomit.

Sarn raced with the speed of the terrified. He passed the window through which he had tried to escape before and as he sped through the next room saw that the closet door was open and no one was there.

"You pig, I'll kill you!" Derxter's voice rumbled.

Sarn did not pause when he reached the outside door but gained speed as he ran down the narrow street toward the square. People turned to stare at the unusual sight of a fair-haired, white-skinned man running around in his underwear.

Reaching the town square, Sarn crouched behind a wagon and fought to catch his breath. Cautiously peering around a wheel, he watched the street from which he had just come. Where were his pursuers? Had he run that fast? Had Derxter taken a wrong turn?

The crowd continued to move around the square. An occasional cart rolled by. People stopped at the well and filled their jugs. Life continued as usual in the town of Gennesaret.

A small group of men came into view, their attention glued on their leader's words. Sarn barely noticed them at first, but a second look identified the speaker as the Messiah, Jesus.

Sarn found an old blanket in the wagon and draped it around himself. He ambled over to the group gathered around the well. Pulling the old smelly blanket around his head like a hood, Sarn stood at the outer edge of the circle of men. hey paid no attention to him, so engrossed were they with what Jesus was saying.

"Jesus, do you know that the Pharisees have taken great offense at what you have been saying?" Sarn did not know what saying had bothered the Pharisees, but clearly the situation was of great concern to the men surrounding Jesus.

Insulting the religious establishment did not make for a comfortable bed on any planet. The disciples were clearly worried about their own skin as well as the safety of Jesus.

"Any plant that is not of my heavenly Father's planting will be rooted up. Leave them alone. They are blind guides, and if one man guides another, they will both fall into the ditch."

Sarn was impressed with the man's manner. Whatever Jesus had said that had upset the Pharisees, the man minced no words and seemed confident of himself.

One of the men—a tall bushy-headed, full-bearded, heavily muscled man—was not satisfied with Jesus's answer.

"Tell us what that parable means." There was some nodding by the others who also wanted amplification of what Jesus had said. Jesus sounded impatient with his students, however, apparently overlooking the fact that his followers were clearly not well educated—if at all. Sarn made a mental note to check the handbook on messiahs. Was there some method in the choosing of common, uneducated men for followers, or was this simply the best a messiah could hope to sign up?

"Are you still as dull as the rest, Peter?" Jesus asked. "Do you not see that whatever goes in by the mouth passes into the stomach and so is discharged into the drain? But what comes out of the mouth has its origins in the heart, and that is what defiles a man."

Sarn nodded and smiled. "A little wordy but good," he muttered.

"Wicked thoughts, murder, adultery, fornication, theft, perjury, slander— these all proceed from the heart. These are the things that defile a man. But to eat without first washing his hand, that cannot defile him."

Vigorous head nodding signaled that the men not only understood but heartily agreed. Sarn found himself nodding, stopped himself, and resumed nodding. *Why not flow with the tide and be one of them? That's the safest route.*

Squirb! Sarn suddenly saw the short fat man staring intently at him. Where was Derxter? Sarn slumped and moved to blend in with the small crowd around the well.

Stepping between two of the men and holding the blanket around his head, Sarn spoke to Jesus, "Excuse me, sir. I have a question."

"Yes?" Jesus's expression invited Sarn to continue.

"Uh, do you expect there to be trouble?" Sarn asked the first thing that came to mind, anything that would engage him with Jesus and his followers.

Jesus looked Sarn full in the face, making direct eye contact. Sarn had never experienced such an open and embracing gaze; it was as if he would be pulled into the liquid-brown eyes of Jesus.

Jesus looked at Squirb who had taken a step forward. His gaze held Squirb in place as he replied, "There will always be trouble. But the farmer does not refrain from sowing his seed just because he knows there will be dry spells during the growing season." He looked back to Sarn. "The man who has a work to do will do what has to be done and pay the cost." Sarn looked uncomfortable.

"Come with us," Jesus concluded simply, turned, and walked out the gate of Gennesaret, his men straggling behind, Sarn in their midst.

As Sarn passed through the gate, he furtively looked back. Squirb was still at the well, gesticulating to Derxter who had suddenly appeared. Squirb excitedly pointed to the band of men leaving the village. Derxter's face was dark and ominous as he glared at the departing group.

Sarn visibly shuddered. He flashed on a sudden image of having one foot in cold water, the other in hot. Such was the contrast between Derxter and Jesus.

The rest of the day was spent leisurely traveling toward Capernaum. When they came to the mountainside overlooking the Sea of Galilee, Jesus stood near the top and spoke to a crowd that had gathered on the slopes.

After the Messiah finished his more formal address, he and his disciples walked toward town, talking among themselves. Sarn mostly listened, choosing to stay on the fringe as an observer. The men were so caught up with Jesus's teachings that they paid scant attention to this new camp follower. Temporary hangers-on were common; out of curiosity people came and went, trailing along with the group for a while and then leaving.

The Messiah and his audience stopped in a grove of trees when they were startled by the sudden arrival of a wailing woman. She was perhaps in her middle thirties, slightly stooped, with a plain face and large brown eyes. She had been running, breathed heavily, and tears strained her face. She scanned the group, saw Jesus, and threw herself to the ground at his feet.

"Sir! Have pity on me, Son of David. My daughter is tormented by a devil."

Sarn noticed for the first time a young girl of about ten years of age standing not far from the group. Her unkempt hair stood out in different directions, and her eyes were wild with fear and confusion. She stood on the balls of her feet as if poised for flight.

Jesus looked down at the woman and then at the daughter.

"Send her away. See how she comes shouting after us," one of the men urged Jesus.

"I was sent to the lost sheep of the House of Israel and to them alone," Jesus said.

The woman was not to be denied and crawled closer to Jesus, the dust sticking to her wet face.

"Help me, sir," she begged.

Moved by the woman's entreaty, Sarn moved closer.

"It is not right to take the children's bread and throw it to the dogs," Jesus said to her.

The woman raised herself to a sitting position, still leaning on her hand. She lifted her face to Jesus and spoke, "And yet the dogs eat the scraps that fall from their master's table."

Jesus's face visibly softened. "Woman, what faith you have! Be it as you wish!" He made a gesture toward the girl as he spoke.

The woman slowly turned and looked at her daughter. Everyone watched as the child's face contorted; deep and unnaturally hard lines appeared. There was a sound, at first like a muted growl and then a pitiful whimper. And then the girl's face relaxed, and her rigid posture softened. The wild look in her face disappeared, and for the first time she saw the group of men. Tears slowly squeezed from her eyes and then became a flood. A cry of release emanated from the depths of her being, and she ran to her mother's arms.

Sarn had the distinct impression that a battle for possession of the child had been waged and won by Jesus.

A battle with what or whom? Sarn pondered.

Chapter 30

LISH

Aleah had lived near the town of Gennesaret for all of her seventeen years. Nothing much exciting ever happened, and playing games with her friends and listening to her mother talk about the latest news were her two favorite activities. Unless you included time with Uncle Lish, and then there was no comparison at all; for Uncle Lish was a warm, caring, and most interesting man.

Actually Lish was a family friend who had been adopted several years before Aleah's birth. Aleah, like her brothers and sisters, had grown up calling him uncle.

"Your father was attacked by thieves and left to die. Lish found him and cared for your father until he was healed." Aleah's mother took time to retell the story whenever asked, for it was clear that she was grateful to Lish.

"Your father and I had been married less than a year. I was large with Yoster, your oldest brother, when your father traveled to Jerusalem. He did not return for a long time, and we all thought he had been killed or abducted by slave traders." Even after many years, her voice still conveyed the concern and sadness she had felt at the time. "One day, on my way back from the well, I head a shout from the gate.

"I could not believe it when I saw your father, Yasha, walking with the help of Lish."

"But why did Lish stay with us?" one of the children would always ask. Actually Lish did not share the same house with Aleah and her family. He had built a small house well behind that of Aleah so that everyone could have their own privacy. Yet he often ate with them and was always available to help with some chores.

"Because he considers our family to be his," Mother would say with a slight shrug, which suggested that she really did not fully understand or considered it important why he stayed. Lish would always be welcome.

And when Lish was asked about himself, he was always vague without sounding evasive. "Where is my family, you ask?" Lish would say, "Why, they are far away. I think of them often."

"Why do you stay with us, Uncle Lish?" Aleah had asked.

"Because I am lonely for my family and so you take their place while I am away from them. And while I am here, you are my family. Are you not, my dear, Aleah?"

Aleah had always prized her time with Uncle Lish. He was not only knowledgeable but very wise. Aleah, brighter than her siblings, had early established a special bond with him. He had expressed his fondness for her by defying tradition and teaching her to read; this became their special secret, although Aleah's mother suspected but looked the other way. It had never made sense to her that only men should be taught to read and write, but she never questioned the way things were. It only made problems when she did.

It was to Uncle Lish that Aleah sped with the stolen scroll. He alone would know what to do with it.

Uncle Lish was tending the garden when Aleah arrived. She ran breathlessly to him.

"Uncle Lish! Uncle Lish!"

"Whoa, my dear girl, slow down and get your breath." He led her to the shade of an olive tree where Aleah promptly plopped to the ground. As she sought to catch her breath, she brought the scroll from her pocket.

"Can you tell me what this is, Uncle Lish?"

Lish took the scroll, smiling as he did so, wondering what Aleah had gotten herself into. "Where did you find this, Aleah? In the synagogue on the altar, no doubt!" He chuckled.

Lish carefully unrolled the scroll and held it before him.

As he read the script, his face took on a serious cast. "Where did you get this?" His voice was flat but with an edge to it. Aleah had never before heard him speak in that tone. She averted her eyes from his piercing gaze.

"A friend gave it to me for keeping."

"Exactly who is this friend, Aleah?"

"Just somebody I met one day. Down at the river."

"Name? Did he give a name?" Lish urged.

"Yes, his name is Sarn. And he is very nice."

"Think carefully," Lish said as he squatted before Aleah and firmly held her shoulders. "Where did Sarn get this?"

"You're hurting me, Uncle Lish! Please let go!"

Startled, Lish released her. "I'm sorry! I wasn't paying attention. I'm really sorry. But I must find out where Sam got this document!"

Aleah rubbed her shoulders. She was frightened as well as puzzled by Lish's behavior.

"I'm not sure, but I think from the two men who were chasing him. One was big, real big, and there was something about him that scared me." Her eyes flashed with fear. "He was mean. That's all I know how to describe him. Mean!"

"And the other man? What was he like?" Lish asked.

"The other man was shorter and ran in a clumsy way. He was fat. The big one was the boss."

"Tell me what happened. Everything," Lish urged.

Aleah told him the entire story of how she had gone to town to shop and had stopped by her aunt's apartment, how she happened to be on the street when Sam ran around the corner, and how he had given her the scroll in case he was captured.

"I don't know if he was captured or not," she said. "But I'll bet it's no secret. They were making a lot of noise."

Lish was thoughtful. "Tell me more about your friend. Was there anything unusual or strange about him?"

Aleah furrowed her brow in thought. "Well, yes, there was something odd about Sarn. I thought it was because he is from another country. Maybe it was the way he talked." Looking full at Lish, she asked, "Why?" She glanced at the document in Lish's hand. "What is on the scroll?"

"Now, now, please don't get excited." Lish smiled, but Aleah knew it was a forced smile. His manner also told her that she would get no more information from him until he was ready to share it.

"Let me keep the scroll, Aleah. If those men are still searching for it, there may be danger. We'll talk about it later." Lish rose and strode toward the small house in which he lived.

Aleah was relieved to be rid of the scroll and yet had a feeling that the matter was not finished. She wished there was a way to find Sarn before morning.

Lish entered the small hut, sat heavily on his one chair, and opened the scroll. He read its contents twice and then stared at the aged parchment for a long time.

He had finally found what he had been looking for.

How many years ago had it been since Lish had arrived on Earth? Twenty-five? Twenty-two? He did not recall the exact year, but it had been a long time. His pre-Earth life seemed like something he had once read about rather than belonging to him.

Lish was, in fact, an archaeologist in the employ of the Xerxes Galaxy, Department of Science History. While finishing his education, Lish had become fascinated by an obscure monograph written about an even more obscure planet. It told of a ship from the Xerxes Galaxy that had mysteriously disappeared about four thousand years ago. It wasn't until a thousand years had passed that its distress signal was received. The message had been bouncing around the universe for all those years, and by some highly improbable statistic, it was finally picked up by an amateur radio operator.

According to the distress message, mechanical problems caused the ship to crash-land on the third planet of a small solar system.

There had been no publicity. The disappearance of the ship had been long ago, and its loss had not been as interesting or important as many other missing ships during that time span. The radio operator had reported his finding to the proper government agency, where a lesser bureaucrat had dutifully recorded it in the central computer. There it was eventually properly catalogued and ultimately discovered by Lish.

The scenario of an entire crew trapped on a primitive planet without eventual rescue had never happened before or at least was not recorded. The question of how they would adjust to such a situation was prescribed by firm and detailed policy but had not been addressed in real life.

Would the crew resign themselves to living out their lives on that planet while maintaining their own exclusive colony?

Or would they fraternize with the natives? Although policy negated such a practice, it was nevertheless Lish's belief that such would happen.

Lish's imagination was fired. If the crew had actually bred with the natives, then Earth presented a fascinating opportunity for research into the effects of outside genetic influences. The ethical code for interplanetary exploration expressly forbade tampering with the evolution of a developing planet, but Lish believed that there was enough of a natural attraction between people of different planets to ensure eventual association.

At the end of his studies at the academy, he applied for a postdoctoral research grant, which turned out to be barely enough to pay for passage to and from Earth. But then that was all Lish had hoped for. A young and romantic adventurer, he was moved more by the challenge of the moment than any consideration of the long-term ramifications of his research or of material reward. And he certainly never stopped to think about the hardships of such an undertaking.

A government scout ship made room for him, his equipment, and his meager personal belongings and on their next trip to the general vicinity of Earth deposited Lish on the primitive planet. He was to send a call beam when ready to be picked up. The desolate arid mountains of a large island were chosen for his base of operations, and there he settled himself in a cave. The population of the island stayed to the lowlands, and the likelihood of discovery was unlikely.

One of the essential parts of his equipment was a small two-person ship, which resembled something like a small wheeled bicycle with oversized wings. Designed for camping, it was lightweight and folded up neatly. Powered by a solar power pack, the simple machine amazingly could fly at almost one hundred miles per hour, which was more than fast enough for its unprotected pilots. It was called a *Dune Hopper*, and most families had at least one to play with on holidays and on camping expeditions. Lish realized it would take a very long time to canvass the planet on such a machine but early on resigned himself to a life of slow progress.

Exploring the area immediately around his base had been initially exhilarating. He had never been off of Bigor, his home planet, and it was exciting to explore a planet thus far officially unexplored.

Soon Lish was making daily forages from his base in the mountains. Occasionally he was spied by natives as he soared across the landscape, but other than causing a little excited finger-pointing, nothing came of it. He found that by flying low, with hills and mountains as a backdrop, he was not easily spotted from the ground.

Lish's cave was high on the eastern slope of a mountainside so steep that anyone below would have been severely discouraged from making the climb. Lish began and ended most days sitting on the ledge outside his cave surveying his kingdom. Occasionally he walked as far as he could without doing any serious climbing and found the exercise to be enjoyable.

By nature, more than training, Lish was a thorough and careful person. Not only was he conscientious about the details of his work, he was also thoughtful about his own safety. There was always an extra water bottle and food ration stored aboard the *Dune Hopper*. Lish did not take foolish risks on the rocky heights surrounding the cave. He knew that if a leg was broken or he was trapped in a chasm, there was no one to help him. Lish double-checked his equipment before leaving on expeditions and always placed something in the mouth of the cave, which he could easily spot from the air upon his return. If the object was disturbed in any way, he would know that someone or something had been in the cave and may well still be there.

There were villages in the valleys of the island. As best as Lish could tell, a little farming was done but mostly they survived by fishing and tending animals. As time passed, he found himself wanting more and more to have a closer look at the people. He was aware that more than curiosity was involved; he was also lonely.

The mountain range in which Lish resided lay across the island from northeast to southwest. A large river began in the foothills northwest of the mountains and ran leisurely toward the sea off the northern tip of the island. There was nothing remarkable about the river. It was fairly straight in its journey seaward, and was not, in Lish's eyes, a particularly scenic river.

However, he had noted a tributary beginning high up in the mountain range and tumbling its way down the crevices and chasms in a riotous, foaming progression until it reached the forested lowlands. Then it continued in a swift curving path through the trees until it reached the main body. Several times Lish had flown down the path of that smaller river, swooping from his cave perch down the mountainside and gliding the course of the tributary until it was lost beneath the arching branches of the jungle. It reappeared briefly on a plain before again ducking into the foliage.

It was on this plain that a small tribe lived. They tended gardens, fished from the river, and raised goats. Lish enjoyed watching them as he soared by, his silent solar-powered motor carrying him above the treetops. On a few occasions members of the tribe had noticed him. At first there was a great deal of consternation and excitement, but after that they seemed to grow accustomed to his infrequent appearances in the sky. It seemed to Lish that once they had ascertained that he was not dangerous, his magical flights were totally acceptable and no longer worthy of any remark.

Early one morning Lish sat in front of his cave and ate his morning fruit. Looking across the island on that clear morning, he easily made out the plain on which the village lay.

Now I wonder, he said to himself, a habit he had taken up the first year of his residence on Earth, *how would it be to visit those people? I would like social contact with humans, it is true, but it is also important that I begin to collect information from the human species on this planet. And I do believe that these are a suitably peaceable group.* He continued eating as he stared through the morning haze, imagining that he could make out the shapes of people moving about the clearing.

How would you people like a visit from a not-so-distinguished scientist from afar?

Lish considered what he would take with him. A quick inventory proved that he actually had nothing he could afford to give away as a peace offering. He decided to take several of the fruits from the mainland. He had not seen those growing on the island, and the succulent fruit might be a welcome gift to the natives.

Several men tilling the gardens were the first to spot Lish gliding above the forest. One of them pointed and called out to a group of children who seemed to find the craft more interesting than did their elders. When Lish circled, coming lower on each pass, it became apparent to the natives that this was not the usual flyby but a probable landing.

Lish glided in for his final approach and found the entire tribe waiting for him as he rolled to a stop.

He cut his switches and looked up at his reception committee. The people were tall, golden brown, solemn eyed, and reserved. They stood in a semi-circle and calmly watched the short pale man climb off his strange bird.

"Isn't anyone going to get excited about this?" Lish asked. He lifted his hands, palms upward, in what he hoped passed for a signal of peace.

One of the men stepped forward, holding out his hand to Lish. He was the tallest man Lish had ever seen, and he had to look up to the native. Lish assumed that this man was the chief and smiled in response to whatever the native said to him. The chief grasped Lish's hand in his, turned, and proceeded to lead Lish toward the village. The other tribal members walked along with them, talking incessantly among themselves about their visitor.

Within a short period of time everyone had satisfied their curiosity and gone about their business, leaving Lish alone with the chief and a few children hanging around in the background. Lish had never done this sort of thing before and was not at all sure what he should do. He had a feeling that the chief was a novice too, for soon they ran out of things to grunt about and gesture over. Suddenly the chief, who claimed Moffat as his name, rose, said something to Lish, and strode away. Lish sat waiting for a time but then decided that Moffat was not coming back. Apparently, Lish concluded, the chief had more pressing things to do than sit and grunt with some short white fellow.

Lish walked around the village and found that he was welcome to come and go as he chose; in fact, no one paid much attention to him.

"Actually," Lish stated to the three children who continued to accompany him on his rounds, "this is rather ego deflating. I expected that I would be worth a great deal more attention than a mere three children. Make that two children," he said as he noticed that one of the boys had stopped off to catch a large yellow-striped caterpillar.

Lish became absorbed in his inspection of the village. The people lived a simple life. Their houses were huts made of woven branches roofed with large leaves to shed the frequent rains. Unlike most of the island, which was quite dry, this low area drew rain clouds almost daily. The men fished, made canoes, and created and repaired tools for tilling the soil and fishing. The women tended the gardens and the children, cooked, and whatever else needed to be looked after. The older children watched the goats and helped with whatever chore required assistance.

"Nothing complicated about you people," Lish said after he had toured the village.

A smiling young woman approached him with a yellow fruit. She held it out to Lish, clearly expecting him to eat it.

"Thank you," Lish said as he took the fruit. He remembered his own gifts, the fruit he had brought with him. It seemed anticlimactic to give them the fruit now; after all, the formalities were over. He bit into the yellow fruit and found it to be sweet and soft. He finished it while the young woman watched, smiling as if his consumption of the fruit was a compliment to her. When he had finished, she clapped her hands and ran away, a simple act that brought Lish much satisfaction.

Eventually Lish made his way to the river. It was every bit as beautiful from the ground as from the air. The green water was clear in the shade of the forest, and fish could be seen swimming by. There were several canoes on the shore, and Lish found their construction interesting. The crafts were made of logs hollowed out by fire. It had never occurred to Lish that boats could be made by burning out the cores of trees, but apparently this was standard practice here.

Suddenly there was a whoop from the stream. Lish turned to see two men in a canoe whipping around a bend in the river. The water was rapid in that place and flowed around several rocks. The men were clearly having fun as they attempted to steer the canoe around the rocks and enter the calm waters of the pool without losing their balance. They lost control as they sped between the boulders and managed to hit the largest rock with the front of the craft. The prow went up in the sky amid a spraying of white water, and the men were thrown into the water. They came up, teeth gleaming and laughing aloud their merriment at their adventure.

Lish watched the men swim toward their upside-down canoe. They pulled it to the shallow water and beached it. Sitting down by their boat, the two men relived the adventure with animated sounds and gestures.

Lish was startled when someone touched his arm. An adolescent boy, taller than Lish, gestured toward a canoe and then pointed at himself and Lish.

"What? You want to do that with me?" Lish made his own gestures as he spoke. The boy apparently understood Lish's meaning and with a wide smile nodded vigorously. Lish found himself nodding and smiling too, and before he knew it, the young fellow was leading him toward a canoe. The youth introduced himself as Dillo, and both had difficulty articulating the other's name, which caused some chuckling among the group of children following in their wake. Lish thought that a group of children must be assigned to follow the adults wherever they went.

What seemed at first like a wonderfully exciting idea turned into a great deal of work. Dillo wanted to take the canoe farther upriver than Lush felt able. It made sense, of course, to go as far upstream as possible so as to maximize the number of rapids one would navigate before reaching the placid pool near the clearing. But Lush was not used to lifting and carrying such loads as the heavy boat, which was made for men larger than he. Fortunately the boy was able to enlist the aid of another young man, and the two of them carried the craft up the river while Lish had to hurry to match their strides.

The river was noisier upstream. After a mile of hiking up a well-traveled path, Lish expected the youths to stop and launch the canoe, but they kept going. It appeared that the trip could be more than Lish wanted, and he hoped that Dillo was an expert boatman. Finally they reached a place that was obviously used for launching boats. One boy sat his end of the craft down, cheerily said something, waved, and walked back down the trail. Dillo motioned for Lish to get in the front of the craft, and he then slid the canoe into the water. The launching place was a relatively still pool, protected from the fast-moving river by a point of rocky land. Dillo produced two paddles, one of which he thrust at Lish. With a huge grin, Dillo pushed the boat out into the current, and they were off.

Lish did not have time to consider that he was a novice at white-water canoeing. Instinctively he paddled on the left side until the point of the canoe swung around and they were headed downstream. Occasionally he used the paddle to fend off rocks or to push from the bank, but mainly he stayed busy trying to keep the boat straight.

The pace was fast and furious for two miles, and then they hit a long stretch of calm, translucent green water. Dillo laid his paddle across his lap and rested while they slowly drifted. Lish did the same, leaned back on his elbows, and watched the verdant undergrowth along the bank. He was having a good time and had come to appreciate Dillo's ability to handle the craft. Both, however, were glad for the respite from the hard work of navigating the white water.

Overhead the trees met across the river, providing a green canopy with sunlight filtering through a soft haze. The effect was almost hypnotic.

A gasp and clicking sound from behind Lush brought him alert. He turned to Dillo and found the wide-eyed youth visually searching the shoreline on his left.

"What is it?" Lish asked reflexively.

Dillo mumbled something as he continued to scan the underbrush. He paddled away from the shore, and Lish did likewise. Apparently Dillo had seen or heard something frightening on the bank.

The brush rustled slightly ahead of them. Lish saw a movement through the leaves but could make nothing out. His attention was drawn back to the river, which was moving faster. From the corner of his eye, he spotted a shape moving through the undergrowth bordering the river. Ahead was a point of land jutting out into the river. It suddenly was clear to Lish that whatever was pacing them on the bank intended to intercept them at that point.

The river moved much faster now. Lish's attention was necessarily absorbed by the duties of navigating around the many rocks in the river, and he lost sight of the shadowy figure onshore. Dillo decided that it was time to beach the craft on the opposite shore and furiously paddled to that end. Frantically searching the left bank for whatever stalked them, he neglected to see the low-hanging limb. With a cry of alarm and surprise, he was knocked from the boat.

No sooner had he hit the water than he began swimming as fast as he could toward the right bank. Lish glanced back at Dillo and saw that the boy was already wading ashore. The boat was in a clear spot of the river, and Lish turned his attention to the shoreline. A few branches quivered in the still air, but he could see nothing else. He paddled faster on the left side of the canoe, sending the boat toward the center of the river. However, the river was so rapid at that point that it was not possible to avert the point of land that lay directly ahead.

Suddenly off to his left, Lish could see a form in the undergrowth. It was large, and for a second he thought he saw eyes glaring at him, great orange and red orbs. Then they were gone, and the form was moving down the point of land to meet him. Lish, whose initial curiosity had already turned to concern, now felt terror. There was something terrible waiting for him on the shore! He paddled in a frenzy.

The river was shallow close to the point. Lish felt the gravel grating against the bottom of the canoe before he heard it. At the same time the dark form rushed through the bushes toward him, making no pretense at stealth.

Lish stabbed the gravel bar with his paddle and pushed with all his might. The canoe came free and slid into the deep water with a sudden surge of speed. Just as he made his next paddle stroke, the canoe lurched wildly as something heavy leaped into the rear of the craft. Lish jerked around to face the creature; a wave of virulent energy almost swept Lish from the canoe and into the water. Large and hairy, it hulked in the back of the canoe and sought its balance, great claws gripping the sides of the boat. Its gleaming eyes fixated on Lish, and its savage mouth opened and closed with a clack of teeth and spray of saliva.

Lish was so terrified that he could do nothing but grasp the sides of the canoe and stare at the monster. The creature moved toward Lish, its noises increasingly loud and agitated.

Fortunately for Lish, it was at this moment that the canoe reached the main surge of the river. The weight of the creature swung the rear of the canoe out into the current so that the craft was floating sideways when it reached the rapids. A sudden dip nearly toppled the creature, but it sat down and again grasped the sides. Eyes still on Lish, as a snake might charm a bird, the creature again began making its way toward him. Lish was helpless, frozen in his seat, hands gripping the sides as if he were a part of the craft itself, a state of affairs that was to serve him well in the moments ahead.

Lish dimly heard a shout of warning from shore. The creature turned its attention briefly toward the sound, and it was at that exact moment the canoe slammed against a great boulder in the middle of the river. The creature was thrown overboard, and Lish was jolted but retained his seat. The canoe balanced against the rock as if it could not decide which way it would go. Finally, with a loud scraping of wood, it slid stern first back into the current, its lone occupant hunched forward.

Above the sound of the rapids came a cry of warning. Dillo stood on the shore and wildly gestured. Lish, who could only move his eyes, followed the boy's point. There, at the end of the canoe, was the hairy hand of the creature hanging on to the side. Lish shifted his gaze to the water, and there was the face of the creature floating in the water, eyes again fixated on him. If there had been a glimmer of hope when the creature fell from the canoe, Lish now felt only a dark void.

The creature made no attempt to climb into the canoe but simply began moving toward Lish, placing one great claw after the other on the side of the boat. Somewhere in the recesses of his mind, Lish could hear a voice urging him to strike the creature's hands with the paddle. But he could not move and watched stupidly as the grizzled paws moved closer, the sharp claws longer than any he had ever seen.

Again the river came to Lish's rescue. The grade became steep, and the water literally tumbled among the rocks. As the canoe bobbed along like a chip of wood on the torrent, the creature was buffeted unmercifully by the tons of rushing water among the rocks. The boat violently lurched, and the creature disappeared under the water, its claws leaving furrows in the wood. Totally helpless, Lish waited impassively for the creature to reappear and pull him from the canoe. Dimly he heard yelling in the background but could make no sense of it.

Lish's next conscious awareness was of the ceiling in a village hut. The light silhouetted the leaves against the branches in a crazy pattern. Sitting beside him was Moffat. After a short time a woman entered the room with a bowl of soup. While Moffat held his head, the woman fed the soup to Lish. After that he slept again, occasionally waking to find someone different sitting beside him, always with a bowl of soup that was gently and firmly spooned into his mouth.

There was no way for Lish to know how long he rested. He vaguely knew that he had not been physically hurt; his injury was an emotional trauma. Each time he awakened he felt a little stronger. It was as if he was recovering from a drug-induced sleep or deep trance where he had been held captive for days. Finally he was able to sit up and attempt communication with Moffat and Dillo.

The last recollection Lish had was of sitting in the canoe and waiting for the creature to reappear. The monster's orange-and-red eyes had hooked onto Lish's very being with a power against which he was helpless. From the gestures Dillo made, the canoe had come close enough to the shore for him to pull Lish out to safety. The creature had not been seen again, and Dillo had carried the unconscious Lish back to the village. He had remained in a stupor for several days, much to the concern of the natives.

Lish tried several times to find out the nature of the beast or where it had come from, for he had never seen evidence of anything like that on the island or, for that matter, anywhere else on the planet. At that point communication broke down, and Lish could not be sure what was being told him. At times it seemed the natives were claiming they knew nothing about the creature and its origin while on other occasions it seemed that the creature was an old nemesis whom they had known for a long time.

Whatever it was, the creature possessed an hypnotic power, which rendered its prey helpless with fear. Lish had never experienced such a loathsome and revolting terror, and he shuddered whenever he thought of it. Needless to say, he decided to be quite careful in his travels from that time on.

When Lish regained his strength, he said his good-byes to the people and took off in his *Dune Hopper*. He had come to be fond of the natives and wanted to visit them again. He reflected on the rule about interfering with primitive people on a developing planet. He decided that one visit was a noninterfering investigation and that so far he had not broken the rule. If he visited again, he ran the risk of influencing the tribe in some way, and then he would be interfering with their development. The argument took the position that a visitor from an advanced culture could and would alter the lives of a developing people in subtle ways, which might not be noted for years or even decades.

Lish had not realized how lonely he had become. It would be difficult for him to keep his distance from the tribe.

Having gained sufficient altitude, Lish circled the peak. He lined up the *Dune Hopper* with the wide ledge, which ran about two hundred feet in front of the cave opening. He started to cut power for his descent when he recalled he had not yet made his approach ritual. *Oh, well, no need to do that,* he heard himself saying. But his compulsive nature kicked in gear, and he automatically gave the plane power and banked to make his turn. From that angle, he could clearly see the cave opening. When he had left the base, he had placed a tin of canned food delicately balanced on a rock where it would be easily dislodged by anyone entering the cave.

It was gone.

Lish felt his heart climb into his throat. He regained his composure and banked away from the peak. After gaining more altitude, he swung back and made another pass. There was no question about it. The tin was gone.

Goose bumps popped out all over his chilled body, and he felt light-headed and ill. He flew away from the peak to give himself time to settle down and think things through. This had never happened before, but he had thought out a next step. What was it? He breathed deeply and sought to control his fear. The next step was to look into the cave from the air as he flew directly at the opening. If something was still in the cave, then Lish would see it.

Turning his craft around, Lish flew toward the peak. Locating the cave opening, he descended to a level even with that of the ledge. He would have only a few seconds of close-up viewing before he had to make a radical veer to avoid collision with the mountain. Lish slowed the plane to near-stall speed. He aimed his light at the cave opening and gripped the controls tightly, ready to veer at the last second. When he was close enough, he turned on the light. The beam stabbed into the cave's darkness. Shadows danced off the walls in time with the movement of the *Dune Hopper*. At the last second he veered away.

Lish saw nothing, but he felt the tracks of something that had been there. He was nauseous, and in an effort to quiet his fear, he repeated the maneuver and once more saw nothing in the cave.

When he landed on the ledge, Lish turned the *Dune Hopper* around so that it was poised for a quick takeoff. He wondered if he would ever be the same after his close call on the river.

Chapter 31

HEALER

Mingling among the Messiah's followers, Sarn enjoyed some sense of safety; yet he knew that if Derxter wanted to harm or abduct him, the natives could not be counted on to lift a finger in his defense. And they shouldn't be expected to, concluded Sarn. He was none of their business.

Sarn left the messianic group at the village gate. He attempted to walk casually but felt as if everyone was staring at him.

A boy, perhaps six years old, fell in behind him. The child was curious about this stranger and had nothing better to do than follow him about for a while. The boy's dog soon joined them, and the three formed a small parade.

Sarn satisfied himself that there was no danger and settled under a scrub in an alleyway just off the main street. The boy squatted at his feet, hugging the tree's late-morning shade. The dog scratched behind one ear and then the other, hoping to dislodge the pesky fleas. To the left and slightly behind Sarn was a house. Actually it was an apartment house, for there were several doors, each opening into small living quarters. The light was dim in the rooms, and Sarn could not see anything but the vague shapes of a few furnishings.

There was a rustling in the darkness of the room nearest Sarn. A head, about knee high, protruded through the doorway, slowly turned, and revealed the lined, worried face of an old woman.

"Is he coming here today?" The small feeble eyes peered into Sarn's face, searching for an answer.

"What? Is who coming?" Sarn was surprised to be addressed by the woman on the floor.

"The man they call Jesus. You know, the Messiah people are talking about," she said. "I think he is coming here today."

A portly woman dressed in worn clothing appeared from the next doorway. Looking up and down the empty, still street, she spoke sarcastically to her neighbor.

"Why are you so interested in the street preacher? He doesn't have any time for a worn-out old woman like you." She snorted an exclamation, wiped her nose with the back of her hand, and dragged it across her ample belly. She scowled at the old woman and went back into her apartment. The old woman did not seem to have paid any attention to her neighbor. She looked at Sarn.

"Well, have you heard anything about the Messiah coming here?" She repeated her question with an urgency that told Sarn how important the matter was to her.

"Yes, I have heard that he is coming here today," Sam answered.

"Good I knew that he would."

Curious, Sarn squatted in order to be closer to the old woman.

"How is it so important that you see this preacher?" Sarn could see her more clearly now. As his eyes adjusted to the shadows, he could make out a thin frail body resting on her knees and leaning forward on her hands. She took her weight off her hands, rested back, and spoke softly, "He will heal me." The creases in her face, testimony to a life of hardships, relaxed somewhat as she spoke of her expectations of healing.

"What? Heal you?"

"Yes, he will heal me."

Reflecting on what the old woman said, Sarn thought that it was too bad that people could be fooled that easily. He had recently witnessed something happen between Jesus and the little girl, but it sure didn't look like a miracle. The girl had seemed to change, but that was a far cry from the actual healing of bodily tissue.

This poor woman will get her hopes up and nothing will happen. Sarn felt a flash of resentment toward the Messiah.

It was cruel to let people get their hopes up when he obviously could not heal everyone. And even if he healed some people, what could be the conclusion of the nonhealed persons?

"What's wrong with you?" Sarn asked.

"It's my legs. I can't walk or support my weight. And I bleed a lot." Her voice rose in frustration. "For twelve years I've been in this condition. I get so tired of hurting that sometimes I want to die."

Sarn focused on a yellow dog ambling aimlessly down the street. Sarn felt sympathy for the distraught woman. Maybe Jesus would heal her, he thought, but doubted it. He tried to think of something to say to the woman but could not.

An hour passed. The neighbor woman appeared again, left, and returned. The child grew weary of nothing happening and ran after the dog that was investigating another dog. Sarn shifted positions several times, occasionally swatting at a fly. The old woman hardly moved as she remained poised, watching the street.

About noon more people appeared on the streets, apparently in response to shouts coming from the direction of the village gate.

Sarn glanced back at the old woman. Body tense, eyes fixed on the movement at the end of the street, she was oblivious to anything but the expected arrival of the street preacher. Sarn wondered how she had known the Messiah was coming to her village today. News traveled fast among these people, he supposed.

By the time Sarn reached the city gate, the crowd was larger than he expected. Sarn spotted Jesus, and there was Simon Peter looming over the crowd. Peter did not appear comfortable with the jostling crowd and kept gesturing for the people to back up. Dogs yelping, children calling out, babies crying, people talking and pushing—the scene was turning into quite a tumultuous affair.

Directly ahead was the home of the old woman with whom Sam had visited. It occurred to him that her rooftop might make a good vantage point to observe the events in the street, and just at that moment he spotted her crawling toward the oncoming crowd.

"Lady, go back to your house! You'll be trampled!" Sarn called to her. She glanced up briefly and resumed her efforts to pull herself into the street. He grabbed her shoulder, and she swatted his hand away with surprising ease.

The crowd was excited and noisy. Street preachers were not rare, and perhaps only a relatively small percentage of the population believed strongly one way or the other about Jesus being a messiah. But because some did and because he had reportedly performed magic tricks, people wanted to see up close this man who was purported to have such grand abilities.

In some ways Jesus was like any religious figure: he was an inkblot, a person on whom could be projected whatever meaning was needed to fulfill someone's hopes and dreams. Some saw in him a political figure, a leader who could pry off the yoke of the Roman government.

Others saw the fulfillment of the ancient prophecies of their religious faith, with Jesus as the embodiment of the national god. Still others viewed Jesus as an answer to very personal needs. The old crippled woman was among this last group.

It was this milling assemblage that washed down the narrow street and pushed Sarn one way and then another like a leaf on a stream of water. The woman, her gaze fastened on the center of the crowd, crawled into its path. A child fell over her, and then someone stepped on the woman's hand. The crowd surged forward, and Sarn lost sight of the fragile woman; he was certain that her lifeless body would be discovered in the dusty road after the procession had passed.

"Who touched me?"

The crowd hushed. The Messiah had stopped and held up his hand.

Peter's voice could be heard. "But Master, the crowd pushes against you, and you ask who touched you? I do not understand. It could have been anyone of these rude people." Peter looked as if he would like to singlehandedly push everyone back.

"I perceive that energy has left me." Jesus's gaze swept around him. He reached forward and waved people aside. Looking down at the ground, he focused on someone. A gentle smile crossed his face.

"It was you who touched me."

"I only touched your cloak," said a frail voice.

People stared at the woman on the ground, the crippled wretch who now held the attention of Jesus himself.

"Look! It's old Reba!"

"What does that sick old hag want?"

"Get her out of the way!"

The shouts trailed off as Jesus raised his hand. "Why did you touch me, woman?"

"I am but an old woman, sir, and I want to be well. If I could but get close to you, perhaps touch your cloak, I thought . . ." her voice trailed off.

An indignant old man opened his mouth to scoff at her presumption. A woman raised her hand to protest this attention being given to the worthless old hag. Several teenagers giggled because they were embarrassed for her. Jesus raised his hands, palms up, and quietly spoke, causing the crowd to fall silent.

"Your faith has made you whole. Rise and walk."

The old woman paused, then slowly pulled herself up, wobbled, and stood straight. The look of determination became one of sheer wonder and then turned into a broad smile that split her face in two. Turning to Jesus, she found him smiling warmly back at her.

"Thank you," she said and threw her arms around his neck. "Go in peace," he replied.

Sam, like the others, watched in shock and disbelief. Was this the old woman he had spoken with earlier in the day? It hardly appeared to be the same person, and yet he knew it was. *Pretty good trick,* he conceded as he watched the old woman walk without pain.

Yet Sarn knew that Jesus was demonstrating something more than tricks. And just who was he representing? Sarn looked up to find Jesus studying him. Their eyes locked for a split second, and then the crowd came between them.

Chapter 32

GAOLL

Gaoll, a large burly man with a bushy red beard, set down his wine glass. He turned to the lady at his side, a tall stately appearing woman. Her hazel eyes connoted wisdom, and her mouth was quick with smile. It was her poise more than that of her husband that was congruent with the Presidential Office of Hoxd Galaxy.

"Maalda, my dear, I am concerned. Travelers have brought word of a strange turn of developments on a small planet on the other side of the universe."

"Oh?" said Maalda quietly as her eyebrows gently raised. Gaoll had often thought that with a minimum of effort, his wife could drag from a man his best-kept secrets.

"Yes," said Gaoll. "It seems that a star was spotted over this planet some years ago—a signaling star, it is thought—and Sathel from Xerxes has sent an expedition to investigate."

"That should be interesting," said Maalda. "Yes, I recall meeting Sathel one time."

"Hmmm. More than interesting, I'm afraid. The scuttlebutt has it that Lybur, head of Xerxes Internal Control, has also sent men—well, trained mercenaries, with the intent of stopping any messiah that might emerge from the populace."

Haalda was puzzled. "Oh? Why would they do that? I don't believe anyone here ever did that."

The queen was referring to an event of many years ago in her own galaxy. An unusual star had visited a planet in the Hoxd star cluster and caused quite a stir in the scientific community. Years after the star's appearance and disappearance, a powerful man had emerged. Farn, the one whose birth was paired with the star's visitation, claimed to be an incarnation of the power, that supernatural force that supposedly created and ran the universe.

Prior to his coming, few cared if such a power existed. The idea was a comforting thought at best, especially attractive in times of emotional distress. However, the idea was totally unprovable, scientifically impractical, and held little credence for the average person.

As it turned out, Farn impacted in an unprecedented way on those who crossed his path. After his life and death on Tsarkn, one of the medium-sized planets of the sun, Tak, Farn's teachings began to spread. It was a slow process, but within a century his influence had reached nearly every populated planet in the Hoxd Galaxy.

His message had been simple and clear. Farn taught that he was the incarnation of the power behind the universe—not just Hoxd Galaxy but the entire universe. His goal was to teach people the secret of getting along with one another.

Cynics enjoyed pointing out that Farn's polemics on healthy relationships were so ineffective that he got himself killed. His supporters replied that any successful instructions about how to get along with one another would most certainly involve major changes, and some people had rather kill than change.

Gaoll was wistful as he reflected on his religious heritage. It had given him a sense of rootedness as if his very being was centered in what he believed about the power. His faith in the ultimate goodness and invincibility of the power afforded him a perspective about himself and all of life, which was both tough and sensitive. Gaoll was a warm man with a twinkle in his eye, a ready smile, and a leader capable of firmness and sound judgment. He was nobody's fool. He considered the Farnian people of Hoxd, for the most part, to be healthy both in mind and body.

"I think this star, the one that Sathel and Lybur investigate, is another in the holy sequence," said Gaoll. With all his being, Gaoll believed that there was a supreme intelligence engaged in the process of making itself known.

He was optimistic about the power eventually spreading throughout the universe. He liked to contemplate such a course of events, yet he felt no need to force his theology on others.

"You may be correct," his wife said. "It always excites me to contemplate the nature of this power. Is there some great plan in action at this very moment?"

"And if so, where will it end? I tell you, Maalda," Gaoll said, "if there was anything I would change about the way the power is doing things, it would be to hurry him up. He is moving far too slowly. The universe needs civilizing now!"

"Perhaps the power is not a he. Perhaps it is a she," Maalda said, baiting her husband.

"No, it is not a she either. It is a committee of both hes and shes. And they can never agree on anything. So they quibble about details and who gets to do what. And before you know it, a hundred years have passed."

Maalda tilted her head in thought. "Yes, I suppose the power could be a committee acting as a united entity. But no one really wants to hold a committee in awe, so everyone automatically assumes that the power is one being."

"I know, and Farn always talked in the singular, never once mentioning a committee. I was just teasing."

"But," said Maalda, inspired, "what if there is one supreme power behind the whole thing and he or she does appoint committees to introduce him or her to each of the planets?"

"You mean each messiah is sponsored by his own committee?"

"Why not? After all, think of the enormity of one being—even a supreme one—with all that is going on in a whole universe."

Gaoll smiled. "I think behind the committees there may be a whole bureaucracy. And the more I think on it, the more I am convinced that I don't want to know all the details."

Since Farn's arrival brought a burst of interest in religion, there had been many books written about the subject. The conclusions drawn so far were short on scientific facts but did find that if ten planets that had experienced an incarnation were matched with ten planets that had not, the first ten became religious and the others did not. The really interesting question had to do with the difference that made in the long run.

After 453 years, conclusions based on field studies and statistical analyses of rates of mental and behavioral aberrations, strong trends, and probabilities were evident. The general conclusion was that messiahs did make a difference in the attitudes of the people toward themselves and others. "Touched" planets did not progress any faster than "untouched" planets and in fact probably were not as progressive in terms of technology and trade. At one time Hoxd and Xerxes, considered sister galaxies, were equals in terms of scientific progress. After the Farnian influence in Hoxd, the two peoples seemed to go in different directions. Xerxes became the more economically successful of the two, and Hoxd, on the other hand, seemed to slow down. Their vista shifted from being almost exclusively outward to the stars, to one aimed inwardly at the self. A visitor would find the pace of living more hectic in the Xerxes Galaxy and might become bored in its sister galaxy. Each seemed satisfied with itself.

The research seemed to show that an incarnation made a difference in people's personal adjustment to life, but it was difficult to evaluate the effects in terms of statistical exactness. Nevertheless, in Gaoll's opinion, planets exposed to messiahs were healthier, stronger, and more robust than unexposed planets, especially under great stress.

"The effects of a messiah are too nebulous," Gaoll had once complained. "The power should be more efficient than that. I couldn't run a government the way he runs a galaxy and get away with it."

"Yes," Maalda answered, "but you may not have the same goals as the power. His may be a little harder to reach than yours."

"Hmm. And neither of us has much to work with in the way of staff."

"Don't knock the race too badly, my dear. After all, we're part of it."

"You can't force people to change," Maalda remarked once after Gaoll complained about certain department heads behaving in stupid ways. "All you can do is plant a seed and hope it grows. If it does, it can make all the difference. It has to be natural and eventual, a growth process."

"That may be so," Gaoll agreed, "but people are so inconsistent that it is difficult to know just what it is they value."

"You mean that the seed sometimes seems to be growing, even flowering, and the next day it is wilted?" Maalda nodded. "Yes, that is disappointing to me too, but that apparently is part of the definition of being human."

In Gaoll's opinion religion could not be exported. People from one galaxy simply would not accept the beliefs of another. It had been tried but with little or no success. If he had thought that religion could be effectively passed around the universe like a drug, he would have done it long ago. He was that sold on the effects of religious faith.

Gaoll sometimes became impatient with the power for moving so slowly and inefficiently, but he could not think of a better method than using messiahs, or "the drop method" as someone once called it. Eventually, he believed, there would be enough incarnations to positively affect the entire universe.

Gaoll's position was simple and consistent with his governmental policies: the power is behind the universe, moving and shaping in slow unfathomable ways and will do what it will as it pleases. Because the power did not know how (some said) to coerce people or because it held free will important (others said), its effect was limited to the influence of a messiah born under a small and strange star.

"Born under a star. That seems strange in a way and yet very nice. It certainly is unique. Who else can claim as much?" Maalda mused about Farn's mission.

"Not me," said Gaoll. "Let's see, there have been twelve messiahs so far—"

"Fourteen," Maalda corrected.

"Yes, fourteen of which we know. Possibly there could have been more before we started noticing the stars. Don't you agree?"

"Possibly hundreds. Or thousands. Who knows how big the universe is? Twelve men and two women, we know for sure," Maalda said.

"As I recall from reading part of that book you gave me," Gaoll said, "all of them came from the bottom of their respective societies." He glanced at Maalda who made a slight nod to indicate that he had recalled correctly.

187

"And didn't it say that there some difference between how the men and women did their work?"

"You remember better than I thought you could, my husband. There did seem to be a difference, but just what it was is vague. As far as we know, the results came out the same."

The two did not have as much time together as they would have liked because of Gaoll's extensive duties as head of the galaxy. Whenever there was time, they jealously guarded it for themselves. Not only were they still much in love, but they remained good companions.

Maalda turned to her husband, concern etched on her face. "Gaoll, I am uncomfortable. No one has ever attempted to stop a messiah before. Not that we know of."

"Not from outside the host planet. There have always been attempts, eventually successful, from the messiah's own people."

"Yes, of course. It seems to me that it is a dangerous business for outsiders to interfere. I don't like it." She sipped her wine. "Is there not something we can do?"

Gaoll's face lit up. "That we can do, my dear. If this latest incarnation is not of the power, then there is precious little we can do to save it. And if it is a gift from the power—messiah number 15—then my dear lady"—he chuckled—"there is precious little for which we are needed."

Maalda's face was serious. She was not sure if her husband was correct. Was it not axiomatic that the power depended on mere mortals to implement its influence? Maalda was troubled.

"I will think on what you say, Gaoll."

Chapter 33

LISH II

For nine years Lish lived on the island. He made numerous journeys to many different lands, some lasting for months at a time. His collections of various data and specimens grew larger, and they threatened to overcrowd the recesses of his cave. He often thought of again visiting the natives in the valley below but did not. He waved to them when he flew over and knew that he would be welcomed should he ever return.

Slowly the evidence came together and yielded three conclusions.

The first conclusion was that the planet had been visited by aliens at some time in the distant past. Lish had flown over areas containing structures that could not have been made by natives. There were giant stone creations made by precision tools, which the natives did not have. There were markings around the planet that clearly did not fit into the patterns of the indigenous populations.

For example, the giant thur, constructed on the desert of the large continent, thousands of miles to the north and west of his base did not resemble anything native to Earth.

On two continents there were pyramids constructed of huge stones cut by laser from solid rock. The sheer size of the building blocks dictated that they were not lifted by human hand. His analyses of the blocks' edges confirmed that laser beams had been used On the walls of ancient buildings he found drawings of spacemen with their bulky suits and air tanks.

As far as Lish could ascertain, the only use made of the pyramidal constructions was as grave sites. Apparently the edifices had been diversions for Captain Aladam and his crew, but he could not see that these activities had made a difference to the natives. As far as Lish could tell, Aladam had arrived, played with the natives, presumably died, and then life had gone on as before. If this thesis held up, it would constitute evidence defending benevolent contact with a developing race.

On the other hand, if he could build a sound case that the visitors' genes had been infused into the native population and that it had made a difference in intelligence, physical size, or some other variable, then there was evidence supporting the other side.

The second finding disturbed Lish, but try as he might, it would not go away. Alive on the planet was a malevolent force. Scientific and rational thought could not rid him of the feeling that in certain places on the planet he was in the presence of evil.

His first encounter had been on the island river during his third year on the planet. At the time he had ascribed his terrifying experience to a large animal with some kind of hypnotic powers. Since then he had another experience that changed his earlier conclusion.

One day he was flying over the jungles of the continent to the west of his home island. Swooping just over the treetops, Lish was suddenly directly over a small barely visible clearing. In the middle was a large flat stone with the shape of a human figure lying prone on it. It was a curious sight, one unlike any he had seen previously. He banked and flew over the place again, this time barely clearing the treetops. And then it began. A chill, goose bumps. Fear clutched his heart and then churned his stomach. The hair on the back of his neck bristled. Palms were cold and sweaty. Deep within Lish an urge screamed for him to flee, to get away as fast as the ship would carry him.

Lish traveled several miles before he stopped trembling and some semblance of reasoning returned. What was it? What had happened? Had it been a chilling wind off the forest floor? Lish shuddered. He circled the area until he felt composed. Finally he smiled at himself. What a silly reaction! Now out of simple curiosity he had to find the place again. He wanted to know what had affected him in such an unusual way.

He brought the silent craft around and headed back toward the clearing. Soon he was in the vicinity and gazed intently at the carpet of green below, noting that the jungle growth was curiously darker than it should have been at midday. Was that a sound? A low primordial groan, which Lish felt more than heard, emanated from the tangled growth below. The jungle moved, undulating as if it was a single live thing.

Lish's fear returned, and he found himself rapidly gaining altitude. *Get away! Get away!*

another voice, not so loud, cautioned him about climbing too steeply. *Take it easy. Don't stall. Just ease up and away. Don't look behind you!*

Lish lost complete track of time. It was much later in the day when he found himself high above a plain, hunched over the control bar, soaked with sweat, and tense as a coiled spring. His head throbbed and his hands ached from having gripped the steering mechanism so hard.

Lish came to grips with the navigation readings and turned toward base, flying high above the jungle. When the island appeared on the horizon, Lish experienced a strong sense of relief. He circled twice, and twice the marker was where it had been left in the cave mouth. It was good to be back home.

A third conclusion was the most nebulous of all. Lish had come to believe that in addition to a force of evil present on the planet, there was also a force of good. Furthermore, Lish posited that the two forces were in almost constant combat with neither having yet established an advantage.

The idea came to Lish while studying the pictures on an old building that had been constructed about the time Aladam and his crew were alive and well on Earth. The hieroglyphics told a story about a good man in a chariot that flew through the heavens. The good man was brought to Earth by an evil force, which permanently disabled the chariot. A battle ensued, and the evil force prevailed. However, even though the good man died, the good force did not, and it continued to live through the lives of other people. The evil force continued to seek out the good and wage war against it. The story ended with no resolution to the battle.

Lish studied the pictures at great length. The theme was age old and found in the histories of most cultures. Lish was not surprised to find a depiction of the story on Earth; indeed, he would have been surprised if he had not. But the saga of the battle between evil and the good man from the starship was graphically told in great detail.

And besides that, the picture of evil very much resembled the creature of the island river. That experience of being stalked by a red-eyed beast was indelibly burned into Lish's memory, and he was startled when he first saw the hieroglyphics; he had to sit down and wait for his nausea and trembling to pass.

The idea of good and evil was as old as mankind itself, and the personal experience of opposing forces seemed part and parcel of the human makeup, no matter which corner of the universe one lived.

Lish believed that an explanation of good versus evil depended on one's perceptions of the world. If one was a scientist of the mind, his explanation would be one thing. If another person emphasized chemical imbalances in the brain, then he would ascribe still more different meanings. And if a third person was religious by nature, his framework would paint still a more different picture.

Lish concluded that there were certain issues humans had to deal with in the course of their lives, one of them being the conflict between the forces of good and evil. And what was the essence of this conflict? Good and evil boiled down to the question of how one person deals with other humans. How much does one person share with another? How much, if any, sacrifice will one person make for the welfare of another? Can a human care for another to any significant degree,

191

or is he consumed by self-interests? Of course one must maintain a consummate interest in one's own well-being, or there would be no survival. But there is always the question of accommodation. How does one protect his own interests while caring about the welfare of his brother and sister? And most importantly, how does a person know how to do this?

That the good and evil conflict was universal Lish found fascinating. Who or what would want to create a universe pivoting on an endless and dreary war between good and evil? Or was that just a given characteristic of the universe, like gravity, which had nothing to do with the quirks of some supreme intelligence?

Primitive peoples found answers simpler to come by: there were good forces and there were bad ones. The two sides were embodied into life-forms, with the bad one described as ugly and dark and the good one as fair and light. Both were to be feared.

In all his readings on the subject, never had Lish come across an account where the force of evil was any stronger than it appeared to be on Earth. It was as if forces unknown to mankind had decided that the planet Earth would be their battleground.

And even if it were true, he mused, what was he to do about it? Was there a government agency on Bigor to which he could lodge a complaint? Could he complain that the forces of good and evil were having a fight in his neighborhood and were making too much noise?

More seriously, when he made his final report to the academy, how would he present his conclusion that the age-old battle was raging on Earth? If he said, "It's there because I could feel it," he would be laughed at. After they laughed, out of idle curiosity someone might ask how evil on Earth feels as compared with the local bad on Bigor. Or someone might ask what good feels like since it was there too.

He had to find some way to present his findings in a believable way, and to do that he would need good, solid evidence. Here he was stumped. The best evidence he could think of was the creature itself, but catching it was out of the question. And killing it was beyond anything Lish could fathom.

Lish had to admit that if he had not personally experienced evil on the planet, he would not believe it either and would, in fact, be the chief scoffer.

Chapter 34

Ticol

Sathel stared across the grounds at the ducks floating on the pond but did not see them. He dratted a pencil against the desktop, sighed, and paced around the office as if looking for something to do.

How long had they been gone? A glance at his calendar showed close to a year had passed. *Damn! How time flies,* he thought with a momentary dash of guilt. *Almost a year!* Indeed, the whole mission had turned out to be more than Sathel had first envisioned.

There was only one thing to do, he concluded. He would send help to Toler. He reasoned that if Lybur's men had won the day on distant Earth and returned to Bigor, Sathel would have heard something about it through his own intelligence network. *Hah!* he thought. If Lybur's men came back the winners, he wouldn't have to guess Lybur would come straightway and tell him! The fact that he had heard nothing only meant that Lybur too had received no news. How the contest was going on Earth no one could tell.

Sathel poised his finger on the call button and then changed his mind. No, he would not call a meeting of his advisory board. He didn't trust them all in the first place, and secondly, the damned board was a headache and more trouble than it was worth. The members were diverse in their opinions and allegiances, which was a strength of the check-and balances form of government. However, when something needed to be handled quickly and with discretion, the board was not the way to go. He picked up his private phone.

Ticol put down his chisel and walked to the phone, which was hanging from the center post. Although he did not get as many calls as he once did, Ticol liked to keep a phone in his workshop. Much of his time was spent there working on sailing craft, his main hobby, and one never knew when something exciting would come up. It wasn't that Ticol did not enjoy his retirement, for he did. But he was a man easily bored, and sometimes tinkering with sailboats was not exciting enough.

"Ticol here," he said into the phone.

"Sathel here, you old fart!"

"Sathel! How is the great leader faring these days?"

"Tolerably well. Most of the time. And you?"

"Also tolerably well. Just finished a thirty-five-footer, the one I've been working on forever. That's kept me busy," said Ticol.

"I'd love to see it, my friend. Can we meet at the boat and you show it to me?"

Ticol paused. This was no social call from his old friend but an invitation to meet for a secret purpose. "Yes, of course, if you don't think you'll get seasick."

Sathel gave him a time, and they disconnected. Sathel did not want any leaks this time.

Later that afternoon Sathel arrived at the Capitol Docks, a marina and dry dock used almost exclusively by present and retired government workers. Security was tight at the docks, and Sathel was able to leave his guard on the pier while he joined Ticol on the boat. Security guards were a nuisance, he thought, but necessary.

Ticol waited on his sleek twin-masted sailboat. It was his pride and joy, but he had not yet taken it out. His satisfaction came more from the building of a boat and not the actual sailing; he was a craftsman, not a sportsman. He didn't like to admit it but sailing itself could rapidly become boring.

Sathel gave his friend a hug. Ticol was tall, graying, and still physically imposing at age fifty-one. Sathel was the same age but shorter and owning a larger stomach than he wanted.

At one time they had been roommates. Each had come to the capitol city seeking his fortune. They had met by accident while trying to rent the same apartment at the same time.

There had been an instant mutual attraction, and they decided on the spot to share the accommodations. Eventually they each married but continued their friendship. As the years passed, each man rose to his own height of competence and interests. Sathel was bright, articulate, and willing to work hard at whatever job needed to be done. He was easy to be with, and his judgment impressed those in power enough for them to give him increasingly more responsibility. Being chosen leader had been a combination of his years of hard work, loyalty to his superiors, and happening to be in the right place at the right time. Ticol had contended good-naturedly that Sathel was leader mostly because of his good luck.

Ticol, on the other hand, was not so good with people as he was with things. It wasn't that he disliked people, for he did—most of the time. It was just that he had a penchant for saying the wrong things. It was easier for Ticol to insult someone unintentionally than it was for anybody else to do it on purpose, Sathel claimed. Ticol maintained that was why Sathel liked him—because he said things Sathel wanted to say but didn't dare. "You are a vicarious insulter," Ticol told him. It was no surprise that Ticol did not go as far in government work as his friend. The important thing, however, was that both ended up doing something they liked and were good at.

Ticol eventually ended up over the Program Consultants Department. It was his job to evaluate government programs and agencies, helping them to figure out their problems and find solutions. Ticol was perceptive about people and willing to be honest about what he saw. Because it was obvious he did not have a mean bone in his body, Ticol could get away with making his critical evaluations of the way people were running things. He was good at what he did but found it tiring to look for how things didn't work right.

When he retired from the government, he told Sathel, "Now I'm going to spend my time building boats that work rather than looking for reasons things don't work." Whereas Sathel was highly personally invested in his work, Ticol had regarded his employment as simply a job to be done.

"Walk this way, your highness," Ticol said and led his guest on a tour of the boat. When they reached the stern, Sathel glanced around and then spoke to his friend in a low voice, "I've got a job for you, my friend."

"With the government? You know I'm retired from that crap."

Sathel smiled. Ticol hadn't changed at all since he quit. "I try to run the place with a minimum of crap, but I guess some does get in under the door."

"Oops. Nothing personal meant. I was referring to the system. You know it is," said Ticol.

"This is a special job. I need a good man I can depend on to do something undercover."

Ticol was intrigued. "Tell me more, great leader."

"I want you to head an expedition to a small planet in another galaxy."

Ticol looked at Sathel incredulously. "What?"

"Do you want to hear more? If you don't, I'll stop right now and you can finish showing me this sloop."

The thought of such a long space journey was uncomfortable for Ticol. He liked the water but had never been a fan of flying. His curiosity overcame his anxiety over space.

"Sure, tell me more. I'm not pledging myself at this point, you understand, but I'd like to hear more."

Sathel sighed with relief. For a second he thought Ticol might refuse him up front. "It's understood that you haven't obligated yourself not until you've heard the whole story."

Sathel then told Ticol about the Star Light project and Lybur's plans to interfere on Earth. "The investigative team has been in place for about a year. I need them on-site to witness whatever Lybur's agents do. There are just two men on my team, both inexperienced with combat situations and one of them is inexperienced with anything. He's just a kid. I need someone to head out there today to make sure things don't get nasty."

"Hell, in a year things could have become nasty several times. What makes you think they're still alive?"

"I don't know. If Lybur's agents had been successful with their mission, they would have been back by now and he would be gloating over it. Of course, there is no guarantee that Lybur's agents haven't already disposed of my men and are just wrapping up the mission." He spread his hands in exasperation. "Dammit, Ticol, I just feel I have to do something. And you could handle it better than anyone I know."

"Thanks for the compliment," said Ticol, "but I'm not a warrior or one of those secret-agent types."

"I know that. I'm not even asking you to carry a weapon. Someone else will do that, and a third person will man the ship. What I want from you is leadership and judgment."

The more Ticol thought about the offer, the more he liked it. It did not sound all that dangerous to him, at least what he understood of it. "You want me to take two men to Earth and—what was it you wanted me to do when I got there?"

"I don't know, Ticol. Not for sure, that is." Sathel shrugged and struggled to find the right words. "I guess I'm counting on you to know when you get there."

"There are no right answers and no wrong answers. Everyone sees something different," intoned Ticol.

"Now, here's what I want you to do when you get there. Locate our guys and let them brief you on the situation. Maybe they'll know something about Lybur's men, maybe not. When you get the situation lined out, you can act on one priority: get our men out safely."

"So do we just walk up to Lybur's agents and say, 'You're under arrest for fooling around with the Earthlings'? They might not like that, and I'll bet they've got weapons."

"No, don't worry about that. Just get our men back, and they can testify to whatever Lybur's agents did on Earth."

"That makes it simpler."

"That's why I want you, Ticol. Nobody can say right now what is the right thing to do. When the time comes, you'll know. And you'll do the best thing."

"I don't have any experience doing this sort of thing, Sathel."

"So who does? Not anyone I know of offhand, and if I did have some names, I wouldn't trust them. You've always been a troubleshooter, Ticol, and you were good at it. This is basically the same thing. You go into a new situation and figure out what is going on and what needs to be done. What's so new about that?"

"The distance, for one thing, and the bad guys' high degree of hostility for another thing. Yeah, Sathel, it's different all right. Real different."

Sathel's face fell. He was clearly very disappointed. He sighed and turned his gaze seaward. "I was being unfair, Ticol. Sorry. I got caught up in the excitement of the moment."

"Wait a minute, fellow. I didn't say I wouldn't do it. I was just airing my reservations. A fellow has a right to that, doesn't he?"

"You'll do it?"

"Sure. Why not? I might get old if I don't have an occasional adventure. Can I pack a bag?"

"Pack one. You won't need much for the trip there and back. While you are there, you'll be wearing native clothing. We'll have everything you need by the time you get to the departure station."

"I do have another question. Who are these two guys I'll be with? My life depends on them," said Ticol.

Sathel nodded. "The pilot, Pitro, is an older guy with lots of flying experience. Started when he was a teenager. He has been around the government—top-security clearance—for most of his adult life. Used to be my pilot before he retired last year. Very trustworthy."

Ticol knew who Sathel was talking about. He had seen the fellow around on occasion when he had been with Sathel. Ticol nodded. "Who is my gunner?"

"That was a little more difficult to put together in a short period of time. It has become hard to know who to trust. The trust level in government just isn't like it used to be."

"I'll bet you, my friend, that the good old days were just as treacherous as modern times," Ticol said. "People are no better or worse than they've ever been. The difference is we're in the middle of it now instead of reading about it through the romantic eyes of historians."

"I pushed a button, didn't I? My, you do get excited about some topics." Sathel smiled at his old friend. "Now the guy I finally picked for your gunner—why am I calling him that? That's your title for him. He is a crew member."

"He'd better be a gunner if I'm going along," rejoined Ticol.

"OK, gunner. His name is Rajol, and he came up the hard way on one of the outlying planets, Kena, I think. His family must have been romantics because they took their small children and left Bigor for Kena to settle the jungles."

"Back in the days when everyone talked passionately about heading out to the frontiers on the new planets. How well I remember those days," said Ticol.

Sathel continued, "I think most of his family was killed on Kena over the years, except for Rajol. He survived the hard way. He immigrated back to Bigor when he was in his early twenties. Worked for a security company as a guard. Probably would have worked for the bad guys just as easily, but he got a chance first with a legitimate company and took it. He did well, established a good record, and eventually got a chance to work for the government when they were putting together a special task force. Maybe you read about it. Their job was to strike bandit enclaves on newly developed planets. It was hard and dangerous work, but it was appealing to him. He distinguished himself before he was wounded and had to retire from the task force. I took him on as part of my personal security guard. He's been with me for three years now, and I'd trust him further than anyone else on staff."

"I'm supposed to entrust my safety to a crippled guy? Next you'll tell me the pilot is blind."

"Rajol walks with a limp, and that was sufficient to disqualify him from that particular task force. They're a pretty elite group. But other than the limp, he's intact."

"And you trust his ability?"

"He's good, Ticol, real good. I've seen his service record, and I'm impressed. That's why I wanted him."

"Where are Rajol and Pitro now?"

"They're waiting for you to join them at the departure station."

Chapter 35

Derxter

Jesus's most faithful followers were personally recruited and came to be known as disciples. Sarn thought they were an odd assortment, ranging from beggars to fishermen to a tax collector.

They maintained closer proximity, often shared intimate conversations with the Messiah, and were clearly more trusted. Sarn enjoyed mingling with them when the chance arose.

By far the largest group of followers was avid "groupies," those who tagged along as close to Jesus and the disciples as they could. They didn't look like they belonged, just that they wanted to be a part. And then there were the inevitable beggars who followed at various distances, usually alone, waiting for mealtime so they could beg food.

After lunch it was decided to go to Capernaum. Since it was in the direction toward Gennesaret where Toler supposedly was and since Sarn still had not resolved the issue of his pursuers, he decided to go with them.

At one point Sarn spotted two figures following at a distance, and he kept his eyes on them the rest of the afternoon. When the entourage passed through the city gate, Sarn sought a hiding place where he could monitor the incoming traffic.

Sarn squatted behind a group of palm trees on the other side of a public well. From there he could easily see the roadway leading into Capernaum. The late-afternoon shadows shrouded him in semi-darkness, and he felt safe from view of anyone entering the gate.

Soon the two figures came into sight on the roadway. Eyes straining, Sarn studied the two. It was Derxter and Squirb just as he feared!

Upon entering the gate, Derxter scanned the open area. Spotting Jesus's group, Derxter strode over to them, pulled one of the disciples to the side, and spoke in low tones.

Sarn could see the man Mark nodding in response to the inquiry, looking around, and then shaking his head. Derxter scowled and headed toward the center of town, trailed by Squirb.

Sarn wondered if covert missions to other worlds were more common than anyone realized. Possibly there could be an opportunity for substantial economic gain. He had heard that there was a flourishing underground slave trade across the Xerxes Galaxy. It was easy to see how unsuspecting individuals could be spirited away from their home planets without anyone ever knowing what had happened to them.

"If I was a slave trader," his young friends used to argue, "I would pluck a few off this continent and a handful off that one, move to another world, and do the same thing. Nobody would complain because people disappear all the time. But if you kidnapped a whole city, you just couldn't hide what had happened." Another would add some business sense to the whole thing. "Besides, I would be choosy about who I took so I could sell them quickly for the best prices."

Everyone knew that slavery existed, that it was carried on discreetly and for the benefit of the well-to-do. Luxury was not complete without servants, and paid servants were not as compliant as slaves, who would do anything their masters asked. And, the rationale went, the savages were better off as servants/slaves in the lap of luxury than they were trying to scratch out a marginal living on their home planets. Slavery was an act of kindness for those people.

Sarn could see how slavery appealed to human nature. Personally the idea did not appeal to him, but if he was in the business, he'd take Aleah for sure. He thought of her and the good time they had at the lake and how she had helped him hide the stolen document. *If only she was here.* He sighed, feeling a tide of loneliness.

He purchased a small loaf of bread and some cheese, took one last look at the street scene, and exited the town. If he was lucky, he would meet Toler on the road before dark. If not, well, he would figure out what to do when he reached Gennesaret.

Darkness found Sarn reclining against a rock near the road. He had walked for a while, decided that he would not make Gennesaret before sundown, and chose a rocky bluff as a resting place. After eating his fill, Sarn pulled his blanket around his shoulders and settled in for the night. The sky was clear, and the stars were as bright as torches.

Sarn wondered what was happening back home. What were his parents doing? Did they ever wonder about his whereabouts? Did they even care? Sarn startled himself with the last thought. Of course they cared! Or did they? It had always been difficult to earn a show of affection from his parents unless he was absolutely perfect in what he was doing. And if they weren't too busy. Sarn felt a twinge of homesickness in spite of the resentment welling up inside him.

The sound of feet on the rocky path broke into his reverie. A dark figure moved in the starlight, apparently heading toward Capernaum. The man was slight in stature compared to the hulking Derxter, and Sam, rising stiffly from his resting place, moved to intercept the traveler.

"Hello," Sarn called out.

The man stopped and silently regarded Sarn. "Hello," Sarn called again. "Who are you?"

After a pause, "And who are you, my friend?"

"Sarn. My name is Sarn."

"And I am Lish," he said and lunged toward Sarn.

Toler searched Gennesaret for most of the day before finding that Sarn had left the village with Jesus. While refreshing himself with a drink from the well, Toler overheard two women talking about the day's events.

"He was a big man, that one, but he wasn't too quick on his feet," said one.

"But strong of arm," the other answered. "Did you see if he caught the young one?"

"No, the boy left the village with the preacher, Jesus. I hear the big one left shortly thereafter with blood in his eyes."

The first woman laughed. "Don't know why he would be so shy of that messiah person. He could have walked right up and grabbed that young one. He was just sitting there pretending to be listening so hard. It was funny."

"From what I hear, that preacher and his friends would not have lifted a finger to help if there had been trouble. Cowards, I guess."

"More like they just know to keep out of other people's business," she snorted. "But then again maybe he was just afraid of that preacher's magic."

Toler made his way to the gate and left. He likely would not make Capernaum before dark, but he could make a start on it.

If there was good moonlight, he might make it all the way.

Toler passed several people, and once he stopped someone and asked if he had seen a young man pass earlier in the day. After finding that his description was too vague to be very helpful, Toler didn't ask anymore.

The shadow of steep hills grew longer across his path as the sun receded in the west. The road was well traveled and in the moonlight easy to follow.

After a while Toler heard noises ahead. Muffled grunts and angry mutterings caused him to crouch to the side of the road and move forward cautiously. The struggle was punctuated by the rasping breathing of combatants.

"Stand still, you little retarded thur!" bellowed a voice that could only belong to Derxter.

"Catch me if you can, you pile of camel grease!" retorted a breathless Sarn.

Toler peeked around the boulder. Immediately before him was stretched the body of a stranger. The acrid smell of a fired laser gun hung in the air. Opposite the rock stood the huge form of Derxter, glistening with sweat as he crouched for one more charge at his opponent. Sam too crouched and waited, hands dangling close to the ground. Derxter charged with a roar, arms reaching for Sam. Nimbly the boy swayed one way as a fake and leaped the other way as Derxter lunged. The large man stumbled in the dark and fell flat on the ground with a garbled noise of sliding rocks.

Toler was speechless. He had never thought of Sarn as a fighter. Or, in this case, one who could survive tangling with a fighter and a professional one at that, although, Toler footnoted, Derxter hardly looked like a professional at the moment.

Moonlight glinted off a metallic object on the ground. It was a laser gun and undoubtedly belonged to Derxter. With Sarn attacking him on the flank whenever he turned to search for the small sleek weapon, he had been unable to find it.

Toler leaped to the laser gun and picked it up. A short burst fired at Derxter's feet exploded sand and rocks into the man's legs. Everyone froze. Derxter glared from beady eyes under his heavy brow. For a moment the only sound was heavy breathing.

"Don't I know you?" Derxter finally asked.

"Stand back with your arms in the air!" Toler commanded.

Derxter did as he was told while continuing to stare at his captor. Sarn slumped against a rock, only now realizing how tired he was. Fatigue kept him from saying, "It's about time you got here!"

"You know how to use my gun," Derxter was saying. "You're not from here. You're one of Sathel's men! That's who you are, aren't you?" Derxter's face had become even redder.

"And you"—he turned to Sam—"you too are one of Sathel's men. And you have the scroll." Turning back to Toler, he asked, "And now what are you going to do? Kill me?" He laughed.

"And bury your body here in the desert where no one will find you. No one would ever know." Toler raised the gun.

"Fool! Of course it would be known. Do you think I would come alone? Kill me, and Lybur will move against Sathel. What is presently a covert political maneuver will become a bloody war."

"He's right," said Sam. "That twerp of a sidekick was with him and escaped."

Toler couldn't help but feel like the thur who chased vehicles on the road: what am I gonna do now that I've caught him?

"Go! Get out of here!" Toler gestured with the laser gun for Derxter to leave.

"But my gun. You must not leave me without an arm. I would not be safe."

"You'll be as safe as we are. You know you're violating travel ethics when you carry an arm. Just be thankful I don't burn a hole in your foot!" Toler aimed a shot into the ground at Derxter's feet. Derxter hopped from the stinging rock fragments and began trotting off into the darkness, muttering to himself.

Toler listened to the retreating warrior until he could hear him no more. He turned to Sarn and grinned. "You were giving Derxter some trouble. You're fortunate he didn't take your head off."

"He had to catch me first," Sarn said.

"Just remember that he is overwhelmed with meanness. One day when we're bored, remind me to tell you about some of the things Derxter has done. Nice bedtime stories, if you don't mind nightmares."

"All right. I'll remember that."

"Who is your friend?" Toler inquired. The man on the ground was groaning and beginning to regain consciousness. He sat up and rubbed his head.

"I don't know who he is, but he probably saved my life."

"Oh?"

"I was resting by that rock hoping to catch you if you passed by or spot Derxter if he came. I didn't know it at the time, but Derxter had sneaked up on me in the dark. It was good luck that I spotted this fellow on the road and hailed him.

"He saw Derxter coming up behind me and jumped between us. He wrapped his arms around Derxter, and I guess that's when the laser gun fired and was thrown loose. Derxter knocked the poor man unconscious, and it wasn't long after that when you arrived." Sarn looked down at the recovering man. "He seemed to recognize my name when I identified myself."

Lish blinked his eyes and attempted to focus his gaze. He had taken quite a blow from the fist of the massive Derxter.

"My name is Toler. And who are you, my friend?"

Lish looked up at Toler and with effort raised himself. "Lish, my name is Lish."

"And I'm Sarn."

"Yes, I remember, Sam," Lish said slowly. "And how are you? Did you escape any damage from the large man who attacked?"

"Well, yes. And with some help from my friend, Toler. Was he a common thief?" asked Lish.

Sarn and Toler looked at each other. "No, I would say that he is more than a thief," said Toler.

As if on cue, Derxter's bellowing voice rolled through the darkness. "I must speak to you before I go!"

Lish watched Sarn and Toler, curious about what was transpiring. Sarn started to speak, and Toler motioned him to be quiet.

"What is it?" answered Toler.

"The scroll," said Derxter, closer now. "I must have the scroll! It is of no use to you."

"What is on the scroll?" Toler asked, searching Sarn's face for a clue. Sarn shrugged. He had no idea of the contents of the document.

"It does not involve you or your mission," replied Derxter. His form could be made out in the darkness.

"Stay where you are," warned Toler. "How do we know what you say is true?"

Lish had been listening intently to the conversation. As Derxter drew closer, Lish again experienced an unmistakable stench of foreboding and felt himself recoiling, the hair on his neck rising in fear and his stomach turning in revulsion. Who was this man, this creature, who sent forth such negative and repulsive vibrations?

"What could possibly be on the scroll that would be of interest to you?" countered Derxter.

"Until I see it I cannot answer," said Toler.

"Give me the scroll, and I'll leave you alone for as long as we share this forsaken planet. I swear it," boomed Derxter. "Besides, I do not know what is on the scroll or what its value is to those back home."

That made sense to Toler. Lybur would not try to explain to his hired guns what was on a scroll. He would simply tell them to get it and kill anyone in the way.

Sarn looked at Toler. "Do you think we should trust him?"

Toler bit his lip in thought. He could not imagine what could be on the parchment that would make much difference to his mission, and besides, it was Derxter's property. Perhaps if they could wrest this deal from Derxter, it would be worth the scroll. As immoral as Derxter was, he considered himself an honorable soldier. Toler mentally kicked himself. Who was he kidding? Derxter was not honorable in any way.

"Toler, I don't have it anymore," said Sarn.

"What?" Toler shot a glance at Lish and then back to Sarn. "You don't have it? What did you do with it?"

"Enough!" interrupted Lish. "It does not matter to whom you gave it or where it was left. Tell the man," Lish commanded in his intense voice, "that you do not have it and you do not know where it may be found. And that is the truth."

Sarn shrugged. "It's the truth with me. I really don't know where it is now."

Toler turned back toward Derxter. "We don't have it. We don't know where it is."

"You lie! You must know. You stole it!" Derxter had come closer, and his angry face was red in the moonlight.

A shot from the gun threw rocks at Derxter's legs. "That's enough. Go! We have no deals to make with you!"

Derxter gave a terrible glare to the trio and turned into the darkness. They listened to his footsteps fade into the distance. Toler turned to Lish.

"Mister, you've got some explaining to do."

Lish glanced at Toler and Sam. "Yes, I suppose I do. And that might just go two ways."

"Let's find a better place to talk. I'm not comfortable here," Sarn said, indicating the direction in which Derxter had gone.

The three men walked down the road in the opposite direction. Occasionally they stopped and listened just in case they were being followed. Finding a small canyon with sheer sides, they settled in and talked without fear of being overheard. If someone approached them through the entrance, he would be seen and heard before he could see them. Because they owned the laser gun, they felt secure.

"Lish is your name?" Toler asked. "That doesn't sound like any name I've heard on this planet."

"My home is Bigor," Lish said. "For over twenty years I have been researching this planet, and I must admit I have been lonely for companionship from home. Welcome to Earth!"

Toler and Sarn were dumbstruck. They stared at this man who calmly peered back at them.

"I have possession of the document. It was given to me by Aleah, the girl to whom Sarn gave it. I have known her for years. I am almost one of the family, I guess you could say."

"Amazing," said Toler. "You just never know who you will run into anymore."

"Yes, isn't that the truth? I am just as surprised to find you here but probably happier than you are."

"I was very happy about you helping me out back there," said Sam. "If you had not gotten in the way when you did, I imagine I'd be close to dead by now. Thanks."

"It wasn't all coincidence," Lish said. "I admit I was looking for you. I was told that someone matching your general description had been seen in the company of the Messiah. I was ready to stop for the night when you hailed me. And then I saw that big guy coming up behind you. If you hadn't given your name, I might not have been so brave."

"That big guy was the one I stole the scroll from. He had just bought it from some local fellow," said Sarn.

"What is it all about?" asked Toler. "This scroll must be a real dandy if it has brought all of us together. Not to mention Derxter. Makes you wonder who will show up next."

"All right, sit back and I'll tell you," said Lish. "First I must give you some background, and that will help you understand why I am here." Lish then began telling about his research into the alleged long-ago landing on Earth. Toler and Sarn listened without comment until Lish had completed the story of Aladain and Evaze and their disabled ship.

"I have traveled over much of this planet in an effort to locate tangible evidence of their settlement. There are physical constructions for which I believe they were responsible. There is no way the natives could have done some of these things by themselves." He opened a sack and offered some food to the others. They gratefully accepted the bread, dates, and cheese; and Lish continued talking while the three shared their meal.

"I can make a plausible and circumstantial case from that evidence, but I was hoping to find something more. Of course, the best idea would be to locate the actual ship. Unless they destroyed it, it has to be somewhere on this planet." Lish paused to catch up on his eating.

"I can see how you would be excited about this business," Toler said. "I find it very interesting."

"I'm fascinated," added Sarn. "I can't wait to hear what the scroll is about, but now I've got a pretty good idea."

"You would expect there to be some direct evidence of the ship even if everything had been eventually destroyed. You know how thieving those locals can be. After living among them all these years, I am convinced that if it was at all possible, someone slipped into the ship before its destruction and took something. A piece of hardware from the ship. Some clothing or a written record."

"And you've been looking for that hard evidence," said Toler.

"Yes, but did you ever think about how hard it is to inquire about something like that? You can't go around asking for information about a spaceship. Nor can you ask for anything pertaining to Aladam and Evaze since the Earthlings have apparently over the years built extensive religious myths around the captain and his crew."

"My guess," said Sam, "is that the scroll had something to do with the hard evidence you have been looking for."

"Right. When I opened the scroll, I could not believe my eyes. Some evidence had finally just plopped into my lap."

"That makes your search successful. Was it worthwhile to spend all those years to prove a spaceship landed here once upon a time?" Toler asked.

"I don't know. I don't think that way about it. I'm here, the years are gone, there is no turning back the clock. If I had not been here, I would have been someplace else." Lish shrugged. "I have adopted a family here, and I'm very close to them."

"What did the scroll say?" impatiently asked Sam.

"The scroll was written by one of the crew members. It's too bad it wasn't written by the captain. That would have been best of all. It was put together by a man named Scribelar. He was a technician of some kind, from what I can tell. He wrote about life with the natives. Very useful material."

"What was life with the natives like?"

206

"One of the most interesting points had to do with the natives themselves. From Scribelar's descriptions, the people back then were very primitive, not nearly as developed as they are now. My guess is that the whole human race on this planet took a giant spurt forward when the genetic stock of Aladain and his men was introduced to the planet."

"I wonder what the Ethics people will say about that," mused Toler.

"I don't know. Maybe some statements about 'This is what you don't do on other planets.' But there is another interesting aspect to the manuscript, and to me it is the most intriguing part. Scribelar wrote about a fellow crew member, an engineer, who was also a sensitive. A sensitive is a person who has unusual powers to sense wavelengths the average person cannot detect. He can feel good and bad vibrations from other people." Lish paused to satisfy himself that his listeners were with him.

"I've heard of people like that," Sarn said, "but I've never known anyone personally."

"What about it?" urged Toler.

"Scribelar wrote at length about the ship's engineer—his name was Uber—who could sense good and bad. The bad part of being on Earth for Uber was that all he could sense was evil. He was a tormented individual who believed that the planet was controlled by the very essence of evil itself. It was so hard on him that he finally killed himself."

"Wait a minute," Toler said. "How do you know Uber wasn't demented? Maybe it was his own pathology he smelled."

"That's an interesting way of putting it." Lish smiled. "I must remember that."

"What do you think, Lish? Do you believe the planet is controlled by evil?" asked Sarn.

Lish did not smile. He solemnly looked at the two men and said matter-of-factly, "There is a very strong evil power present on this planet. I have felt it more than once."

"Are you a sensitive?" Toler asked.

Lish nodded. "It is not a pleasant thing to be. There are some things better not known. Scribelar lived out a good life to a ripe old age because he knew nothing about the evil on the planet. Uber, on the other hand, died miserably because he could not shut it out."

"Is it better not to know what you can't change?" said Sarn.

"That's an interesting question to debate," added Toler. "Tell me, Lish, what do you sense about this planet?"

Lish sat back. "I'll tell you some more stories." He told about his experiences with evil since he had been on Earth. Sarn and Toler listened carefully, for Lish was helping them to understand the nature of their mission to the planet.

Not all the pieces were in, but they knew more than before.

"And one more thing," continued Lish. "When I was around Derxter, I felt strong evil vibrations! It was almost nauseating. That man is totally bad his boss back home!"

"What do you mean by that?" asked Sarn.

"This is not my field of expertise," he said, "but I have developed some opinions since I've been here."

"You believe that Derxter is controlled by the forces of evil?" asked Toler.

"I said this is not my area of specialty, and I am not good with the words. But what I believe is that there is a force of evil, sort of a general power that sometimes gets focused in places and people. For some reason it became focused on this planet and in that man Derxter."

"This is the opposite of what is called the power, which is how people talk about a good god?" asked Toler.

"That's how I look at it. Good and evil are polarities of the basic life energy. Most people vacillate in the middle, controlled by some good and some evil. Regular folks, we call them. Some people are lightning rods for good or evil. This Derxter probably was ready made to draw evil energy." Lish shuddered. "I did not like him!"

"Then the Messiah could be a focal point for good energy?" asked Sam, who was finding the conversation most intriguing. "It's as if this planet is a battleground between the forces of good and evil," he said.

"Yes," said Lish, "and the natives are the pawns in the war or game, whichever it is. That's a dirty trick to pull on the poor wretches."

"Us poor wretches is more like it," said Toler. "I feel like I'm caught up in the middle of a war, and I don't even belong to either side. Not by my choice, anyway. I'm not even sure who is fighting. A homespun messiah against who? The force of evil? Not much contest there, is it?"

"If this god is omnipotent, as the Jews maintain, then why hasn't he taken charge and done away with evil?"

"Maybe," said Toler, "this god is not omnipotent. Maybe he is flawed. Maybe he just does the best he knows how to do and hopes that he can get enough humans to work on his side."

"If you gave most people a choice, they would choose to mind their own business and stay out of any such conflict," said Lish. "The average person on this planet is just trying to eke out a living and doesn't really want to be involved in some cosmic struggle between good and evil."

"How do they make any sense of it?" asked Toler. "These people must experience both. They go listen to the Messiah, and then maybe there are bad people like Derxter who intrude into their lives from time to time."

"And they all experience their own vulnerability to both positive and negative forces," said Lish.

"So how do they explain all this?" asked Toler.

"How do you explain it for yourself?" asked Lish. Sarn wanted to hear Toler's answer to the question, but Lish continued, "The people on Earth, they explain it just like the human race has always explained what they don't understand: they use myths. The concrete manifestations of the local myths are God and devil."

"Are those myths? Could they be real?" asked Sarn.

"Myths are an attempt to explain something that is very real but not understood. Whatever I saw stalking me on the riverbank many years ago was quite real. The natives there explained its existence through a story they made up over generations. So far I haven't evolved a myth, and therefore, I don't have an explanation to offer. It was just there, and it wanted my hide!"

"I have trouble tying all this in with the reason for our mission to Earth," said Toler. "If the Messiah was placed on Earth to do battle with an evil force, which has been here at least as long as Captain Aladam and his ship, then how do Lybur and Sathel fit in?"

"And us, don't forget us," said Sarn.

"Oh!" said Lish. "Another bit of information in the scroll was most enlightening. Scribelar gave a description of their landing site, and I think I know where it is."

"Close by?"

"No, although I do think Aladam's ancestors migrated here. It's a place north of here. I flew over it a few times. Beautiful valley where two great rivers meet. There, my friends, is where Aladam and his crew bred with the human race of Earth."

The faint light of dawn could be seen in the eastern sky.

The men decided to get as much sleep as they could before the new day came upon them. Their conversation had lasted almost all night, and it was difficult for any of them to shut down his mind and sleep.

When they finally woke up, the sun had been in the sky some time. After a breakfast together, Lish wished his new friends good luck and implored them to please stop in whenever they were in Gennesaret.

"That would please Aleah too," he said, looking at Sam.

"One last question," Toler said. "Whatever happened to the *Dune Hopper*?"

Lish smiled. "It's put away and safe. One day I may need it again. Who knows? Maybe never or maybe tomorrow."

Chapter 36

PIGS

After Lish departed for Gennesaret, Sarn suggested to Toler that they return to Capernaum and locate the Messiah.

"I heard them talking about a boat trip over to the eastern shore of the Sea of Galilee. Maybe we could go along if they haven't already left."

Toler was agreeable to this idea; a boat ride sounded like a pleasant diversion after their recent excitement.

In Capernaum they went to the waterfront and had no difficulty finding Jesus and his band, whose departure had been delayed. The word about the healing of the old woman had a crowd clamoring for another miracle. Peter, often a spokesman for the Messiah, was impatient.

"Let us cast off, Master!" said Peter.

The disciples escorted Jesus into the boat and prepared to cast off. Just as the last disciple boarded, Toler and Sam reached the edge of the wharf.

"May we go with you?"

The disciples ignored them as they did the begging crowd. Jesus, however, looked up. Recognition came across his face when he saw Sarn, and the two locked gazes for a full five seconds.

"Let them come aboard," he said.

"What? But, Master, we are full already and there is no room," complained one of the disciples.

"Then make room for them!"

Toler and Sarn were allowed to make the journey across the Sea of Galilee to Gergesa in the land of the Gadarenes.

Jesus was quiet most of the trip, lost in his own thoughts. The disciples discussed fishing, which Toler found mildly interesting; but when they began their theological palaver, he tuned them out. Sarn, on the other hand, preferred the theological discussions and kept tuned to the Messiah lest he say something.

Their goal was the town of Gergesa in the region of the Gadarenes, which they would reach about midday. Jesus moved to the bow where he seemed to enjoy watching the boat plow through the sea.

The disciples were more relaxed and conversational in their tone when Jesus was not listening. Although basically honest and straightforward men, they nevertheless were not sophisticated in any philosophical or theological sense of the word. They strained not only to understand Jesus's teachings but to relate the business of the Messiah to the real world as they knew it and to the Jewish law in which they had been faithfully trained.

Toler wondered if Jesus knew what he was doing when he chose this collection of uneducated men. Yet he recalled Hextor's requirements for the launching of a messiah. It was essential that the common people be reached or else the movement would not have a broad-enough base of believers to make it successful. No one could have done a better job of choosing common people than had been done with this bunch, Toler thought. They would provide a real test to the pedagogical skills of the Messiah.

On the other hand, they knew the traditional Jewish law very well. Their lives seemed quite structured by ritual and practices.

Toler had become increasingly aware of something else about this company of men. There was a spirit about them, a feeling of camaraderie, and yet more than that. They shared a common loyalty, built around a "presence." Toler found he liked these men, which was out of character for him, for he didn't like many people.

I must be getting old, he ruminated and then surprised himself with the thought, *I wish I was one of them.* He shook his head. *How absurd! The men are undisciplined, crude, and often loud.*

The band of men possessed a magnetism and at some level of awareness Toler wished he was one of their number.

Toler reproached himself for behaving so nonprofessionally and stopped to adjust his sandals. He was a member of a vastly superior race of beings. There should be no difficulty keeping a distance between himself and the primitive natives. He had seen things and been to places these moribund creatures could not even guess at. There was no reason for him to be impressed with these men. Rather, if they had any idea who he was, they would be awestruck!

Having cleared his thinking, he caught up to the group. Even before he could make out what they were saying, Toler felt it again. It was an unmistakable presence. A power. It was like entering a room of fragrant flowers after existing in the barren and lifeless air of a desert. Toler had the fantasy that he could reach out and touch the presence, fold it, and place it in his pocket. And yet when he came closer to the men, he became a part of it and it a part of him. *There is a power here, I can tell, and it becomes part of me and I feel stronger than when it is not with me,* Toler thought involuntarily. He added a footnote, *I'm glad I'm with them.*

The band stopped to eat and rest near the local burial grounds. It was an eerie place, and Toler could not make out what lay in the shadows of the tombs. As he leaned against a rock, absently staring, he felt a cold, prickly feeling as if a wave of cold air had just passed down his back. He thought if he had hackles, they would be fully erect. He glanced at the other men. They too had felt something and exchanged glances, uncomfortable, grimacing, distaste vivid on their transparent faces. *There is something down there that I do not like and it scares me in spite of anything I tell myself,* Toler thought.

A shout from the tombs startled him. He could make out a figure and then two shadows. One of the disciples stood and pointed below.

"Look! It is those demon-possessed men!"

"I knew it was something foul," said Peter.

The two figures loomed into the pathway and became distinct from the deep shadows of the tombs. Never had Toler seen such dirty and unkempt persons. Clothes in tatters, skin scaling off like dirty snowflakes, and dirt-flecked spittle caked in their beards, they stumbled toward Jesus and his group. A yell suddenly turned growl came from one of the men. The eerie and menacing noise was an icy blade held against Toler's backbone, and yet it was a pitiful and despairing plea for deliverance, the kind of sound Toler would expect the damned to make after all hope had been lost. Chill bumps formed on his arms, and his skin crawled. Toler moved closer to the disciples, who were now shoulder to shoulder. With steady eyes Jesus watched the two come up from the tombs.

The grotesque figures stumbled closer. If Jesus and his disciples carried a presence with them, the men from the tombs also had a presence but one that reeked of evil and went before them, generating revulsion and fear.

The disciples instinctively edged even closer to one another. Toler put a hand on James's shoulder, an effort to join forces against whatever was coming their way. As he did so, he experienced a nefarious image of dark waves breaking on and around the presence that was with Jesus's group, flowing over, around, and past, but never quite into. Faint and shrill wailings were audible, and Toler wondered if the others could also hear them. An image flooded his mind: he and the disciples were behind a wall of sandbags, daring to peek over the top at the dark, putrid green waves washing up against their fortress. Higher the waves came, seemingly with a mind of their own, their one goal to tear the wall down and cover the men, beating them into the ground until they could rise no more.

Never had Toler known such an experience. He was certain he was in the midst of a skirmish between two mighty forces. He was startled as the wave from the tombs crashed against him. Although it was a hot afternoon in the desert,

Toler shuddered from the chill of his fear and held tightly onto the arm of the man next to him.

The cursed men stood in the middle of the path. The arms of one gesticulated in the air as if the limbs had minds of their own and moved without any purpose known to their owner. The second man was tall and broad of body, a huge fellow who stood with bowed head peering at the disciples from under his heavy brow. His hands were held in tight fists, menacing and yet telling of the tightness within him. Spittle drooled from the corner of his mouth.

Jesus stepped forward and stood before the men. Toler almost thought he could see the clash of two auras as the vileness surrounding the wretched men rose up against the presence of the Messiah.

The second man's face was bathed in perspiration, and his glazed eyes rolled upward in his head. The mouth opened, sputtered, and spoke in an unnatural guttural voice, "What do you want with us, Son of God?" The mouth twitched, moved as if the man was chewing on his tongue, opened again, and another voice, whiny and shrill, spoke, "Have you come here to torture us before the appointed time?"

Jesus stood his ground and held a level gaze on the two.

The tension grew stronger. The tall man swayed as if being buffeted by winds. The robe Jesus wore began flapping in some strange and arcane gale. The battle was joined!

The tall man suddenly lost his balance, stumbled, and fell to one knee. The guttural voice spoke, "If you drive us out, send us into the herd of pigs!"

Toler had noticed earlier that there was a herd of swine on the slope facing the Sea of Galilee.

Jesus seemed to stand up straighter, even appeared to grow in size. *He's getting ready to do something to those guys,* Toler thought.

"Go!" Jesus said with a voice possessing power sufficient to overcome the energy of the two men. A cry leaped from the throat of the tall man, a scary, chilling scream that caused Toler to tremble. The man kneeled before Jesus, head thrown back, rotten teeth peering from his open mouth, eyes glazed over, and arms trembling. The second man fell to the ground and convulsed, flopping wildly in the dust like a frantic fish out of water. Jesus stood still, his robe beat harder, beads of sweat stood out on his forehead, and the lines on his face drew more tightly. He swayed, almost stumbled, and regained his balance. The demons were not giving up their hosts easily!

Suddenly the other man fell to the ground, the two of them limp and panting in the dusty path, as if they were puppets whose strings had been cut.

The Messiah, bent over with his hands on his knees, breathed heavily. His gaze lifted from the men on the ground and toward the swine moving down the hill. His brow furrowed with concentration. Toler thought the two bodies quivered at that moment, but he was not sure. Suddenly there was a squeal from down the hill, and one of the pigs jumped up in the air, almost doing a backward somersault. A cry from the swineherd to his sons was too late and probably would not have made any difference anyway. The other pigs ran in a wild frenzy, and despite the best efforts of their keepers, the animals made toward the cliff beside the lake. The men chased the squalling pigs to the edge of the steep bank only to watch helplessly as their charges tumbled into the water. Instead of swimming, the pigs appeared to make no effort to save themselves. Soon all had sunk beneath the surface and were gone. Their owners stood gawking in disbelief.

Clearly tired from his effort, the Messiah sat down heavily on a rock. One of the men offered him a drink of water, and he gratefully accepted it. The strain had been great, and his followers gathered close to him, thought Toler, as if to draw energy from his presence.

Chapter 37

Pigs II

Curious, Toler walked over to the two men lying on the ground. Strings of muddy saliva connected their dirty cheeks to the ground while open mouths drooled into fresh, silent puddles. *The sleep of the postepileptic seizure,* thought Toler. Soon the men would awaken and probably not recall all that had happened. They would go about their business like anyone else until the next seizure hit them. And yet Toler felt that he didn't really understand all that had happened.

Peter announced it was time to move on, and his group gathered themselves together and turned toward the road. Toler waited behind to see what would happen with the two possessed men. Sarn joined him.

"They seem to be taking the whole thing in stride," said Sam, indicating Jesus and his disciples. "They've probably been through similar situations before."

They are taking things much better than I am, Toler thought as he noted that he was still feeling shaky. He glanced at Sarn, whose face was pale.

They found shade and sat down to wait. Neither said anything; words simply were not expressive enough to discuss what had happened.

It was not too long before the men began regaining consciousness. Their faces, which had been grotesquely drawn into hideous masks, relaxed. The stench of evil dissipated, and Toler almost imagined he could see it lifting. The two fellows rubbed their eyes, scratched their heads, and seemed genuinely puzzled about where they were and what had happened. The pair seemed to be just a couple of common goatherds with no memory of what had occurred. If they were fortunate, he thought, they would never recall wandering half-crazed around the tombs.

"I wonder how long they have been possessed," whispered Sarn.

"Possessed? You mean ill, not possessed."

"Looked like possession to me," said Sarn, shrugging.

The men spoke in greeting as they passed. Toler presumed they were heading home. He flashed on a scene where one of the men walked in the door of his home and his wife nagged, "Well, just look at you! Don't tell me you've been playing in the tombs again!"

Toler and Sarn were able to catch up to Jesus and his band before they reached Gergesa.

"I have never seen this group move quickly," Toler commented. "No, they always have a lot of talking to do."

Gergesa was not a large place and, in fact, was much like the other towns around the Sea of Galilee. As they drew near to the outskirts of the village, shouts greeted them, but no one could make out what the villagers were saying. Seeing that they were not being understood, someone left the village and briskly made his way to greet the party.

The man looked the group over and decided that Jesus was the leader. He walked directly to the Messiah and spoke in a calm and authoritative voice, "I am Mosha, head of the village of Gergesa," the man announced. "We wish you no ill will, but we ask you to not come to our village."

In his impetuous manner Peter stepped forward and took charge.

"But why? We are hungry and tired and would stay overnight. Besides that, this is the Messiah, a great preacher whom you have surely heard of."

Mosha raised his hand to quiet Peter, who paused for breath. "We have heard who you are, and we had looked forward to hearing your leader speak. But just awhile ago, we"— and he gestured toward the village—"were told of what happened to the swine at the lake. The swineherds are understandably upset over losing their herd."

"But we will pay for them," offered Mark. "That is only right, I suppose, although we were doing everyone a favor by disposing of the demons."

Matthew muttered under his breath, "Who has the money to pay for the swine? Not us, I think!"

"But that is not the main reason we ask you to bypass our village," Mosha continued. "You see, we are afraid. The demons."

"But, you fool!" Peter retorted. "The demons have been drowned with the pigs. It would seem more sensible if you welcomed us as heroes!" His face was red, and he began to pace.

"My friends—and I hope we will remain friends," Mocha continued icily, "I am afraid you do not understand. We had the demons safely put away, restricted only to the two wretches in the tombs. And then you came. Now we are afraid that you have loosed them, and their wrath will be on us if we welcome you."

So! thought Toler. *Perhaps the demons, who had asked to be placed in the swine even before the battle, had outwitted the Messiah.*

"But the demons are gone. Go see the two men who had been possessed. When they awakened, they will no longer be captive to the devils," argued Mark.

"I am sorry," said Mosha and turned away. The men looked to Jesus, for he was the final word. He seemed sad. "Come," he said and turned away.

It was late in the day when Jesus and his followers threw camp on the coast just south of the town. Everyone seemed deflated and too tired to try to make it to the next village. Prior to Mosha's confrontation, there had been an air of quiet confidence among the group. Now there was only fatigue.

Even Peter had stopped his complaining about their treatment at Gergesa.

These were exciting times for the disciples. Mostly from common, uneducated backgrounds, they had never before been the center of attention. They took pleasure in their association with this preacher who could work magic and at the same time were uneasy at being identified with a man who enjoyed such notoriety. Events like the conflict at the tombs was not understood but were accepted as part of the price of their discipleship.

The disciples held a simple literal understanding of what it was that Jesus was about. They considered themselves as part of a fledgling political movement designed to eventually gather strength sufficient to throw off the weighty yoke of the Romans. As such, they were ready to fight if necessary but often were perplexed by the teachings of the Messiah with regard to violence. They were wanting victories in this world; he spoke of triumphs in a kingdom yet to come. They were ready to sweep aside their tormentors; the Messiah taught that they should love their enemies. It was usually more than they could understand or agree with, but they hung on, often overlooking or ignoring Jesus's teachings in the interest of an eventual political victory for their homeland.

"I tell you," said Judas, "the man is no fool! He knows that to move too quickly will bring strong resistance before he is ready to launch the final attack." Jaw thrust forward, Judas seemed to be daring anyone to question his conclusion.

"I think you're wrong," said Nathanial, a quiet, thoughtful member of the group. Tall, with a prominent forehead and a receding hairline, Nathanial was stout with a barrel chest and thick arms. Among his other jobs he had once been a stone mason and possessed enormous strength. Of all the disciples, he was perhaps the most physically capable. Yet he lacked the assertiveness of Peter and the leadership qualities of John. He seemed content to bask in the background and ponder what he had gotten himself into.

"One thing I believe about Jesus is that he is no deceiver. There is more than we are understanding," continued Nathanial.

"Bah! You do not know what you are talking about!" groused Judas. "He said himself he is here to deal with evil." Several men nodded solemnly. "And what greater evil do we have in our land than the Romans?" He glared, challenging anyone to answer his question. Dark complexioned, with rich black hair and a medium-length beard, Judas was a lean and wiry fellow. He had been accused of sneaking around more than once when he was actually just innocently walking by. He spoke with a nasal quality, which became shrill and even more unpleasant to the ear when he became excited as he was now. A chronic complainer, he tended to be critical of his fellow disciples. He was neither liked nor trusted by the others, and more than once they had wondered how come he had been chosen for their mission.

"Judas, for the good of us all, you must be patient and take Jesus at his word." Nathanial swept his gaze around the group, appealing to their logic. "The Messiah does not expect us to read his mind. I for one could not read anyone's thoughts. And if I thought he was misleading us, playing us for fools, I can assure you I would be on my way very quickly."

Matthew nodded vigorously. Nathanial had stroked his logic cord. "Yes, that makes sense. If he deceives any of us, I hope we will all be gone."

"As for me, I am not a mind reader. I cast my lot to trust Jesus and so far he has not double-crossed us. Not that I understand everything he says or does—I don't—but he has been honest." Mark moved away, satisfied that the issue had been settled for the moment. It had been settled many times "for the moment," but no permanent answer had been found.

"Yes, you are fools. That is what I say!" said Judas. "We are soldiers, warriors who will be called upon to defeat the enemy."

"Is he training us to fight without weapons against the Romans who have very fine ones? If so, then he is the fool, for I won't be around to engage in that," quipped Nathanial. He held his finger up to his face. "My sword is not so sharp. How about yours, Judas?"

Judas scoffed. "Don't you see! Of course we are not to be the frontline troops. We are his generals. We will not do the actual fighting. And then when we have won, he will give to each of us a section of empire, each with our own army."

Judas had worked himself into a broad smile as he talked. He was first of all a patriot, and if power and property came with riding the country of the Romans, then so much the better.

"Me? A general?" John raised his brows in mock amazement and let his mouth fall open in shock. "Why, Judas, I never knew I had such an aptitude. And here all this time I was fishing, I could have been a general and had my own kingdom with my own lake and the fish that would jump into my nets when I gave the word."

Nathanial smiled at John. Several of the disciples snickered in amusement. "Mama, can I be a real general when I grow up?" John continued, "Fishing is too hard, and being a general is lots more fun."

Judas scowled and strode away in anger as the men broke into laughter. The chuckles continued for a short while and then died out. Behind Judas's convictions

218

and their own unanswered questions, the men were anxious about their mission. What was it they were getting into with this Messiah?

Toler lay awake that night thinking about the day's events. The losers had been the pigs. No, Toler corrected himself, the pigs would die soon anyway at the hand of the butcher. The ultimate losers were the owners of the swine. Poor fellows likely had no insurance. No wonder they were mad.

But that was not the complete story. If it had been so simple, Mosha would have said that the swineherds were mad and wanted to be paid for their animals. But Mosha had expressed not anger but fear. He was afraid that Jesus's little trick had disturbed a balance, opened a can of worms, loosed something that had been bound, and made the villagers once more vulnerable to something they felt powerless to defend against, an evil force they thought they had somehow relegated to a couple of peasants wandering in the tombs.

It just did not add up. There was too much unexplained to suit Toler.

Toler considered cornering Jesus and asking him to explain what had happened, but he was not comfortable calling attention to himself. The Messiah was no fool and would immediately know something was awry. Toler didn't know what he would say if the Messiah asked him, "Are you from another galaxy?"

Before going to sleep, he concluded that the only way to find out more about what was behind the day's events was to ask the villagers.

The next day Toler left the messianic group. He told Sarn to stay with Jesus while he was gone, which the young man was more than glad to do. In less than an hour Toler was in Gergesa where he made his way to the center of the village. There he was able to get a drink from the well and buy something to eat. Leaning against a date tree and munching dried figs, he studied his surroundings. It was a scene common to most small towns in that part of the world. Toler spotted an obese man with a bushy black beard dawdling at the well. The large rather pleasant-looking fellow seemed to be killing time.

"A drink for your thirst?" the fat man offered as Toler ambled over to the well.

"Thank you. Yes, I need a drink of cool water." Toler hoped that his manner of speaking was sufficiently native to not arouse distrust. People from outside the village were not easily trusted, and those from another country were viewed with outright suspicion and contempt.

Either Toler handled himself passably well, or else the fat man was amiable enough not to care. He held out the bucket for Toler. With a nod of appreciation, he took a sip from the ladle.

"That is good water." He took a long drink and made a complimentary smacking noise.

"I heard that someone's pigs drowned today," Toler said. The fat man chuckled. "I too have heard that."

"How did it happen, my friend, that someone's pigs would drown? Does that happen often around here?"

"Not often," the fat man said. "Only when the Evil One possesses them."

"Hmm. An Evil One? Gergesa has an Evil One? Where is he usually kept?"

"I could tell that you were not from around here even before you spoke," the fat man said matter-of-factly.

"You are very observant. No, I am not from around here, and I do have a great curiosity about the men in the tombs," said Toler.

"Why do you want to know?" The fat man's voice carried a slight guardedness. He was wary of this stranger.

"I saw the men on the road before the demons were cast out, and later I saw them again." Toler decided that the best tact with this wily fellow was to be straightforward. "They were different people when I last saw them."

"Yes, I suppose they were. Without the Evil One residing in their minds, they would be different."

"Can you tell me, my friend, who this Evil One is?" Toler asked. "Has he been around here a long time? And why would he ever want to stay in those two fellows?"

The fat man leaned against the wall. "You are curious, aren't you?"

"Yes, please, but only if I am not being too forward. It's just that what I saw today is such an unusual incident."

"Do not worry. It is simple. The Evil One has been here longer than anyone can remember. If someone enters the tombs, he is likely to be possessed by the Evil One. When that happens, the rest of us are left alone. The men you saw stayed in the tombs in order to protect the rest of us. We did not like this sacrifice of two men to the Evil One but then were not asked. It just happened one day when they visited the tombs. We were sorry, for they were good men, and we were thankful, for then we knew where the Evil One was." He chewed thoughtfully on a date. "Next time it may be me who is caught up by the Evil One. If it is, then as long as I am possessed, the others will be safe." He shrugged. "It must be God's will."

Toler opened his mouth to speak, but the fat man raised a hand. He had not expressed the most important part of his thought. "But now, we do not know where the Evil One is, and once again we are all afraid. And no one who is smart will go to the tombs."

Toler nodded understandingly. "Yes, I see," he said, "but tell me, does anyone know where this Evil One came from?"

"My name is Dov," the fat man said and settled back against the stone wall.

"I am Toler. It is my pleasure to meet such a friendly man as you."

Having adjusted his body against the stones as best he could, Dov began his account of how the Evil One came to be.

"A long time ago, before the time of Father Abraham, there lived a troll on the hill overlooking what is now the tombs. He was called a troll because no one knew for sure what he was or even from whence he came. It seemed like he had been there forever.

"No one lived nearby because of their fear of him. It was said that the Troll could merely stare at people and burn holes through them. Those travelers who were unlucky enough to be caught by his evil eye were killed and their bodies dragged to a pit. There the bodies were eaten by the troll. It was said that at night when the wind was right, one could hear the crunching and snapping of bodies as they were eaten."

Dov glanced at Toler to see what effect the story was having on his listener. Toler's face had taken on a look of revulsion as he imagined the hulking form of a troll gnawing on human bones in the moonlight.

"And that place, where the Troll consumed its meals, later became known as the tombs.

"But there came a time when people stayed away from the hill of the troll," Dov continued. "No longer could it stalk the unwary traveler and kill him before he could escape. The power of the troll diminished without food. Years passed until he was seen no more. Only his spirit remained as it does today, possessing those who are careless enough to stray too close to the tombs."

"Excuse me, Dov," interjected Toler, "but when people stopped going near the tombs, why did the troll not go looking for them? With its powers, surely there would be no problem catching anyone it wanted."

Dov shrugged. "It is said that the troll was limited to the area on the hill overlooking the lake. In ancient times, when the troll first came to our land, its carrier, the chariot in which it rode, sunk into the ground where the hill now is. The troll could not leave the hill because its source of power was buried there."

Dov noticed Toler's quizzical expression. "Or so the story goes." The myth was not too much unlike many others Toler had heard or read about. Ahna occasionally recounted such myths for Toler's entertainment if she found them unusual or interesting. What made this one different was the mobility of the evil spirit.

"But how is it, Dov, that this man Jesus could order the troll's spirit out of the men?"

"It is said that the Evil One is not as powerful as it once was. For another thing, the man you call Jesus is powerful in his own right." He looked squarely at Toler. "Did you not know that the confrontation today between the Evil One and this messiah was a major test of strength?"

Toler was surprised, for Dov's statement was similar to thoughts he had already had. "Oh, I'm not sure I know what you mean."

"Did you think that the meeting was chance? That no one was watching to see the outcome? It was an exciting day for us in Gergesa. Some of us have looked forward to this meeting for some time."

Now Toler had the feeling that he and Dov were talking about two different events. "You knew that Jesus would meet up with the two possessed men? And you were watching?"

Dov smiled at his listener's incredulous expression. He was both amused and satisfied with himself, for he loved to tell stories and a good audience was hard to come by these days. "Was it not logical to believe that Jesus would approach Gergesa from the south? And was it not to be expected that the noise of this group would awaken the men who lived by the road to the tombs? And further, is it not the nature of the Evil One to be compelled to challenge someone with the power of Good?" A smile crossed Dov's face. "And of course we did not want to miss any of this. So we watched from a hillside opposite the tombs."

Toler contemplated all that Dov was throwing at him and was sure that the man was embellishing the facts as he knew them. Dov clearly liked to tell a story, and he no doubt found a story a bit more delicious if flavored with a generous dose of fancy.

Yet he was a genuine fellow.

"Does this happen often?" asked Toler.

"What does what happen often?"

"Someone with the power of good meeting up with the Evil One?"

"Oh," said Dov, "no, not at all. There are just not very many truly good men around anymore." He raked a molar with his nail, seeking to dislodge a date skin. "Once there were prophets, powerful and good men, but I do not recall if they ever came across the Evil One." Dov paused. "Now that would have been a battle! Amos or Ezekiel head to head with the Evil One at a time when its power was greatest." He obviously relished the idea of such a confrontation and would have watched from a front-row seat. "But here, among the Gentiles, they have no great religious prophets. Their religion does not have the rich heritage we Jews have."

Dov looked at the sky. The sun was descending, and shadows were long. It was a good time of the day to go home. Standing straight, he said that he must be going.

"One more thing, Dov. Please tell me how come the villagers would not let Jesus come into the village? Was it because of the swine that drowned? I mean, whoever owned the animals must have been angry."

Dov frowned, looking more serious than Toler had seen him thus far. "It is like this, Toler. We enjoy a good joust as we saw today. Perhaps it was too easy for the Messiah and it could have been more interesting. But it was still something to watch. We kept our distance, and whatever cheering was done was not very loud. We handled the whole business discreetly.

"But," continued the man, "suppose Jesus comes into the village, sits in our house at our table, and we like him and he us And suppose further that the Evil One is not dead but only wounded. And mad too. It makes notes of who shared food with this Jesus and later takes its revenge."

"Or suppose the Evil One recovers enough to rejoin the battle tonight. When we are all comfortably sitting around in our homes, here he comes. We are all killed by his terrible power, even our children. And all because we broke bread with the Messiah."

"I see your point," said Toler. "It's just better to not be involved with these conflicts between good and evil."

"Much better," said Dov with feeling. "You live longer."

People are the same everywhere, Toler thought, returning the man's departing wave.

It was dark when Toler arrived back at Jesus's camp. Sarn and the disciples were sitting around the fire. Peter was loudly making a point to one of the other men who persisted in shaking his head in disagreement. Peter's voice became louder as if an increase in volume would change the mind of his adversary. Several of the others were quietly engaged in their own discussions. Jesus sat, chin resting on his knee, staring into the fire, his mind far away.

Toler stopped in the shadows and observed the scene. So this gentle man was a messiah. He was not an imposing figure, certainly unassuming, and did not sport a loud authoritative voice. Yet somehow he exuded a charisma that drew people to him and caused some of them to even leave their families for the opportunity to follow him around.

Most of what he taught was not new but reworked and dressed-up teachings already in existence. The closest he came to a clear departure from the old established religious law (at least that was what Sarn told him; Toler didn't pay much attention to theology) was his emphasis on love rather than a legalistic moral system. Toler didn't know if that was the main attraction for the followers, but he doubted it. Although the idea of extreme love had some appeal to it on paper, Toler quite frankly doubted that such a strategy was practicable at all in real life. The preaching of love most likely raised the disciples' eyebrows, and they stayed with him in spite of such impractical theology.

Surely Jesus could see that his men did not totally agree with what he was preaching, but maybe he figured he could not be choosy. Toler wondered what method the preacher had employed in screening the men. Whatever it was, it did not seem very efficient or productive. That Jesus was not always happy with the disciples was evident to anyone who followed the band for any length of time. Patience wore thin on occasion and Jesus berated his men, expressing frustration over their lack of faith and understanding of what he was about. In the short time Toler had been observing from within the group, he had decided that most of the disciples should have been fired long ago. But again maybe Jesus figured that replacements would not be any better and he had just as well work with what he had.

As for Toler, he thought Jesus for the most part had some good ideas about how people should go about getting along with others. In fact, what Jesus was preaching could well be taught on any planet and the people be better off if they heeded what he said. But that was the catch. No one would follow his advice—not for any length of time. Not in the real world. The real world was too cruel, and men like this messiah were no match for it. There was a spirit of evil alive and well on the planet, and it had the power to corrupt men's best-planned intentions. The fact that the Messiah had bested the evil spirit in the tombs may have been a small battle in a larger war, a conflict he could never hope to win.

Toler studied Jesus as he sat by the fire. His thoughts seemed far away. Never had Toler been around such a man. His caring for those around him emanated from the depths of his being, and even Toler—with his trained, objective posture—felt warm and comfortable around Jesus.

What did this messiah have that affected a person in this manner? *Similar to a hypnotic trance,* pondered Toler, *and yet why couldn't he do a better job of influencing these natives?* The answer to that question may have to do with the quality of the people. Perhaps they were incapable of consistently following a code of behavior designed not only for their own good but for the welfare of the group.

Toler had the disturbing thought his race was little better. If not as bad. From Lybur at the top to Derxter at the bottom, his people had their own rascals. And what about himself? Toler had never thought about himself as a moral or immoral creature. He had just assumed that he was a good person and found justification for whatever he did.

In his more candid moments he admitted that the Messiah exerted an influence over him; if pressed, he would have to admit that he felt drawn to Jesus and his band.

"He's doomed, this Jesus!" said one of the camp followers one day as they were settling down for the night. "The day will come when all his pretty talk isn't enough. They'll get him then, and it won't be pretty!"

"Not too bright when it comes to practical matters," another said. "If he's not making the Romans nervous, he's making the rabbis furious with him."

"And the people he leaves confused. I don't understand much of what he is talking about."

"But I will say this: the man does impressive miracles." The camp follower hitched up his robe and sat down on a rock, assuming his storytelling posture.

"Did I tell you about the time he raised this man from the dead? The corpse had been in the tomb for days. We were sure there would be a terrible stink when the door was opened. But no, Jesus called out for the fellow to come forth. And he did."

The second man had appeared bored. "Yes, you told that already. Twice, three times at least. If only he would do more of that kind of miracle, then it would be easier to stay around. My complaint is that it's too long between miracles."

"Why don't we speak to one of the disciples, ask him to persuade Jesus to do at least one miracle a day?"

"Yes, but not tell us when, so we'd be trying to guess, is this it?'"

The first man grinned. "That would be a great setup. I'd take bets on what kind of miracle it would be. Will today's trick be a resurrection? A lame leg healed? Vision restored?"

His companion looked worried. "Hey, I want in on that. I'll help you with those bets."

Conversations such as this made it hard for Toler to like Earth people, and he wondered how Jesus could. Toler concluded that Earthlings really did need help from a messiah.

Curious about Jesus's method of selecting his inner band of followers, the twelve who came to be known as disciples, Toler brought the matter up in a conversation with Mark.

"It seems that Jesus has great confidence in you, Mark. How is it that he came to choose you? And the others?"

Mark rubbed his chin thoughtfully for a long while. "That is a good question, I suppose, and I don't know the answer. I was fishing. He walked up and said something about following him. He said, 'Come with me and be fishers of men' or words to that effect. And I just got up and went with him."

"You didn't think about it? You didn't take time to say good-bye to your family? Or get your affairs in order?"

Toler was perplexed. Not only did he wonder how come Jesus chose this common fisherman, but he also wanted to know by what power of persuasion had the Messiah been able to draw these men away from their jobs and families.

And were there any men who turned Jesus down? Or women? No, he was sure no Iwoman was asked to join up. That was not allowed in this primitive society. *If Ahna was here, I'm afraid she might find it hard to keep her mouth shut,* thought Toler with a grin.

He felt a tug of loneliness for Ahna. He did not recall being away from her for so long a time. True, he had been busy, but occasionally something happened to jar his memory; and there she was, her face, warm and yielding, as real as life itself. He missed her!

One day Toler was washing at a stream. James strolled down to the water's edge and squatted, washing out a cloak. Being on speaking terms with most of the disciples, they chatted for a while.

"James, I have a question about something. If it is too personal, I'll understand." James looked at Toler expectantly. "When Jesus invited you and your brother to join him, did you hesitate?"

"No." James's answer was simple; his expression was one of puzzlement as to why the question needed to be asked at all.

"Do you suppose that Jesus asked other men who turned him down?"

"Why?" James was still puzzled.

"When you go about selecting volunteers for a project, you certainly don't expect everyone asked to agree to go, do you?"

"When Jesus asks, I think so." James turned his attention back to his washing. Toler did not know what to say. Recruitment was such a simple matter to these men. Jesus asked, and they said yes. But surely he had been turned down by someone.

"Did you feel"—Toler realized that James would not know the word *hypnotized*—"uh, overpowered as in a trance?"

"When?" James had already gone on to other thoughts. "When Jesus recruited you."

James reflected on the question. "Yes, I suppose so."

"Do you ever come out of it? I mean, do you ever think of leaving Jesus and going back to your family and job?"

James wrung water from his cloak. "Most days I think about it. I miss my family. And fishing is a hard life, but in some ways it is not as hard as following after him." His eyes rolled over his shoulder toward Jesus and the camp. "But I guess I'll stay with him. There is something about the man. I feel like a puppy dog following an all-wise and wonderful master. He has a power over us. I don't know if I could break away if I wanted to."

Toler sat back on a rock and finished with his washing, now fascinated with James.

"I think he is changing us. I know he is changing me." James looked squarely at Toler as he spoke, "I don't agree with all he says, don't even understand it all. And I know I disappoint him at times. But"—James shrugged—"you can't be around him all day and not be affected."

They watched the water ripple against the stones. Toler knew that Jesus had power over these people. He had seen it happen, and now he had heard James acknowledge this influence. They knew they were being changed, even though they lacked the insightfulness to define the change.

"Isn't he changing you?" James's voice brought Toler out of his reverie.

Toler smiled. If only James knew who he was, that he was a space traveler from across the universe. Could a primitive inhabitant of a young planet, even a so-called messiah, place him in a trance? Of course not. His smile became smug.

"I think so," James said. "I have seen you change since joining us." He stood, gathered his cloak, shook it, and turned back up the path.

Toler's smile faded. He experienced a first doubt about his immunity to these Earth happenings and put it out of his mind.

Chapter 38

THOMAS

Inevitably the Earth messiah was sentenced to death. In the end it was the voice of a fickle crowd that clinched the Roman government's decision to end the short-lived messianic venture.

Even though Sarn and Toler believed from the beginning that the Messiah's death was a foregone conclusion, the news was nevertheless a shock.

Toler and Sarn were in Samaria and happened to hear word from a traveler that Jesus's capture was imminent.

"The authorities cannot ignore him any longer!" Shevach spread his hands in a gesture of helplessness. "It seems he just keeps saying and doing things that get him in trouble with everybody. Even his own people complain, but I think the Pharisees and Sadducees put them up to that! They don't like it because he is too popular."

"What happened?" Toler asked.

"This time he went too far! So many pilgrims had come to Jerusalem for the Passover. They say over one hundred thousand. I know it was many! Jesus, with the others, went to the Temple Mount. There the animals were kept in the Temple precincts and sold to the pilgrims for sacrifice."

"What happened?"

"Jesus came across people engaged in selling oxen, sheep and doves, and many others, seated around tables, changing coins. So he made a whip out of strands of rope and caused a big disturbance. I am told he drove them out and overturned the moneychangers' tables!" Shevach wiped away a grin.

"Isn't that usual practice?" asked Sam. "The pilgrims don't want to haul their sacrificial animals all the way from home, so it is simpler to buy them when they arrive. What did Jesus not like about that?"

The man raised his finger and jabbed the air to make a point. "I tell you what Jesus did not like about that. Number one, Jesus did not like the sacrificial ritual so much. Number two—and this is the big reason—the moneychangers were cheating the pilgrims with high prices. Who makes all that money from the selling of sacrificial animals? The high priesthood of the Temple, that's who!"

"Jesus was getting in their pockets. It was the last straw!"

"Yes," said Shevach, "and I personally think it was a good thing that somebody finally did it. Why, you could not go to the Temple Mount without being offended by the filth and smell of the animals kept in those little pens. That is not right! Besides that, the pilgrims must buy their animals only from the priests. It is a well-protected monopoly, which makes them wealthy!"

"You can say lots of things about people and get away with it," said Toler. "But if you get in their pockets, you've got trouble."

"There is no doubt that there is a turnover of hundreds of thousands of shekels during the Passover. His attack convinced the Sadducees that Jesus was too dangerous to be left at large." Shevach was visibly agitated. "These men who are the priests—they use us for their own gain. They control everything. But at the trial they will not say the real reason for condemning Jesus! They are too clever."

Sarn felt empty inside, and his voice quavered. "Will they execute him?"

"Yes, I believe they have no choice. He has become too dangerous to them."

"When?"

Shevach put his finger to his jaw as he thought out loud, "Passover was on Tuesday. That was the day they arrested him. The trial was today. I wanted to stay for it, but I had to leave the city. I am sure it is over by now. Then he will be given one day in jail before his execution—if death is the verdict. That means his death would be on Friday."

Sarn turned to Toler. "We must go! If we leave in the morning, we can make it by Friday."

"All right. We need to be there anyway to observe the crowd."

Sarn looked at Toler, astounded at the captain's reason for going to Jerusalem. Toler read the meaning in the boy's face, looked away, and said, "That is the official reason for going. There are personal reasons too."

Admittedly he did not have the interest in the Messiah that possessed Sarn. Whereas Toler was content to gather information from the people, Sarn preferred to be present with Jesus whenever possible.

"If you were a native, you'd be one of them," Toler once remarked.

Sarn thought about that. "Probably. No, not probably. For sure I would!" He shrugged. "What can I say? I feel like I am one of them."

Toler didn't share the fact that he had experienced the same feelings about wanting to be one of the disciples. Sometimes it was hard to maintain his professional distance from the Messiah and his men.

By traveling fast, they were able to arrive before the execution. Jesus had been tried and condemned to death, and his crucifixion was to take place at Golgotha, a large rock that somewhat resembled a skull. It was west of the old city, and it was to this place that Toler and Sarn went.

By the time they reached the crowd around the base of the hill, Jesus had arrived along with the crosspiece. The upright post had been taken down from its socket in the rock and lain on the ground so that the crosspiece could be attached. In the background two other crosses stood in place with men hanging from them.

"What are they doing to Jesus?" Sarn asked. Neither could see from behind the pressing crowd.

"Attaching him to the cross, I suppose. Stay back here. We don't need to be in the middle of this."

The sound of a hammer striking metal echoed across the crowd, bringing a cheer. A man beside Sarn said to his companion, "They're nailing his hands to the crosspiece! Did you hear the first two men holler when they nailed them?" His lopsided grin contrasted absurdly with the grotesque expressions of excruciating pain on the faces of the men drooping from the crosses.

Sarn nudged Toler. "Look!"

A large figure had stepped forward from the crowd and leaned toward the figure lying on the cross. He stared into the face of the stricken messiah and nodded. One of the soldiers turned and said something to Derxter, who growled back. The soldier stood to face him, but Derxter faded back into the crowd, a pleased look on his face.

"He's doing his body count," said Toler. "Maybe that means he'll go home now."

With the help of several soldiers, the third cross was raised. Its silhouette made a grim specter as it tilted against the morning sky. The post trembled as it reached the vertical and slithered into its socket, jarring its victim. Jesus's arms were stretched wide with large nails through the palms holding the hands in place. There was a small platform on which he sat; otherwise, his body weight would have ripped him loose from the nails. His legs were together and turned to one side so that a single spike could pin both ankles to the post. Crucifixion was a method of execution exquisitely designed for painful torture and slow death.

Sarn stood with Toler on the fringes of the crowd and watched the ugliness of the crucifixion of Jesus and the two thieves.

"How can these people be so barbaric?" Sam asked.

Toler tried to be more philosophical about the matter. "Here they use wooden crosses to eliminate undesirables. Makes for a slow death in the public arena where the grisly spectacle supposedly is a lesson for others. Don't know how effective a deterrent it is, but it apparently has good entertainment value." He glanced around at the jostling, loud crowd.

Sarn pulled his hood closer around his face.

"I'm glad we're not like this back home," Sarn said with disgust.

"What makes you think we're not?"

"We don't do stuff like this. We're civilized."

"True, we don't use wooden crosses. We're much more efficient. We use blasters. No bodies to dispose of. Vaporize the undesirables!"

"But that's in wartime. I mean, these people are not at war," Sarn protested.

"In a way they are at war. Don't forget the Roman occupation. Anytime a person is threatened, he tends to—"

"Toler, do you realize how you shift into a nonemotional gear in times like this? I mean, this is really tearing me up inside, and you're starting on one of your rational discourses about psychology and philosophy." Sarn felt hot tears rolling down his cheeks and made no effort to hide them. He looked directly at Toler who could not hold eye contact. Sarn opened his mouth to say more and then shut it.

Their attention was drawn to the small hill where the three crosses silhouetted against the sky. A solider had speared Jesus in the side, causing heavy bleeding. The sight of Jesus's torture was too much for Sarn, and he cried openly.

Was Toler denying his feelings? He shook his head and stopped the self-analysis before it could get started; he then listened to himself. As if a button had been pushed, tears began flowing, and he allowed himself to appreciate in the fullest sense Sam's pain, to experience it as his own.

He awkwardly placed a hand on Sam's shoulder. The boy leaned against Toler, gratefully accepting the consolation.

"I really came to like the guy," Sarn said through his tears. "He's not your everyday kind of fellow, is he?"

Sarn glanced at Toler and did not seem surprised to see the captain's sadness plainly revealed. "Jesus said some things I'll always remember." Sarn needed to talk. "Unrealistic, sometimes, I guess, but good. But it was more than that. There's just something about the man. If this was my planet, I'd have been a disciple," Sarn said.

Toler looked at the young man for a long time and nodded gently.

"But why? You and I are so advanced compared to these people it is incredible. And yet I'd follow this guy. It's crazy!" Sarn tried to laugh through tears streaming down his face.

Toler was thoughtful for a long time. "When someone comes along and promises to help raise up the good in us, we become hopeful." Toler was surprised at his words.

"I have the feeling that there is something else going on here on this crazy planet," Sarn said. "Something bigger than our personal battles. It's like Lish said that night when we talked. Every time we turn around there is a war between the good and the bad."

"I think this sort of thing goes on all the time. On every planet." At one time Toler would have smiled at the naïveté of his friend, but now he didn't. "If you're right, and this planet is a battleground between the forces of good and evil, then the force of good uses him." Toler indicated the slumping figure on the crossed beams.

For a time neither said anything as they watched the Messiah dying on the hilltop cross. Sarn finally uttered, "The force of good is not very impressive right now."

They were silent for a while, while they soaked up the sights and sounds. The scene was a statement in weird contrasts. Some people mourned aloud, sobbing and wailing. Many more stood around, curious, craning, their necks to see what was happening. For them, "wonderful" would be the occurrence of something even more exciting and dramatic than that which had already transpired. The crowd was in constant movement. Children chased one another around the legs of their elders.

Adolescents alternated between staring in shock at the three dying men, becoming bored, and moving in closer for a more interesting vantage point.

"Look at them. They have no understanding of the significance of Jesus's dying."

"If they did understand, what would they do differently?" Toler asked. "We have an idea, and what are we doing that's so great?" Toler doggedly hung on to the role of objective researcher but wasn't very successful.

"We could stop it," Sarn said, although he knew that such a course of action was unthinkable.

"With laser guns? Fly in on the shuttle, take Jesus up into the clouds? That would give them some delicious legends, wouldn't it? And what good ol' Jesus say as we accelerated him through the clouds at 2Gs?" Toler smiled wryly. "Try to make the rescue a little quicker. Next time, fellas."

"Or 'I always thought you two guys were strange, but this—whew!" Sarn shook his head. "I know we can't do anything, but I'd sure like to."

Toler chewed on his lip. "Yeah, me too."

Finally Jesus uttered a few words, and his head fell on his chest. After a while, the soldiers took the body down and carried it off. Toler and Sarn melted into the crowd and followed at a discreet distance as the procession made its way to a nearby tomb, a place that had been hewn out of the rock. Their family and friends took the body and prepared it for burial.

According to Jewish law, the body of an executed person could not remain on a cross overnight, and Roman law allowed the relatives to claim the body the same day after the soldiers had ascertained death. A friend, Joseph of Arimathea, who lived a few miles north of Jerusalem, petitioned Pilate for Jesus's body so that it could be buried before the Sabbath.

He offered the use of his own tomb for the burial.

Preparation for burial consisted mainly of washing and wrapping the body in shrouds. It was first anointed with oil to clean it and then given a bath of water to rinse off the oil. A second anointing perfumed the body. However, because it was late in the day, Jesus's body was simply wrapped in linen clothes with spices.

The body was brought to the grave, a niche hewn from the rock of the cave belonging to Joseph. A heavy round stone was rolled into place across the opening. The tomb was then left with the understanding that relatives would revisit in three days after the burial. This custom prevented the possibility of premature interment and allayed all doubt about the person's death.

Aware that Jesus had claimed he would rise from the dead after three days, a contingent of soldiers was assigned to accompany the procession so that no one could steal the body. At the tomb the responsibility of guarding the body was turned over to the priests, and a guard of four soldiers was put around the tomb twenty-four hours a day. Any appearance of the prophecy having come true could only mean more problems for both the Romans and the priests. Jesus had already caused enough disruption without coming back from the dead.

"Is he really dead?" Sarn asked. He and Toler followed the procession and from a distance watched the body being placed in the tomb.

"Yes, I'm convinced he is. There was too much loss of blood for him to survive. I thought he stopped breathing for some time before they took him down."

Standing in the shadows, the two watched four men roll the great stone door into place with a whump. Soon most of the people had gone, and the guard was placed two on either side of the stone door. Except for the weeping of a few people, everything was quiet. Toler and Sarn were painfully aware that there was nothing else to do. It was over.

As they made their way back into Jerusalem, Sarn quietly said, "You know what the messiah manual says, don't you?"

Toler thought a moment and said, "Oh, you mean the resurrection part? Forget it. He's dead."

"You think the manual is wrong?"

"Yes, guess I do. I've never known anyone to come back from the dead, and I suppose I'm too old to expect to see it now."

"But just supposing it did happen, Toler? What would we tell them back home? That we missed the resurrection of the Messiah because we decided on our own that it could not be done? You put that in your report, not me."

"Look, Sarn. I just want this whole business to be over so we can go home. I'm tired of living on this planet, and I'm lonesome for Ahna. I am so weary of these primitive natives and their strange ways of doing things." He paused to catch his breath. "And I've had enough of following an itinerant preacher around this dry and hot land. And most of all, this . . . this . . . crucifixion has just done me in!" He bit his lip.

"But you're right," he finally said. "We have to see it through."

The next two nights were spent near the tomb huddled against a wall waiting for something to happen. The guards of the Temple priests initially made hostile and suspicious stares but then decided the pair was no threat and forgot about them. "Just two more of the idiots waiting for the Messiah to rise from the dead," said one guard.

On the second night a large figure walked across the open space before the tomb. One of the guards challenged him, and the man passed on into the darkness. *Derxter!* Sarn thought.

It was before dawn after the second night that they were jarred into alertness by the sound of the stone moving. Eyes straining, they watched the ponderous stone roll back but could not make out who moved it. A figure appeared in the doorway, paused, moved silently away, and disappeared into the darkness. The guards were nowhere to be seen.

"Quick! Follow him. We've got to have a positive identification," said Toler, and the two ran in the direction where the shadowy figure had been.

Sarn and Toler searched thoroughly and found no one. By the time they had satisfied themselves that the figure had successfully eluded them, the empty tomb had been discovered by the women.

Sarn and Toler watched from a distance as the guards stood around the tomb talking excitedly among themselves. Occasionally someone in authority arrived, made another search of the tomb, and left shaking his head.

"They don't know what to make of it," Sarn said.

"They don't? I don't either," said Toler. "I know this is what the manual said would happen, but I'm still surprised."

"The manual said that a resurrection would help a lot to make a messiah's mission successful," said Sam. "I guess he could have done without it."

"I doubt it. He'd be remembered as only one more preacher who said clever things. No, I think he had to pull off a resurrection to make it worthwhile."

In the next few days Toler and Sarn wandered around the city, listening to the public reaction to the recent events. Some claimed that Jesus had risen from the dead while the priests put out the story that his followers had stolen the body. Another theory was that Jesus had not really been dead but only in a "swoon." It was a confusing time with each person believing what he or she preferred as an explanation of the empty tomb.

Increasingly Toler and Sarn thought of leaving Earth and knew that they had gathered just about all the useful information available.

But then they heard that the Messiah had appeared to the disciples. They wanted badly to believe that this was true but nevertheless were skeptical.

"If I was one of the disciples, I might spread that rumor too," said Sarn.

"They need something. They are a dispirited band if I ever saw one. Hiding out. What better tonic than to believe that their leader has returned?"

"But," said Sam, "if Jesus can come back from the dead, he can certainly appear and disappear whenever he wants. That shouldn't be hard to believe."

"Maybe, but we'll still investigate."

Toler had come to know all the disciples by name but none of them intimately. One evening Toler happened across Thomas sitting by himself.

"The crucifixion was terrible!" said Toler.

Thomas looked up, paused for a long time, and asked Toler to sit with him. Late into the night Toler listened to Thomas's doubts about Jesus and the mission of the twelve. Toler had the impression that although Thomas was obliged by his nature to question matters, he nevertheless was as loyal to Jesus as any of the disciples. A bond of sorts was established between the two as often happens when people talk late into the night about their innermost thoughts and feelings. That was the closest Toler came to any of the disciples.

Later, when news of the return of Jesus to the disciples reached Toler, he sought out Thomas for confirmation.

"I'm sorry, my friend. I was not there. I was detained by other matters." His dejection was clear.

Toler's disappointment was evident. "Thomas, I must have confirmation that Jesus is the man who appeared to the others."

Thomas regarded him thoughtfully. "Toler, my friend, I believe that you are having problems with your own faith." He smiled.

"Faith? I'm talking about simple verification of the identity of a man who supposedly appeared and disappeared after being reportedly resurrected from an allegedly dead state. I just want to take away some of the iffiness of this situation. Listen, Thomas, it is hard for me to believe it, even though I want to."

"You are the doubter now, but"—and his expression grew serious—"your doubt may become contagious."

"Don't give me that, Thomas. Your doubt is your own," said Toler. "But if you hear anything from the others, which would clarify what happened the other night, let me know."

Eight days later Thomas sent word to Sarn and Toler to meet him in the small house on the edge of town. There he told them of Jesus's second visitation and of his own unshakable belief in the authenticity of Jesus's resurrection.

Thomas leaned forward as he spoke, a look of ineffable joy radiating from his face. The dim light partially hid his features but could not disguise his elation.

"Yes, I saw him I was there. It was Jesus." "You are sure?"

"There is no doubt. I asked to touch his wounds, the ones he suffered from the crucifixion, and I have no doubt it was him." Thomas stood up. "It is as they say. He has come alive." Thomas was deeply moved.

"What happened?" asked Sam. "I mean, when you and the others met with Jesus?"

"It was a long meeting. There was so much he taught us. I only wish I had been at the first meeting. There must have been many teachings I missed." He shrugged. "I am by nature a doubter, and sometimes the others label me a cynic. But that is my way of being certain about something." His voice quavered with emotion. "And, my friends, I tell you that this was him, in the flesh. His voice, his way of looking into your soul. And his wounds too."

"All right, we believe you," said Toler. "Did he say what his plans are? We'd like to locate him ourselves."

Thomas raised his brow. "Oh? But you were not his disciples. Yes, you often followed us, but you were not involved. Not really. Your role was spectator. So why would you want to see him?" The look in the disciple's eyes was one of suspicion and guardedness. There had been enough treachery to last him a lifetime, and mistrust came easily. Besides that, now that he stopped and thought about it, these two men were not your ordinary camp followers. There was something different about them.

"It's not easy to explain," Toler answered. "I guess you could just say that we'll be more believable when we report to our own people if we can say that we were firsthand witnesses."

"He really believes it," Sarn said as they watched Thomas leave. The disciple's step seemed lighter than before.

Toler nodded. "Yes, he does. It could be true, but then it could be a group trance or mass hysteria. The disciples want to believe so badly that they are susceptible to just about any kind of suggestion. But we're getting paid to document, not speculate." Toler cleared his throat and walked away.

Chapter 39

DERXTER AGAIN

"Who is that?"

A tall woman, face barely visible behind her toga, stood beside the temple door. Her straight nose and large brown eyes marked her as pretty, but it was her grace of movement that caught Toler's attention.

"I don't know," said Sam, "but she spent a lot of time with Jesus. I saw them together many times."

"Come on."

"Pardon me," Toler said as he caught up to the woman and gently pulled at her sleeve.

The woman regarded Toler and then Sam, her expression puzzled. "Yes?"

"I think I know you, but I am not sure. Were you not present at the recent crucifixion?"

The woman's eyes narrowed, and she visibly tensed. Her voice lowered, and she glanced from one to the other. "Whose crucifixion?"

"That of Jesus," said Toler. "The fellow who called himself a messiah. Weren't you there?"

"Please don't be frightened," added Sam. "We were there too. Besides, we followed him and his group for a while and saw you many times in his company. He seemed to be quite fond of you."

"Oh? You were with him when?" The woman was cautious. "There were so many who drifted in and out of his life I hardly paid attention to them."

"We followed him on several of his preaching trips. We saw him do some incredible things." Sarn groped for something he could say that would allow the woman to trust them. "Look, we were on his side."

She studied them, but her guarded expression also contained curiosity. "What is it you want from me? I have done nothing."

"Just to talk. We saw you at the crucifixion, and well, we knew Jesus meant a lot to you."

"Say," said Sam, "Weren't you also at the tomb that morning?"

She looked at him. "How did you know?"

"We were there too," said Toler. "Now that he mentions it, I think I recall seeing you too."

The woman glanced around the public street, suddenly feeling very self-conscious. "Could we go somewhere private to talk? Please."

"Certainly. My name is Toler, and this is Sarn. Where shall we go?"

"Follow me. There is a place by the creek, under a bluff, where we might be alone and talk. Oh, my name is Mary. Mary Magdalene."

As they walked down the dusty street toward the edge of town, Toler found himself absorbed in his conversation with Mary Magdalene. Sarn followed closely, trying to listen to what they were saying. Once he thought he saw a strange movement down an alleyway, but a second glance discovered nothing.

"You knew Jesus since you were children together?" Toler was delighted at his good fortune. He had not counted on being able to interview someone from the Messiah's past.

Leaving the city, Mary turned off the road and led them down a path, around a hill, and toward a line of trees. They saw no one as they drew near the bluff. It seemed that Mary had picked her place well.

The trees formed a shady, cool cover for the small creek. There was barely any flow at all, but opposite the bluff was a large pool of placid green water. The three settled on the bank under the bluff and continued their conversation.

"Did you see Jesus after his resurrection?" asked Toler.

Mary nodded. "Yes, it was after he had been with his disciples. He was concerned about them, afraid they would disband and forget what he had taught them. But later he appeared to me."

"And what happened?" Sarn asked impulsively. Toler scowled at the question but was glad it had been asked.

Mary lowered her eyes and blushed. "We talked about what had happened and what might come next. We reminisced about old times together. And then we said our good-byes." Her eyes became moist, and she dabbed at them.

"Excuse us for probing into your private life," apologized Toler. "We had no right to ask something so personal."

Mary looked up at Toler and barely smiled. "Don't worry, I didn't tell you everything."

Sarn was too embarrassed to say anything. He felt like hitting himself over the head with a club.

It was almost dusk when they left the bluff on the creek.

"I hate to break up a good party," said Toler, "but it's getting late. Why don't we meet again tomorrow? That is, if you don't mind my prying questions," he added with a twinkle, hoping Mary would take his comment lightly.

She smiled and nodded. "You are such unusual men," Mary said. "I don't know what it is about you, but you are somehow different."

"I hope that is different in a good way," said Sarn.

"It is neither good or bad—just different."

Sarn led the way around the bluff and up the trail. He was paying more attention to the conversation behind him than to where he was going when suddenly he was knocked backward into the water. Stunned by the blow, he struggled to surface. A heavy body came down on top of him before he could get a breath and took him to the bottom. Clutching hands went to his throat. Sarn reached to the face of his assailant, trying to find something to gouge, but the man dodged and pushed him under farther. Without any breath in his lungs, consciousness began to fade. Through a window, he fixed on the image of Jesus hanging on the cross, wondered why he was thinking about that, and then a black curtain was suddenly pulled and all was darkness.

Toler was in midsentence when he heard Sarn's woof and saw his friend topple into the creek. The man who had knocked Sarn into the water swung a fist at Mary, knocking her against the bank, and then leaped into the water after Sarn. Caught totally by surprise, Toler instinctively stepped forward, only to be caught by the collar and yanked backward by a huge hand. Off balance, he was not prepared for the blow to the side of his head. Before passing out, he heard Mary screaming.

It was later—how much there was no way of knowing—when Toler slowly emerged from his dream. He was blindly staggering down a steel tunnel. A swinging clapper barely missed him as it thonged into the tunnel wall; the clang almost tore off the sides of his head. As he struggled toward consciousness, he found the throbbing was even more real. All he could do was lie still and wait for the world to come into some kind of coherence and hope he survived the pain.

"Toler, can you hear me?" A voice from far away could be heard echoing as if through a long curved metal pipe.

"Toler?" A hand was on his head. It was as heavy as a large brick. Maybe a cube of lead. Was this a torture test?

He tried to open his eyes, and a cloudy slit appeared. A blurred form was before him, connected to the hand banging against his head. Toler opened his mouth to ask the person to stop but could not make a sound. He felt consciousness slipping away again and did not fight it. Maybe he could dodge the clapper in the tunnel better this time.

The sounds of birds greeted Toler when he next rose to consciousness. He lay still, eyes closed, a dull throb reminding him of his pain, but it was nothing like before. He drifted off again while trying to tune out the chirping, which pecked against his head like a dull chisel.

The next time he came to, Toler felt strong enough to open his eyes. It was dark, and his first thought was that he was blind. Before his dismay could register, the full moon filled his vision. He lay staring at the sky for a long time, wondering where he was but did not have the strength to move. When he turned his eyes to either side, he thought he saw the tops of bushes but in the dark could not be certain.

He entertained the thought that he had been left to die in the wilderness. Or maybe it was the middle of the night, and everyone else was asleep. He wondered if he would spend the rest of his life lying in darkness formulating questions having to do with where he was.

Footsteps sounded somewhere off to his right. There was a woman's stifled cry followed by a gruff and demanding voice. Toler had heard that voice before, and as recognition slowly came to him, his body tensed in terror. It was Derxter!

"Where is he?" Derxter hissed.

"They took him away. They wouldn't tell me where," Mary Magdalene said in a quavering voice.

"Who? Who took him away?" Derxter was angry, and Toler could imagine the look of hatred on his face.

"Some men. Some of them were soldiers. They said something about him stealing the body of Jesus." Toler listened, wondering if she was talking about him or someone else.

The sounds of someone approaching became audible. "Who is that?" asked Derxter.

"The soldiers. They said they would be back tonight. They are looking for others who might have been involved with the grave theft."

"Do not tell them anything about me. If you do, I will kill you." Toler listened but could not hear footsteps. Either Derxter was still there with Mary, or he had very quietly stolen away in the darkness. In the distance were the sounds of horsemen making their way toward him. Before they arrived, he had drifted off to sleep again.

The sun was halfway toward midday when Toler next woke. Or was it halfway through the afternoon? He had no way of knowing. It was hot, and the bushes provided little shade. He heard people occasionally passing by, not too far from where he lay. He felt weak as if all energy had been beaten from him. His head still hurt, and now he became aware of pain in his shoulder and back.

He tried to reconstruct what had happened. Sam! Where was he? He had been knocked into the water by someone who had then leaped after him. No, the man had first struck Mary.

Was she all right? He struggled to recall what had happened since the ambush. It was Mary he had heard last night. Derxter was looking for him and had threatened Mary. That's why he should lay still and wait. It was beginning to come together now. Had it been Derxter who had attacked him from behind?

Toler was startled at Mary Magdalene's sudden appearance above him.

She did not smile. In the shadows of her kerf, Toler could see that her face was bruised and her eye was black. "I see you are awake. You had a most nasty beating Can you get up?"

Toler rolled to one side and felt excruciating pain in his neck and back. He stopped and waited for the pain to pass.

"I know it hurts, but you must get up. We have to leave this place. The man who beat you wants to kill you. I told him you had been taken away by the soldiers. He will find out I lied and come looking for both of us. We are not safe here." She reached to help him, pleading in her eyes.

Gritting his teeth, Toler managed to pull himself to his hands and knees while trying to ignore the pain washing over him. He was nauseous and thought he might vomit. Mary put her arm under him and gently pulled. Together, they were able to get him on his feet without passing out. She had brought a donkey, and with much effort they finally got him onto the animal's back. Toler found that it required his full attention and energy just to remain astride the animal. She put a cloak over his head and shoulders to disguise him as much as protect him from the sun. Walking beside the ass, Mary helped support Toler lest he fall off. After traveling down the main trail for a half mile, she veered off on a less-traveled path, which led into the foothills to the southeast of Jerusalem.

The sun continued to rise, and its rays bounced mercilessly off the rocky ground. Toler barely hung on to consciousness, although he was sure he drifted off into a stupor several times. He considered it nothing short of a genuine miracle he did not fall off the animal.

Before long they had come to Bethany, a village located to the southeast of Jerusalem and in reality a suburb of the city. Mary asked directions of an old man, and he led them down backstreets. Villagers stared curiously at the strange pair following the old man. Mary had pulled her shawl around her face to hide the bruises, but there was no mistaking Toler's condition. He had the drunken wobble of a wounded man who was barely hanging on to his seat.

After snaking down several twisting alleyways, they were deposited in front of a house. Mary thanked the fellow and without further delay knocked on the door. Almost instantly a man appeared, glanced toward Toler, and spoke to Mary in muffled tones. Toler knew he was the object of much of the discussion and was relieved when he was finally helped down from his precarious perch. He was half carried into the house and passed out just as he was lowered into a bed.

Over the next few days Toler drifted in and out of consciousness. He was ministered to by Mary Magdalene and a brother and his two sisters in whose house they were staying. The man's name was Lazarus, and his sisters were Mary and Martha. Only after he had begun to recover did he realize how badly he had been hurt.

"What did that man hit me with?" Toler asked Mary Magdalene.

"I am not sure. Things were happening so quickly. It looked like a large stone."

"I wonder why he didn't kill me when he could have. I certainly could not have stopped him."

"I think," Mary said, "that my screaming frightened him away. He was afraid someone would come, and he did not take the time to be sure you were dead. It was terrible the way he beat on you and kicked your back." She shuddered at the recollection.

"What happened to Sarn?" Toler dreaded hearing what she would say and had put off asking the question.

"I do not know. I think he probably drowned, but I could not be sure. After he was knocked into the water, his attacker hit me in the head, and all I could do after that was scream hysterically. I recall seeing the man jump into the water after Sam, and I never saw Sarn come up. In a little while the attacker came up out of the water, gasping for breath. He left when Derxter did." She shook her head sadly. "It is so unfortunate about your friend."

"Did you see a body floating? Any sign of him?"

"No. As soon as the two men left, I tried to get you up. I was afraid that they would be back to finish the job on both of us as soon as they found no one was coming. Fortunately someone was coming, two men, and I was able to persuade them to carry you from the creek and lay you in the brush. It was not much of a hiding place, but it was the best I could do. Twice I went back to the pool and looked for Sarn but saw no one."

Toler swallowed hard. "Derxter believed you when he returned that night?"

"Yes, I was afraid he would kill me." Mary pulled her cloak around her. "I am scared of that man."

The death of Sarn was like a weight on Toler's chest. Mary seemed to read his thoughts.

"Don't blame yourself for Sarn's death. You know better than that. There is no way you can prevent evil men from ambushing you if they are determined to do so." As she spoke, Mary put a finger on his chest as if driving home her point.

He knew she was right, and he also knew it would take awhile to get over the loss of Sarn.

Within a week Toler was moving about the house. He came to know and enjoy his hosts, who turned out to be a rich source of information about the Messiah.

JESUS THE 15TH MESSIAH

"Yes, I knew Jesus well. He ate many a meal with his feet under our table. He was a good friend. Liked to eat, too. Didn't see him all that often, but it's sad just knowing he's gone."

"He was more than a friend," said Martha. "He brought Lazarus back from the dead."

Toler raised his brows. At first he thought maybe it was a joke but then saw that they were serious. Lazarus looked at his hands in a solemn way while Mary, his sister, nodded at Toler.

"I do recall hearing something about Jesus bringing someone back alive, but I never thought I should be so fortunate as to meet him." He hesitated before going further, afraid he would be misinterpreted. "I would be most interested in hearing about it. Would you mind?" said Toler.

"Not much to tell," said Lazarus. "I got sick, bad sick. Mary and Martha then sent for Jesus. He was only a few miles away at that time, but he was busy. It took him two days to get around to coming. By then I had died and been buried." Lazarus gestured behind him. "On the hill out there, in the family tomb."

"He was dead," Martha said. "We had no guarantee that Jesus could have prevented his death, but we were hurt that he did not come see Lazarus when he was so sick."

"When Jesus finally came," Mary said, "Martha met him on the road and gave him a severe tongue lashing. She was angrier than I had ever seen her."

"I was hurt! I knew how much it would have meant to Lazarus to see his friend before he died," Martha said.

"Next thing I know I'm walking out of the tomb with people pulling away the grave clothes. I felt like I had just woken from a long sleep. Didn't feel like I had been dead." Lazarus reflected a moment. "I felt terrible before I died. Just sort of drifted off into a black tunnel. There was a light at the end, I recall, and that made it not so bad. So I just drifted with it like I was a leaf floating down a creek. Felt peaceful and good after being so sick." Lazarus enjoyed telling the story even though he had no understanding of what had happened.

"How did you happen to bring me to this house?" asked Toler of Mary Magdalene.

"I knew of them through Jesus. He told me many times of his love for them. Since you had been sympathetic to Jesus's cause, I thought I could use that as a ticket to get you inside the door. If whoever attacked you was also part of the powers that killed Jesus, I knew they would help."

Mary B, for Mary of Bethany as Toler had begun calling her to distinguish her from Mary Magdalene, had questions of her own. "Toler, tell us about you. You ask the questions and keep us talking, but we never hear you telling us anything."

Toler nodded. "You are right. And there is much about myself that I cannot tell you. I wish I could, but I simply cannot." Toler was as honest as he could under the circumstances. Better to do that than to have them see through his thin disguise and consider him a liar. He needed their trust and goodwill if he was to survive.

Toler's main injury was the blow to his head, which still caused him pain for weeks afterward. He was bruised in the kidney area, his sides, and his neck. It did not appear that he had any internal damage, and he considered himself fortunate that his skull had not been cracked. It seemed clear that Derxter had intended to kill him.

Several days later Toler and Lazarus were sitting at the kitchen table working on sandals. Suddenly Martha slipped into the house, breathless. After shutting the door behind her, she leaned against it, wide eyed.

"What is it?" asked Lazarus.

"He's here! In Bethany!"

"Who is here?" asked Lazarus in his slow, patient manner.

"That man. What did you call his name? Derxter? He is at the market asking questions."

Toler felt a sinking in his stomach. Not that he was surprised, for he had known that Derxter would be coming after him. Whatever else he was, the man was a professional and as dogged as they came.

Probably Derxter had gone further than his orders allowed and now needed to cover his tracks by getting rid of Sarn and Toler. Sarn had been disposed of, and that meant Derxter would come after him.

Lish! At some point Derxter would be searching for him as well. Toler felt a need to be with Lish. Together the two of them would be more of a match for Derxter than either alone. Besides that, Lish may still have the laser gun, and that would be the equalizer they needed.

"Is there any way he might trace me to your home?" Toler asked. He had not been on the streets in daylight since he had recovered enough to get out of bed. He had taken short walks at night but did not think he had been seen by anyone.

"I don't know," said Martha. "I think Mary told someone about you being here. Where is she?" Martha moved to the bedroom door. "Mary!"

There was movement in the bedroom, and Mary B came to the door, distress written on her face. "I heard what you said, Martha. Yes, I did tell someone at the market that we had a sick guest, and that was why I was making soup. But I didn't mention any names." Mary B was obviously flustered at the idea that she had leaked vital information to the enemy.

"I'm afraid all he needs to know is that a sick man is being kept here and he will come to investigate," said Toler. "I am afraid that the time has come for me to leave. Your hospitality has been greater than anyone could ask, but I must not place you in danger."

"He is right," said Lazarus. "If this man is as ruthless as Toler says, then there is no way we can defend against him."

Toler was already up and gathering his belongings. Within a few minutes he was at the door.

"Wait," said Martha. "Would it not be better if you left in the night?"

She was right, Toler conceded. In his condition he would not have a chance of getting away from Derxter if he was seen.

They were interrupted by the sound of someone running in the street. Toler grabbed his things and climbed up the ladder into the sleeping loft. He had just flung himself down when the door opened and Mary Magdalene ran in.

"He is on his way here! We must hide!" Mary said as she gasped for breath. "I was coming from the market when I heard two women talking about a big angry man who was looking for a wounded person in our village. One of the women said she told him that there was such a person in the home of Lazarus."

"I have an idea," said Martha. "Mary, get your things together and hide in the loft with Toler. Quickly!"

Mary B had been peering through the window. "A big man is coming down the street. He looks like he means business!"

"Quick, Lazarus, you get in the bed here." Lazarus did as he was told, and Martha threw a cover over him. "You are the sick one, brother." Lazarus understood what Martha had in mind and promptly lay down.

"Yes, I am sick," he uttered and moaned. "Don't overdo it, my dramatic brother."

"Now he's close," said Mary B. "He is asking someone which house is ours."

The sound of heavy footsteps paused outside the door, and then a loud knock reverberated through the room. Mary B opened the door a crack.

"Yes?" she asked in a timorous voice.

"I am looking for a sick man, one who has recently suffered injuries. The man who caused the injuries has sent money to pay for his inconvenience." Derxter held up a purse and jingled it.

"Oh, we have a sick man here, but he was not injured. He is just sick," said Mary B.

"May I see him? It may be the same man." Derxter stepped forward and put his hand against the door. Mary B tensed and braced her frame behind the door.

"Let him in," whispered Martha. It would not be smart to act as if they had something to hide.

"Yes, why don't you come in?" asked Mary B. "You may want to leave part of that purse with our sick brother. It would make all of us feel better, I assure you."

Derxter pushed into the room. His hulking body made the room seem small. "Where is he?"

"Here," said Martha, seated on the edge of Lazarus's bed.

"This is our brother, Lazarus, and he has taken ill. We have had to nurse him for two weeks now. You can see he is sleeping now."

Lazarus took his cue and moaned. He opened his eyes slowly as if he had been sleeping heavily. He focused on the scowling man above him. Slowly Lazarus raised a hand and touched Derxter's sleeve.

"Please, sir, are you a doctor? I need help." At that, Lazarus began coughing. He pulled up off the bed and coughed violently on Derxter's chest.

"Oh, I am so sorry," said Martha. She picked up a dirty cloth that had been used for cleaning and wiped Derxter's face and neck. Derxter leaped backward and stood by the door.

"Is there no one else living here who is ill?" He asked.

His eyes traveled around the room, searching for a clue. He spotted the sleeping loft with hay spilling over the edge. "May I look in your loft?"

"There is no one in the loft," Mary B said.

"Let me see for myself," insisted Derxter. His steely gaze caused them to hold further protests.

"Be careful then," said Martha, "for that is where Lazarus was sleeping when he came down sick. There seems to be something about the loft that causes illness. Our parents came down with the same sickness before they died."

Derxter's step slowed as Martha spoke. He climbed the stairs and stood as high as he could. Martha reached the table behind her, grabbed a knife, and held it under the edge of the bed. Derxter turned his head in all directions, taking his time to let his eyes grow accustomed to the dark.

"Are you a physician?" Martha thought it might help to keep talking with the man, but Derxter had tuned out the people downstairs and focused on the dark recesses of the loft.

"I say, are you a physician?" Martha rose and tugged on Derxter's cloak. Her knife was hidden beneath the folds of her shawl. She had never stabbed anyone before and looked up at the huge body above her on the ladder. She debated where she would stab and decided that she would push the blade straight up into the man's body from between his legs. Even as she made that decision, she was surprised at herself for electing such a drastic and potentially deadly target. And yet, it seemed only appropriate for the man who had beaten Toler almost to death and who was probably somehow associated with those who had their beloved Jesus killed.

"There is no one there," said Derxter and came down the ladder. He took several coins from the bag and flipped them to the floor. "For your trouble," he said and left.

Mary B watched him stride down the street. "He is gone." Martha sighed with relief and dropped the knife in her lap. Lazarus sat up and asked if anyone wanted to hear him cough some more. The smiling faces of Toler and Mary Magdalene appeared over the edge of the loft.

"If he had come up here and poked around, he would found us under the hay," said Toler.

"That was smart thinking, Martha, about the sickness in the loft. I think that is what discouraged him from searching harder," said Mary.

"You were all good. You make a good team," said Toler. "I will leave you when dark arrives, and your lives can go back to normal."

"And I will leave too. You have been wonderful friends to us," said Mary Magdalene. She and Toler climbed down the ladder.

"He is a disgusting man, that Derxter. The evil poured out of him like sweat from a desert hog," said Martha. "I think I would have tried to kill him if he had spotted you in the loft. I never thought I could say that about anyone, but there was something about him that made the decision easy."

"You too?" Mary B asked. She held up a knife for them to see. "I had the same plan, Martha. Where were you going to stick him?"

"I don't want to know," said Lazarus. He held up a hammer that had been under the covers on the bed. "I guess this hammer wouldn't have done as much damage as those knives, but maybe together we could have discouraged him."

"Five against one would make even the stoutest man think twice," said Mary Magdalene, "especially if some of them were armed, and there were neighbors close by who would help out."

"Let me be a wet blanket for a minute," Toler said quietly. "If I was Derxter and I believed that my man was hiding in here, and furthermore, I thought that I would have to fight all five people who might be armed, then I think I would quietly excuse myself just as he did."

Everyone looked around at the others.

"I hate to admit it," said Lazarus, "but I think we overplayed it. Maybe we were too obvious."

Mary B nodded and sat down on a stool. Martha slumped and appeared dejected. "You are right, brother, and I think the man is no fool."

"He is definitely no fool," added Toler. "He is smart and deadly."

"So what does that mean?" asked Mary Magdalene. "That he will wait for us to leave tonight and then pounce on us? That is what I would do if I was him."

Mary B said, "But then again maybe he was fooled and we will never see him again."

"Maybe," said Toler, "but I don't intend to give him another chance to come up behind me."

"Nor me," said Mary Magdalene.

"One thing is for sure," said Toler, "and that is Mary Magdalene and I must leave this house. There is no good in us staying any longer. You have been wonderful, but it is time you were taken out of the picture."

Mary Magdalene nodded. "The question now is, how do we go about doing it?"

"Surely you will not be going by yourself, Mary," said Mary B. "That man or his friends could catch you in a minute."

"Perhaps," said Mary Magdalene, "but they can't make me tell something I don't know, and I don't know where Toler is going."

"Don't underestimate the evil of this man," said Lazarus. "Do you think he will say 'Thank you anyway. Now you may go' after you tell him you know nothing about Toler? No, my friend, he will first torture you to make sure you are telling the truth. And when he has discovered that you, in fact, knew nothing, he will then kill you so there will be no witness. That is how they work."

Mary looked to Toler, who grimly nodded. "That's how they work," he said. Mary blanched.

"What are we to do?" asked Mary B.

"I see only one option," said Toler. "If Mary and I are to be away from here tonight, then we must travel together."

Mary thought about that for a moment. "And where will we be going?"

"Leave that to me. I'll let you know after we are on our way."

"But," said Lazarus, "if we are asked, where shall we say you are going? Would it not be best that you tell us something? Can't you give us a false destination?"

"Hmm . . . good point. So if I were to say that we are going to the coast, it would not be my fault if you overheard. Yes, Mary, we will travel to the coast. Perhaps there will be a boat we can board."

"Ah, so to the coast they are going. Did you hear that, my sisters? They will go look for a boat," said Lazarus.

That evening, after dark had fallen, neighbors began dropping by to see Lazarus and his sisters. When there were seven present, all pulled their cloaks around their faces and left, each going in a different direction. Lazarus and Martha and Mary B also left, and then Toler and Mary Magdalene departed separately. The plan was to confuse anyone who might be watching the house.

Two of the men had been instructed to walk with a limp and a third had a natural limp. Two of the women walked stooped, and Mary Magdalene also walked hunched over. Unless Derxter knew Toler and Mary Magdalene well and was also able to get a close look at the figures, it would be very difficult for him to make a positive identification.

Of the total of twelve people leaving the house, Toler was fifth and Mary Magdalene seventh. There were one-minute intervals between each departure, which would give any pursuer a hard time staying with everyone since they were going in different directions. Each person walked away from Lazarus's house in roughly a straight line, like spokes going out from the hub of a wheel. Toler and Mary Magdalene had agreed to meet in a manger Lazarus had described to them. Entry into the manger could be made from either of two parallel streets, allowing Toler and Mary Magdalene to arrive separately.

Toler left the house shortly after the fourth person. There was plenty of moonlight, which Toler decided would be more of a help to Derxter than to the pursued. However, that advantage was offset by the number of people, mostly children and adolescents, who were walking and playing in the streets. Toler found himself extremely afraid and was surprised at how he had been traumatized by Derxter's beating. He trembled as he approached one dark alley.

Fifteen minutes later he could see the manger. Lazarus had told him it would be on the left with doorways large enough for wagons to pass through. The doors should be open as the owner seldom closed them. There was no sign advertising the location, but Toler had no trouble identifying it.

At that moment Toler noticed two men talking on the street corner. He nodded a greeting to the pair, who eyed him suspiciously as he passed. The sound of running feet on the other side of the street echoed off the close walls. Toler involuntarily turned his head to see who was racing toward him. The boy slapped him on the arm as he passed and started down the street perpendicular to the one Toler was traveling. He gestured for Toler to follow him.

Toler stopped and turned around. The two men were still on the corner a few paces behind him, and Toler hoped they would not think him odd for passing them again. They stopped their conversation and regarded him questioningly.

"Good evening," said Toler.

They grunted in response and resumed their conversation.

The boy waited in a doorway, his eyes seemingly larger than they should be.

"Yes?" Toler said.

"Are you Toler?" He licked his dry lips and glanced nervously up and down the street.

"Yes. What is it?"

"Lazarus sent me to warn you. Don't go into the manger."

"What? Why not? What about Mary Magdalene?" Toler suddenly had many questions that demanded immediate answers.

"There is danger at the meeting place. Now I must go find Mary Magdalene and warn her." The boy turned and trotted off down the side street, blending into the darkness and suddenly Toler could see him no more. The next street over was the one Mary Magdalene was to have traveled as she made her way to the back entrance of the manger, and in that direction the boy ran.

Toler limped awkwardly after the boy, alarmed about Mary's safety. He figured that if she left about two minutes after he did, then they should be able to intercept her before she arrived at the manger unless she had walked faster than Toler.

When Toler arrived at the corner, the boy was waiting against the building, hidden in the shadows.

"You wait here," he said breathlessly and trotted up the street toward Lazarus's house. Toler stepped back into a doorway, hidden in the shadows; he felt helpless to do anything else.

From his position on the connecting side street, Toler could not see down either main street and therefore had no sight of either door of the manger. To his left the two men still stood on the corner talking. Occasionally there were the usual neighborhood noises drifting down the streets: mothers calling to children, people laughing, children screaming at one another, dogs barking, doors slamming. Toler began to relax, feeling safe in the dark doorway.

He tensed as he heard someone approaching from the direction of the manger around the corner to his right. The sound of pebbles under sandals stopped around the corner just out of his sight.

What if Derxter was standing around the corner a few feet away, and Mary and the boy walked up the street, right into his grasp? The scenario chilled Toler. He reasoned that the two would not be so foolish as to just walk up the street without first letting the boy scout ahead. He waited impatiently.

The footsteps began again, and Toler froze as Derxter moved into sight from around the corner, his attention riveted down the street where the boy had gone looking for Mary Magdalene. Derxter leaned against the building only a few feet from Toler. Neither could then see the other even if they had looked because Toler had melted back into the darkness of the doorway.

Derxter murmured a curse and walked down the side street.

As he passed in front of Toler, his head was facing toward the main street, still searching for his quarry. Toler could see an old scar on Derxter's cheek shining in the moonlight. Derxter stopped three feet from Toler and scanned the street. *If he sees me, I am dead,* thought Toler.

Derxter spotted the two men at the corner and walked in that direction. As soon as Derxter took several strides, Toler stepped from his hiding place and walked in the opposite direction, matching his footsteps with those of Derxter. He had almost made it to the corner when he heard Derxter call out. Toler jerked his head around, poised to run, but Derxter was calling to the two men who were hidden from Toler by Derxter's bulk.

"Hello," said one of the men in response to Derxter. Toler turned onto the next street and peeked around the corner at the men. He could not hear what they were saying, but there seemed little doubt about the subject of their conversation. One of the men gestured in Toler's direction, apparently indicating the direction Toler and the boy had taken.

Toler wanted to be out of Derxter's way but also wanted to be in a position to see Mary Magdalene if she arrived at the manger. He crossed the street but could not retrace his steps toward Lazarus's house without crossing the intersection in full view of Derxter. He considered hiding in the manger but decided that was a dumb idea; he had no desire to be trapped there with Derxter and his henchman. Toler noticed a narrow and crooked alleyway opposite the manger. Taking a chance that he had not been observed from the manger, Toler hid in the shadows behind an old cart parked in the mouth of the passage. He was able to see not only the manger door but the street Mary Magdalene had planned to come and the corner he just left.

The faint sound of the men's conversation died away, and there was silence. Toler was puzzled as to why Derxter had not appeared from around the corner. He glanced behind him; the alleyway turned out of sight, and he fought the urge to make sure he was not trapped in a dead end.

The lively talk of two boys rattled down the street, and before long the two figures could be seen coming in his direction. They passed a few feet from Toler as he crouched behind the cart. Neither looked his way, but Toler was able to catch a glimpse of their faces. One of them was the boy who had warned him!

"I'm here," Toler whispered as they passed. The boys continued on, but there was enough of a hesitation in their gait for Toler to know he had been heard. Soon they passed out of earshot, and the streets again were quiet. Nothing to do but wait.

Chapter 40

Sᴀʀɴ Rᴇᴛᴜʀɴs

Squirb nervously waited for the three people to come up the bank. Not one to enjoy physical violence, he would rather have avoided the whole scene. But since the only option was Derxter's wrath and an almost certain beating, Squirb determined to do his part.

He hoped the woman would come first as she would be the easiest for him to take down while Derxter handled the other two. Sarn, however, was in the lead. Squirb turned and opened his mouth to suggest that Derxter attack the boy while he waited for the woman. With a disgusted scowl, Derxter pushed his assistant forward.

Squirb's feet slipped on the steep bank, and he lost his balance. Instead of grabbing his victim by the neck as he had been instructed, he careened into the surprised boy and knocked him into the water. In an attempt to avoid falling in after Sarn, the clumsy Squirb pirouetted and grasped for the shore. His hand caught the woman a hard blow on the head, knocking her against the bank. He then lost his balance and toppled into the water on top of Sarn, who had not yet come to the surface. Terrified that Sarn would drown him if he came up, Squirb grabbed him by the neck and sought to hold him under until Derxter could help.

As soon as the boy's body went limp, Squirb thrashed his way the few feet to shore. One of Sarn's hands had become entangled in the fat man's belt, and Squimb unknowingly pulled Sam's limp body to the bank. As Squirb hurriedly clambered from the water, Sarn's body was lifted just enough to be dropped over tree roots growing out of the bank. Upset by the screaming woman, horrified at his own murderous action, and most of all afraid of Derxter's impatience, Squimb barely glanced down at Sarn's limp body. On the shore he found Derxter beating the other man while the woman continued screaming.

"Derxter, I think I hear someone coming!" said Squirb. He was not sure if he heard anything or not, but more than anything he wanted to be away from the place.

Demxter gave one more kick to the limp body and scrambled up the bank. "Come on!" he commanded.

Caught on the roots just above the water line, Sarn could not be seen from directly above on the steep bank. With his torso over a large root and his face downward, water drained from his lungs. It was two hours later that he regained a dim consciousness. He lay there for a while longer, not sure what had happened, and tried to gather his scattered wits. Finally, still confused, his strength returned sufficiently for him to drag himself off the roots and into the water. Sarn stood in the chest-high pool staring blankly around him. Eventually he moved along the bank until he stumbled up out of the water onto a gravel bar. Exhausted and disoriented, he huddled under the overhanging bank. Once he saw a woman appear and look around, but he pulled himself farther under the embankment and hid there until before dawn. Then, brought awake by some sound, he staggered up out of the water and began walking.

All that day Sarn walked south, not knowing where he was going but nevertheless filled with a sense of urgency. By midday he passed to the east of Herodium, and by nightfall he had come to the outskirts of Engedi on Lake Asphaltites. He stopped momentarily and gazed blankly across the expanse of water. Although he had seen the sea before when visiting Masada, no recognition registered on his face. Without showing any interest, he turned and continued walking, this time angling toward the west.

Later that day, when the sun was about to dip behind the horizon, Sarn stumbled into a sheepherders' camp on a plain just outside the city. The men squatting around their cook fire looked up at Sarn, noted his dirty and exhausted condition, and motioned him to join them. He plopped down just outside their circle and watched with eyes that did not see. One of the men handed him a chunk of bread with roasted mutton. Sarn accepted the gift without acknowledging it and mechanically chewed the food. No one said anything to him or expect him to speak. They had seen men like him before. Sarn hardly had time to eat his meal before he fell asleep on the floor.

If the boy had been alert, he would have noticed that one of the men in the group did not look much like a sheepherder. The man was short and dressed better than those with whom he sat around the fire. Although the man turned away when he saw Sarn, it would have been no problem to recognize the guide. But Sam's mind was not working well, and Arie went unrecognized. Soon after Sarn was asleep, the wily guide gathered his belongings together, felt something under his robe as if reassuring himself it was still in its place, and left.

When Sarn woke the next morning, the sun had been up for a while and he was alone. Sam did not know where he was or, for that matter, who he was. He simply picked himself up and started walking to the west.

253

Chapter 41

TO GENNESARET

Several hours passed without any further activity on the streets. Toler nestled down among some trash and dozed off and on. Once he heard angry voices dueling in the manger, but they were too muffled to be understood. Another time he was awakened by the sound of footsteps on the street but when he looked could see no one. He knew he would have to move when dawn came; but meanwhile he was safe, and as far as he could tell, so was Mary Magdalene. After a while he dozed again.

Toler was awakened at dawn by a shuffling street beggar searching the street for salvage. All he needed now was some beggar to spot him and start pointing and hollering. The beggar paused at the entrance to the alley and poked in the trash. Toler was surprised to hear Mary Magdalene's voice coming from behind the shawl.

"Go to the end of the alley. I'll meet you there."

She picked up a few things from the street and placed them in her bag. Using her to shield his movements, Toler slid backward, got to his feet, and ran down the alleyway. At the first turn, a backward glance saw only empty street in the coming dawn.

Toler continued down the winding alley until he came to the next street. He crossed it and leaned back into a doorway so that he could not be surprised from behind. After a long wait the beggar appeared, wobbling down the street toward him.

"Follow me," the beggar said as she passed Toler.

The next alleyway led in the opposite direction from the manger, and she ducked into it. Toler followed the beggar down the crooked alley and suddenly was face-to-face with Mary Magdalene.

"I am so glad to see you," he said. "I didn't know whether to come looking for you last night or stay put."

"You did right. We located Derxter and yourself, and it was a lot easier if you didn't go wandering off. It was hard enough keeping up with him."

"How did you know the manger was an ambush?" asked Toler.

"Right after I left, a few minutes behind you, one of Martha's friends came by. She wanted to know who that big man was who had been listening outside the window of the house earlier in the day."

"What a wily creep!" Toler said.

"It didn't take much imagination to figure out that he had heard our plans and would be waiting for us to meet at the manger. So they sent someone after us."

"It was close." Toler glanced around them. Two old women ambled down the alley. There was no one else in sight. "Where is Derxter now?"

"He came out of the manger for a while last night."

"Yeah, I got a good look at the back of his neck. He talked to some men on the corner. That's the last I saw of him."

"It must have been after he talked to the two men that he began roaming the area. The boys that followed him said he can move very well for his size. He eventually gave up and went back into the manger. As far as I know, he's still there now."

"Maybe he's catching up on his sleep. I'd like to catch up on mine."

"Me too," said Mary Magdalene.

"What is the plan now? At least we have gotten away from Lazarus's house. Is there a plan to get out of town?" Toler had learned not to underestimate these people. They were very resourceful.

"If at all possible we should leave on our own. To make further contact with Lazarus and his sisters would only complicate matters unless there is no other way."

"That seems logical," said Toler. "Now that we are alone, I'll tell you where I am going. You can go with me, or you can go wherever you want."

"My home is now in Jerusalem, and I live by myself. There is no one to go to there. If I can be of help to you, I'll go with you. I'd also like to hear more about you and Derxter. It sounds like an intriguing story."

Toler's first reaction was an inward groan for he did not want the burden of taking care of a woman while he traveled. On the other hand, he admired Mary Magdalene's resourceful cunning. And she knew the people and the country better than he did. Besides, now that Sarn was no longer with him, it would be a lonely trip by himself.

"I must go to Gennesaret," said Toler.

"Gennesaret? That is a town in the north, by the Sea of Galilee."

"Yes. Will you go with me?"

"Of course. There is nothing more pressing to do. That is very near my old home, at Magdala, which is just south of Gennesaret. I have not lived there in years, not since my parents died. When I was in Capernaum with Jesus, I sometimes stopped and visited with old friends, but after a while I stopped. You know how that goes."

"Do you still have family in Magdala?"

"No. They either died or moved away. There is no one there with whom I am close."

"We'd better get started. Do you know how to get out of Bethany?" Toler asked. "I guess we can head north until we find a road out of town."

"Instead of going through Jerusalem, let's go up the Jordan River valley. It's easier traveling than across country. Besides, I think Derxter might expect us to go back to Jerusalem."

"I am glad I did not give my destination while in Lazarus's house."

"Your caution paid off," agreed Mary Magdalene. "Let's go to Gennesaret."

Chapter 42

DERXTER RECRUITS

The Kidron Valley, just outside the walls of Jerusalem, was a deep and rocky ravine where men could gather without being seen. If someone had been on the wall at that moment, he would have been privy to such a meeting, but that would not have mattered to Derxter. It was time for drastic action.

Seven rough-looking, impatient men waited for Derxter to speak.

"Tell us the deal! It is getting too hot to stand around waiting for something to happen," said one who was stouter than the others. His name was Haj, a man who rode a fast horse and was wanted for murder and robbery in his home country to the north. He had come south along the trade route that passed close to the Great Sea on its way to Egypt. Occasionally he found opportunities to rob travelers but had not come across any large prize in a long time. There were too many Roman soldiers to suit him. He considered himself a much more experienced and worldly robber than the local wretches surrounding him and felt it only natural that he should become their leader.

"Yes! Tell us. Now!" came a chorus from the others.

Derxter held up a hand. "Wait! Someone else is expected very soon. The pay is good. It will be worth your wait."

"If I wait any longer, I want more pay!" said the self-appointed leader. He glanced at the other men and pressed his demand. They were more than willing to have someone push the case for my more pay. On their own, they would not have thought of it. After all, they had already been offered a sum greater than any had ever seen at one time. But they were able to quickly readjust the estimates of their worth and, in fact, began to believe that they were on the verge of being cheated unless the fees were raised. Men who would likely spend the day uselessly, as they did most days, now believed they deserved better than top pay.

Derxter was enraged at the men. "You slime! You don't deserve what I'm paying you! Wait!"

The men seemed cowed by Derxter's outburst. Haj, however, pushed forward and revealed his flawed judgment. "Pay us more or we walk!"

Derxter stood with arms crossed. He said nothing, but the glare of his eyes would have halted most men. Haj, however, didn't look at Derxter's eyes, and that was his fatal mistake. Haj believed that a dramatic exit would likely bring Derxter around, and he intended to casually brush him aside as he departed.

"We walk—" was cut off by Derxter's huge hand around his throat. The man was lifted off the ground, eyes bulging.

"Your services are terminated!" Derxter hissed and threw the man against the wall of the ravine. The noise of Haj's head smashing against the rock sounded like a ripe melon being dropped off a wagon onto a paved street. His body crumpled loosely to the stony ground; the fingers on one hand tremored violently for a few seconds. The kerf, which still covered his head, became dark red as blood poured from the crushed skull.

The remaining men held back, demonstrating more common sense than their recent leader. None of them spoke as they milled around and waited silently, all the while keeping their distance from Derxter.

It was not long before there was a noise of someone coming.

Rocks rolled down the side of the ravine, followed by a cloud of dust, in the middle of which was Squirb sliding on his behind. He unceremoniously dusted himself off as he reported to Derxter.

"Vashil said he would do it if you paid him enough! He wants a larger fee if he catches them."

"Tell him it is a deal. Tell him to start now!" With a gesture Squirb was sent on his way to meet with the bandit Vashil and his men.

Derxter turned to the six men. "All right, we are ready to start. Your job is to catch four fugitives for me I will pay you one-half now and the rest when they are caught. If you personally catch one of them, your fee doubles I want all of them alive."

The men mumbled among themselves, for it was easier to kill someone than to catch and deliver them alive.

"If you accept this job and then quit before it is done, you will become a fugitive yourself. Others will be paid to hunt you down. If you don't have the stomach for this kind of work, now is the time to leave. If you betray me in any way, you will join your friend." Derxter indicated the still body of Haj.

Derxter produced a sack of coins and shook it. He had dealt with men like these all his life, and nothing motivated them so much as fear and greed. One of the men hungrily eyed the bag of jingling coins and made his way to Derxter, who doled out half of the fee. The others followed suit.

"You have been assigned to cover the roads out of Jerusalem. You have a description of the four people. If you need to, recruit more men to assist you. Just catch them!"

Meanwhile, Squirb met with Vashil. Whereas the men whom Derxter hired were to guard the roads, Vashil and his group of bandits were to go anywhere necessary to track down the fugitives. Vashil was a rangy, dark-complexioned, unpleasant man with a perpetual sneer on his face. His black eyes appeared to be darting back and forth at all times as if afraid that he would miss something if he was not looking directly at it. His large strong hands were never still, nervously fidgeting, usually with a knife. Reared in a Bedouin family, he had been treated coldly and harshly while growing up. This was the standard Arabic approach to child rearing and produced adults with unusual capacities for violence and cruelty. Vashil was known as an opportunistic and ruthless person, and it had been an easy matter for him to become the gang's leader. Although he had an "understanding" with the local authorities, he was sometimes bothered by the Romans, who wanted criminals taken out of circulation. Lawbreakers only caused trouble, and the Romans wanted a peaceful occupation.

"It is agreed," Squirb said. "If you catch them, your fee will be doubled. But they must be caught alive."

Vashil smiled crookedly. "Alive? It is more fun to catch them dead." He laughed.

"If they are dead, then you will not be paid double," Squirb said.

"If we catch them anyway, then I expect to be paid double. Or I will take my fee out of your friend's hide."

Squirb bit his lip to keep from laughing aloud. He wouldn't mind seeing Vashil take on Derxter. That would be a no-lose match from Squirb's viewpoint. It would be an interesting fight, and he would be satisfied no matter who won. It would be best, of course, if they killed each other.

"That is between you and Derxter. I only relay to you what he says are the rules. You are free to take or leave the deal." Squirb turned to leave. He did not like dealing with people like Vashil. They were deceptive, manipulative, and obnoxious, not to mention lower class. Squirb didn't really care if they made a deal or not. He knew that Derxter was moving not only far beyond the limits of propriety for planetary visitations but was becoming irrational; Squirb was especially nervous about that. The sooner they could leave this awful place, the happier he would be. Meanwhile, he just wanted to stay in the background as much as possible.

"All right. It is done." Vashil signaled the deal was closed.

"We start now. They already have too much head start."

Squirb nodded and stood aside. Vashil left the small house and whistled. Within moments he was surrounded by his band of fourteen men and began giving instructions.

Chapter 43

ON THE RUN

Toler and Mary stopped for the night at Jericho near the Jordan River. Behind them was Jerusalem, and to the east, the mountains formed a dramatic backdrop to the flat plains of the river bottom. The Jordan River itself was not a great river and would be called small by many people. But it was life giving and allowed the farmers to have green fields all along the length of the valley to Lake Asphaltites or the Dead Sea. From Jericho the Jordan was not visible, although if one knew where to look, he could make out the flat banks snaking their way from north to south on the level plain.

To the south, Lake Asphaltites, cradled by mountains on the east and west, stretched into the haze on the southern horizon. The waters were a medium blue and contrasted pleasingly with the beige-yellow mountains.

"This river country is much greener than the desert," said Toler. "Better crops too. I like the higher ground myself, especially around Galilee. The air is thinner and fresher."

Toler nodded. "Jericho itself is a pleasant place."

"It is our oldest city, perhaps the oldest in the world," said Mary. "Or so the story goes."

"Yes, I believe Lish mentioned that during our all-night conversation," said Toler. He frowned. "We must warn him before Derxter gets there."

"You're certain Derxter will be after him?"

Toler nodded. "Yes, and I can't tell you why. Not now."

Mary nodded. She was very curious but respectful of Toler's need to be secretive.

"I may sound paranoid, Mary, but I prefer that we not spend the nights in the usual mangers."

"What is this word *paranoid*?" Mary looked at Toler with puzzled eyes.

"It means to be unnaturally mistrusting. More cautious and suspicious than necessary. That's how I'm feeling these days."

"If your mistrust is more extreme than is necessary for the situation, then is it good to be paranoid?"

She caught that one, he thought. "I feel safer that way."

"If Derxter comes after us, he will inquire first at the usual places people stay when traveling. Would it be so difficult to recognize the description, a woman and a dashing, handsome man?"

"No, a man and a beautiful, sexy woman."

Mary blushed. "You no doubt say that to all the women."

"No, I have only said that to one woman, I think. Maybe I just thought it. I'll ask her next time I see her."

"Don't ask her if you have said it, you silly man. Just say it no matter if it is the first or the twentieth. You know that deep down a woman had rather be called sexy and beautiful than anything else."

"I disagree, Mary. That's not true everywhere. Not with my woman."

"You jest. What would be the best compliment to your woman?"

"Ahna would rather be told that she is intelligent more than anything else." Toler smiled at Mary's surprise. "And her second choice would be for someone to appreciate her sense of humor. She is not especially funny herself, but she appreciates good humor." Toler smiled as he recalled Alma's laugh.

"My! Where is this place you come from? It sounds most unusual. It might be a very interesting place for a woman to visit."

Toler smiled noncommittally. It was not easy to lie or even be evasive with this keenly perceptive woman.

"But what about you, Toler? Regardless of what Ahna values about herself, what is it that you like most about your friend? It is beautiful and sexy, right?"

Toler stopped walking and furrowed his brow in thought. What did he value most about Ahna? He had never before sought to put it into words. "Mary, I really do like a beautiful and sexy woman, and I would rate that second in terms of Ahna's value to me. First would be our companionship."

"Companionship? I am not sure what you mean. Companionship in the bedroom?" Her face showed genuine perplexity.

"No, we just enjoy being together. Our times in bed are very intense, but quantitatively that is only a small fraction of our time together." He noticed that Mary's face was bright red. "I see that I am embarrassing you with this talk about sex. Please excuse me."

"Oh, don't stop." She blushed even a brighter red. "It is just that I have never heard anyone speak of it before. It happens, obviously, and everyone knows about it, but it is not talked about especially between men and women. I cannot believe

I am standing here and listening to what you are saying. About your woman and the bed."

"Then we'll stop." Actually Toler was feeling somehow disloyal to Ahna for having talked with a strange woman about their private life together, although, he reflected, he had not revealed anything he or Ahna would consider very personal.

"That is not necessary. To tell the truth, I enjoy it—the conversation, I mean." And she laughed at herself. "I am proud that I am able to handle our discussion so well. Most women would have fainted with embarrassment or acted horrified or walked away indignantly. Why do I handle it so easily with you?"

"Because," said Toler, "you are unusually intelligent. It is possible for you to talk about emotional topics without losing your power of reason. That is difficult for many people to do." Toler didn't really know why she talked easily with him but took the opportunity to compliment her intelligence, which he did admire. She looked at him, her expression suggesting that she probably didn't accept as truth what Toler had just said but didn't think it important enough to pursue further.

They walked on, each lost in their own thoughts. Toler was aware of how much he liked Mary, and it was amazing to him that she was a member of a primitive culture. She made more sense than a lot of women he knew back on Bigor. Mary was resourceful and not overly dependent on him, maintained her own opinions, and was a good conversationalist. And to put the icing on the cake, she was a good-looking woman. He resisted the urge to compare her with Ahna. Better to let each excel in her own unique way on her own respective planet.

Mary thought her step was lighter, and she felt more attractive than before. It was quite flattering to her, a mere woman in a paternalistic and chauvinistic culture, that this unusual and attractive man found her company desirable. Other than Jesus, she had never talked with a man who liked her for her thoughts more than for her body. She could count on one hand the times she had ever laughed with a man, she had been laughed at, but not with. With most other men she had known, Mary always kept her sexuality hidden or else ready to use as an equalizer or as a manipulative ploy. That was her only source of power. With Toler that was not necessary, for he treated her with respect.

There was another who had treated her with respect. Sadness clutched her chest as she thought of Jesus. How she loved him! There had not been much time to think of him lately, and she knew that there was much unresolved grief to be dealt with. That would have to come later. There was too much to do now.

Martha had a friend whose sister lived in Jericho and a few discreet inquiries located her house. She was a friendly woman who was more than happy to take in friends of her sister. She enjoyed conversation, talked a lot, and, in Toler's opinion, would put anybody up for the night if they had ears and would sit still and listen to her.

The next morning found Toler and Mary on the road by daybreak. They had estimated a long day of steady travel would put them at Coreae by sunset. That would leave them two days of travel to reach Gennesaret.

"She was very curious about where we are going," Mary said of their hostess of the night before.

"You didn't tell her, did you?"

"Yes, you don't think I would be rude enough to tell her it was none of her business, do you?"

Toler stopped and stared at Mary. He was surprised that she had told anyone, especially someone as talkative as their recent hostess.

"I told her we were going to Ascalon to be picked up by a ship. Ascalon is a small town on the sea, to the southwest of Jerusalem by two full days." A smile played at the corners of her mouth.

"Why, you!" and Toler laughed with relief. "I feel like shaking you. My, but you gave me a start!" They walked on for a while, Toler still chuckling. "Say, lady, I think you like this spy business."

"It's different," she admitted with a wry smile.

Before noon they reached the wide flatland of the river bottom below Archelais. Mary had been watching the higher ground to their left.

"Can we go over there? I think I see some berry bushes. Berries would be a nice addition to lunch, don't you think?"

"That does sound good."

The detour to the berry bushes required about five minutes' walking time, and there they spent the next thirty minutes picking the fruit. The berries were ripe, juicy, and a sweet compliment to their meal, which they ate on the spot in a shady area overlooking the river. Crops of several varieties surrounded them, and people could be seen tending the fields.

"Toler, sometimes I want to hear more about you. You have never told me much about where you are from and what you did there and why you are here. I don't really know who you are." He opened his mouth to speak, but she put up a hand to hush his protestations. "If you cannot tell me, don't say anything. Please just do not hand me a convenient fabrication. I would feel insulted."

Toler lay back on the grass to think about Mary's statement. Before he could say anything, she grabbed his wrist.

"Look!"

Two men on horseback galloped to the north, leaving a cloud of dust behind them.

"It is unusual for men to be galloping their horses in the heat of the day unless there is an uncommon reason. Do you suppose they are looking for someone special?"

"Probably. Do you feel like someone special?"

"Maybe too special."

Long scimitars in the men's belts flashed in the sun. The sound of hoofbeats was muffled in the soft earth, and the horses and their riders appeared to glide soundlessly across the stretch of bottom land, their shapes almost ghostly as they shimmered through the heat waves.

"I still don't think they know where we are going. I've racked my brain. There is no way they could know unless they somehow knew Lish was from Gennesaret and figure we'll be going to meet him. But I don't think they know that Derxter saw Lish with Sarn and myself. But he had no reason to think he was one of us—"

Mary raised a brow. "One of you?"

Toler bit his lip. "A friend." Mary's expression said she did not believe him. "He's more than that. Please don't ask me to tell you more. Not now."

Mary nodded. She understood without understanding. There was something very different and special about Toler and Sarn and apparently this man Lish. Whatever it was, she half hoped she never found out what it was because it was likely more than she could comprehend. The same had been true with Jesus. He was different in a way she could never adequately describe. *Why am I always attracted by these different types?* she asked herself. *There is just no future with them!*

"If these guys knew where we were headed, I think they would have sent more than just two. Probably they have sent scouts in all directions just hoping to find us."

"Do you think they are the men of Derxter?"

"They have to be. No one else would be after us. I just can't believe he would disturb things like this. He has to be desperate for some reason. I never thought he would bring natives into the situation."

Mary continued looking at him strangely and then visibly put aside her curiosity. It was time for practical matters. "What is our plan if we are spotted by these two henchmen? Do you have a weapon?"

"No. Mine was stolen by a tour guide. Then I had Derxter's at one time, but I gave it to Lish. He said he could get rid of it." He shrugged, feeling silly.

"Why would you want to get rid of a weapon you could use for your own defense?"

Toler looked at Mary's quizzical face. "Sorry, but I can't tell you that either."

Mary shrugged. "What will we do if they spot us? Talk ugly to them?" Mary's sarcasm did not hide the anxiety she felt, and her insecurities were not helped by Toler's apparent indifference toward his inability to defend himself.

"I suppose we should arm ourselves. Do you know where we can get knives?"

"Probably in the marketplace at Archelais. Should I get one too?"

"Can you use one?"

"Probably as well as you, my fearless leader."

Toler grimaced. He had not instilled much confidence in his troop, he thought, and decided he should take more interest in the matter of self-defense.

"We'll get knives as soon as we can. Now let's get started. We'll stay close to the brush cover and keep our eyes peeled. Unless you have a friend or relative with whom we can stay, we'll have to find a place outside the town."

"No, Toler. We're on our own from here northward."

For the rest of the day Toler and Mary kept a close watch on the road ahead of them. Several people on foot passed, but they saw no one on horseback.

"Derxter probably figured we'd be walking and sent the horsemen ahead to wait for us. That gives them the advantage."

"Except," pointed out Mary, "that they don't know we saw them."

"Let's keep that advantage."

There was an hour of daylight left when they spotted Coreae in the distance. Leaving the river bottom for higher ground, Toler and Mary walked to the west of the town. They passed several farmhouses before choosing one. The farmer was suspicious of travelers, especially those off the main road. However, he took a liking to Mary and finally agreed to let them sleep in his barn and even fed them as a bonus.

In spite of their anxieties, the pair slept soundly after their hard day on the road. It was past dawn when they were awakened by the farmer feeding the chickens.

They bought food from him and thus found it possible to bypass Coreae altogether. The rough going across the countryside was partly compensated for by the scenic view. Toler enjoyed the hillsides with the farmhouses nestled on their slopes. Herds of sheep and goats occasionally dotted the landscape, and people tending their farms waved to them as they passed. On several occasions they stopped briefly for a drink of water and a word with the farmers.

Once Toler asked a farmer if he had heard any news of Jesus and his followers.

"I heard he was killed and his disciples went into hiding. That's all I heard. News doesn't get around much. Do you know any news?" The bearded man looked eagerly at Toler.

Mary spoke up, "Jesus rose from the dead and met with his disciples several times."

The farmer looked at Mary and then to Toler. "Is she telling the truth?"

"The tomb was found empty in spite of being guarded by the Romans. I have talked to people who saw him alive after his death." The man's mouth dropped open as Toler spoke.

"And I was one of them who saw him alive," Mary added. The man's mouth dropped open even farther, punctuating a rather florid gawk. Although such a claim sounded outrageous and defied belief, the farmer preferred to believe it. He would have something to tell his wife.

"Thank you for the water. We must go now," said Toler. He wanted to get away before the man started asking the many questions that were no doubt forming in his mind. He had enough information to pass on to interested neighbors but not enough for detailed stories. Unless he was creative.

"I suppose we should not bring up that topic again," Toler said after they left the man by his well, mouth still open.

"I know, but I feel disloyal letting people think Jesus was killed like a common criminal and that was the end of it. He was a great man—and a god too—and it just wasn't fair the way he was treated."

"You were very close, closer than I knew." Toler put his hand on her shoulder. "I wish I had known him better, but he was always so busy instructing his disciples and teaching. And I just hung around on the fringes of the crowd. I often thought he would make a good friend, but he seemed distant. Or I was distant. I don't know. It seemed like he was beyond me."

"He would have liked you too, Toler. Both of you are different from any man I have ever met."

"I hope you mean that in a positive way."

"Yes, of course. Neither of you put me down because I am a woman. Nor did you pressure me in any way. That is most unusual."

"You said he was a god, Mary. How was that? I thought he was an unusually intelligent and sensitive man, but I did not find myself thinking of him as a god."

"He told me. He was sent by his Father in heaven, he said. He did miracles. Real ones. He came back from the dead. What else does he have to do to be a god?"

"I'm not disputing the possibility that Jesus was a god, Mary. It seemed clear from the beginning that he had been placed here by some power—or god. I just never thought much about Jesus himself being a god. Anything I ever read about gods made it easy to know one when you saw one. They fly through the air on clouds, turn invisible, shoot rays from their fingertips, and stuff like that." He sighed. "But Jesus—he was a man for sure—at best, a mixture of God and man. Didn't you say you had met his mother?"

Mary nodded. "She is a sweet woman."

"And she is human, right? The way I understand things, a real god—someone who is only a god—doesn't have humans as his parents. The parents are gods too." It suddenly occurred to Toler that he didn't know what he was talking about. He had done no serious reading about gods and was only commenting from stories he remembered reading as a child. *Everyone knows what a god is, and yet no one knows one when they meet him,* he thought.

"Even though I cannot put into words exactly what he was," said Mary, "I know who he is, and that makes all the difference to me."

They planned to make it to the town of Scythopolis by the end of the day. Toler remarked that they had forgotten to obtain knives at Coreae and now would be unable to buy any before the next day unless they arrived at Scythopolis before dark.

"There is only one thing to do," said Mary, "and that is to be very careful. We must spot them before they spot us."

"I am hoping that they are still back at Coreae waiting for us to amble into town."

"But you know they won't stay there long. If this Derxter is as determined as he seems to be, they will go ahead of us again and wait. We must be watching behind us as well as ahead," she said.

The morning was uneventful, and they stopped to eat and rest in the shadow of a boulder on the river. Toler lay back on the grass for a short nap, and Mary excused herself and went back into the brush. The shade next to the river was cool and comfortable. It did not take long for Toler to drift off to sleep.

The sound of men's voices brought Toler out of his nap. He opened his eyes and without moving his head could see two men on camels approaching his resting place. Toler could not understand what was being said but decided to take no chances. He sat up and made a move to hide behind the boulder. He was too late.

One of the men said something to his companion and pointed at Toler who had frozen his position halfway behind the rock. The two men kept their animals coming toward the river while they warily kept an eye on him. Toler relaxed and eased back into full view of the men, casually covering his face. They apparently meant no harm, and it was better not to appear afraid. He squatted by the boulder and flipped a small rock into the water, trying to appear casual.

The camels went straight for the water's edge and drank. The two men kept their seats on the animals' backs and watched Toler. When the camels had their fill, one of the men gestured to Toler.

"Scythopolis?" and pointed to the north. He repeated himself before Toler realized the man was asking for directions.

Toler nodded and pointed upriver.

The two men waved appreciatively and headed their steeds toward the town of Scythopolis. As Toler watched them go, he heard Mary come up behind him.

"What a strange pair," she said. "Didn't you think so?"

"Oh? How was that?"

"They were barely able to stay on those camels. And their accent. He could hardly pronounce Scythopolis." She shrugged. "I suppose they are just traveling through the country, but I get spooked easily these days."

"We'll keep an eye open for those fellows too. If many more suspicious-looking people come by, we'll have to hire a scribe to keep track of all of them."

Resuming their trek, Toler and Mary talked little during the long and hot afternoon. About two hours south of their destination, they came to a small river flowing into the Jordan. It began in the highlands near Ginae and flowed easterly until it joined up with the larger river on the plain.

Mary stopped and, shading her eyes with open hand, scanned the flat area ahead of them. "I see someone. I think it's the two men we saw on the camels."

Toler could make out forms in the distance but could not identify them. "Your eyes are better than mine."

"They are off their camels for some reason," said Mary. "It does not look right to me."

As they drew closer, even Toler could discern that normality did not reign for the two men and their camels. One man stood and held onto the bridles of the two animals as if he was afraid to let go lest they run away. The other man sat on a rock rubbing his leg. He said something to his companion and gestured toward Toler and Mary. The first man glanced at them with little interest.

"I think they are having trouble with their rides," said Mary, "and it looks like the one has hurt his leg."

Toler suddenly and firmly took her arm. He began a wide detour around the pair.

"What is it?" she asked. "Do you want to help them?"

"No. Just come with me," he said through clenched teeth. He hoped it would not be too obvious that he was avoiding the two men. He raised his hand and pointed toward a hill.

"See! I told you that hill was there," Toler spoke loudly to Mary as he led her toward the rather common-looking knoll.

The two men watched them curiously for a while and then resumed their discussion about how to handle recalcitrant camels. When Toler thought they were safely away from the men, he released his grip on Mary's arm and slowed his pace.

"My, you are paranoid," she said. "Just two men who probably can't get their camels to cross the river with them, and one fell off." She looked at his face and saw that he was very serious. "What is it, Toler?"

"I saw something—a weapon in the man's belt. When he rubbed his leg I saw it—just like Derxter's. We must stay away from those men." A laser gun was the last thing Toler expected to see, but its shape and metallic glint were unmistakable. The man appeared to be unaware that he had pulled back his garment far enough to reveal the gun.

"Do you know for certain they are with Derxter? Is Derxter the only one with weapons like that?"

"No friendly party would have such a weapon. I'm afraid Derxter has armed the locals to come after us."

"If so, then how come they did not come after us when they had the chance two times?"

"I don't know. Maybe they didn't recognize us. One thing I know for sure: they're not anybody I know."

After walking away from the Jordan for a mile, they found a place where they could cross the tributary by stepping on strategically placed rocks. They continued northward and saw Scythopolis in the distance as darkness fell. Rather than look for a friendly farmer, they walked back into the trees and found a grassy spot. After a light meal, it did not take long for both of them to fall asleep, and both dreamed about two men on camels.

The next morning found them in good spirits and ready to resume their journey.

"Let's go through Scythopolis and buy a couple of knives," Toler said.

"Oh, why not just go around the town and avoid seeing anyone? Or being seen by anyone, I guess, is what I really mean."

"It was your idea about acquiring weapons. If you're satisfied being unarmed, it's all right with me. I'm not much good with weapons, anyway."

"Did you never have to defend yourself?"

He thought a moment. "No, guess I haven't ever been in that position until Derxter ambushed us at the river. A weapon would not have helped." The recollection of the beating was unpleasant. "I won't let him surprise me again, and in that case, I might need a weapon." The thought of having to tangle with Derxter while unarmed was a chilling thought. Toler realized he would have no chance at all. The man was a killing machine.

"Let's get some knives," said Toler.

They stayed off the main river road and approached the town from the west. Once into the village, they left the main street and worked their way on the backstreets to the center of town. Scythopolis was a sleepy, rural town with a small marketplace. The main asset of the town was the fact that it was a day's walk south from Galilee and a handy place to spend the night for those traveling to Jerusalem. Most of the people in the area lived outside of town and were self-sufficient on their small farms and with their herds of sheep and goats.

"Let's just stand here in the shadows and get our bearings," Toler said as they emerged from an alleyway into the town square. In the center of the square was a well. Scattered around the open area were carts filled with food and other products for sale. Before the morning was halfway over, the carts would be largely depleted and the sellers gone. Shopping was done early to avoid the heat.

Neither noted anything strange. Mary had picked out a shop likely to have knives for sale and was ready to leave their hiding place when Toler put his hand on her arm.

"I think our friends from the south are here."

"Which ones?" She followed Toler's gaze. Standing in a side street were the two horsemen they had seen on the road, behind them their steeds. Scraggly and unkempt, the two men looked over the marketplace as if searching for someone.

"They look mean!" she said.

Toler and Mary pulled back into the shadows and waited. The men seemed to be in no hurry to leave.

"Mary, can you walk over there and buy those knives? I doubt that they know what you look like, and if you are alone, with your face covered, they cannot possibly tell you from anyone else. Besides, you can hobble like a street beggar."

"Give me some money."

"If they spot you—or if anything happens—I'll meet you where we slept last night." He handed her several coins.

Mary walked into the square, stooped, and displayed a slight limp. Toler thought she would have made a fine stage actress. It occurred to him that he was watching the drama unfold as if he were in an audience watching a play.

So engrossed was he that Toler did not notice the two men come up the alley and stand beside him. The snort of a camel caught his attention, and he turned to find the two inept camel riders at his elbow. They were looking at the square and had apparently not recognized Toler, who quickly turned his face away from them. If they didn't recognize him the day before, they wouldn't today, he reasoned, and relaxed as much as he could.

Knowing that at least one of them carried a laser gun was disturbing. Toler could imagine an untrained native becoming excited and shooting up the place with the high-tech weapon.

Meanwhile, Mary ambled into the flow of people and made several stops at various shops. She bought some food, Toler was glad to see, and eventually made her way to the stall she thought might have knives for sale. The two horsemen maintained their vigil in the side street, and the camel men kept their positions beside Toler.

Toler had a feeling of unreality as he watched the drama unfold and had to bite his lip to keep from laughing out loud. He could no longer ignore the comical aspects of the situation. Mary was limping around trying to buy knives with which to defend herself while surrounded by two currish-looking horsemen with long swords on the one side of the square and on the other, two clumsy camel men with laser guns standing beside the pilot of a spaceship. And it appeared that no one knew anyone else. *This has to be the absolute height of incongruence,* thought Toler.

Mary completed her transaction and turned toward Toler. She immediately spotted the two camel men standing beside him. Instead of turning in the opposite direction, which might call attention to herself, she veered to her right, toward the street parallel to Toler's alleyway. Toler left the shadows of the alleyway and made to follow her. He had not walked far when he heard the clop of horses' hooves on the cobblestone. Glancing up, he saw the two horsemen walking toward him, leading their horses. He continued walking, hoping to appear as one of the local townspeople. Another glance at the horsemen found them staring intently at him.

"Toler?" one of the horsemen called across the square. It caught Toler by surprise; and he hesitated at the sound of his name, looked up, and then realized his mistake.

"You! Toler! Stop!" The men mounted their horses. Toler reached the street and ran, almost immediately tripping over an old woman. Sprawled in the street with the woman on top of him, Toler looked up into the leering faces of the horsemen with drawn swords.

"You are Toler! Get up. You come with us!" Toler was numbed. How could it be that he was suddenly a captive of these two sleazy men, no doubt sent to bring him back to Derxter? The thought of being taken to Derxter triggered an immediate and involuntary revulsion and fear. He would not do it! He would not allow himself to be taken to Derxter! He pushed the woman off him, stood, and found himself face-to-face with one of the horses. Reflexively he slapped the horse in the nose; and when it leaped backward, startled, Toler ran back into the square, dodging people and carts.

The horsemen barreled after him, swords raised above their heads. It would be a delight to them if they could justify killing him; they detested the thought of taking prisoners.

Toler leaped to the side just as a broad sword swished by his head. There was barely time to crawl under a cart before the second man made his pass, sword flashing in the sun. Toler crawled out from under the cart and ran as fast as he could toward the alleyway. He was halfway across the square when the horses again closed in on him. The swordsman screamed triumphantly as he raised the gleaming scimitar.

Through his blurred vision, Toler saw the two camel men standing impassively in the alleyway; then one raised his hand with a shiny object in it. There was a flash of light and a burning sizzle from behind Toler. The horse galloped past Toler with its rider tilting limply to one side. The man's hand opened, and the sword clattered on the cobblestones at Toler's feet. The swordsman's foot caught in his stirrups, and he bounced on the cobblestones like a sack of cabbages until his horse slowed to a walk. Everyone in the square stood still as the horse circled the market dragging his dead owner behind him. The second rider reined up and stared at the camel man with the gun and then at his comrade. He turned his horse and galloped down the street toward the city gates.

Even though his pursuer had been shot off his mount, Toler kept running at full speed and entered the street down which Mary had disappeared. He ran until his lungs felt they were bursting. A wagon full of hay suddenly appeared from a side street, and without thinking, Toler leaped at the hay, spearing it with his body. Pulling himself onto the wagon, he let the straw fall down over him. As far as he could tell, no one had chased him from the square; but once he had begun his run, he could not stop. Fueled by his uncontrollable fear, his body acted with a mind of its own.

Lying in the wagon fighting for his breath, Toler only then became fully aware of just how intense was his terror. He trembled uncontrollably, became aware of his wet crotch, and discovered he was crying. He hated himself for being so terrified.

Chapter 44

LAST LEG

Toler was not certain how long he had been in the hay wagon. Possibly he had dozed off; he was not sure. The warm, moist smell of freshly cut hay was all around him. Straw poked his neck and tickled his nose. Voices of gossiping women drifted from down the street. The sounds of an animal munching hay echoed unnaturally loud. The blurred forms of several people moved about the street not too far away.

The smell of urine and perspiration wafted over the aroma of hay, and Toler cringed in embarrassment. Eyes squeezed shut, he fought his fear. The threat of being captured by the man was enough to cause a veritable panic attack.

So what would you expect after the beating he gave me? Toler reasoned with himself. But there was something else besides fear; there was repulsion: Derxter was evil.

He remembered the camel man firing a laser at a pursuing horseman. The other horseman had stopped, not sure what to do. It seemed clear that the horseman and camel man were not members of the same team.

The horseman had to be Derxter's men, but if so, then who were the two men on camels? He ran the possible answers through his mind.

Had Lish entrusted the laser gun to friends and sent them south to keep a protective eye on Toler and Mary? That seemed doubtful since Lish did not know they were headed northward and pursued by Derxter.

Was it possible that someone had come across the laser gun by accident, fortuitously happened to be in the square at the time Toler was being chased down, and shot the horseman because he felt in danger himself? That seemed more plausible since the camel men obviously did not know Toler. Or if they did, they concealed their recognition extremely well. Toler wasn't satisfied with that explanation either, but he could think of no others.

Unless—he paused at the unlikeliness of the possibility—the camel men were agents from Sathel, sent to protect Toler. But if that was the case, then why hadn't Sathel said he was sending backup agents? And if Sathel later made the decision to send backups, after Toler could no longer be reached, then surely the agents would have been able to recognize him. Or would they? He had grown a beard and gained a suntan since being on Earth. If those were backups sent from Sathel, then Toler was indeed fortunate that the horseman called out his name.

Now he was most curious about the identity of the camel men.

He left the hay wagon, got his bearings, and made his way to the south of the city where he and Mary had agreed to meet.

She was waiting for him on the grassy knoll under a large tree and did not see him approach. Toler looked at her for a long time before he called out. Mary was a striking woman in any case, but Toler had not seen the softness of her beauty before that moment. Sitting on the grass, legs curled up beneath her, dark hair covering part of her forehead, she seemed quite feminine and vulnerable.

Mary looked up, uttered a cry of relief, and scrambled to her feet. She ran to him and spontaneously threw her arms around his neck. He was equally relieved to see her; and they embraced, feeling comfort in the warmth of the other, until Toler became uncomfortable and pulled apart. Mary looked up at Toler, eyes inviting, giving rise to conflicting emotions.

"I'm glad you're safe," he said, breaking the spell. "Sit down and tell me what happened."

They brought each other up-to-date on what had happened. Mary had encountered no problems after she entered the side street.

"I was going to wait for you to follow me down the street. But then I heard horses running and all this shouting and screaming. After a while things in the square seemed to calm down, and I made my way back to look for you. The camel men were gone. One horseman was lying dead on the ground with a ghastly wound in his chest. Several townspeople were gathered around his body, fascinated by the sight. I must admit I have never seen anything like it either. What caused it?"

"The horseman was about an inch from lopping off my head when one of the camel men killed him. You remember me telling you about the weapon I spotted on the camel man? That's how he made the hole in the horseman."

Mary was concerned and puzzled. "Who are these people? If the horsemen are Derxter's men, then who are the camel men?"

Toler shrugged. "I don't know. Do you have any ideas?"

To suggest that the camel men were Sathel's agents would only hopelessly confuse Mary and put him in the position of being overly evasive.

"No. But I'm glad they saved your life. Does that mean they are on our side?"

"I would not count on it. Right now there is not much I would count on. It's all pretty confusing."

"Perhaps your friend Lish can shed light on the situation."

Toler stood. "Let's go find out. But first I want a bath." He headed for the river. Mary watched him until he was out of sight among the trees. He was an unusual man, and she liked him more than she wanted to admit.

That night was spent on the road north of Scythopolis. An early start and a long day on the road placed them at the Sea of Galilee by the following day. Once Mary thought she saw the silhouettes of camels with riders ahead of them, but the sighting was not confirmed. There was no sign of the horseman or expect to see him. No doubt he had gone south as fast as his horse would carry him and reported to Derxter what had happened.

"Do you think Derxter will give up the chase?" Mary asked.

"No, he'll redouble his efforts. He can't let me go back home. Not if he expects to go home too."

"Your people are unusually ethical. I have never heard of punishing one's citizens because they abused their hosts while visiting another country. That is admirable, I am sure." Her expression said that the idea was so novel that she was not sure what she thought of it.

The afternoon was spent walking around the west bank of the Sea of Galilee. The view was beautiful, and they occasionally stopped to enjoy the panorama. The city of Tiberias spread on the hill overlooking the sea, its white walls and houses bright in the sunlight. Rather than enter Tiberias, the two passed to the west.

They traveled not too much farther north before they came to Magdala, nestled on the coast.

"Do you want to stop here?" asked Toler.

"No, there is nothing left for me here."

The sun was halfway across the western sky when they came to Gennesaret, located on the northwest shore of the Sea of Galilee. It did not take long to find someone in the village who knew where Lish lived. There was still an hour of light left when they found him sitting in the shade of his small house studying a scroll. He looked up as they approached, and a smile of welcome lit up his face as he recognized Toler. He gave an admiring look to Mary Magdalene.

"Welcome, my friend! Bring your companion and join me. Would you believe I was thinking of you today?" He gestured for them to sit in the shade of the building. "While you are resting, I will get you cool water to drink. You appear to be tired and thirsty."

"It is good to see you again, Lish," said Toler. "This is my friend, Mary Magdalene. And yes, we would like a drink of water."

The three talked until late into the night. Lish and Mary took an instant liking to each other, and by the time they ended their discussions for the night, they felt they had known each other for a long time. It was awkward for Lish and Toler to discuss some issues with Mary present, but she politely and patiently ignored their allusions to things she did not understand. Toler wished they could tell her the whole story, for she more than anyone they had met on the planet could have dealt positively with the fact that Earth was a stage for a deadly conflict between extraterrestrials.

But that would have been against the rules, and it was better not to complicate matters any more than they already were.

The next morning Toler and Lish rose early and had a chance to speak alone. They walked down to a ridge overlooking the Sea of Galilee where a few fishing vessels could be seen plying their nets in the blue water.

"Does she know anything?" Lish asked Toler.

"No. She is suspicious. She's too bright not to be. But she knows nothing. I think the idea of visitors from another planet is something so totally alien to these people that they would not believe it if you told them. She simply believes that we are from a faraway, very different land."

"Good." Lish had successfully hidden his identity for the many years he had lived on Earth. There were times, such as when he sat peacefully on the ridge with a full stomach and watched a sunset or when he sat with Aleah and her family at table, that he could easily forget that he had another life.

Lish knew that from a practical standpoint, it would be easier to continue on Earth than to pick up the threads of his previous life. Nevertheless, it was important to him to maintain the belief that one day soon he would be returning to Bigor with the results of important research.

"How soon do you think Derxter will be coming after us?"

"I figure about five days," said Toler. "It would take the horseman two days to return to Jerusalem, and it is about three days from there to here. Assuming the horseman returned. Those kinds of people have limited commitments."

"Unless they were promised great rewards or sure death."

"Or both, which is probably what Derxter did," said Toler. "Good pay if you do the job, death or worse if you don't."

Toler told Lish about the camel men and the laser gun. "What did you do with Derxter's gun? It occurred to me that someone may have found it after you tossed it away."

Lish was very puzzled. "No, I didn't just throw it away. I have it safely put away. Someday, when I'm on the lake, I'll drop it in, about the middle."

"Then you don't have any idea of who they were?"

Lish shook his head grimly. "If they are headed this way, maybe I'll find out. I'll keep my eyes open for two camel men."

"Who don't ride very well."

Lost in their own thoughts, the two watched the fishing boats for a while.

"What do you plan to do now?" asked Lish.

Toler shrugged. "Go home, I suppose. My job is done. I have collected the data Sathel wanted, and there is no reason to stay here."

"Which of the data will be of most importance to Sathel?"

"First of all, he will want a firsthand confirmation of the existence of a messiah. Second, he'll want as much detail as possible about what the Messiah did and said."

"Did you record what Jesus said?"

"No, we didn't want any devices on our bodies that could possible arouse suspicion if they were found. Sarn and I repeatedly talked about what Jesus said as sort of rehearsal for writing it down later."

Toler peered across the sea, lost for a moment in his thoughts of going home without Sarn. "I came to you because I thought you should be warned that your life is in danger if there is any way Derxter can trace you down. And, Lish, I thought you might want a ride home."

Lish watched the cloud bank gathering on the horizon. It looked like rain, but chances were that it would not. He tried to construct an image of what the horizon on Bigor looked like but could only get fuzzy outlines. It had been a long time.

"Yeah, well, I'm not sure it's time to return."

"Oh? From what you said before, you've now established what you came for."

Lish continued watching the cloud bank. Maybe it would rain. That would cool things off, help the crops. "It may not be time. Not yet."

Toler joined Lish in watching the clouds. Their reflection could be seen clearly in the lake and made a beautiful sight. Toler could understand what Lish was telling him: this is his home. Slowly, without Lish realizing it, Earth had become his home and Bigor his place of origin.

"I'll be leaving Gennesaret in the morning," said Toler.

"From where will you leave Earth?" asked Lish.

"A few days from here. Perhaps it's best I don't tell you just where."

"Right. I'll be careful, but you never know." They stood on the ridge for a while longer before Lish asked him about Sarn. "I suppose there is no hope for your friend?"

Toler looked at the ground and shook his head slowly. "Afraid not. I'll be leaving without him. Good kid."

"What about Mary Magdalene? Will she be returning to Jerusalem?"

Toler shrugged and raised his brows. "Ask her."

Mary had walked up behind them, unseen by Lish. "Ask me what?"

Lish turned, startled. "Oh, I was wondering what your plans are. Will you be returning to Jerusalem?"

Her eyes darkened. "I have thought about that. It will be hard to go back now that Jesus has gone. There are so many memories."

"Then why don't you stay here?" Lish's eyes were bright, and his smile begged her to say yes. "It gets lonely without good conversation, and you are a good talker."

Mary was flattered, but her glance at Toler made it clear where her allegiance lay. Toler caught the meaning and felt both pleased and disappointed. He had grown to like Mary very much, and he knew that if he stayed on Earth with her very long he would probably not want to go back. He and Lish could then form a colony of ex-Bigorites, he thought.

"I'll be leaving in the morning, Mary, back to my own people. You would likely be very happy here." He gestured toward the lake. "It's beautiful."

Her face fell. Toler would be going by himself, and he was inviting her to stay with Lish.

"I don't know. Maybe in a day or two."

"Why not give yourself a week here on the Sea of Galilee, a vacation designed to refresh and renew, and ending in a decision for the future?" Lish spoke in a phony salesman voice, which brought laughter from the others.

"All right. I'll stay for a few days." The three made their way back to Lish's house. There was still a great deal for them to talk about.

Late into the night they talked. Lish had a good supply of wine, and the conversation was mostly festive. Wine and friendships—they agreed nothing could be better. Mary kidded with them, an unusual trait for an Earth woman, but one the men enjoyed.

"If you are with Toler and somebody chases you, be ready. He runs very fast," Mary said with a smile.

While Lish chuckled, Toler frowned and looked down at his glass.

"I was just kidding you," said Mary.

"What? Oh, I know that I was just thinking about how scared I was the day in Scythopolis—when the horsemen almost captured me. They were going to take me captive to Derxter, and that really scared me. I would have died before allowing that to happen. And almost did."

"That was because of the beating he gave you, don't you think?" pointed out Lish.

"Partly. Mostly it was something else. Something to do with the kind of person Derxter is."

Mary nodded. "I know what you're going to say. He has an attitude about him—more than that, a presence. It's like he is the focal point for badness."

"The word that keeps coming to me is *evil*," said Toler. "I experience a total revulsion of the man. He is so completely evil that I find myself unnaturally frightened. *Terrified* is more accurate."

"Yes," agreed Mary. "Just as Jesus was the embodiment of all that was good, so Derxter stands for just the opposite."

"When a messiah appears, then a counterforce also appears," mused Toler.

"Things have to be kept in balance, you know," quipped Lish, "or we'd go spinning off into the far reaches of the unknown."

"Interesting point, Lish," Mary said. "Maybe things do have to be kept in balance."

"If so, then a messiah's appearance becomes a magnet for the arrival of an anti-messiah," Toler said.

"Or the opposite," said Lish. "Maybe the so-called anti-messiah was here first, and that's why the Messiah was called in." Lish thought about the contents of the document Aleah had brought him. The author of the ancient scroll had spoken about a force of evil being present even then. From his own experience, Lish knew that a malignant evil had been on the planet when he arrived, and that was years before Jesus made his move. Whoever was in charge of messiahs took their own sweet time in dispensing them.

"Where is a messiah when you need him?" Lish asked.

Toler left early the next morning after saying his good-byes. It had been hard to bid farewell to Lish and Mary, two people whom he had come to love. He was sorely tempted to change his mind and stay with them a while longer, each evening sharing the warmth of their friendship. Instead he turned, walked away, and did not look back. He knew that the longer he stayed, the harder it would be to make those good-byes.

The first day of his travel south was uneventful. Toler walked on the east bank of the Jordan because it was more deserted. He and Mary had used the road on the west side for their trip to Gennesaret as it was the more convenient. The less traffic he had to deal with, the more easily he could recognize Derxter and his men when they came north. Toler had no doubt that on the second or third day he would pass them. Most likely they would be traveling fast, but they would also be alert for anyone who appeared familiar, no matter which way he was going.

The night was spent restfully in a rented manger in Scythopolis. As he made his way south the next morning, he knew that he would have no more peaceful nights. From then on he would be watching nervously, trying to anticipate the time when his path would intersect that of Derxter the Dreaded.

In the afternoon of the second day Toler stopped off at the small town of Amathus where he bought food. As he shopped, he wondered if Mary had ever bought the knives she had set out to purchase in Scythopolis. On impulse he bought a knife from a man who was selling chickens. With only a four-inch blade, it was not much of a weapon, but Toler felt safer with it hidden in his belt.

Later in the day he reached a point across the river from Coreae and looked for a spot to bed down. Under a ledge was a hollowed-out place, and from the look of the dried droppings, sheep had found shelter there more than once. Toler brushed the litter out; sat down, back against the cool ground; and relaxed. It had been a long day, and he was tired.

From where he sat, Toler could see the lights of Coreae across the Jordan. It was here that the Jabbok River flowed from the east into the Jordan while another river, whose name Toler did not know, came from the west. From here southward to the Salt Sea, the Jordan would become wider.

It was not long before Toler noticed a group of travelers moving upriver on the west bank. He tensed and retreated back into the shadows of the overhang, although he was far enough away not to be seen. The band of eleven men stopped directly opposite him and set up camp. He could not see anyone resembling Derxter, and since these men were on foot, he was convinced they were not hostile. However, these men had been traveling hard, which would raise the possibility they were in pursuit of someone.

After a while they gathered inside their tent, and Toler became even more curious about who these men were. If this was Derxter's posse and he could get past them now, he would not have to worry about them anymore. By the time they could pick up his trail in Gennesaret and follow him back down to Jerusalem, he would be gone from Earth.

After a while the camp settled down for the night and Toler crossed the river. Except for a deep place in the middle, he was able to wade most of it. The camp had posted no guard, and all the men were in the large tent. Toler made his way to the back and put his ear to the side. There were several voices speaking at once, some of them excitedly.

"I still think this is a wasted trip! Who wants to travel all the way to Damascus?"

"There is a job to be done. Listen! Think about this a minute. Suppose that they build a stronghold in Damascus. When they get strong enough, they'll start taking over other villages. Where will it end?"

"Saul, you are overestimating these people. That is the foolish part. Their leader has been killed. They claim he returned from the dead, and now they want to meet together and play church. So what? Let them! They bother no one!"

Clearly having lost his temper, Saul bellowed back, "You are in charge of keeping the church pure just as the rest of us are. We must purge these splinter groups, or they will dilute the one church, and none of us will enjoy the power that comes through singleness of purpose."

"But all the way to Damascus?"

"Yes, and farther than that, if necessary!"

Satisfied that the group had no relation to Derxter, Toler returned to his shelter across the river. Before drifting off to sleep, he shook his head in wonderment at the conversation he had overheard. *People just won't leave one another alone,* he thought.

He wondered what Peter was doing these days. If he was in Damascus, his connection to the Messiah might turn out to be a costly affair. As he drifted off to sleep, he was trying to remember what the book said about messiahs starting things and not finishing them.

Chapter 45

LISH AND MARY MAGDALENE

The clear and sunny morning was cooled by the breezes blowing off the Sea of Galilee. Lish, Mary Magdalene, Aleah's mother, Darene, and two of her children leisurely made their way to Gennesaret. They had started out along the town road, but Mary asked if they could go down the hill and walk along the water's edge. She exclaimed that this had to be the most beautiful lake in the world.

It was this side trip that prevented Derxter from finding Lish and Mary Magdalene as they made their way to Gennesaret.

From the cove, Lish and his friends walked along the shoreline toward town. It was a pleasant stroll, and several times they stopped to watch fishermen repairing their nets.

They came into Gennesaret on the waterfront. One large dock protruded into the lake like a thick thumb, and onto this the fishermen unloaded their baskets of fish. The fish were then carried to the market building on shore. It was there that the buyers came each day to inspect the fresh catches. It was a busy place with a good deal of quibbling over prices. Lish and his party were enjoying the activity of the market when a man walked up to him.

"Lish, how are you this day?" said the man.

"Well, my friend, Droka, how are you? Let me introduce you to a very good friend of mine. I think you know this other lady and her terrible children." Darene made a mock scowl while Lish made the introductions and asked Droka how he was doing.

"I am doing as well as old legs and sore knees will allow," he said. He was becoming infirm with age, and if occasionally someone would ask how he was and then let him list at least one of his infirmities, he was satisfied. *What more can a man ask?* he told himself. *No one wants to hear about my aches and pains, but if I can sometimes mention them without being told to shut up, then I feel much better.*

Droka asked if he could speak privately with Lish. Lish excused himself and followed Droka to a corner of the building.

"Someone is looking for you, my friend," said Droka solemnly.

"This man asked for you this morning in the square. He got directions to your house not long ago. I came here from town and was surprised to see you. Did you come here by the shoreline?"

Lish nodded. "Who was it?" He was afraid he already knew.

"A big man was the leader, but he did not give his name. There were perhaps fifteen riders with him. I did not like the looks of them, and I worried for you."

"Did they go to my house?"

"I think so. They left in that direction."

"Thank you, Droka. You are a good friend." Lish rejoined the others.

"We must leave now." He led them outside and said to Darene, "You must go stay with someone in town—your sister—until you hear from me again."

"But—" Darene was alarmed, but she trusted Lish and protested no further.

"Take the children with you. Do not go back home until you hear from me. Do you understand?" Lish looked at her firmly, for she was sometimes a willful woman.

"Yes, Lish," and she clucked to her children to go with her.

Mary read the concern in Lish's face and dreaded to hear what he would say. The past several days had been some of the happiest she had ever known, and she hated for them to come to an end, especially if by the hand of Derxter.

"Is it Derxter?"

"Yes. He was in town asking about me. He got directions to the house and is probably there right now."

Mary was truly alarmed. "Aleah is there by herself! We must go help her!"

"I'm afraid we're already too late for that. I just hope she recognized him and hid. She saw him before when he was chasing Sarn. Aleah is no fool. She knows danger when she sees it."

"I hope you're right. Can't we go see?"

Lish and Mary retraced their steps on the shoreline. They planned to approach the house from the southeast, directly from the Sea of Galilee, rather than from the road that ran south from town to the house.

As they made their way up the hill, moving from one clump of plant cover to another, Mary found herself caught up in the excitement of the moment and moved with a grace and speed she did not know she possessed. Lish was impressed with her agility and had to hurry to prevent her passing him.

At the top of the hill a grove of olive trees bordered the road from town. They kept the trees between them and the road as they followed it toward Aleah's home. Soon they could make out the house through the trees. As they drew nearer, the sounds of men swearing and throwing things became audible.

"I'm afraid they're wrecking my place," Lish said grimly.

"Look! Some of them are coming this way!" They crouched down behind the bushes as several of the men rode up to Aleah's house. They dismounted and knocked heavily on the door. When there was no answer, the door was kicked in. Within seconds the men began destroying the inside of the house.

Lish was livid. "There is no reason for that!" he said more loudly than he intended.

"Except to distract you while we came up behind you!" bellowed Derxter from behind and below. Two men stood beside him, knives in hand, and laughed heartily, their curling lips framing rotten teeth. "We saw you coming up the hill, you fools."

"It was me what saw you," chortled one of the men. "I was the lookout down there—" He was cut off by Derxter's backhand across his face.

"Shut up, you fool!"

The man was lifted off his feet by the force of Derxter's blow. He sailed through the air for an inordinately long time because he was going downhill. The second man, startled, turned to watch as his comrade hit the ground and rolled down the hill.

"Catch him! Catch him!" the man shouted hysterically as he pursued his rolling companion.

At the instant the second man turned his attention to the first man, Lish grabbed Mary's arm and whispered urgently, "Run."

Lish ran down the hill, but on a line angling away from their would-be captors. Mary passed him, and the two sprinted at top speed across the slope of the hill. The ground was rocky and treacherous, but they were uncaring as their fear propelled them down the slope toward the Sea of Galilee.

Meanwhile, in his effort to stop his companion from rolling down the hill, the second man lost his balance and fell on the first. Together they rolled down the hill, a tangle of arms and legs aided by the many round rocks on the hillside.

Derxter, face red, looked as if he might explode. He stepped up to the road and called out to the others, and within moments his men were in pursuit of Lish and Mary. Derxter himself bounded down the hill and in passing kicked at the two benumbed men who had rolled into a dazed heap against a boulder.

"Catch them, you fools! Spread out!"

Another man lost his footing on the rocky ground, twisting his ankle. The others slowed from their initial onslaught of the hill as did Derxter. Instead of pursuing directly down the hill, they began moving along the slope parallel to the lake in an effort to form a net around the two fugitives, thus forcing them down to the shore.

From his vantage point, Derxter occasionally glimpsed Lish and Mary as they neared the bottom of the hill. He thought the pair was stupid for having gone directly to the water, allowing him to cut off their escape along the shoreline. That was their only chance, after all. If they could have reached the village and rallied a few townspeople, it would have been difficult to take them without an extremely ugly scene.

Unless he had his laser gun. Then it would have been simple. Derxter had hoped that his men would find the weapon in Lish's house but had met with no success. Perhaps the man had disposed of the weapon as he had told Toler he would, but Derxter doubted it. The temptation to hang on to the laser gun in a primitive society would be great. The promise of instant power—if ever needed—would be too tempting for anyone to ignore.

But now he didn't have to worry about Lish making it to the village because he and his friend were trapped on the shoreline. After they were caught, it would be a simple matter to get the gun from Lish by torturing the woman while he watched. He motioned for his men to move farther down the hill and close the net.

Mary and Lish reached the shore and headed north toward town. They had not gone far when they came across a fisherman who was about to put out into the lake.

"Andros!" called Lish.

The fisherman turned and regarded Lish and Mary. "Why, it's Lish and his lady friend. How are you on this beautiful morning? Say, I heard some shouting up the hill a few minutes ago. Do you know anything about it?"

"Andros, we must have your help!" Lish gasped, trying to catch his breath. "There are terrible robbers and thieves coming down the hill after us. We are surrounded!"

"They have already torn up Lish's house. And Darene's too," Mary added. "They will probably tear up your boat."

Andros's face switched from horror to anger and back to horror as he listened. He glanced up the hill and then at his boat. "Quick! Get in my boat. We will make a run for it."

The three pushed the boat away from the shore and clambered aboard. Andros hoisted the sail and sought to catch a breeze. Lish picked up an oar and rowed. Mary looked for a second oar while Andros played with the sail and rudder, trying to get some movement.

"Ah! There it is. Not much but a little. Maybe we will find a better wind." The craft, about twenty-five feet in length, had a single mast with a square sail attached to a crossbar, which was raised by rope and pulley. Andros was able to handle the boat by himself, although it was tedious rowing if the winds failed him.

Andros's fishing boat moved slowly out into the lake. Derxter stared, disbelieving his eyes. There were three figures in the boat, and two of them bore an amazing resemblance to Lish and Mary Magdalene. Uttering curses, he ran down the hill and called his men. Within a short time they were gathered on the shoreline watching the sailing vessel move slowly away from them, carrying their quarry with it.

About fifty yards down the coast was a fisherman mending his nets. He sat on a piece of driftwood, lost in the concentration required to repair the tears in his nets. Since he was hard of hearing, his attention had not been drawn by the shouting from the hillside; and he continued to work, silently cursing the submerged rocks and limbs that almost daily created this wretched job.

He did not notice when Derxter and his men appeared along the shoreline and made for his boat, which was anchored just offshore. A few minutes later he happened to look up, only to see his fishing boat, loaded with strange men, moving away from the shore. Mouth open, he stood and stared. What was he to do? He hurled an insult after the thieves, threw down his net, and strode toward town.

Lish had little optimism that they would escape unnoticed but hoped to gain a lead. They had traveled about sixty yards from shore when Andros spotted the other boat.

"They have taken Vater's boat!" Andros spoke bitterly, for fishing boats were prized possessions and the key to one's livelihood. A person who would take away one's tools of his trade was to be despised.

Vater's boat was roughly the same size as that of Andros. There was no skilled sailor aboard, but there were two oars and many strong arms. In the light breeze Vater's boat began to make some gain. After a while the distance between the two boats had been cut to half. Lish was not only growing tired, but rowing with one oar was inefficient; he had to keep changing from one side of the boat to the other in an effort to keep the course straight, a time-consuming and tiring process in itself.

"It is too bad I have only one oar," said Andros as he squinted at the sail. "One of mine broke. I should have replaced it, but I told myself, *I am only one man, so why do I need two oars?*"

"How is it that Vater has two oars in his boat?" asked Mary.

Andros shrugged. "I don't know. Maybe he takes his son-in-law with him to help row when there is no wind. It would be good if that son-in-law could do at least something."

Mary stood by Andros in the stern, trying to stay out of the way. "Isn't there any way I can help? They are getting closer."

Andros had intended to sail down the coast to one of the villages where help could be obtained. However, because of the light wind, he had been unable to make much progress; and when the pursuing boat appeared, Andros felt compelled to sail in whatever direction the wind was favorable.

Vater's boat had drawn even closer, and Mary could clearly see two of the men in the bow. One had drawn his sword and held it ready for boarding while the other leered at her across the water. Mary shuddered.

"I don't see Derxter," said Lish, struggling with the oar.

Mary looked again. Vater's boat was close enough now that all the faces could be clearly seen.

"I don't see him either," she called back. "He must have stayed onshore."

The straining and grunting of the men in Vater's boat could be clearly heard across the water. The two men in the bow readied for boarding as the gap between the two craft narrowed. When only ten feet separated them, one of the men crouched on the side, sword drawn, ready to leap.

"Kill the sailor first!" called one of his comrades. "Then it will be easy to capture the others."

"You'll have to catch us first!" muttered Andros just as a gust of wind filled the sail. It was at that exact moment the boarder with drawn sword decided to jump. He made a good leap and landed on the railing of Andros's boat. The sudden wind moved the boat from under him a slight bit, enough to cause him to lose his balance. Waving his arms wildly, he struggled to grab onto something but was hit in the face with a fishnet. He tried frantically to unwrap the net from his head and keep what balance he had. He dropped his sword just as a sudden poke in his chest sent him backward into the water. He surfaced in time for Vater's boat to crack his head and run over him.

"Aaaahaha!" cheered Andros as the wind continued to pick up. "That was close! And look, we now have us a weapon." He picked up the sword and holding it above his head shook it at Vater's boat. "Where are you pirates now?"

Mary sat down, pale. "I'm sorry I threw your net overboard. I didn't know what else to do!"

"Not to worry," said Andros. "You make a good team. One throws the net. The other pokes him with the oar. The man falls into the sea and leaves us a knife. That is a good trick you do. Have you practiced long?" He laughed at his wit and was very relieved they had not been caught.

Lish sat down beside Mary, put an arm around her shoulders, and together they watched their pursuers. First the rowers began putting on the brakes so they could recover the man overboard. At the same time the wind picked up, filled the sail, and left the man farther behind in spite of the rowers' efforts. The rowers then tried to make a circle and come back for their companion, who was still entangled in the net and floundering badly. The other men, however, seeing the wind come up, promptly forgot the man in the water and turned the rudder toward Andros's ship.

"After them!"

"But Nazrof is still in the water!"

"Forget Nazrof! There is no reward for catching him!"

By the time Vater's boat resumed its chase, Andros had picked up a full sail of wind and was expanding their lead.

Although the pursuers had rowers in addition to the sails, they did not know how to take full advantage of the wind.

Lish and Mary found themselves laughing at the spectacle behind them. "Did they ever pick up the man?"

"I don't know. Did you ever see anything so disorganized?" In the next hour they had no reason to laugh. The men in Vater's boat gradually began to understand how to handle the sailing and coordinate it with the rowing. Once more they were closing the gap although not as quickly as before.

In order to take full advantage of the wind, Andros directed the boat straight from shore. Both boats were nearly in the middle of the lake when suddenly the wind died and Andros's boat sat still in the water.

Lish picked up the oar and began rowing again.

"Wait! We're getting another wind!" Andros was right, but the wind had changed and now came from the opposite direction. The sail picked up, and the boat began turning to accommodate the easterly wind. In a moment they were headed toward Vater's boat and picking up speed.

Lish and Mary watched, dumbfounded. It did not make sense that they should race toward the other boat. "What are you doing, Andros?"

"We take a chance, see? The lake has lots of little winds that come and go, this way and that. We have one now, a good one that takes us back to the west. And they don't have one. Not yet." Andros pointed to the water behind and immediately around them.

"See the water? You can tell where the wind is by looking at the surface. The wind is friendly to us right now, and I don't see any gathering in their direction. So we take a chance."

They studied the shimmering of the water. If they kept their heading at their present speed, it appeared they would miss the other boat about twenty-five yards. If the wind also caught up Vater's boat, then it would have to be turned around before coming in pursuit. Hopefully by then they would have enough of a lead to make it back to Gennesaret.

And Derxter.

Andros steered toward Vater's boat at an angle that used half the wind. The men shouted and waved their fists. Several of them leaned over the side of the boat, ready in case they drew close enough to board. The helmsman veered the boat slightly in an effort to intercept Andros. For a few minutes the two craft were on a collision course, which brought even more shouting from the men on Vater's boat.

And then, like the experienced sailor he was, Andros cut his rudder to the right. The boat turned, and the sail billowed with a full pocket of wind, causing them to leap forward. They came abreast of Vater's boat and then past it, missing by about five yards. The wind spilled against the pursuing ship, which unfortunately for them was headed in the wrong direction. Certain that the two craft would collide in midlake, the rowers had laid down their oars in order to be part of the boarding party.

By the time the men on Vater's boat had reorganized enough to turn around, Andros had almost a hundred-yard lead. Over the next two hours the wind came and went, allowing Vater's boat to gain on them.

"Do you think we'll make it?" asked Mary.

"Who knows? This wind is so unreliable that it's hard to tell."

At one point Vater's boat was within ten yards and gaining, but another breeze appeared, and because of Andros's superior handling skills in the lighter boat, they were able to increase the lead. The game of cat and mouse continued, with Andros becoming increasingly anxious and the pursuers growing more frustrated.

"There is one good thing," Andros announced. "The winds continue to take us to the west."

"How is that good?" asked Mary.

"Look!" answered Andros and pointed ahead of them.

Mary and Lish turned. About a mile away there were several boats with sails down.

"Who are they?" asked Mary.

"My friends!" Andros said proudly, fist to this chest.

Lish stood and shaded his eyes. "Yes, I can recognize several of the boats. They are fishermen from Gennesaret."

The men in Vater's boat also spotted the fishing boats ahead but did not give as much significance to their presence as did Andros. It was the wrong time of day for the fishermen to be on the lake fishing, Andros knew, and the boats were waiting for him to come to them.

The wind slowed for several minutes, barely pushing the boats along. It was a time that gave Vater's boat the advantage because of their oarsmen. This had happened several times, but the wind had picked up before the gap closed to less than ten yards.

This time, however, the wind did not start up when the gap closed to thirty feet. When there were eight yards between the craft, the men on Vater's boat crowded to the bow and leaned out, cursing and threatening. Having decided that his lopsided efforts at rowing were slowing them more than helping, Lish stood with the oar poised as a weapon. Mary had another bundle of fishnet ready. Andros held the sword in one hand and the rudder in the other. Occasionally he laid the sword down so he could tender the sail to a more efficient angle. There was nothing else they could do to get ready for what appeared to be an imminent boarding.

"I'll fight to the death rather than be captured by Derxter's men!" muttered Lish.

Mary nodded. She was not sure but thought that death would be preferable to capture.

One of the more daring pirates pushed his way to the bow. His more cautious comrades made way for him, eager for a triumph of some kind. The man placed his dagger between his teeth, held on to a rope with one hand, and leaned forward, readying his leap. The other men cheered him on.

For the next few minutes the race became a chess game between the two helmsmen. Twice the gap was small enough for the leap to be made; but each time, just as the man bunched his legs for the jump, Andros veered away. This had the effect of momentarily widening the gap and costing the would-be boarder his balance as his boat too changed course.

The third time the pursuers pulled close enough for a boarding attempt, there was about an eight-foot gap. The helmsman of Vater's boat had been roundly cursed by his crew for having allowed them to be outmaneuvered twice before. This time he was determined not to be fooled. He carefully watched Andros, trying to anticipate when the old sailor would veer.

"I think the helmsman is going to veer with you this time, Andros," said Lish. "He's watching you like a hawk."

"So? Let him watch. I watch too. I watch that ugly man with the knife in his mouth."

The man was coiled on the bow, leaning forward, his eyes gauging the distance between the two boats. The other men urged him to jump as the distance narrowed by another foot. He bunched himself for the leap, and at that instant Andros made a shoulder fake to the right, as he had done twice before, while, in fact, he pushed the rudder to the left with all his strength. Two things happened in the split second following Andros's deceptive move: the helmsman in Vater's boat veered sharply to the right, and the boarder leaped out from his boat.

The leaping man seemed suspended in air before landing flat on his belly in the lake. When he surfaced, the knife was still in his mouth. As his boat passed, he grabbed an oar and held on; he was determined that he would not be left to drown as Nazrof had been. His weight caused the boat to swing around, resulting in an even louder uproar. The men had been cursing the helmsman for his error but now turned their attention to pulling in the swimmer and resuming the pursuit.

By the time the men on Vater's boat had reorganized, Andros was within hailing distance of the fishing boats. And by the time Vater's boat had joined the pursuit, Andros was among the fishing boats, which pulled in to make a protective circle.

"How is the fishing?" one of the men called to Andros. "Or is it racing you have taken up?"

"Only with a bunch of thieves!" Andros said in disgust.

Vater's boat gained quickly now that Andros had stopped among the other boats. When they were a short distance away, the spokesman for the crew called out to the fishermen.

"Move aside! It's only the man and woman we want. The rest of you can go free."

Andros said to the other fishermen, whose boats had come in closer, almost within touching distance, "Now they don't want me. My feelings are hurt."

"Mine too," said another.

"What's wrong with us that you don't want us too?" shouted someone.

"We're coming in! All we want are those two! Move aside, and we'll cause no trouble!"

"Say, whose boat do you have there?" someone called out.

"That's my boat!" yelled Vater from one of the boats. "You men get off my boat this very minute!"

The men on Vater's boat were becoming confused and unsure of what they should do. After a brief conference, they continued rowing toward the fishermen while they prominently displayed their knives and swords.

"Here we come! Just move over!"

A fishing boat blocked their way. "Move that boat, or I'll move it for you!"

"Did you hear that? The man is courteous now. He wants to move my boat for me."

One of the men on Vater's boat lost his temper and jumped into the fishing boat, knife drawn. There were three fishermen waiting for him, and others were on their way, leaping from one boat to another. All of them carried clubs. In all there were twelve fishing boats carrying about fifty men.

"Let's get out of here!" commanded the leader on Vater's boat. The oarsmen began rowing backward until someone noticed they were surrounded.

"This is your last warning!" called out the leader.

His warning was drowned out by laughter from the fishermen.

"Let me give you a warning, my brave man. You and your men will have to give up poor Vater's boat. How do you expect the deaf old man to make a living? We will escort you back to port."

"You can't push us around! Move aside and let us go!" Thoughts of taking Lish and Mary back to Derxter for a bonus were now replaced by thoughts of just getting back to shore in one piece. The leader craned his neck as he looked at the shoreline, seeking Derxter, not sure if he wanted him to be there or not.

"Would you like a demonstration of being pushed around?" The fishermen began moving in, clubs at the ready. Sure-footed from a lifetime of being on the water, they moved from one boat to another with ease, a sight that intimidated Derxter's gang.

It did not take long to convince them that they were better off allowing themselves to be taken back to Gennesaret. By the middle of the afternoon, the flotilla had come into the harbor, where many townspeople crowded the dock. Once Mary thought she saw Derxter duck behind a house, but she was not sure.

"Andros, may I use that sword by your side? I have to return home, and I'm afraid there may be danger waiting there."

Andros handed him the weapon. "Wait until we've tied up, and I'll go with you. There is no reason for you to go by yourself."

"Me? What about you? You have been most courageous and a brilliant sailor on top of that! I don't want you in any more danger on my behalf."

"Ha! Don't worry about me. It was exciting, and my grandchildren will enjoy hearing about it. Besides, I will ask others to join us, so none of us will really be in danger."

After docking, Andros recruited two other men to accompany them to Lish's house. They were about to leave the dock when shouts caught their attention. A fight had broken out on the dock after Derxter's men had come off the boat. Not knowing what kind of punishment the people of Gennesaret reserved for thieves and not wanting to stay around and find out, they made a break for freedom. Catching the fishermen off guard, several of the men were able to escape. Others were subdued and bound after fights, which resulted in several serious wounds. Fortunately no one was killed. Enraged at this apparent assault on their peaceful village, the fishermen thought long and hard about how they might torture their captives.

Andros, Lish, and the others hurried back to the fracas; but it was settled by the time they got there. The town leader, Shamil, had taken charge and spoke loudly to the townsmen, "We should track down those who escaped. Otherwise they will be breaking into homes and stealing whenever they have the chance. We will hunt for them until we are at least satisfied the thieves have left Gennesaret and surrounding area."

There were shouts of approval from the crowd. The thought of a thief sneaking into someone's house that night was enough to mobilize the community into action. When someone pointed out that he wasn't leaving his family alone until the thieves had been caught, there was another wave of enthusiasm. Shamil then organized the men.

Afterward Andros and Lish found themselves part of a sweep operation whereby it was hoped the thieves would be flushed out if they hadn't already left the area. Similarly the women were also organized so they could assist one another in the event one of the thieves appeared at their homes.

"Looks like we won't be going to your house tonight," said Andros.

"I'll ask Shamil if I can be part of the group that searches in that direction. I must find out what happened to Aleah."

"We didn't see her this morning," said Mary. "I think she got away. When those men went into Darene's house and tore things up, we would have heard her scream if she had been there. I think she left when she saw them go to your house. That's what I would have done."

"You're probably right, but I still want to be in that group. I know the area better than the others, and that would be a help."

Lish approached Shmil and had no problem getting himself assigned to the group that would search south of town.

"Just be careful, Lish. Those men may still want you."

"I'll be careful. I'm not worried about those men who were in the boat. They're totally disorganized now. But I am worried about their leader. He still wants me now more than ever."

Chapter 46

Sᴀʀɴ Lᴏsᴛ

Water from the well was cool on Sarn's parched lips. Standing in the shade of spreading tree fronds, he again lifted the cup to his mouth. The water level of the well was several feet below its rim, and a rope attached to a wooden bucket dropped loosely over the rock ledge. Once his thirst was quenched, Sarn turned his attention to the date trees. Since being on Earth, he had learned to eat the fruit, even though it was too sweet to suit him. Under the circumstances, he thought they were delicious and ate until he was nearly ill.

He sat beneath a tree and listened to the quietness of the oasis. The sun filtered through the motionless fronds and made an intricate ribbed pattern on the ground. His tired body began to relax and mold itself into the sand.

A fly lit on Sam's nose. He swatted at it with his hand, and it directed its attention to his feet, circling just out of Sarn's reach.

All right, which foot will it be? Since you, fly, are no fool, you'll land on the left one, the one out of the sun. Sarn didn't recall talking to himself in a long time maybe since he was a kid. The stress of being lost together with the pressure of a new assignment on a strange planet was enough to make anyone talk to himself, Sarn reasoned. Not to mention the thugs who tried to kill him. And don't even consider the emotional drain of dealing with a pretty girl.

And let's ignore all the trouble that Jesus had caused.

No sir, there is nothing to be upset about. Nothing at all.

Sarn watched the fly. *And you, my little friend, will find out about stress in just a short time 'cause I'm gonna get you.*

The fly made two false landing approaches on the sunny foot, lifted off, and made a nice pinpoint landing on the big toe of Sam's left foot. Before the fly could turn around, Sarn had swung his head cloth at the insect. The fly easily dodged the cloth, which possessed the velocity of a parachute, made a circle over Sam's head, and indigantl disappeared to the other side of the well.

You were lucky that time!

There was no breeze, and the fronds hung motionless on the trees. There was no sound, and it occurred to him that this was probably the quietest place he had ever experienced. It was interesting for a while, but then the silence became annoying.

If I have to make my own sounds, well, I'll do it. The thought that he needed noise was absurd, and yet Sarn knew it was true. *Where is a shrieking native when you need one?*

He opened his mouth to sing and found his lip trembling and his eyes filling with tears. Face turned upward to the sky, he poured forth the sobs of loneliness and fear. In some ways Sarn was still a little boy, and he was lost in the desert on a faraway planet. He cried himself to sleep.

Sarn woke up enough to notice the sun was almost behind the horizon. The pink-and-gold colors were beautiful but not impressive enough to prevent him from falling asleep again. It was two hours before dawn when he woke again, feeling rested but thirsty. After quenching his thirst, he again looked for a container in which to carry water but found none. The bucket was briefly considered, but it leaked too badly. He placed a supply of dates in a cloth, soaked it in water, and wrapped it with a fold of his robe. He knew it would dry out in the heat of the day, but it would provide him with some food, and he could wring some moisture from the cloth.

With a last look at the oasis, Sarn walked in the direction where the sun had set the night before. The stars were still visible, and he made a note of their positions. Surely he could count on them for the short time before dawn. There was enough light to see the rise and fall of the dunes but not much else. The air was dry and cool, and Sarn felt good. It was only after he had walked for a while that his mind came clear.

Sarn recalled the terror of being held under the water and losing consciousness. He could not remember much else after that except for vague recollections of steady and tired walking. He was not certain how long he had been on the road but reasoned it must have been at least a day, maybe two. He was not sure where he was but thought he should travel to the west. There was a sea, not villages as he had erroneously recalled the day before, and from there he could get his bearings.

He had no idea what had happened to Toler and Mary Magdalene. Probably his best bet was to find his way back to Jerusalem and locate the disciples. Perhaps they could help him find Toler.

Why was it that life never seemed to go right for any length of time?

The sun came up behind Sarn, and he chased his shadow for several hours. At late morning he opened his package of dates. The cloth was still wet, and after eating dates, Sam sucked moisture from the fabric. He continued walking, the sun growing hotter each minute. After two more hours of trying not to think of the wet cloth under his robe, Sam again pulled it out and sucked moisture. It tasted so good that he wanted to put the whole cloth in his mouth and chew on it until it was as dry as his mouth now felt.

By late afternoon Sarn was certain that his brain was frying in his skull. He could no longer think clearly or focus on a thought for any length of time. All his energies had to be concentrated on walking westward, one foot ahead of the other.

About three hours before sundown Sarn was convinced that he would not survive. He longed to just let his body yield to gravity, fall headlong into the sand, and never have to move again. He had eaten half of the dates but could not stand to eat more of the sweet fruit without water.

Another hour passed before Sarn saw the sea. At first he thought it was a mirage and then had trouble seeing it because of the sun's glare. He was elated and knew then that somehow he would keep on until he reached the water.

Dusk came, and he seemed no closer to the sea. Perhaps it was a mirage, he fretted as the light began to fade. Sarn had presence of mind to look at the emerging stars for a bearing, but it was difficult to focus his vision. Soon it would be dark, and he doubted his ability to maintain a heading toward the sea.

Sarn plodded on, exhausted, thirstier than he had ever been in his life. In this stupor he did not care if he lived or died. He was no longer capable of holding a straight course, but the downhill grade and his own will kept him headed toward the sea.

Sarn had no idea how much time passed before he felt something cold against his feet. Sarn looked down to find that he was standing calf deep in the surf, waves gently pulling against him. He sat down, feeling the waves wash his chest. Lowering his mouth, he let a wave fill it with cool but salty water; he could swallow only a little, but he knew that he would now survive.

Refreshed, Sarn stumbled back to the shore. He was sorely tempted to lie on the beach and be cooled by the wet sand. Maybe he could keep going for just a little while longer, he told himself, and continued walking until his body simply gave out and collapsed onto the sand.

The sun had been up two hours when Sarn awakened. His throat and mouth were parched, and he felt nauseous, but otherwise he seemed intact. The night's rest had refreshed him surprisingly well, but Sarn knew he could not last another day without fresh water. After washing out his mouth with seawater and soaking his garments for coolness, he continued northward along the seashore.

About noon Sarn spotted a few trees in the distance. What appeared to be a shallow riverbed wound among the trees and met the sea. A few houses were scattered along the riverbank; the residents had already spotted him and were coming to meet him before he saw them. Two women and an adolescent boy helped Sarn to the nearest house where he was lain on a pad. He looked up into the face of an old woman, face wrinkled in concern, as she slowly gave him fresh water.

"Where am I?" Sarn managed to say in a voice that sounded strangely squeaky. "You are not far south of Gaza," she said. "Less than three days from Jerusalem."

"Thank you," said Sam and drifted off to sleep. He woke intermittently over the next two days as his body healed from the ordeal. Each time he woke up the old woman was there with soothing words and soup. Finally, on the evening of the third day, he sat up and looked around, for the first time comprehending his surroundings.

The old woman appeared in the doorway. "Well, I see our patient is looking better." She smiled, revealing the gaps of several missing teeth.

"I am indebted to you. You saved my life." He felt a lump of gratitude swelling in his chest. When he had arrived on Earth, Sarn felt distant toward the people. They were primitive and ignorant by his standards, and there were times he could not help but feel superior to them. And yet, he had been rescued and nursed back to health by a thin old woman with only half her teeth.

"Are you hungry? I have some soup ready."

Sarn nodded. The mention of food reminded him that he was very hungry.

"Could I have some bread with it?"

She brought Sarn a bowl of soup and a large chunk of dark bread, both of which were delicious. As he ate, Sarn wondered if everything tasted so good when one was extremely hungry. He had once heard a crewman say, upon his return from a particularly long assignment, that after a few weeks in space any woman looked good to him. At that moment Sarn had no appetite for a woman, but he felt like he could eat anything placed in front of him.

Sarn came to know the woman better. Her name was Larna and she was a widow. She lived with her son, about sixteen, and a sister, also a widow. They were barely able to scratch a living out of the desolate land, and Sarn wondered how come they had not moved to Jerusalem or at least the town of Gaza where it might be easier to make a living.

Standing at the doorway, Sarn could view the bright blue of the sea to the west. To his right was a small stream snaking out of the hills and emptying itself into the ocean. A few anemic-looking trees bordered the stream, and a garden spot outlined a nearby flat area. Calmly standing under the trees was a small herd of lean goats. Lying across the sand was a long net drying in the sun.

"Isn't it hard to make a living out here?" Sarn asked Larna.

"We have lived here for many years," she said. "It is a hard life, but we are accustomed to it. In the city I would not know how to make a living. Here I know. The goats, a garden, fishing—the food is simple but we always have enough.

Sometimes a ship will anchor offshore and send its crew to get fresh water from the stream. We trade with them, if possible, and in that way we can get a few things we need. Besides, we enjoy the news they bring. It is about the only news we get unless someone like yourself wanders by, and that is not often."

"How long have you been a widow?"

Larna's eyes stared across the sea as she remembered her husband. She did not think of him so much anymore; but when she did, the same feelings were still present, undiluted by time.

"Elihoj was a good man," she said. "He lived a good life, but it was too short. He was not yet thirty when he was taken."

"How did he die?" Sarn asked. "If I'm not being too personal, that is."

"No, it is not too personal to ask how Elihoj died. It was quite a public event." She paused, lost in thought. After a few moments, Sarn thought she had decided not to continue.

"He was taken by the Great Demon," she said simply. "The Great Demon?"

"I don't suppose you would know him by that name since you are from a far country, but I am sure you know him by another name. Here we call him the Great Demon."

"Who is he?" asked Sam. "The name does not sound familiar."

He racked his brain but could not recall reading any reference to a demon. Surely, if the Great Demon was a significant factor in the lives of the Earth people, some mention would have been made in the literature.

Sarn could only conclude that the Great Demon was a local god, an opposite to whatever good god was worshipped.

Larna glanced at Sam, surprised that he seemed so ignorant of the matter. "The Great Demon lives in the sea. He knows of what we do, and sometimes he makes us do things we do not want. He made Elihoj to drown."

"How did that happen?"

"For several days Elihoj had been moody, lost in his thoughts. I could not talk to him. Something seemed to possess him, and he did not hear me when I spoke. He told me he was fighting a battle for his soul. I wanted to help, but there was nothing I could do." Larna's body tensed as she recalled the events leading up to her husband's death. Sarn became uncomfortable, but it seemed that once she had begun the story she could not be through with it until it was told.

"There was a storm, and the waves were coming in strongly. That made Elihoj even worse, and he paced wildly. His eyes flamed, and mostly I could not understand him. Once he said that 'it' had come for him. I asked what he meant, and he said the Great Demon. Then I did not know much about the Great Demon, and he would not tell me anything." Larna clasped and unclasped her hands.

"And then when the storm was at its worse, I felt it too." She clenched her fists and held her eyes shut as if reliving the event of some twenty years before.

"It was not much at first like the water that seeps around the wall of the house. But then I began to notice it. I asked Elihoj what it was, and he just looked at me with a strange expression on his face."

Sarn leaned forward. "What was it you noticed, Larna?"

"It was a feeling that someone, or something, was trying to take control of my mind. Bad thoughts began sneaking in, wanted to do things I had never even thought of before."

"Like what?"

"Like—" She looked at him, face shot through with pain. "Like hitting people I love and hurting them. I wanted so badly to smash my sister's face with a club. She ran over in the storm to our house, and when she came in the door, I had the club by my side. She knew something was wrong. I fought the impulse to raise the club and hit her. Before I could do anything, she ran out the door."

"Did you ever talk with her about that—later, I mean?"

"Yes. I tried to tell her that something was taking over Elihoj and myself, and she would not say much, only that she had understood that all was not right. We never talked beyond that. It is not a pleasant topic."

Sarn waited for her to go on.

"I found myself hating my husband. I caught myself watching him with great contempt, even though he was in the depths of his own agony. I wanted to take the club to him but was afraid I would not be fast or strong enough to finish him before he turned on me." Larna winced at the memory. "I spent one whole day debating with myself about how I could best kill Elihoj."

"How did he die?"

"On the fourth day of the storm it was almost intolerable to be in the same house with Elihoj. I hated him so much. And for no reason. It was the Great Demon that made me hate. It was him that took over my husband's mind and drove him mad. I know that now. But it affected us differently. I was driven to hate him and my sister. He was driven to hate himself, or so it seemed, for he never turned against me."

Tears streamed from Larna's eyes as she continued the tale, "Late on the fourth day Elihoj left the house and walked toward the sea. The storm was at its worst. I remember thinking he would be killed if he went to the beach, for the waves would take him out to sea. I also thought, 'Fine! It will be good if he dies!' And so I stood there at the door, where you are standing now, and watched him walk into the sea. I never saw him again." Larna leaned against the house and sobbed quietly.

"I doubt you could have stopped him," offered Sam. "A man in that condition has great strength."

Larna looked at him through tear-filled eyes. "But I didn't even try to stop him! I was glad! I will never forgive myself for that!"

They were silent for a while, each lost in their own thoughts. Sarn still did not have the complete picture.

"How did you find out it was the Great Demon who made all this happen?"

"I saw him."

"You saw the Great Demon? Where was he?"

Larna turned her gaze toward the sea and pointed toward the horizon.

"He came up out of the ocean?"

She shook her head. "No, he was in the sky. I watched Elihoj walk into the surf, and above him the clouds were dark. But then there was a face, a large evil face in the sky. It smiled as Elihoj waded to his death. The eyes then looked straight at me, into my own eyes, and then it laughed. At that moment I felt evil and dirty like I was part of something abominable and unclean. It was like for a moment I became a part of that evil leering from the sky. I was bathed in the force of the Great Demon. It so repulsed me that I fell to my knees and began vomiting until I thought I would turn inside out." Larna was pale as she spoke, "When I could finally look up, Elihoj was gone. I never saw my husband again after that." She sobbed, still overwhelmed by her grief.

"The face of the Great Demon laughed one more time and then was gone." Her expression turned from grief to one of hatred as she relived the image of the Great Demon taunting her from the clouds.

"You sound angry."

Larna nodded. "He took my husband. I'll never have another."

"You said your sister is a widow. How did she lose her husband?"

"He too was lost at sea. Romma had a fishing boat, and one day after a storm, he did not return. Such is the risk of the fisherman. I do not have reason to believe that the Great Demon took him too, but he could have," she added in response to Sam's unspoken question. "With the help of my son, we manage all right. There are neighbors too, you know. It is not like we are alone."

"Have you ever seen the Great Demon again?" asked Sarn.

"My goodness, young man, you are a curious person. Why are you so fascinated by the Great Demon?"

"It's just so . . . unusual. I have never seen anything like that before."

"And you'll not want to again, believe me."

"Besides that," added Sam, "I have seen a man who claims to be just the opposite of the Great Demon. The Great Demon you tell about sounds like total evil pulled together in one face while the man I saw was supposed to be totally good. It sounds like the difference between black and white." He shrugged. "Anyway, I find that interesting."

"Who is the good man you refer to? I have heard of one such person. He is called a messiah, but I cannot recall his name."

"The man I am referring to was called Jesus," said Sarn.

"Yes, that is it. Jesus. Some fisherman stopped by some months ago and told stories about Jesus's preaching. These fishermen always blow up their stories—make them bigger than life itself—but it was clear that they had been impressed by this messiah. Whatever happened to him?"

"Well, you may not believe this, but he was executed by the Romans and then was resurrected. Just as he predicted, I might add."

"What do you mean by that?" asked Larna. "Resurrected, I mean."

"Just that he was killed by hanging on a cross, and then his body was placed in a tomb. Three days later, in spite of guards watching the tomb, his body disappeared."

"So who said he was resurrected? I mean, grave robbers were not invented yesterday."

Sarn smiled at the woman. Life's hardness had molded her into a hard-core doubter. But her question was legitimate.

"I did not see him alive myself after the resurrection, but I have talked to people who did."

"Like who?" Larna asked.

"One of the disciples. Thomas by name. He is quite a skeptic himself. And Mary Magdalene, one of Jesus's friends. She saw him near the tomb right after the resurrection."

"Ah. But the impartial observers. How many of them saw this messiah come out of the grave? After all, if Jesus predicted that he would rise from the dead, surely some unbiased observers were placed close by just in case." Even though her eyes twinkled in fun, her points were valid and discomfiting to Sam in spite of what Thomas and Mary Magdalene had said.

Sarn shrugged and smiled, signaling that he could not satisfy her doubt.

"So what did you see this Jesus do? Tell me quick. In a world where demons come out of the clouds and take away one's husband, I need to hear about someone who can do good things." Her face said, "Believe me, I do need to hear some good news."

"I saw a few things, but my favorite was the old woman he healed."

"He had time for old women? A strange man, in this day and age. Tell me about it."

Sarn related to her the events surrounding the healing of the old woman with the bleeding malady. Larna listened closely, savoring each word. When he had finished, she sat back and smiled.

"That was good. I like to hear about good winning over bad. It happens so seldom, you know. If it was a contest, I would say that the forces of evil are much stronger than those of good. At least I notice them more. But tell me more news. I would like to hear all you know about this man."

Sarn and Larna talked about Jesus long after the stars had come out. Later Sarn would remember one thing more than anything else about Larna: he had never known anyone so hungry for news of the power of good.

The next morning found Sarn ready to depart his friends by the sea. He accepted a few food supplies, made sure he was clear on directions, and walked to the northeast. He turned to wave at them and found himself tearing. They, especially Larna, had come to be very dear to him. He would always remember them as poor people who yet were rich.

By noon Sarn had reached Gaza, and by sundown he came to Belzedek, a small and depressing village. He stayed in someone's manger without charge. The owner didn't seem to care as long as Sarn didn't bother the livestock, which consisted mostly of chickens. By the time Sarn settled down, the chickens had roosted high in the beams of the barn and he couldn't have bothered with them if he had wanted to.

The next morning he started early and walked hard all day. By nightfall he had arrived at Jerusalem's outskirts. He was too fatigued to make inquiries about Toler or the disciples and turned in early. Again he stayed in a manger but this time had to pay a small fee. In Jerusalem there were many more travelers, and the room in barns and mangers was scarce. The owners found it to be a profitable sideline to rent spaces for wayfarers needing a bed for the night.

He tried to make small talk with the other men in the manger, but they were either too tired to talk or didn't know any news.

Morning found Sarn feeling optimistic and ready to begin his quest for Toler. He did not expect that anyone would know who Toler was, but he thought he could trace his friend by asking for Jesus's disciples.

A chilling thought suddenly knocked the props out from under his optimism: what if Toler thought he was dead? If that was the case, then Toler could be anywhere; he could have already left for Bigor.

The thought was almost too much for Sarn, and he leaned against a wall to steady himself. How would he like to spend the rest of his life on a primitive and alien planet and never again see anyone from home? His early-morning confidence turned to chalky depression.

He had to try to find Toler. He began by visiting every synagogue he passed. He asked whoever seemed to be in charge if they knew where the disciples were. He was invariably answered by evasion and denial. From what little he picked up, the disciples were in hiding and association with Jesus's band had become highly unpopular. The Messiah's mission had become politicized to the point of having to go underground to survive.

Finally satisfied that the church leadership would not be of any help to him, Sarn inquired of the people coming and going around the temples. Most of them sincerely did not seem to know anything; others surreptitiously glanced around them before saying that they did not know.

Sarn had the dull feeling of someone whose day had started well and then turned to ashes. Loneliness tugged at him. *No friends here,* he told himself with a tinge of self-pity. Unless it was that girl—what was her name? Aleah? Yes, that was it. Aleah. What was the name of that place where she lived? He could not recall. It was somewhere to the north, on the Sea of Galilee. He would never forget the morning she had come across him bathing in the lake.

He sat up straight. Lish! Sarn had forgotten about the researcher who had lived on Earth for many years. Aleah would know where he was. Didn't she give him the document he had found? Just the thought of finding a fellow traveler, someone else from Bigor, was a relief. Even if Toler had already gone home, Lish would have a means of going back.

And if he didn't, well, things wouldn't be quite so bad with a friend.

And Aleah too. He had liked her a lot but had not been able to get to know her very well. She was a spunky girl, a quality he appreciated. He recalled the name of the village, Gennesaret, and figured with steady travel he could be there in three or four days.

It was then that he thought of the rendezvous cave where he and Toler had stored their gear. If Toler had already left the planet, Sarn would discover the cave empty, but he would at least know. If Toler had not left, Sarn could leave a note for him.

Sarn walked to the east and after several hours of searching found familiar landmarks. Soon he was back in the barren foothills between Jerusalem and the Dead Sea, and finally in a small canyon he found the cave. As far as he could tell, no one had disturbed the area.

Nervously Sarn entered the cave, afraid of what he would find. He sighed with relief when he discovered everything just as they had left it. On a shelf was the device that would call the scout ship down to pick them up. If his mentor was dead, then Sarn would have to return by himself, a possibility he had not contemplated. If he could figure out how to work the ship.

Sarn left a note saying he was on his way north to Gennesaret, and if he did not find Toler there, he would return to the cave.

He chose the river route to the Sea of Galilee and spent the night at Nearaa, just north of Jericho.

Chapter 47

FIND ALEAH!

The stable owner turned out to be a talkative fellow who wanted to know where Sarn had come from and what his plans were. The man traded on news, and he plied his customers for the latest. Sarn offered little, and after the man concluded that his customer was a poor source of information, he was more than glad to tell Sarn what he knew, which was much.

Although the man related a good deal of common gossip, Sarn was able to glean a few items of interest. Jesus had appeared to his disciples several times, the estimates ranging from four to twenty-six. After the most recent appearance, Jesus purportedly departed by dramatically rising into the sky.

Whatever Jesus told his disciples during those visits had made an appreciable difference in their attitudes.

The crucifixion had left his followers demoralized and confused. Although Jesus's alleged resurrection was a wonderful affirmation for them, it provided no cohesion or direction; they remained disorganized and lost. Jesus's visitations in the weeks following his death and resurrection gave them a new understanding of themselves and their role in the post-Jesus world.

Central to their beliefs was the divinity of Jesus, whom they called the Christ; he was considered to be the messianic deliverer for whom the natives had been waiting all these years. The community branched out into other places beside Jerusalem. As far as the stable owner knew, the followers met regularly, took care of one another, and were generally considered to be a closely knit group. They didn't bother anyone and talked a lot about Jesus returning when the world ended, which could be any day.

The stable owner's brother had joined up with the local Jesus group, as he called it. He did not see his brother much anymore but when he did sought the latest news of the group's activities. Although having no interest in joining the group himself, the stable owner found the whole phenomenon a fascinating saga in progress.

Sarn recalled Hextor's book on messiahs, which predicted excitement. In his opinion there had been more than enough drama and if it was true that Jesus had resurrected, reappeared to the disciples, and flown away into the skies an ample supply of magic.

"Do you think the movement has a future?" asked Sarn.

"No. People will get tired of it. And if they don't, the Sadducees won't tolerate it. They get touchy about splinter groups like this."

"There's not much they can do about it, is there?" asked Sam. "I mean, why would the Sadducees care? They're not hurting anyone."

The stable owner sat down, settled his bulky body, and faced Sarn. He had just been given the opportunity to make one of his favorite lectures, and he liked to be comfortable whenever he did that. One never knew how long it would take to render these services to mankind, and he tried to remain humble. Sarn remained standing; he was not sure how much education from the stable owner he could tolerate.

"Why should the Sadducees care? Two reasons, as I see it. One, they consider themselves to be entrusted with the spiritual welfare of the people. Without the Sadducees, no one would know how to act. People would do terrible things to one another," he said with obvious sarcasm, "and we'd all end up going to hell in a handbasket.

"Second, they lose power and influence if their flock starts straying into other camps. It's a political matter about power issues. And financial. They need people who will give money to the Temple. In that sense, the Temple is just another business. It has to have a cash flow, or it closes the doors."

"Do you belong to the Temple?"

"Oh, of course. Almost everyone does. We are Jewish, and being Jewish is having the Temple. It is very dear to me, but that does not keep me from seeing things as they are."

Sarn nodded. He liked this man for his frankness and his knowledge. The stableman would make an excellent teacher. "What will the Temple leaders do about the situation?"

"Oh, different things. They will make fun of the Jesus groups and urge their flocks to stay away from them. They might have a trial in which they label the Jesus groups as heretical. That would give them license to outlaw the meetings. And then there is always the ploy of inciting people to use force.

"Who knows, they might think of something new. Meanwhile, do you know what the Christians, which is what they call themselves, use as their symbol?"

Sarn shook his head.

"A fish." He drew in the dirt with his toe two curved lines open to one another and crossing at one end.

"Why a fish?"

"Because when they meet one another, they need a code. Theirs is 'Jesus Christ is Lord', and in Greek the first letters of the words in that phrase spell *fish*. It is simpler to leave a picture of a fish somewhere than to leave the word *Christian*.

"But you asked what those wonderfully intelligent people who run the Temple will do if they really are smart," he continued. "They won't do anything. They'll ignore the whole thing and give it time to wither away."

"Do you think they'll do that?"

"Probably not. They get fleas in their pants and can't sit still. They'll decide they have to do something today. And that will only make the Jesus groups stronger."

"What do you think will be the ultimate outcome?" Sarn asked.

"Hmmm. I do not have a peephole into the future, of course, but I can make a guess. I think it will grow stronger for a while, especially if there are those who actively oppose its growth. Then the men and women who knew Jesus will start to die off. Exit the messianic charisma factor. Since the world will not come to an end and Jesus will not return to rejoin his followers, as they are claiming, it will be seen as a hoax.

"Then people will laugh at them, and that will do them in. If you persecute a cause, it will flourish. If you laugh at it, it will die because everyone wants to be taken seriously."

"Has there been any persecution yet?" asked Toler.

"Nothing organized, I think. There was a hothead, though, here yesterday. With him was a group of men from a synagogue south of here, and they were on their way to the north."

"To the north? Do you know where they were headed?"

"Damascus. Some of the men were disgruntled about it. Too much of a trip to suit them. Can't blame them. If I had to chase around after Jesus people, I'd want to be home at night. What I think is this fellow Saul wanted to make a name for himself and thought if he made a regular campaign of it, he might become famous overnight."

Rather than being bored, Sarn found himself fascinated by his discussion with the stable owner. Later it occurred to him that he had never even known the man's name. Their conversation was ended when the man's wife came to the stable to fetch her husband.

By dawn Sarn was on the road headed north. He traveled less than ten miles before coming to the sleepy village of Archelais. Although past midmorning, Sarn had not yet eaten and decided to stop for a meal. He typically bought bread, cheese, and fruit since their quality was usually reliable.

However, in the marketplace Sarn caught the aroma of roasting meat and soon tracked down its location. An old man squatted by a small fire over which a chicken had turned golden brown. Hypnotized, Sarn watched the man slowly turn the bird. With a slight nod, the fellow gestured for Sarn to come over.

"Sit down, young man," the cook said. "My name is Moora."

Sarn squatted beside Moora. "My name is Sarn. I smelled the chicken and came to see. It is not often I smell such good roasted meat."

"Would you like some? I was just about to eat, and there is more than enough for the both of us."

Sarn doubted that but quickly agreed. He placed two coins on the ground by man. It would have been bad manners to have offered money for a man's courtesy, but it was all right to leave a gift. Moora removed the chicken from the spit and deftly pulled it into several pieces with the aid of a sharp knife. The pieces were lain on a palm leaf, along with a loaf of bread, and the two feasted together.

With his back to the square, Sarn did not see the men on horseback enter the village. Moora looked up and said, still chewing, "They almost look like soldiers. But I think they are looking for someone. That is the way they look when they are chasing someone."

Sarn froze and then with one hand to his ear as if he was scratching slowly turned his head. Peering through his scratching fingers, he watched the band of grim-faced men make their way across the square. His heart leaped as their leader came into view.

Derxter!

Trembling, Sarn forced himself to turn back to Moora and the chicken. He was afraid he was going to lose his meal.

Moora looked at him with a curious expression. "Do you know these men?"

Sarn shook his head and then nodded. "Just one. The big one. He is bad. Dangerous."

Moora seemed to hunker down lower, eyes squinting. "Yes, I can feel him. He is evil."

After the men, about fifteen in all, had passed out of sight, Sarn thanked Moora and went to the edge of the village. In the distance Derxter and his men loped their horses to the north, clearly in a hurry to get somewhere. Would that be Gennesaret? He did not know, and without a mount, there was no way to keep up with them. The only reason he would want to keep pace would be to warn Lish and Aleah; otherwise, he was more than glad for Derxter to put distance between them.

The rest of the journey north was uneventful. In the afternoon of the third day Sarn walked into the picturesque town of Gennesaret. It was a simple matter to find directions to Lish's house, and before too much longer he spotted the small hut.

Although he had never been there, immediately, at a subliminal level, Sarn sensed that something was wrong. The door was hanging askew, and several objects were lying about in the yard. Tense, he stopped and looked around, carefully studying the little house and the surrounding area.

"Lish! Anyone home?" The only response was a heavy silence. Finally he made his way to the doorway. Inside the house everything was in disarray. Furniture had been destroyed and clothing strewn about. Boxes were ripped open and their contents scattered around. Sarn searched through the debris thinking that Lish or Aleah might be lying unconscious on the floor. He could find no one.

Sarn had earlier passed a house about a hundred meters up the road, and it was there he went to seek help. No one answered his knock, and he had departed but a few steps when he heard the door open. Turning, he tried to make out who was looking at him through the cracked door.

"Pardon me. I am a friend of Lish's. I have come a long way to see him. His house is wrecked. Is he all right?"

The door opened wider. "Sarn? Is that you, Sarn?"

It was a familiar voice. "Hello. Who is it? Yes, I am Sarn."

The door opened, and a figure came out. "Sarn, it's me, Aleah."

She ran to Sarn and threw herself against him. He awkwardly put his arms around her, more to steady himself than anything else. Her eyes were red and her face tear stained.

"I am so glad to see you. I was afraid no one would come, and I was afraid to stay here tonight by myself. I think they might come back."

"Just slow down and tell me what happened. Is there some place we can sit down?"

Aleah led him into her house. Sarn could tell that it too was a shambles.

"Where is a light?"

"No! No light! Come with me." She led him to the stairs, and soon they were sitting cross-legged in the loft. An opening in the window covering allowed them to see the road leading to the house. While they talked, Aleah frequently glanced outside, clearly quite nervous.

"Several days ago your friend and a woman came to see Uncle Lish."

"Toler?" Sarn asked excitedly.

"Yes, Toler was his name. And his friend's name was Mary Magdalene. Do you know her?"

Sarn nodded. "Yes, a little."

"I asked Toler where you were. He said you were dead, Sarn. I am so glad you are not." She cried. "What happened?"

"No, you go on and tell me what happened here. There will be plenty of time later to tell you about that."

"All right." Aleah composed herself. "Toler left two or three days ago—I don't recall—just when Mary—she is a very nice lady, and I like her lots—stayed here with Uncle Lish. They seemed like close friends. I don't mean that they did anything wrong."

"What happened next?"

"This morning Uncle Lish and Mary came by to see if my mama would like to walk into town with them. They had some shopping to do. My sister and brother went with them, but I stayed here to finish baking bread. Not long after they had gone, I heard horses come up. Someone hollered out front, and I opened the door to see what they wanted." Aleah shuddered, and her voice cracked. "It was that big man and his friend, the ones who chased you that day."

"Derxter!"

"Yes, Derxter. That is what one of the other men called him. They asked me—no, they demanded to know—if Uncle Lish lived here. Before I even thought about it, I had looked down the path toward Uncle Lish's house. That's all they needed.

"They took off in a gallop to his house." She leaned to the window and satisfied herself that no one was coming.

"I could tell there would be trouble, especially after they found out he wasn't there. I figured they would come back and make me tell them where Uncle Lish was. So I ran into the woods and hid. I stayed there a long time after I heard them leave. Finally I came back to the house. I've been here ever since, afraid to do anything."

"You haven't seen anyone since they were here?"

Aleah shook her head. "I wanted to go into town—it's not far, you know—and look for them. I don't know what happened to them. They haven't come home!"

"But if something did happen to them in town, surely people would have come here looking for you."

Aleah stated the obvious, "Unless no one saw Derxter get them. Anyway, if they haven't come home, where are they?"

"I don't know, Aleah. We can go look for them."

The girl nestled against Sam, finding in his warmth a sense of security she so badly needed at that moment. Sarn felt her need and placed his arm around her. She sniffled, and within minutes her breathing had slowed. Not wanting to disturb the exhausted girl, Sarn let himself relax too, although he had many questions. He told himself there were too many unknowns to make plans, and besides, he too was tired. Before the late-afternoon sun, bathed in orange and pink hues, began its last leg of descent, the pair was sound asleep.

The dream seemed to go on forever, and Sarn, as the participant-observer, wondered why it didn't end. He watched himself walk across the desert as he had done when lost.

Like then the sun was terribly hot and the sand stretched endlessly in all directions toward the horizon. Sarn discovered a water bottle in his hand. He took a draw on the bottle but could not discern a taste as the liquid tumbled down his parched throat. Water was not his primary concern; he turned and watched the top of the dune behind him. The pounding of footsteps reverberated through the sand, causing shimmering waves of rock granules to dance. Over the edge of the dune appeared a giant blob of inky wavering colors, which moved in rhythm to the sound of the footsteps. The blob took shape as shoulders, and then a head became discernable. Sam in the dream felt himself shudder with fear and then run across the sand. His strides were long and lazy. His feet were sinking in the sand, and he was rapidly losing his lead over the blob-which-walked. He looked over his shoulder at the mass flowing across the dunes in his trail. The small head became larger and took on features.

It was Derxter! Sarn in the dream felt an icy wind rattle his stomach, and he gasped for breath. There was a pain in his groin, and he doubled up. Derxter came closer, and a huge hand reached for Sarn, grabbing his neck. How it hurt! The grip was so powerful.

Sarn opened his eyes and could not focus. His head was filled with cotton, and the sharp edge of something hard pushed into his face. Was his hair being pulled out? What—who—was pulling his hair out?

Sharp pain wrenched Sarn awake. Derxter kneeled over him, one huge hand holding his head, the other twisting Sam's arm behind his back. The boy could not move, so powerful and heavy was the man. He heard his own breath wheezing in and out and became aware that there was something against his windpipe.

Aleah! Where was she? His eyes sought to scan his surroundings and locate her, but he could not move his head. Aleah could have been directly behind him or nowhere near. He had no way of knowing. He tried to make a sound, to ask about Aleah, but could not breathe. Suddenly the face in his vision blurred and began spinning. He felt himself being sucked down a vortex of dark sand, and then there was blackness.

Derxter felt Sarn's body go limp. He turned to the other body, that of the girl, which lay just behind the boy. She was still unconscious from the blow to her head. A purple knot was already making an angry appearance on the side of her head near the temple. She lay akimbo, like a rag doll carelessly tossed across the room, and saliva drooled from her open mouth onto the rough wood floor.

Pulling the girl upright by her hair, he slapped her face repeatedly.

"Wake up! Foolish girl, wake up!"

Slowly, groggily, the girl came to her senses. When she saw Derxter, she attempted to scream but was hushed by his rough hand over her mouth. He had first struck her while she still slept, and until he brought her to, she had not seen him.

"Now listen to me, you fool!" Aleah turned her frightened gaze to Derxter, then closed her eyes, and sobbed in horror. Another slap to the face, this time much harder, brought her eyes wide open and full attention to her captor.

"Listen carefully! Soon the others will be coming up the path. We will make this as quick as possible. When they are within shouting distance, I will offer them a trade—you for Lish and Mary Magdalene and Toler. Maybe they won't have any problem making such a deal, for all those three are not from around here, and you are." He squeezed her more tightly.

"And if they don't make a deal, then *cluk*." He made a popping sound as if something had broken.

"And now we wait," Derxter said. He leaned against a wall with Aleah, back to him, sitting on the floor between his legs. One hand he kept on her neck.

Aleah softly cried. Once she was able to look to the side and spot Sam's inert body but could not tell if he was alive.

She tried to think of some plan, something she could do to help matters, to save the people she loved; but she simply could not focus on anything long enough to evolve a strategy.

Derxter watched the road through the window. He fully expected a rescue party to come before darkness fell. There had been time for everyone to return from the sea chase and organize into pursuing groups. Derxter was reasonably certain that was how things would be done. When he thought back on the spectacle, he felt his insides wrench. What a pitiful spectacle! These people were so inept as to be laughable. Derxter thought he would have had a good laugh over the sea chase had those not been his own hired men. Instead he was filled with rage toward the bumbling creatures. He wiped saliva from his chin.

It had been a long time since Derxter was so filled with hatred and rage. A scene from years past, when he was a young boy, flashed across his mind. His father came home drunk and could not find a favorite shirt. Blaming the loss on Derxter, his father severely beat the boy with a branch from a tree. The switch raised welts and even cut the flesh several times, but Derxter refused to cry. Protesting his innocence would have done no good because his father was intoxicated and totally unreasonable. So the boy absorbed the terrible beating, made the worse because he did not beg for mercy or cry out in pain. All the while, he felt hatred building in him, a fiery, explosive rage that drowned out the pain and gave him the will to endure the ordeal. Derxter recalled vividly how the rage had allowed him to feel powerful but at the same time had scared him because it was so strong. He had felt some wonderment at the rage, which seemed so alien and yet so comfortable. It was like a drug high, almost exhilarating, a state of mind Derxter had come to like, although it was seldom that he felt as much hatred as he did then.

The thought of being traded for her friends was more than Aleah could bear. It would be better that she die now than to live with the knowledge that she had been responsible for the capture and death of those dear to her.

The solution was simple, she finally concluded. She would run down the path and warn them before they could be caught. If she could get free of Derxter for just a moment, perhaps she could outrun him.

"I have to go to the bathroom," she said.

"Then go!" Derxter whispered harshly in her ear.

She started to get up and felt herself rudely pulled back down to the floor.

"I mean go where you are if you must! You are not leaving my side!"

Aleah felt her face turned red. She was too modest to urinate while sitting beside Derxter. She doubted that she could relieve herself even if she wanted to, so strong were her inhibitions.

"I can wait," she said. "May I shift positions?" Without waiting for his response, Aleah moved to put her legs beneath her body rather than stretched out in front as they had been.

"I like your legs, little girl. Show me some more!" Derxter reached over her shoulder and pulled her robe up, exposing half of her thigh. "Hmm! I like that!"

The unexpected move by Derxter caught Aleah by surprise but more than that made her angry. No one had the right to pull her robe up and speak to her in that manner. Without thinking, she pulled her legs under her, stood up, and slapped Derxter across the face, all at approximately the same time. Her leap backward was thrown off by his grasping for her legs, and she fell down. Before she could roll out of his reach, one giant hand pinned her ankle to the floor.

"You little bitch!" His eyes glazed over and yet seemed to be sparked by red fire. He pulled her toward him with the ease of a cat reeling in a sparrow. Derxter could feel the rage, which had subsided during the last hour, building back up to a new crescendo. His hatred centered on the girl. He would make her pay for all that had gone wrong, and even if it would not undo his recent bad luck, beating her would make him feel good. Derxter licked his lips in delicious anticipation of the pain he was about to deliver to the girl.

"Come to Daddy, little girl," he crooned.

And that was the beginning of Aleah's beating. What brought it to an end before she was killed were the sounds of someone coming up the hill toward them.

"Be still!" hissed Derxter. "Let them get closer before you speak out." The fact that Aleah was barely alive and incapable of calling out to anyone was unnoticed.

Sarn regained consciousness just as Derxter came to the end of the beating. He lay unbelieving as he watched the huge man viciously strike the young girl. At first he felt helpless to make any intervention but then, in his own anger and disgust, discovered a strength he had not been aware of. Reaching behind him, he located a stout board. Slowly he gathered his arms and legs under him and pulled back his club. Fortunately, at that moment Derxter's full attention was caught up with the sounds of someone coming up the hill.

Propelled by desperation and anger, the board bounced off Derxter's head. Dazed, he gasped, put a hand to his head, and looked at Sarn in amazement. That pause was long enough for Sarn to unload another blow against the man's head. Derxter swayed and then fell unconscious, knocking Sarn into the wall where his head struck the edge of the window; and he, like Derxter, was rendered unconscious. Derxter's body fell across that of Sarn, and the two lay still.

Addled, Aleah half fell down the ladder and crawled to the doorway. Slowly pulling herself up, she unsteadily made her way down the path. She had heard someone coming, someone she must warn, and that was all her groggy mind could grasp at that moment.

Sarn had the sensation of being weightless in the darkness of space while a dull pain throbbed in the back of his head. He did not want to come awake because he would then have to deal with the pain. Somewhere in the depths of his mind, a warning voice called out for him to come awake and flee. Danger! Danger! Slowly like a weak fish struggling to swim upstream, he labored into consciousness. He became aware of a deadening weight on his body, one that breathed and had an odor about it.

Derxter! And where was Aleah? He could see nothing in the darkness. He blinked his eyes, making sure they were open, and then began to make out the shapes of things in the room.

Sarn was lying on his back, head against the wall at a painful angle. His arms were free, but the hulk of Derxter lay facedown across his thighs, pinning him down. Slowly he began wiggling and pulling, trying to get free from Derxter without waking him. Twice he thought the man was waking, for he made guttural sounds in his throat and moved, but nothing more. Sarn continued working against the weight of the heavy body until he had pulled his legs free. A quick look around the room revealed that Aleah had gone. Before he could make any plans, Derxter's eyes opened, shining red in some stray light, boring into him.

Without pausing to think, Sarn leaped backward, turned in midair, took the ladder in two steps, and landed running out the door. Propelled by raw terror, he flew through a thicket of trees, branches clawing wildly at him. The only sounds he could make out were that of his own running, and this served to fuel his terror even more.

Finally, when he could run no more, Sarn stopped. Reason finally caught up to his fear, and he decided to hide rather than continue his aimless running.

Behind him, about ten feet from the steep hillside, was a large tree. Sarn found it to be a good climbing tree, and it did not take long before he was perched in a fork high in the branches. Soon his breathing calmed, and he listened to the night sounds. Crickets, a few birds, a slushing sound he presumed was the sound of the lake on the shore, and nothing else. Occasionally during the night, he thought he heard someone walking below him, but he could make out no forms.

Chapter 48

Look for Derxter

Five men, Lish one of them, resolutely marched down the main road to Aleah's house. Another group took the shore path and planned to join up with them at the top of the hill.

"Stay quiet as you walk," advised Shainil, "and you may surprise the scoundrel."

Mary Magdalene watched as the several parties of men left the town to search for the pirates. She felt useless remaining with the women and children and wished she could somehow slip away and join the menfolk. Of course that would not be allowed, and she made no effort to join them. Not that Mary thought she could provide much muscle power, but she knew she was quick of mind, and that was often worth more than a few muscles. *Every group of hunters should contain at least one woman, maybe two,* Mary thought. It was her opinion that because women operated from a different mind-set than did men, they were more alert to some kinds of actions and more apt to see options men missed. When you were weaker than nearly all the men in the world, then you had to think in terms of quick wit and varied strategies.

Sometimes Mary chaffed under the strict rules of proper behavior according to gender. It never occurred to her that being born in another time would have made a difference, for things changed so slowly that progress could hardly be seen from one generation to another. More than once she thought about how it would be to live in Toler's country. Clearly Toler was accustomed to treating women much differently than the men she had known. Mary concluded long ago that she had been born somehow different from the average woman. How else could one explain her independence and spirit of adventure? How many women would have taken up with a rebel like Jesus? Oh, plenty would have followed him as long as he was popular, but after his popularity declined and he faced death, it was Mary who supported him to the end.

Mary wondered if there would be political repercussions for her as a result of her close friendship with Jesus. It did not really matter. She was at a stage in her life when she did what was important to her—within bounds—and let the chips fall where they might. At present her allegiance to Lish and Toler was high priority. She knew that she would likely never see Toler again unless she went to his country, but that was improbable. Neither of the men had ever expressed any hint of that being a possibility.

Mary joined the group of women headed for the synagogue where they would wait for word of the hunt. As always she would make the best of waiting. She glanced at the western sky, which was bright orange and pink in the setting sun, and felt a tinge of alarm over the encroaching darkness. Somehow she knew that the night would be an advantage to Derxter, for he was a creature of darkness.

The fishermen were confident after their easy victory over the men in the boat. This was their town and the culprits they pursued were foreigners, which gave rise to the juices of whatever territorial imperative they possessed. The men of Gennesaret had been called to battle on their own soil against invaders, and they shared a feeling of power and rightness as they ventured forth in search of the gang from the south.

Lish drew strength from the company of men. By nature a loner, he had seldom been a part of a cause, much less a member of a pack of hunters whose prey was other people. He found it exciting, almost exhilarating, and yet was uncomfortable with the role. There was comfort being a part of an armed band, yet he was fearful because he knew something about Derxter, a man who was, in Lish's opinion, more than a man.

The leader held up his hand for the band to stop. There were the unmistakable sounds of someone walking toward them. The men crouched by the side of the road and waited.

A lone figure came slowly into view from around a bend in the road, walking stiffly, occasionally stumbling. At first glance, Lish knew that it was not Derxter, for the figure was not large enough. Transfixed by the strangeness of the shuffling gait, the men waited for the distance to close.

"It's Aleah!" Lish leaped to his feet as he recognized the girl. The men followed him as he ran to the teetering girl just in time to catch her as she fell. As they gently laid her down, the moonlight illuminated her face.

"My god! My god! Look what they have done to Aleah!" exclaimed one of the men. Another turned to the side of the road and threw up. Lish's jaw worked, but no sound came forth. His eyes filled with tears as he looked into the girl's tortured eyes and then he held her close.

"We will take her to the village!" someone said. "She must have medical attention." Aleah was picked up, and with Lish holding her head, the group made their way back down the hill toward town. Thoughts of catching Derxter were temporarily put on hold as the men focused on the girl's injuries.

Lish knew without being told what had happened. Derxter, frustrated after watching the futile boat chase, had gone back to the house, found Aleah alone, and out of spite had beat her almost to death. It was his style to not kill her but to maim her so badly that it would be kinder if she was dead.

Aleah moved her mouth as if trying to say something, and Lish leaned closer.

"Is . . . big man," she said haltingly through her pain, swollen lips barely able to move. "Find Sarn . . . he hurt." Her one good eye reflected the concern she felt for Lish in spite of her own grave injuries. "Please be careful," she whispered and passed out.

It was all Lish could do to keep himself together as they made their way to the village. His chest was swollen, and his heart felt it would burst. Eyes burning, he fought back his sobs and was distantly aware of the hot tears running wildly down his cheeks. Consumed by a mixture of rage against Derxter and concern for Aleah, he nevertheless remained mindful of his nagging fear of Derxter.

And in that instant he made a clear decision for himself: he would find Derxter and make his best effort to destroy the man, no matter the cost, no matter even the low probability of success. Lish was tired of running scared from evil. He knew it was time to take a stand not just for the sake of Aleah or the others but for his own. In that moment of decision, he felt a relief he had not known in many years, perhaps in his whole life: Lish would stand firm.

By the time they reached Gennesaret, one of the men had run ahead and alerted the women who had come up the road to meet them. Mary and Darene, Aleah's mother, reached them first.

"What have they done?" Darene wailed as she tried to take the unconscious girl from the men.

"Move her back," said one of the men, "and we'll take her to Darene's sister's house."

Mary Magdalene held Darene and felt her sob and shudder uncontrollably as she saw her daughter's face. Mary bit her lip and had to work at keeping her composure, for the sight of the brutally mauled face had unnerved her. She had not seen anyone beaten that badly and had never expected to see a young woman in that condition.

"Come, Darene, we'll go ahead. Quick! There is much to do." Mary was dimly aware that she was needful of keeping them both busy. Darene, strong woman that she was, visibly pulled herself upright.

"I can walk," she said. "Let us go ahead quickly!" And she took the lead back down the hill.

Now that Aleah had been placed in the care of the women, the men, very angry by this time, eagerly joined in the renewed hunt for Derxter.

Most of the night was spent scouring the countryside for Derxter and his hired men. Before dawn seven of the henchmen had been caught, but Derxter had escaped.

Lish found his way back to his own house shortly before the sun peeked over the far hills. Moving cautiously in the morning shadows, he kneeled on the west side of the house and pried a stone loose from the corner. Lish pulled the laser gun from the cavity. From there, it did not take long to find his mattress and collapse on it. He kept the gun in hand, hidden under a cover. Before drifting off to sleep, he wondered why Aleah had mentioned Sarn. What had she said?

Sarn need help? The boy had already been killed by Derxter, according to Mary and Toler, and most likely Aleah had been talking out of her head.

Tomorrow would be a new day, one in which he would resume his search for Derxter. His resolve to take direct action against the evil Derxter still felt good, and Lish slept soundly.

Chapter 49

THE DECISION

In spite of his discomfort, Sarn was exhausted and slept late in his tree perch. Finally roused about midmorning by the sounds of men loudly talking, he slowly and carefully stretched his aching body.

The voices drifted up from the lakeside, and through the limbs Sarn could glimpse men moving around on the shore. Their discussion seemed to center around a boat and something about fishing. Occasionally their voices rose as they argued or made a joke. He was surprised that life seemed to be going on as usual for someone.

From his vantage point in the tree, Sarn scanned the area as far as he could see, but other than the figures on the beach, he could spot no movement. After stiffly making his way to the ground, he was surprised at how easily he had climbed the tree the night before, a feat, he concluded, that testified to the ability of the terrified.

The fishermen stopped talking and stared curiously as Sam walked onto the beach.

"Hello, can you direct me to the village?" Sarn asked.

The oldest of the fishermen spoke, "And which village did you have in mind, young man?" The other men smiled.

"Gennesaret. I have lost my way in the night and am turned around."

"Aye! You look as if you have done more than that. What happened to you?" This was asked by the tallest of the five men, a well-built, bearded fellow with a thick shock of hair hanging across his forehead.

"I slept in a tree," Sarn replied. He thought he should be grinning sheepishly at the absurd admission but was feeling increasingly upset about the events of last night and had little patience with social niceties.

"A tree?" the man said and grinned at his friends who were enjoying this diversion from their morning work. "And why would you sleep in a tree?"

"I'll wager the view is better," said one and laughed.

"Tell me, young fellow, did the birds roost on your ears?" asked another, and the others hooted in delight.

"Or on something else you have?" which brought loud guffaws from the men.

In spite of himself, Sarn almost smiled. The men were clearly in a fine mood and meant no harm.

"That way up the shoreline, and you'll come to Gennesaret," said the oldest. "And be careful. There was trouble last night."

"Oh? What kind of trouble?" Sarn asked.

"Some fool rogues from the south turned pirate. Stole a fishing boat and chased some folks around. My brother-in-law came by early this morning, said it was quite a sight to behold. Things looked bleak for the people being chased until the townsmen got into the act. Folks stayed up practically all night looking for the pirates, caught some of them too, but I don't think they know what to do with them. Would have been easier if they had all gotten away, but now they have to do something with them."

"Did anybody get hurt?" The men had turned their attention from Sarn to the old man.

"Some girl got hurt pretty badly. Don't know why they would beat up a girl. Besides that, some of the pirates got bunged up while being captured. Must have been quite an exciting time last night."

"Yeah! We don't ever have anything like that happen around here."

"It's so boring!" moaned another.

"Where did you say we are? Sarn asked, directing his question to the oldest who seemed more able than the others to stay on track.

"I didn't say, young fellow, but I'll tell you. We're about halfway between Gennesaret and Magdala. Gennesaret is to the north." He indicated with a sweep of his right arm. "Magdala is that way," he said with a gesture to the south.

"Thanks," Sarn said and walked up the beach toward the north.

He was surprised at how far he had fled in the dark and concluded he must have ran in a fairly straight line to the south. Although he was certain that in the night he had heard someone pass below his perch, he didn't know if it had been Derxter; it could have been the townspeople pursuing the pirates. Or even the fleeing pirates. Or all of them.

Things seemed normal on the waterfront in Gennesaret.

Several fishing boats were tied up along the main dock while their owners stood around discussing the events of the night before. Sarn approached the nearest group of men.

"Excuse me. I am looking for Aleah. I understand she was hurt last night. Can you tell me where she is?"

"You a friend of hers?"

"Yes."

"What's your name?" another asked.

"Sarn."

"Sarn? What kind of a name is that? Where you from?" The men were not in a good mood. Their village had been invaded and one of their number hurt. Outsiders were not to be trusted.

"Look, I was with Aleah last night when she was hurt. I've got to know how she is."

"What! You were with her? You weren't the one who beat her, were you?" The men moved menacingly toward Sarn.

"No! I stopped the man from beating her any worse. He would have killed her. He's crazy!"

"Who? Tell us who he is." The townspeople had decided that Derxter, the large muscular man who had come into town asking about Lish's whereabouts, was the culprit or at least the one behind the day's events. His identity was still a mystery to them, and they had no idea how to go about locating him.

"A big guy. His name is Derxter."

"Derxter," one of the men repeated. "Another strange name. Where is he from?"

"Far away is all I know," said Sarn.

"What does he want? Why would he come to Gennesaret and start in on our people? Is Lish the one he's after?" There were murmurs of assent.

"I don't know why Derxter wants Lish. Or anyone else. I just know he hurt Aleah, and she is a friend of mine." He looked at them pleadingly. "Would you please tell me where she is?"

"All right," one said and gave him directions to the house of Darene's sister.

His knock brought a cautious opening of the door. A single eye blinked at him through the crack, and a voice asked what he wanted.

"I have come to see Aleah."

There was a long pause. "She is sleeping. Come back another day."

"Listen, I know she's hurt. I want to know how she is. Is she going to be all right?"

The sincere concern in Sam's voice convinced the doorkeeper that he was a friend, and she opened the door.

"Come in but just for a while. She is sleeping. And she is hurt." The woman who opened the door was a tall broad woman with a square jaw. Sarn thought that she probably had never been pushed around very much and was quite capable of keeping anyone out of the house. She looked Sarn over as if assessing his intentions. "My name is Nemna. What is yours?"

"Sarn. I am a friend of Aleah's."

Nemna led Sarn to a small room at the back of the house where a bed and small table took up nearly the whole space. Aleah lay quite still, eyes closed. Much of her face was black and blue from her beating, and her lips and one eye were swollen grotesquely. Sarn could guess what her back and shoulders looked like. He had watched the whipping with the strap. His eyes burned with tears, and he felt like he might throw up. Sarn wanted to reach out and touch her, to somehow fix her body and make it all right. But he felt helpless to do anything but stand rigidly by her bed and fight to control his tears.

Two more women appeared from other rooms.

"This is Sarn. He says he is a friend of Aleah's," said Nerna by way of introductions. "This is Darene, Aleah's mother."

Darene was gaunt, stooped, and haggard. She had been through the worst night of her life and, in spite of being a strong woman, was much the worse for wear. Sarn wondered if she, in fact, was as old as she looked or if she had just aged since the night before. She nodded at Sarn.

"I think she has mentioned you," she said. "No, it must have been someone else. She said Sarn was killed, but that couldn't be." She smiled wanly.

"Yes, it probably was," said Sam. "It was thought that I had been killed by the same man who tried to kill her."

Darene gasped. Nemna's mouth opened, closed, and asked, "You know the man who did this to Aleah?"

"His name is Derxter," Sarn replied, feeling distinctly uncomfortable. He was becoming too involved in the lives of the natives and was probably violating a whole volume of rules about the proper conduct of visiting a primitive world. But he couldn't help it. He was involved. Sarn felt an obligation to warn people about Derxter. *To heck with the niceties of interworld visitations,* he thought. *We're talking about survival. Derxter kills people!*

"Ooh, he scares me so!" moaned Darene.

Sarn glanced at Aleah's mother questioningly. She spoke as if she knew Derxter.

Nerna interpreted Sam's glance. "He was here in the middle of the night. We think he is your man. Derxter is a rather large well-muscled man with an unpleasant face?"

Sarn nodded. "That sounds like him. What was he doing here?"

"We were woken up by someone knocking on the door. Darene here went to the door and asked who it was. A loud voice said that he wanted to see the 'girl who had been hurt.' It scared her, and she said no and told him to go away. He started banging on the door—he was going to come through the door one way or the other—and woke the rest of us. I told Darene to open the door before he broke it down. She did, and there he was, looking right at us. I guess there were five or six of us. And I said, 'Come on, let's mix it up!'"

"That stopped him."

"But he sure didn't like it," added Darene.

"We were all still mad about what had happened," said the other woman, "and then being woke up like that—it was enough to make us spoil for a fight. If he was the man who beat up Aleah, I wanted a piece of him!"

"So he looked us over real good, decided we meant business, and left," said Nerna.

Sarn could understand that Nerna was built like an ox, and the other women, with the exception of Darene, were rather heavy. Derxter clearly had no compunctions about hitting a female, but he had assessed the odds and called it a nonwinnable situation. Even if he could have overcome the women, the noise of the fight would have brought help.

Sarn chuckled to himself. He would like to have seen Derxter backed down by the women. Even better, he would like to see Derxter take on Nerna and her friends. Now that would be worth seeing!

"Now why do you think he wanted Aleah? He beat her up and then wanted her back. Maybe he wasn't through with the beating?"

"You know how some men are. They can't get a good night's sleep without first beating a woman."

Sarn watched as the women worked themselves up. They were a closely knit group and would tolerate no foolishness from any man.

"Will she be all right?" Sarn asked. Aleah had not moved.

"Maybe," said Nerna. She seemed to be in charge and the most able of the group. "Of course her skin will heal and the bruises will go away. But we cannot be sure of what was hurt inside her. That will take time."

Sarn thought about getting her into the *Sprint*, which was high above them at that very moment, waiting to be called. There was sufficient medical equipment aboard to make a correct diagnosis and begin treatment. He dismissed the thought, tempting as it was. Even if Toler would go along with the idea, these women would not let the girl be placed in a strange flying craft and taken out of their sight.

"Hello," came a greeting from the front of the house. Sam thought he recognized the voice. Lish's face popped into view from the front room. He saw Sarn and immediately did a double take.

"My, but you look healthy for a dead man!" He smiled broadly and clasped Sam's hands. "It's a strange world. We almost lose one"—he indicated Aleah—"and another returns. Welcome back, my friend!"

"I see you two are acquainted," said Nerna.

"We have met before," said Lish. "Have you seen Toler? Does he know you are alive?"

"No, I haven't seen him, but I did leave a message for him. So he will find out I am alive. For a while, anyway. Derxter nearly got me again last night. I was with Aleah when he found us." Sarn then brought Lish up-to-date on what had happened the night before.

"So he was going to use Aleah as bait—to trade for us," said Lish after listening to Sam's story. "Poor girl! Just an innocent bystander."

"No, I disagree with that, Lish. She is innocent. That is true enough. But Aleah is no bystander. She may not have told you about how she saved my skin from Derxter once before. She doesn't mind getting involved."

"Do you think that is why Derxter beat her? Did he recognize her as the one who helped you?"

"No, I don't think he ever saw her that other time. He just thought the people would trade you, Mary, and Toler for Aleah since she was local and you three weren't."

"I consider myself local," protested Lish.

"Maybe so," snorted Nerna, "but you still wouldn't be worth much in a trade."

"In terms of weight, it would take about seven of me to trade even for you, my dear Nerna."

"Wanta fight?" she asked, assuming a crouched position. "No, thank you, and neither do I want the plague."

Darene grabbed them by their arms and ushered them out. "You are too loud and not very funny with your jokes. You'll disturb Aleah. Go outside and fight."

Lish and Sarn went outside. The sun was moving up to noontime, and the air was becoming hot.

"So," said Lish, "Derxter thinks that Toler is still here. That is good. At least he won't be looking for him any other place."

"I've been thinking about that," said Sam. "Derxter doesn't really need you or Mary Magdalene. Not if you plan to stay here. He really just needs Toler and myself because we can go back and report on him."

"I'll tell him that next time he comes after me," said Lish. "Or when I find him."

Sarn raised a brow. "What do you mean?"

"When I find him. As long as he's on this planet, I'll look for him. And if he leaves the planet, I'll have your assurance that you'll take care of him back on Bigor. If not, then I'll return to Bigor myself." Lish had a stern, determined look about him. "Somebody has to stop Derxter."

"It is wrong for him to be allowed to go about hurting people." Lish's wet eyes were evidence of the depth of his feelings.

"I respect what you're saying, Lish, but what are you going to do if you catch him?"

Unsmiling, Lish looked straight into Sam's eyes. "Kill him."

There was a long pause as Sarn assimilated Lish's intentions. "But how are you going to kill him? Come on, he's a trained fighter. You and I together wouldn't have a chance against him."

Lish slightly pulled back his robe. Sarn caught the glint of gray steel.

"You've still got his laser gun!"

"And until he's gone, I'm going to keep it!"

"Do you have a plan?" asked Sam.

"Yes, and how would you like to be a part of it?"

Chapter 50

LISH LOOKS

"Now why do you suppose Derxter is here on this planet?" Lish asked Sarn.

"Why are you asking me?" Sarn shrugged. "I don't know. Humor me. Give me the best answer you can."

"I barely know what I'm doing here. I sure don't know what he's supposed to be doing," said Sarn. "But it has something to do with the Messiah. That's what started this whole thing as far as I know. If a messiah had not been planted on Earth, then Derxter or Toler or me would never have set foot on this planet."

"I agree with you. Now, since the Messiah is gone—"

"At least, we think he's gone," added Sarn.

"Off and on, I hear. He's still making occasional visits with his disciples. People just don't die like they used to."

"Not Jesus."

"Now that Jesus has completed his public work," Lish corrected himself, "what keeps Derxter around?"

"I hate to sound conceited, but I think it's me and Toler."

"Again. I agree. Anything else?"

"You and Mary Magdalene—to a lesser degree. But if Toler and I were gone, I think Derxter would leave you alone."

"I'm not very good with this sort of thing," said Lish, "but see if you can follow this line of reasoning. The forces of badness owned this planet for untold eons. Then one day, in the guise of a messiah and heralded by a strange star, the forces of good arrived. There was a battle of sorts, and a beachhead was established by the Messiah. Right now he's shoring it up, I suppose."

Sam's face lit up. "Are you saying that the forces of evil have taken the guise of Derxter?"

Lish twisted his face. "Maybe it's one of those things that sound strange after you hear it spoken."

"And if that is the case, Derxter may need to stay around to stomp out the beachhead." The two pondered this for a moment. "But why him? Why must the forces of evil, whoever they are, import someone from Bigor?"

"Because Derxter is so good at it!" Lish answered. "Besides, it's a dirty job, and somebody has to do it." He shrugged. "Seriously, I think the forces of evil—I feel so melodramatic using that term—are totally opportunistic and will use whoever happens to be available."

"Are you saying the forces of evil—that is beginning to sound weird—are unorganized and opportunistic? Maybe the forces of good are well organized. After all, a lot of planning had to go into getting a messiah planted here. That's not something you do overnight. Did you know Jesus's appearance has been anticipated here for hundreds of years?"

"Hold it, Sam," said Lish. "Don't get so wound up. Yes, I know that. I've been around these people for a while, you know. But you may be making an unfair judgment about the forces of evil. They may have planned for thousands of years before taking over this planet, and we just don't know about it. And the forces of good may be just as opportunistic as the other side."

"How's that?"

"Just suppose you were in charge of the forces of good. Like a god or the power."

"Right. Our terminology is lacking, Sarn. Anyway, if you were in charge and your plan called for a messiah, wouldn't you want a large supporting cast?"

"A messiah couldn't do much without it, could he?"

"So you would use whatever—whoever—was available. Like you. Or me. Or, more likely, Mary Magdalene and the disciples."

Sarn squatted under a tree by the well and pulled a weed to chew on. "I gotta think about that, Lish. Somehow I just never thought of the power needing to use me for anything. Or you either, no offense meant."

"None taken. But if the forces of good and evil are locked in combat on this planet, and if Derxter is the embodiment of evil, then how will good have a chance—now that the Messiah is gone, more or less—unless it's through us?"

"Is that why you're going after Derxter? Because you want to be a player for the good side?"

Lish shook his head. "That's not my reason. My cause has to do with disgust. And fear. And loyalty to my friends."

"Aha! And the power doesn't really care why you're willing to go after Derxter—just that you do it. You're being used," said Sam. "I don't like that it sounds dishonest."

"Why? We haven't been misled. I am still a free agent and can back out of this adventure anytime I please."

"Misadventure," Sarn corrected. "What if your free will is an illusion and you are in reality a pawn of the power?"

Lish reflected on the question. "I guess it doesn't matter. As long as I believe my will is free, that's all that matters to me. Is there a better option?"

Sarn leaned forward and abruptly changed the subject. "Did Toler tell you we're missing a laser gun?"

Lish looked up, raised an eyebrow, and shook his head.

"We think a guide has it but don't know for sure. If he doesn't, maybe he knows who does." Sarn told Lish about their trip to Masada, the loss of the gun, and the strange slaughter of the soldiers.

"There was a rumor about some soldiers being slain, I recall that. Overheard someone in town telling about it. But you hear those kinds of rumors all the time." He rubbed his jaw and contemplated the scene Sarn had painted for him. "Interesting!"

Mary came out the back door of the house and headed in their direction.

"We've been blabbing so much I haven't told you my plan," said Lish. "Here comes Mary. I think she needs to be in on it too."

Mary walked up, smiling broadly. "Aleah just woke up for a short time. I think she is going to make it. Just thought you'd like that report." She looked from one to the other. "Am I interrupting something?"

Lish and Sarn both sighed as one. "I am so thankful she will live," said Lish. "Can you tell yet if she will fully recover from her injuries?"

Mary shook her head. "It's too early to know. She may always have a limp, and we're not sure about her left eye."

Sarn bit his lip. The image of Derxter beating Aleah was almost more than he could bear.

"Now what did I interrupt?" asked Mary.

"Wanta hear a plan, Mary?" Lish asked in his best conspiratorial voice. It was obvious that his attempt at humor was forced, but then none of them were ready at that moment to deal directly with their real feelings.

She narrowed her eyes and joined the intrigue. "I'd love to. If I can be part of it."

"Of course! What would a dangerous plan be without the brilliant and irrepressible Mary Magdalene? Have a seat." He indicated a bench by the well, and Mary sat down.

"I'll get right to the point of the plan. Mary, I'm going to kill Derxter."

"Right. And I'm going to fly across the lake this afternoon and drop eggs on the fishing boats."

"He's serious," said Sam.

329

"Don't play with me, Lish. It's a bad time to make jokes like that."

Lish shook his head. "It's no joke, Mary. The man has been hurting people, and I don't think he is through yet. Do you remember our discussions about good and evil? I think Derxter is the physical manifestation of evil, the opposite of Jesus, and his job is to stamp out what's left of Jesus's work."

"Are you certain?"

"No—yes. How does one become certain about that sort of thing? How did you become certain about the goodness of Jesus? You were probably as close to him as anyone, but how are you certain that he was the embodiment of good?"

"Well, he just said good things. He was helpful to others. He cared about what happened to people. There was just something about him that felt good."

"And the opposite holds true for Derxter. There is something about the guy that just feels evil."

"I'll vote for that!" said Sarn.

"It's scary to talk about fighting that man! Look at what he's done to Aleah." Mary was becoming upset.

"I have looked, Mary," said Lish, "and that's why somebody has to do something. If you and I had been at my house when Derxter came yesterday, we would probably be dead by now."

"I suppose you are right. But," she had a thought, "I don't think Jesus would have done it this way."

"Or course not," said Lish. "He has to be true to his teachings in order to maintain credibility with his followers. And those teachings, in spirit, are quite good. They just don't always work in practice." Lish shrugged. "That's why he needs perverted and sadistic fools like us to do his dirty work for him."

Mary was clearly disturbed by this line of argument. She had come to love Jesus with all her being, and she respected his teachings of nonviolence and forgiveness of enemies. Was it possible that he had not known of what he spoke? She didn't want to think so, but Lish was being most persuasive. The thought of the hulking Derxter savagely beating on the young girl made her decision for her.

"You're going to kill him? How do I fit into this plan?" she finally asked.

The three spent the next several hours discussing the details of their plan.

"I see no reason to put it off," said Lish. "Let's go ahead with it today. Agreed?"

The others nodded, and they set about putting the plan into operation.

Aleah woke again for a short time. She seemed to recognize the women around her bed and attempted to say something before she again drifted off into sleep.

"Next time she wakes up, we'll get some soup down her. She needs to eat something." Nerna turned to Mary. "Are you going to stay here tonight? We can make room if you want."

"No, I think I'll stay at Lish's tonight. He and Sarn are expecting Toler to arrive tonight, and it may be late when he comes in. I want to be there too. There is so much we have to talk about."

"Hah!" said Nerna. "What do you talk about with three men? They put you in the corner and maybe let you listen while they talk. Better you stayed here."

"No, it's not like that. These men really do listen to me. They're not like most men."

"Why should they listen to you?" asked Darene. She did not trust this business of men and women sitting together and discussing matters. As much as she had loved her husband, he had never cared much about her opinions. He had always expected her to take care of the children and the household while he took care of the important things.

"I don't know. I guess because they think I'm intelligent." Nerna and Dame glanced askance at Mary as if she had grown another head.

"Don't look at me like that. I am intelligent. Is there anything wrong with that? You're probably just as intelligent as I am, but you're afraid to show it."

"But," said Nerna in her motherly I-know-what-I'm-talking about voice, "be that as it may, that is not what men want from a woman."

"They don't want a smart woman," chimed in Darene. "They want someone to bed them and have children and cook."

"And do the dirty work they don't want to do," said Nemna.

"When did you start thinking like that?" asked Darene. She was becoming intrigued with the possibilities of which Mary spoke.

"After I got to know Jesus. He was the first man to treat me like that. He used to talk for hours. He would ask my opinions on all sorts of things. He would listen to my ideas without saying a word, think about them, and maybe ask me some more questions. Then we'd discuss our ideas. I really felt like I was important when we talked. I had never felt that way before, and I haven't been the same since."

"Once the goat gets out of the pen, it's hard to keep him in. Yeah, I know what you're saying, Mary, but it just doesn't seem right." Nerna crossed her arms, making an exclamation point in the conversation.

"I would like to help you fix supper before I go. Darene, if I give you some money, will you go to the market and get a chicken? Some chicken soup would be most good for Aleah."

"I don't mind. You ought to stay tonight. I'm sure not going back to my house with that madman on the prowl. I do hope you'll be safe tonight."

Darene was grateful for the opportunity to get out of the house, and besides that, she liked to shop. She knew just about everyone in Gennesaret and was known for her long-winded conversations in the marketplace. Some thought she was an interesting person to know while others thought she was simply a gossip.

Mary was counting on her being a gossip.

Lish picked up a lake bass from the basket. He hefted it, estimated its weight, and offered the fisherman a price.

"Ha-ha-ha! Do you think that fish just swam up to my boat, knocked on the side, and said, 'Mr. Fisherman, can I come get in your basket so you can give me away to someone?' No sir! That fish was a hard one to catch. He even ripped my net. He caused me a lot of trouble, that one! No, must have twice that for him."

"You keep him then. I would be afraid to cook a fish who had caused so much trouble. He might make even more trouble for me. What if he jumped around in my stomach after I ate him?" Lish winked at Sarn who had never become accustomed to the idea of bartering for goods.

"I tell you what," said the fisherman. "You chew him real good before you put him in your stomach, and his troublemaking days will be over."

"For that price, maybe you should throw in another fish. You see, my guest from the far country is coming to see me this evening. We will have a party. Have you met my friend, Sarn? Sarn is from the far country too. We thought he was dead, but he is not. So we are having a celebration tonight. And Mary. Have I not introduced you to Mary? She has been staying with me for almost a week. Surely you have seen us together on the docks."

The fisherman looked blank. He had never heard Lish, usually a very private individual, talk like that before. Oh, well, maybe having a party loosened his tongue.

"A party! Well, why didn't you say so? All right, who am I to interfere in a party? Sure, you take two fish for the one price. If you hear of anyone else having a party, send them this way so I can give my fish away to them. Has not the God of Abraham decreed that I should provide for all parties? Indeed, I have been blessed with this role."

Lish chuckled as they walked away from the still-complaining fisherman.

"If he thinks he is cheated, why didn't he just say no?" asked Sarn.

"He doesn't think he was cheated. That's just part of the game these men play. Most of them seem to be frustrated actors, and they love to entertain themselves with these little routines. I think they must practice while out in their boats. It's not just the fishermen. The vendors in the marketplace do it too. It's a cultural thing. He would have been disappointed if I had not haggled with him. Making the money from the sale is not the whole thing, although it is the most important part, I grant. It is expected that we will match wits, and however the deal is cut, he will come away lamenting how he has suffered so that I may have a better deal. Suffering seems to be an important cultural ingredient with these people."

"Almost sounds like martyrdom," observed Sam. "Come to think of it, Jesus ended up a martyr."

"Always acting the martyr, whether it is true or not, has some nice protective aspects," said Lish. "If you always say you are getting the short end of the stick, then you are never disappointed. And—"

He was interrupted by another fisherman who had just caught up with them.

"Hold on there, Lish. It's me, Ilor." Lish turned and smiled at the old fisherman with a long white beard. "Hello there, Ilor. It's been a few days since I've seen you. What can I do for you?"

"I got something for you, Lish." He held up some fresh turnips. "I heard you're having a big party tonight and knew you'd be wanting some of these. Right out of my garden. Cheap too."

Lish smiled at Sam. "Well, I guess we will need some of those turnips for our guests, won't we?"

"Of course," Sarn answered.

"My, how word does spread," observed Lish as they walked on down the waterfront.

"Let's just hope it spreads to the right person," added Sarn.

"I have a feeling it will. I don't think Derxter will leave the area until he gets rid of a few people. And you can bet he's not just sitting around somewhere playing with himself."

"I'm hungry," said Sam. "Let's get Mary and go eat that fish and turnips." Actually he wasn't sure he could eat anything. The thought of Derxter coming for dinner was more than enough to kill his appetite.

One mile southwest of Gennesaret, a quarter mile from the lakeshore, was a small old house, almost hidden by an overgrowth of vines and bushes. It had once been lived in by a family, but after the children had grown, the woman died and her husband left for parts unknown. Since then it had been used as a storage building for hay, a clubhouse for some local boys, a meeting place for lovers, a temporary residence for transients, and now as a hideout for Derxter.

The late-afternoon sun beamed through the cracks in the wall and highlighted rays of suspended dust particles. Nawaf's one good eye glinted in the dim light as he stopped in the middle of the room. He couldn't make out the form of Derxter, although he knew the giant was in there somewhere. Nawaf didn't know if his eye was losing its acuity or if Derxter just had some special way of blending into the background.

"Derxter?" Nawaf scanned the room but could see no one.

A hand on his shoulder caused him to jump. He turned to face up to Derxter towering above him. Instinctively he backed away, his heart bouncing all over his chest. His voice faltered as he spoke, "I have news that may be of interest to you."

"What is it?"

"Lish, the man whose house is not too far from here—he is having a party tonight."

"So?"

"Did you not want to hear any news at all about him?"

"You fool! Who will be at the party?"

Nawaf resented the degrading way Derxter treated him but had learned long ago to swallow his pride in return for a few coins. It had not been easy to make a living since losing his eye, and Nawaf had been reduced to making ends meet any way he could. His scruples had disappeared as his desperation had increased. Although the townspeople had once sympathized with him, they had offered no tangible help; Nawaf no longer wasted any allegiance on them or anyone. He had made his peace with himself: he would do whatever it took to survive.

"A woman. And two friends from the east. I am not sure where they are from, but it is a long distance away."

If you only knew how far, thought Derxter. "What else?"

"Nothing. Just that Lish is having friends over for fish. Surely that information is worth something?"

"Here!" Derxter tossed two coins into the dust. "Now leave. Bring me more information if you can."

"Two pennies? But—" Nawaf shut his mouth. There was something about this man that frightened him. He wished he had never agreed to do business with Derxter and in that moment decided he would take his two pennies and not come back. Nawaf went to the floor and felt in the dirt for the coins. He suddenly felt a viselike grip close around his head and he was lifted off the ground. Derxter's massive arms twisted the head to the left, to the right, and backward. Nawaf heard the crisp popping sounds at the same time he felt his neck breaking. Sudden excruciating pain, then no feeling, just a brief waiting period while life quickly ebbed from his brain. He was already dead when his body landed in a heap in the corner of the old house.

Derxter stared out the window at the late afternoon light. He was irritated with himself for having killed Nawaf. Why had he done that when the man might have brought him more information? Derxter had been seized by an urge to kill Nawaf as he picked up his coins. *Killing is indeed enjoyable,* he chided himself, *but be more discriminating.* He shook his head as if to clear it.

Getting involved in that massacre at Masada probably had not been a good idea, but then the Bedouins had so easily got caught up in his bloodthirst. It had been almost like a feeding frenzy, he recalled, again feeling some of the excitement of that night.

In the past few weeks he had become quick to lash out and hurt someone in order to get what he wanted, and that had lessened his effectiveness. He would have to do better than that against Lish and Toler. He smiled as he thought about the final struggle with the men from Bigor.

Derxter would visit Lish's party that night. It was time to kill all four of the fools and be done with it. His chuckle turned to a gurgle and startled him; he was becoming little more than a bloodthirsty animal. How he wished he had the laser gun. That would make the killing so much faster, but then he would miss out on the kinesthetic satisfaction of crushing their skulls. Derxter shook his head in disgust at his loss of professionalism. Whatever was driving him was becoming more powerful. A creature had surfaced, which even Derxter did not like. He cursed himself and left the house.

Walking toward Lish's house, Derxter remembered the camel riders. One of his men had reported back that someone on a camel had used a strange rather deadly weapon on one of his hired men. From the description it could only be a laser gun, and the obvious conclusion was that Lish had come to rescue Toler just as his hired men were closing in. But who was the other camel rider? The man had been terribly frightened when he reported to Derxter, but repeated questioning brought an insistence that there had been two camels and two riders. Could the second rider have been Sarn? What mattered most to Derxter at that moment was not the identity of the camel riders but the fact that Lish had a laser gun and he didn't.

Maybe if he went to the party early, before anyone else arrived, he could find the laser gun. Derxter smiled in anticipation.

"You're going to cook this fish yourself?" asked Sarn. "Which means, I guess, that you are going to dress it yourself? And the logical conclusion is that you have done this before?" The expression on his face revealed his obvious distaste.

Lish nodded; and then, adopting the voice of the fisherman at the wharf, he added, "No, the fish just knocked on my door and said he would dress himself if I would just please eat him."

Sarn smiled in spite of himself. "I'm glad you know how to do that because I sure don't. And from the way they smell, I may just wait outside while you take care of them."

"You know the house rule. He who doesn't help with food preparation doesn't get to eat. But I understand how you feel, and I certainly don't want you to do anything that would upset you in the least. There may still be some bread in the house you can munch on while Mary and I dine on exquisite fish cuisine." He shook his head. "How have you existed on this planet without learning how to clean a fish?"

"It wasn't easy." Sam's face took on a somber expression. "That reminds me. How do we know that somebody isn't already there, eating the bread and preparing a welcoming party for us?"

"First of all, I doubt that there has been time for word to get back to anyone like our infamous friend. And second of all, we'll just be real careful because that occurred to me too."

"Let me carry the fish," offered Sarn. "I want you to have both hands free to handle that laser gun. You do still have it, don't you?"

"Here." Lish passed the fish, wrapped in palm leaves, to Sarn. "Thank you, my friend. Those babies were getting heavy, not to speak of smelly."

Soon they were in sight of Darene's home. It still had the appearance of a deserted house. A few pieces of clothing scattered in front of the house gave testimony to the carnage that had recently taken place inside. They passed by, the silence of the house loudly ominous. Lish's house came into view down the path, and it too appeared deserted. Neither spoke as they made their way toward it.

Lish was in the lead, one hand held near the laser gun concealed beneath his garment. He had no apologies to make for his paranoia. Derxter was deadly serious about killing him, and the only way to survive was to be extremely careful.

He was already hyperalert as they drew near the house and immediately noticed the movement through the window. He knew it could be a bird, a village boy having fun going through the deserted house, or simply his imagination. It could also be Derxter.

"There may be somebody waiting for us inside," said Lish out of the side of his mouth. "Don't do anything different. Just follow me."

Sarn said nothing and contained an urge to stop and stare at the house. He tightened his grip on the tail of the larger fish, ready to use it as a club.

When they reached the house, Lish said loudly, "Spread the fish out on the ground while I get a knife to clean it!"

Sarn didn't know what else to do but kneel, lay the fish out on the palm leaf, and wait. Lish continued to the house, paused at the door, and, with hand under his garment, pushed the door open with his foot. It swung open easily and banged against the wall. Crouching, Lish leaned in, peered through the dim light, and saw nothing. He waited in the doorway, carefully scanning the room while his eyes adjusted to the darkness.

He saw no one in the single-roomed house. The back door was ajar, and Lish knew that he had closed it when he left the house early that morning. Whoever—or whatever—he had seen move in the house had gone out the back. If it was Derxter, he must have sensed that Lish had the laser gun with him and decided not to ambush him in the house. Instead he went outside possibly to—

Lish turned and ran to the front door. "Sarn!"

Sarn's face, mouth open, looked at Lish. Behind the boy, moving quickly toward him, was the hulking figure of Derxter. Lish pulled the laser gun.

"Get down!"

Without hesitation, Sarn threw himself flat across the fish just in time to be missed by the swooping arm of Derxter.

"Stop or I'll shoot!" ordered Lish, aiming the laser gun at Derxter.

Derxter froze, unexpectedly finding himself in the sights of Lish's aim. He breathed hard, and his eyes wildly darted around him, looking for an advantage. Derxter feinted to the right and then lunged to the left, rolling on the ground to the shelter of the house. Lish was not prepared for the quickness of the man. He let off a shot to his left, completely missing Derxter, then another shot to his right after Derxter had made his move. Although off the mark, the shot hit Derxter on his left forearm, severing it above the wrist. A wild cry of pain and rage followed him as he sprinted off behind the house.

Ashen faced, Lish and Sarn listened to Derxter's maniacal wailing and the thrashing of the underbrush as he fled. When everything was quiet, they looked at each other and dared to begin breathing again. Lish walked over to the hand, still sizzling, and prodded it with his toe. The fingers made a convulsive grasping movement.

"It smells terrible!" Sarn said. "Will he bleed to death?"

"No, the laser cauterized the wound. A lesser man would have fainted from the shock."

"Maybe we should follow him. He may be unconscious and dying out there," said Sam.

"Not me." He shook his head grimly. "I'm not eager to follow a wounded beast into the woods."

"What do we do now?"

"Hmmm. I've never been in this situation before. I think one thing we don't do is eat the fish."

Sarn looked down at himself. One of the fish was poking its tail out of his robe. The smell of fish covered him.

"I've never wallowed with a fish before."

"Let's go to town. At least we can intercept Mary if she is on her way here."

The two men encountered Mary just outside of town. She could tell from their expressions that something exciting had occurred. They told her what had happened at Lish's house.

"I guess that kills tonight's party," she said with a straight face.

Lish glanced at her and smiled. "Guess we'll have to postpone it to another time."

"Actually I don't feel that good about it," said Mary. "Of course I'm glad you are safe—I'd rather him be hurt than you—but I'm glad you didn't kill him. I just don't want anyone killed."

Lish spoke in a low voice, "I will still kill the man if I get a chance, and that is not meant to be offensive to you, Mary. But we must not underestimate his danger to us."

"With one hand? Surely you don't think he will continue to try to kill anyone! He is probably already on his way back to his homeland. Don't you think so, Sarn?"

Sarn slowly shook his head. "I wouldn't spend the night at Lish's house for a long time. Derxter will want revenge more strongly than you can imagine. I'm more scared now than before."

Mary looked questioningly at Lish. "Is that right?"

Lish nodded. "I'm afraid he'll be looking for a way to get back at us."

"I think we ought to get out of here," said Sam. "Let's go south and leave him here."

"Won't he follow?" asked Mary.

"Only if he knows where we are going."

"I'd rather stay here and fight it out," said Lish. "This is my home, and that's an advantage. On the other hand, that would probably bring danger on my friends. I can think of no better way for Derxter to punish me for shooting off his hand than for him to do something to Darene or Aleah," he paused, looked at Mary, and said, "and especially you, Mary." She lowered her gaze and blushed. For once she did not know what to say.

It did not take long for the three companions to negotiate a plan. They spent the night crowded in Nerna's house and early the next morning packed a few articles and said their good-byes.

"We'll be back, Nerna," said Lish. "We just want to go south for a while until this blows over. Be careful. If you see Derxter at any time, call for help. And please, don't let Darene and Aleah go back home for a while, not until you are reasonably certain Derxter is no longer around. It will be helpful if you will spread word around that we have left."

They then left town, taking the shore road southward. Soon they came across a fisherman repairing his nets on the shore. Without a word being said, all of them got into the boat and pushed off into the Sea of Galilee.

"Thank you, Harvel, for carrying us across the sea. It will make our journey easier."

"For you, Lish, I will do it. I owe you for the times you have been of help to me. And I will say nothing to anyone about it."

"Thank you. At least we can start our trip without looking over our shoulders on the first night."

"Have you ever been on the eastern shore?" asked Sarn.

"No," said Lish. Mary shook her head.

"Not as many villages on that side," offered Harvel. "Slower traveling too."

By noon Harvel had deposited his guests on the far shore and begun his return to the western bank. When he landed later that afternoon, just south of Gennesaret, a large one-handed man surprised him from behind, took him to the ground, and demanded to know where he had taken his passengers. Not a particularly heroic man, Harvel told Derxter, who then cut the fisherman's throat with a dull knife and stepped back to watch him die. Harvel tried to call out but only gurgled blood. He attempted to stand, made it to one knee, and fell face downward where he promptly died while his blood pumped bright red onto the sand.

Derxter became aware of a grin on his face and shook his head. He was surprised at how much he had enjoyed watching the man die. *I must do that more often, but I must find a sharper knife,* he thought as he left.

Derxter headed south. He would wait for Lish and his companions at Philoteria, where the Sea of Galilee emptied into the Jordan River. They would indeed be surprised to see him again.

Chapter 51

To the Cave

If Toler had been on the west bank of the Jordan River, he would have encountered Derxter and his band of men traveling to the north, but on the east shore he was oblivious to most of what happened across the river.

For the same reason, he missed Sarn following in Derxter's wake.

Toler mentally rehearsed the details of his coming departure from Earth, and by the time he reached Jerusalem, he was feeling a tremendous sense of relief; he was ready to go home. By the time he reached the cave, he had already emotionally left the planet. He had survived a clash with death and survived. He could go home now. The job was over.

He was not ready for the note he found.

Toler was ashamed of his first reaction: bitter disappointment, for now he could not immediately leave the planet. His second, and the stronger response, was a great relief and happiness that Sarn was still alive. He would return to Gennesaret and find Sarn.

And probably Derxter too.

He checked the supplies in the cave, looking for a laser gun. No, they had brought only one, and it was lost somewhere on the planet.

Toler found himself filled with fear and dread about returning to Gennesaret. Wouldn't it make sense to just wait at the cave? After all, since Sarn was probably already on his way back, there was no sense in risking the chance that they might accidentally bypass each other on the road.

Then Toler wouldn't have to face Derxter again.

Before he drifted off to sleep, he decided that in the morning he would go to Gennesaret, find Sarn, and face Derxter if he had to. After that he fell into a deep and restful sleep.

The first rays of daylight found Toler in a brisk walk on the road to the north. Not only was he eager to rejoin Sarn, but he found himself possessed by an unfamiliar recklessness.

I just can't run forever from guys like Derxter, Toler thought. *It's too fatiguing.* His sense of relief was tempered by an occasional heavy cloud of foreboding.

Toward the end of the second day, Toler was near Scythopolis and pleased with the rate of his progress. He had even stopped long enough to buy a knife with a longer blade than the small one he had been carrying.

The next morning Toler almost overcame the two camel men. He had resumed his trek with the first rays of dawn and had not traveled too far before he could see someone breaking camp ahead of him. The silhouettes of the camels immediately caught his attention, and Toler slowed his pace. He wanted to get close enough to identify them as the same mysterious camel men he had previously encountered but not so close that they might recognize him. Although one had saved his life, he nevertheless did not trust them. In fact, there were very few people he trusted anymore.

When Toler was about a hundred yards away, the two men mounted their animals and turned to the north. Toler was glad for the opportunity to follow and perhaps find out more about them, but it soon became apparent that the long-legged camels would easily outdistance him. By noon he could no longer spot them, and he remained as puzzled as ever about their identity.

By the middle of the afternoon he had neared the Sea of Galilee. There was a ferry on the Jordan River just south of the sea for the convenience of those traveling to and from Philoteria, which was situated on the eastern side of the river. The Jordan was not that wide, and many people simply waded across it. However, others carried goods or simply did not want to ford the river. As a result, the ferry was a welcome option, and most people chose to use it rather than get wet.

Owned and operated by an old man and his wife, the ferry was irregular in its trips. Although the couple owned the ferry itself, a flat barge-like craft, they had to depend on others for its power. The fare was reasonable enough, and most travelers did not mind the bit of labor required to move the craft. Therefore, it only operated when there were enough passengers to pole it across the river. It was common for people to give up waiting for the ferry to become operational and just wade across. The owner-couple was never certain where they would spend the night, for more than once they had ended the day on the other shore with insufficient passengers to get the ferry back.

It was at the landing that Toler again spotted the camel men waiting for the ferry. It was delayed on the other bank because of the difficulty someone was having loading his flock of sheep onto the craft. Some watched the scene from the other bank and occasionally called out suggestions.

Toler hung back in order to escape notice but was close enough to hear a man speak loudly to the camel men.

"Ask the old man on the ferry. He might know." The man shrugged and headed for some bushes. Several other men were already standing around the unfortunate shrubs, which served as a toilet for the travelers.

Curious, Toler altered his course and arrived at the bushes with the man. He casually relieved himself into the bushes, wrinkling his nose at the smell.

"Have you been waiting long?" Toler asked.

The man looked up. "Yes. Someone's sheep didn't want to ride on the ferry. But it's on its way back. I almost just walked across, except that I enjoy standing around with the other people and talking." He grinned at Toler. "Besides, I like to ride the ferry, even if it is such a short trip."

"Who are those camel men? I've seen them someplace, but I can't place them."

"Oh, them? I forgot their names. Kind of strange sounding. They've been asking about someone. They didn't say so, but it sounded to me like they are after someone."

"Is that so?" said Toler. "Who are they asking about?" He expected the man to say, "They're asking about somebody named Toler." He was therefore stunned when the man answered.

"Some big guy named Derxter. Or something like that. I'm not good with names. Never was."

Toler was speechless. The man looked at him strangely, shrugged, and walked back to the ferry.

What was going on? Were the two men attempting a link-up with Derxter? That seemed unlikely since one of the camel men had saved Toler's life by killing Derxter's henchman.

Was it possible the camel men were in pursuit of Derxter? It was possible if Derxter did not know about it, for he was not the kind to run away from two men on camels, riders who could barely control their mounts.

And why would Derxter be headed to Philoteria?

Toler pulled his shawl around his head so that his face could not be recognized from the side. He was about to return to the landing when out of the corner of his eye he noticed a man duck behind some bushes. *The drama at the ferry landing unfolds further!* Toler thought in exasperation. Quickly stepping around the brush, he confronted the hunkering man.

"Arie!"

The little man performed a squatted leap, but Toler was too quick and took him to the ground.

"Let me go. I'll scream for help!"

With his left forearm across the man's neck and the other hand holding a handful of hair, Toler hissed, "Try anything and you'll be sorry!" He leaned his forearm into Arie's neck as a demonstration.

Arie coughed and managed to whisper than he would not try anything.

"I don't have much time to fool with you. I'm going to ask you some questions, and I expect honest answers."

Eyes bugging, Arie nodded.

"Where is my laser gun, the weapon, you took?" He tensed to apply more pressure.

"I don't have it anymore," Arie rasped.

"Where is it?"

"In the Sea of Galilee I swear it!"

Surprised, Toler eased off.

"After I left you with the weapon that spews light, I tried to figure out how to make it work. I didn't even know what it was."

"Why did you take it?"

"It looked valuable. Never had I seen a metal like that. I thought maybe I could sell it."

Toler relaxed his grip and leaned back. If the laser gun was in the lake, then there was no need to threaten the little guide any further, even though he would like to thrash his hide for having stolen the gun.

"What happened?"

"I followed some travelers to the north and sat around their campfire with them. One night just south of here, I must have accidentally discovered how to work the weapon, for suddenly there was a burst of light and one of the donkeys started hollering. Everyone stopped what they were doing and looked in the direction of the animal and then at me. Nobody said anything, for it was an amazing occurrence, that beam of light. The owner walked over to his beast and saw that it had a hole in its side. There was nothing he could do but stand there while the animal died and fell at his feet. The man started cursing and turned on me. His friends came after me. What could I do? I made the light come out again, and it went into the ground. Before they could reach me, I caused the light to hit one of them across the leg, and he fell down screaming. The others were frightened back, but they swore they would catch me. Then I got scared."

"And so you threw the gun in the lake?"

"Not on purpose. It is too valuable for that. I left the camp that night and traveled north. By dawn I had reached the lake and paid a fisherman to take me out on the water. He and a friend agreed, and I thought I could then lose the men from the night before because they would not expect me to take a boat.

"It turned out the two men on the boat were crooked and had it in their mind to rob me. They were big and simply said to me, after we were away from the shore, that I should give them my valuables because they were going to rob me and throw me into the sea!"

"So you shot holes in their sides?"

"Only one of them. The other man was so afraid that he jumped overboard. He then remembered he could not swim and called for help." Still lying on his back, Arie shrugged. "So me the softhearted one, I reached over the side of the boat to pull him in. It was a trick, and he pulled me in. Somehow the weapon came loose from me and fell into the sea. I can swim and got away from there, leaving the man still trying to climb back into his boat."

Toler didn't object while Arie sat up and dusted his tunic.

"I am sorry. I should never have taken what was not mine. But it was a wonderful treasure, for one who knows how to use it."

"What about Masada? What happened up there?"

Arie's eyes widened and filled with fear. "That was a terrible thing. Never have I seen anything like it!"

"What happened?"

"I left you in the storeroom and looked around. No one was in sight, so I kept exploring and found the soldiers heaped in the basement of the apartment. It was terrifying the way they were killed. So I thought I should get out of there as soon as possible. That's when they caught me."

"Who?"

"Strange people. Some Bedouins, others trashy men, all led by a huge man. He was a monster! His eyes were not clear, and he didn't talk rationally. I don't know what was wrong with him."

"What was his name?"

"I am not sure. He ordered his men to capture me, and then before they could search me, he told them to mount and ride out. He was in a hurry."

Could it have been Derxter? Why would the man kill several soldiers?

"They obeyed him without question. They were as afraid of him as I was, maybe more. I figured they had seen him kill the soldiers."

"So they took you to Qumran?"

"In a way of speaking. By the time we got to Qumran, I think the big man had forgotten I was along. I was on the back of one man's horse and slowing him considerably. I think he saw a chance to kick me off on my head and took it."

Someone called out that the ferry was on its way. Should he follow the camel men or head on to Gennesaret? He could be at Lish's house before dark, he thought, and briefly flashed a warm image of Lish, Mary, Sarn, and himself sipping wine and talking until late that night.

Toler stood and turned his back on the little guide, who promptly scurried away into the bushes. Toler had no use for him anymore and did not bother to turn around.

The ferry ground onto the shore. The old man threw a line someone caught and fastened to a stump. Several men and a woman stepped off of the craft and onto the planking that formed a crude landing. Right behind them the nervous sheep spilled onto the shore, followed by their owner.

One of the camel men stepped up on the wharf and said something to the old man, "Why do you wanta know that for? My memory just ain't what it used to be. You know what I mean?"

The camel man pulled out his purse and offered a coin to the old ferry man.

"Well, what do you know? My memory just sharpened up a bit." He handed the coin to his wife, a misshapen yet hardy old woman who apparently handled the finances. "Yep, I'd say he came through here this morning. Matter of fact, it was on the last run I made. One hand gone too."

The camel man looked at his companion who shrugged. They were clearly surprised at the news.

"How did he lose his hand?"

"He didn't say how he lost it. He looked mean. Didn't no one want to fool with him."

"He was evil!" snapped the ferry woman.

"Are you coming? We can't just stand around here and jaw at each other all day. Got lots of folks who want to go."

Toler made his decision. He stepped aboard as the ferry shoved off and handed the woman his coin. He found a long oar and helped pole the ferry away from shore. The camel men were on the opposite side of the raft and paid no attention to Toler.

Derxter without a hand. Now how would that have happened? Toler knew one thing for sure: the man would be enraged and more dangerous than ever.

Lish may have an interesting story to tell, Toler thought, and smiled in anticipation.

When they reached Philoteria, Toler sidled off the ferry and followed the camel men into the town. His shawl hid his face, and Toler was less concerned about being recognized by the camel men than by Derxter, who would be watching the road behind him. *He could be staying in that barn or looking at me right now from that window,* Toler thought. Despite his best resolve, he felt the icy hand of fear gripping him. He drifted closer to the camel men; after all, they had laser guns and had protected him before.

People in the town seemed to move slowly in the bright sunlight. The camel men walked ahead of their animals and made their way to the town square where they could find food and drink. Toler was grateful for that, because he too was hungry. He bought bread and cheese from a toothless woman.

"Have you seen a one-armed man here today?" he asked her.

"Yes, there was one here today. He was missing a hand. A big man too."

"That's the one. Do you know where he went?"

"He ate—a messy eater, that man—and left to the north."

She gestured behind her where the main street headed through town and became the road to Hippus. "He didn't make sense when he talked, that man." She shook her head.

"Thank you," Toler said.

"Is that man sick? Sick in the head, I mean. He had the same look I have seen in sick animals as if they were possessed by demons."

Toler noticed that the camel men had also gathered information and were moving down the main street to the north. Apparently Derxter had not been exactly inconspicuous.

At the edge of town there was a large stable by the road with a grizzled fellow mending a bridle outside the doorway. The camel men approached the man and asked questions. Meanwhile, Toler leaned back in the shadows of a doorway to watch.

The bridle mender nodded and gestured toward his stable. The camel men stiffened and turned their full attention to the barn. One of them put his hand to his side as if checking his weapon. Slowly they made their way toward the double doors and peered into the dimness of the barn. Framed in the doorway, they waited for their eyes to adjust to the darkness. Above them the loft window slowly swung open.

Derxter, with a scythe in his one hand, balanced in the window above the two unsuspecting camel men. Toler opened his mouth to scream a warning just as someone shouted.

"Look out! In the loft!" Derxter was distracted by the shouting from the road, long enough for the camel men to turn and spot him. He swung the sharp blade downward and caught the sleeve of one of the men. The other camel man leaped backward and fired his laser gun. His shot was high, and Derxter disappeared into the loft.

"Watch the front! We'll go around back!" the voice shouted again.

It was Lish! And Mary and Sarn. Lish, laser gun in hand, ran around to the back of the barn with Sarn close behind.

The camel men entered the front door of the barn, and it appeared Derxter was trapped. Suddenly there was a whooft, and the two camel men rolled through the doors onto the street. Derxter lunged out of the barn and was upon Mary Magdalene before she could move. With his left arm around her neck, his right hand held a knife to her throat. Shielding himself with his hostage, Derxter faced the barn.

"That's far enough, you poor, wretched fools! Come any closer, and this cow will die!" The camel men had regained their feet and stood in the doorway, immobilized by Derxter's threat. Lish and Sarn came around the side of the barn and froze.

"Now it's reckoning time for all of you!" Derxter's voice slurred, and there were flecks of spittle on his chin. His eyes were wild, and there was a tremor in his hand. The stump of his left forearm was a deep red orb jammed under Mary's jaw.

"Throw the laser guns to me. Both of them!"

One of the camel men, hands in the air, stepped forward. "In the name of Sathel of Xerxes Galaxy I ask you to stop this madness."

"Sathel! A poison word! Yes, of course we'll stop this madness just as soon as you give me your guns." He hitched up his grip on Mary, and she grunted in pain.

"If we give you the guns, you'll kill us all," said Lish.

"That's just a chance you'll have to take, isn't it? Or else watch me carve this pretty woman's face." He pressed the knife under her jaw and made ready to pull it across her jugular.

Toler remained in the shadows of the doorway. Events had happened so quickly that he had not been sure just what to do. Now Derxter and Mary, backs to him, were perhaps five strides away. If he attacked Derxter, Mary would probably be killed. It seemed to be a no-win situation, and the only logical solution was to sacrifice Mary since that was the only way Derxter could be taken. To give him the guns would assure that they all died, including Mary. But under the circumstances, the men were not thinking very logically.

They were not prepared to watch helplessly as Mary was tortured.

"Let her go," said the camel man, "and things will go much better for you."

Derexter laughed-sputtered. "You fools, time is running out!" He drew the knife up Mary's cheek, leaving a crimson line from her jawline to her temple. "Would you like to see her eyeball speared on my blade?" He laughed. "I might even eat it while you watch!" Again he laughed, spraying the air with spittle.

Lish could take it no longer. As Derxter poised the knife point over Mary's right eye, Lish threw the gun to the ground several feet in front of Derxter.

"Thank you. And now the other one."

"Let her go!" pled the camel man.

"An eyeball on my knife," Derxter chortled, and then his words became incoherent.

The camel man was a professional, thought Toler. He would never give in to Derxter, who by now had gone totally insane. That meant Mary would die unless he did something. He stepped out of the shadows so that he could be seen by the four men facing Derxter. He hoped they didn't give his presence away, but then Derxter was not entirely alert any longer. The camel man spotted Toler with a quick glance and then riveted his attention on Derxter and Mary. Lish and Sarn gave no indication that they had noticed the shadowy figure in the background.

"All right, here's my gun. Now let her go!" and the camel man tossed his gun a few feet from Lish's gun.

Derxter laughed hysterically and staggered toward the weapons, dragging Mary with him. Crouching, Toler moved closer.

Standing above one laser gun, Derxter seemed torn about what to do. He wanted the gun but seemed captivated by the power the knife gave him. The blood on the side of her face thrilled him, and now that the guns were his, he could continue to cut her up while they could do nothing but watch.

"Before I kill you with the gun, I want first to chew her eyeball for you."

Toler was horrified. Derxter would not lower the knife and give him the moment he needed. It was now or never.

Derxter poised the knife above Mary's eye socket when Toler hit him behind the knees with his shoulder. Derxter fell backward, releasing Mary Magdalene as his arms flailed out for balance. Cursing, Derxter dropped the knife and reached for the gun. Toler, caught up in a tangle of legs, also grabbed for the weapon but was a split second too late. Just as Derxter raised it to fire, reinforcements arrived in the forms of Lish, Sam, and the camel men, who quickly wrested the gun away from the vituperating giant. The men were barely able to hold the crazed Derxter spread-eagled.

The dust made mud on Derxter's sweaty body, and he gave off a foul odor. Features deranged, eyes unfocused, he called out strange words and sounds and then cried and moaned. Toler glanced at the others; all seemed to be repulsed by the evil hulk they held to the ground. The evil blasting from his mouth carried the stench of death; even the sweat pouring from his pores was so viperous as to cause them all to feel contaminated and unclean.

Sarn was the first to become aware of the light, and then the others saw it. Even though it was midday, the light shone so brightly that they could not look directly at it. Toler turned his face away, afraid that he would be blinded. He heard Mary exclaim. When he tried to look again, the light had dimmed some enough that he could make out a figure in its midst. Mary said something else and began softly sobbing, rising from the ground where she had fallen.

"Jesus!" Mary stumbled toward the figure in the light.

A voice, so authoritative and yet melodic and kind, floated from the light and touched them. There was no other way to describe the voice, for it was like the dew that settles on the leaves, and it was like the deep reverberations of the earth itself, and yet it was like music. And time stopped while the voice spoke so that Toler was not certain if the words had been spoken unhurried and aloud or simply transmitted telepathically in a split second.

Later none of them could relate what the words had been, yet all agreed on the meaning. The voice had caressed them and provided comfort. There had been a gentle chiding for not doing better; hope had been offered, with a promise that in the end the power of good would triumph.

It was then that Derxter began a horrible screaming; a terrible agony distorted his face. In the next instant his features contorted, twisted, and vomited mad rage. With a burst of energy Derxter raised the men off the ground and flung them aside like rag dolls. Pulling himself to his knees, Derxter, his eyes red coals, stared hard at the Messiah, hackles bristling and growls erupting from deep inside him.

Somehow—no one could ever say how—the sunlight dimmed in the cloudless sky and a sudden wind whipped their garments and stirred the sand into little whirlwinds. The light surrounding Jesus dimmed too and then brightened again as if a heavy load had been placed on its energy supply. Toler thought that the crazed Derxter was preparing to charge into Jesus and attempt to physically destroy him; but both remained still, facing each another, oblivious to anyone else. The light continued to vacillate, and the wind turned cold and picked up to a roar. A rumbling came from everywhere and nowhere, growing louder until the men thought their ears would pop.

When they thought they could stand it no longer, Derxter suddenly brought his hands to his head and cried out in terrible pain. His eyes bugged until it seemed they would pop from their sockets and roll down his chest onto the ground. Jesus swayed, and even in the gale large drops of sweat stood out on his forehead. Derxter threw back his head and let out the longest and most woeful moan any of them had ever heard. After the wail had echoed off the barn and been scattered by the wind and etched itself forever in their minds, Derxter the Dreaded whimpered and died.

His body fell backward, legs still under him, convulsed a few times, and was still. A green substance gobbled itself out of his mouth and mixed with his beard before tumbling into the dirt.

The light surrounding Jesus glowed brightly once more, and by cue the wind died and the sun reappeared.

Chapter 52

Summing Up

The *Sprint* knifed its way through the emptiness of the universe on a course toward Bigor and home base.

Toler studied his crewman who had grown so much during the mission. No longer a boy, Sarn was broader in the shoulders and generally seemed more mature. He had kept his beard, a reddish-blond affair, which was much thicker than his first wispy effort. Sarn's self-confidence was evident in his voice and even in the way he moved.

The boy has grown up, thought Toler. Sarn noticed the captain looking at him, and the two exchanged a long look, full of meaning. There was so much to say and yet no way to say it adequately.

Finally Sarn smiled and said, "Some trip!"

Toler nodded, smiled, and said, "It was that!"

"Do you suppose that Lish and Mary will stay together?" asked Sarn in between mouthfuls of government-prepared food.

"I was thinking about them too. They seem to be kindred spirits in a strange land. They'll stay together. It's not often you find two people so closely attuned to one another. When you do, you'd better hold on to them."

Sarn thought about that awhile. "When you put it like that, maybe we all four should have stayed together. I have never felt so comfortable with people as I did when we were together. I think Aleah would have fit in too." He frowned. "I hope she will recover from that beating."

"She'll have wounds for a long time, and more than surface scars, that was a traumatic experience." Toler felt very sorry for Aleah.

"I think I could have become very close to her," said Sarn. "Maybe someday we'll meet again."

"Sometimes you have to travel to other planets to find kindred spirits," Toler said. "That's the downside. The upside is to be able to say that there are kindred spirits somewhere!"

"Do you have any close friends back home?" Sarn asked. "I mean people that you feel close to."

"Two." Toler was very homesick to see Gen and Ahna. None of them had any idea he would be gone for so long. Yet he fully expected to reenter their lives as if he had left yesterday.

"I'd like to meet them," said Sarn. "I don't know anyone like that back on Bigor." He supposed Tull was a friend but not anyone he felt really close to.

"It takes time to find friends. And sometimes it just happens when you're not looking for them. The harder you look, the more difficult it is to find them."

"That sounds paradoxical," said Sarn.

"It is. There are some things in life you can't force to happen."

"When we get back to Bigor, I'll have one close friend. I know you're the captain first of all, but I can't help but think of you as a friend," said Sarn, embarrassed at saying something so personal. He had felt a kinship with Toler for some time, an affinity that now didn't seem complete without expression.

Toler looked at his young crewman and realized that Sarn was right! A bond had been formed, which would remain important even after they returned home.

"And I'll have three good friends when we get to Bigor," Toler said.

"Toler, do you think you were affected by being around Jesus?"

"Why do you ask?"

"We were talking about the effect friendships have on us, and I was remembering what Thomas said to you one time that he had seen some change in you."

"Maybe." Toler thought back to his days as part of the Messiah's entourage. At the time, every day seemed dusty and hot and filled with tiresome travel from one town to another. There was always an endless procession of needful and wantful people, all seemingly too greedy, and Toler found himself resentful of their never-ending requests. And yet, when Jesus greeted the people clamoring about him, he was sympathetic and accepting. Although he might become impatient at times, for the most part the Messiah apparently genuinely cared for the wretches who came to him. Watching Jesus reach out to these people, most of whom lived on the bottom of society, did have an effect on Toler.

"You can't watch someone care for the unlovable riffraff of life without being affected. Maybe the most unlovable people are those who need love the most. Yes, Jesus made an impression on me. In certain circumstances I'll be different because of my association with him." Toler looked at Sarn. "What about you?"

"No question about it," said Sarn. "But not just him. I'll be different because of my friendship with Lish, Mary, and you. Maybe especially you, because we spent so much time together."

Toler nodded. "Yes, we did."

"Do you think there is a power?" Sarn asked. "We saw some weird things happen. I felt like we were in the middle of a good-versus-evil battle."

"Call them what you will, Sarn, yes, there were powers on Earth I have never before experienced. They apparently were personified in Jesus and Derxter."

"I wonder who won. Derxter died, but the force of Evil will take the form of someone else—or pigs." Sarn smiled as he recalled the pigs running into the sea. At the time it had not seemed funny, but now it did.

Toler smiled too. "Those pigs put on some show."

"Maybe there is some truth to it when people say, 'It's not my fault. Evil made me do it.' It's all right to place the blame on some external evil force when we've done badly but not when we've done good. Then we claim the credit for ourselves. If we were going to be consistent, after we had done something good, we would say, 'It's not to my credit. Good made me do it.'"

"I certainly wish the forces of good would prevail on you to get us something to eat!" said Toler.

"That is a no-win situation," said Sarn. "If the forces of good arrange for me to bring food to you, you'll then claim that the forces of evil compelled me to make it taste bad."

Toler chuckled. "The good part of it is that after my stomach is full, I won't care whose fault it is."

"Did you ever wonder how things would have come out if Sathel had not sent his two men to look out for us?"

"That's easy," said Toler. "We'd both be dead right now. Along with Lish and Mary. And Derxter would likely be on a killing spree. And Sathel would wonder what happened on Earth, and if he sent someone else, Derxter would have done his best to kill them."

"Maybe that's how the force of evil meant to get rid of Jesus's followers: turn Derxter loose."

"I doubt that would have done it. In the end, Derxter became irrational and scattered in his thinking. He wanted us dead, but otherwise I don't think he cared who he killed."

"Maybe his circuits were overloaded by the force of evil. It thought that he was such a fine killing machine that it demanded too much of him and he couldn't take it."

"Now, that's an interesting thought," said Toler. "Have you considered that the force of good may overload some people?"

They pondered this possibility for a while. Finally Sarn said, "Maybe so, but I've never seen anyone like that. The people I've known could have used a strong shot of good. Have you known anyone overloaded with good?"

"Just one," mused Toler. "I once knew a woman who wanted to do so much good for other people that she ended up just meddling where she wasn't wanted. People learned to stay away from her, but if she saw them coming down the street, she would head straight for them, determined to do some good. It soon got to the point where people wouldn't come out of their homes unless they knew where this woman was. Sometimes families didn't venture out for days at a time, and there were cases of near starvation when people couldn't get out to buy food. It became an epidemic of goodness fatigue, and soon people were hoping for a return of evil."

Sarn looked askance at Toler. "You wouldn't be putting me on, would you?"

"If I was, it was because evil made me do it."

"What are the politics of this business?" asked Sarn. "Does Sathel win? Is Lybur out of government?"

"You're asking me? I'm anything but a politician."

"You don't have any ideas about what's going on right now on Bigor?"

"Not much, because I don't understand what Sathel and Lybur have to do with the situation on Earth. I really don't see why they care about what happens back there."

"I've got an idea, but I don't want you to laugh at it."

"Go ahead," said Toler. "I'll not laugh unless evil makes me do it."

"What if the force of evil is using Lybur to stir up trouble even to the point of sending Derxter to Earth? And what if the force of good is countering with Sathel?"

"Yeah? Well, if that's true, and if Derxter is the agent of evil, then I guess that makes you and me the agents of good."

"Not just us. There's Lish and Mary and the two undercover men who saved our lives."

"And maybe a lot of people we don't know about."

"Just think," said Sarn. "The whole universe, since the beginning of time, may be a big never-ending contest between good and evil. You and I and everyone else are just pawns in the game and don't even realize it. And while ol' good and evil are enjoying themselves matching wits, people get pulled in and pushed out, influenced to be good or made to act badly. We create blame and guilt and forgiveness as ways to try to understand and control these forces that whip us around, but we never feel like we have attained control. Just when our lives feel good, here comes evil, and away we go again. Or just when we're ready to give up on ourselves, *wham*! Here comes good and lifts us up. Maybe our responsibility for being good or bad is an illusion we create, and in reality we have no final say."

"You've been doing some heavy thinking."

"When I think about it like that, I get angry," said Sarn. "If the power would leave us alone, then maybe evil would have no interest in messing in our lives. Did you ever think what it would be like if there was no good and no evil?"

"Can't say that I have. Sounds a little bland to me."

"Maybe that's because we've never known anything else. It might be nice to not have ups and downs all the time."

"I've never known anything else," said Toler, "so I guess I can't evaluate that statesmen. On the surface, sounds boring to me."

"Think of the headaches you would avoid if you didn't worry about right and wrong."

"I don't worry about right and wrong," said Toler. "Do you?"

"Not so much anymore," said Sarn. "I used to when I was living at home. My parents thought everything I did was wrong. I worried lots, trying to figure out how I could be good in their eyes. Turned out I was wrong for them. Period."

"They sound like unhappy people."

"I don't know about that, but I was sure unhappy. They asked me to leave home, said it was time for me to find out about the real world. They barely said good-bye when I left. They showed more emotion when the plumber left. At the time I thought the world had come to an end."

"But here you are, returning home from the deep reaches of space, having successfully completed your first assignment!"

Sarn smiled. "Do you think I'll get asked again? To go into space, I mean?"

"Oh, probably. You now have experience and a good reference."

"Thanks. And if you ever need any help with figuring out good and evil, call me."

"You remember what you said about good and evil having a fine old time pitting wits against each other, using us as the pawns?"

Sarn nodded. "What do you think about that?"

"It's interesting, but let me give you a slightly different way of looking at it. Suppose good and evil are natural forces that balance back and forth, just like light and dark, or hot and cold?"

"Physical laws?" asked Sarn. "Like positive and negative polarities?"

"Maybe. Maybe laws like survival instincts are laws. Maybe it's like germ warfare, where space—all space—is filled with both good and evil gas. They push back and forth, each adjusting its presence, seeking an advantage. People are affected by these gases and begin placing values on how they make people act."

"When in reality they are not good or bad but just neutral gases pushing and pulling against one another, not even aware that anyone might be breathing them."

"Something like that," Toler agreed. "And if that's the case, then there will never be a resolution to the question of good versus evil. That would be like saying that someday cold will overcome hot or light will take the place of darkness."

"If you have one, you've got to have the other," mused Sarn. "They are ends of a continuum, and without their opposites, they have no meaning."

"So if that is true, then it's a waste of time worrying about good and evil, right?"

Sarn thought about that for a while. "If we could leave it on a theoretical level like you just explained, maybe so. But it doesn't stay there. Those gases get breathed and change the way people act . . . people we care about and people who hate us. And we just can't leave it on a theoretical plane. We're too involved."

"You're right. I just don't think Derxter would have let us alone if I had explained all that to him.

"We'll dock in a few hours. Do you have your things together?" asked Toler.

Sarn nodded. "Will we be the first to return? I don't know how our ship compares in speed to that of Sathel's men."

"Ticol and Rajol left before we did, and I suspect Sathel gave them a first-rate ship. I bet they've been home a while and have already briefed Sathel."

"Sathel doesn't want Lybur to know we have returned. At least on Earth things were simpler."

"True enough," said Toler, "but you and I don't have to get involved in complications on Bigor. We've done our job, and we're through with it."

"But aren't you curious about what's behind all this? I have a lot of questions. I know where we went and what we did, but I have no idea how come. That bothers me a lot."

"I'm curious, but I'll not let it bother me."

"Another thing: why did they bring back Derxter's body? It would have been much easier to bury it."

"We never want to leave things behind that don't belong. Simple planetary etiquette."

"But Lish is still there. He'll be there until he dies, don't you think?" asked Sam.

Toler nodded. "Officially he is still doing research."

"And nobody will know—or care—when he dies. He has become one of the natives for all practical purposes."

"All right, I agree. But what about that little fellow—what was his name? The one who followed Derxter around. Squirb. Wasn't that his name?"

"All, yes, Squirb. I wonder what did happen to him," said Toler. "He just dropped out of the picture somewhere along the way. We'll never know, I suppose, although I wouldn't be surprised if in a fit of anger Derxter killed him."

"Or what if Jesus put an evil spirit in him and he stampeded off a cliff into the sea!" Sarn laughed at the thought.

"He already had an evil spirit in him," Toler said.

"What's the first thing you're going to do when we dock?" asked Sarn.

"Check in with Sathel. Find out if he wants to see me or if he just wants me to send in my report." Toler lifted an envelope. "It could have been longer, but I'm not that good with words. However, it's longer than what I usually write. I should have let you write it. It would have been more than plenty long then."

Sarn ignored the humor. "I would have gladly done it."

"Now you tell me! Why didn't you tell me before I labored over it so long and hard?"

"You sound glad to get back home. What are you going to do after you check in with Sathel?"

"Call Ahna. If she's on Bigor, she'll come pick me up and the two of us will disappear for a few days. If she's not available, then I'll call Gen and he'll pick me up. He and I will proceed to Dak's Bar and catch up on news. What are your plans?"

"First thing is find a place to live. I was rooming with a guy before I left, but he had to replace me with someone who could help pay the rent while I was gone. He can be glad he didn't wait on me! Then after I find a place and get settled, I'll be back on the steps waiting for another assignment. I can see how people get hooked on space travel!"

"Will you call your parents?"

"I hadn't thought of it. Do you think they'd want to hear from me?"

"Probably. They might be glad to know you've been off the planet and done some work for the government. Most parents would be proud. Have they been off the planet?"

"Hmmm. I don't think so. Imagine that, me leaving Bigor before my parents."

"Where would you like to go next," asked Toler, "if you could choose your destination?"

Without hesitation, and to his own surprise, he answered, "Somewhere in the Hoxd Galaxy."

"Oh? Why there?"

"They've been through the messiah experience before, and from what I've read, it did make a difference. I'd like to see what a planet is like after the messiah has come and gone."

"I suppose that would be interesting, especially since we've been through the first stage ourselves."

"I'm fascinated!" said Sam. "And someday I'd like to return to Earth and see our friends."

"I'll give you my phone number. Let me hear from you when you get settled. Next time I need a crew member, I'll give you a call. It may not be to the Hoxd Galaxy and certainly nothing to compare with what we've just been through, but it'll be somewhere."

"Thanks! Somewhere is better than nowhere, I always say."

"Buckle in now. We're almost home."

Chapter 53

HOME AGAIN

Puzzled, Toler asked for a repeat of the landing instructions.

"Repeat, Craft Rd. 1375 *Sprint* to land in bay 236, pad 7."

"Is that bad?" asked Sarn.

"I don't know. My pad is in bay 75. I've never been down to 236. I didn't even know they still used it."

"Maybe Sathel is trying to get us in without anyone knowing about it," offered Sarn.

"Maybe. Sure seems like the head of government could bring us in without hiding us. This is new to me, and I don't like it."

The ground control guided the *Sprint* down to one of the landing sites and then directed them to taxi to bay 236. Toler panned the area with the scanners but could make out nothing but older deserted hangars.

"There's not even a light on at this end of the field," Toler fretted. "I wish it was at least daylight."

"If you had let me plan our schedule, Captain," Sam quipped.

The bays were quite large hangars constructed in long rows along the taxiways. Several of the older bays were not in use any longer.

A sign with the numbers 236 came into their lights. It needed repainting. The doors in the enormous building had been rolled back, and the doorway gaped open like a huge mouth waiting to swallow them. There were no lights in the hangar, and the Sprint's beams stabbed through the thick darkness like a laser through a muddy pool of water.

"We're looking for pad 7," said Toler.

"I don't see any other ships around. This place is deserted. Is someone supposed to meet us?"

"Who knows? This is already different from anything I've done. If no one is here to meet us, we'll leave." Toler was very uneasy. He couldn't explain just why other than the procedure was unorthodox. He strained his senses as they made their way down the main aisle of the hangar. Their scanner picked up only empty pads, lonely walkways and the echoing sound of the *Sprint* rolling along on the concrete.

A sign with the large number 7 suddenly appeared in the *Sprint*'s beams. Pad 7 was simply a parking space for a ship and was big enough to accommodate craft much larger than the *Sprint*. Toler parked the ship, checked the scanners again but found no movement in the hangar, and shut it down.

"Do you have everything?"

"I'm ready," said Sarn.

The door opened and dropped steps to the floor. Toler led the way, and Sarn followed, closing the door of the Sprint behind them. For a few seconds they were in total darkness; and both stood still, listening, tense, and not sure why.

All was quiet, and Toler turned on his light. Above them, on the walkway, was a door; and Toler headed for it, Sarn on his heels. Halfway up the stairs Toler suddenly stopped, causing Sarn to bump into him. Toler turned off the light. Directly ahead of them, at eye level, was the bottom of the door, defined by a thin slit of light. Shadows passed back and forth across the light.

"Back down!" Toler hissed. Without saying anything, Sam quickly retraced his steps, followed by Toler. There were sounds from behind the door.

Toler grabbed Sarn's arm, flashed the light once to get his bearings, and pulled the youth with him under the walkway.

"Quiet!" Toler whispered as they moved behind several drums stored under the walkway grid. Frozen, they waited.

For a long time nothing happened. Whoever was behind the door was likely waiting for them to emerge. They probably thought the two had not yet finished unpacking the *Sprint* and would wait a while longer. Toler resolved to outwait them. He placed a hand on Sam's arm and indicated for him to remain where he was. Toler flashed a quick beam in the direction of the *Sprint* to get his bearings and made his way to the ship. The sound of the ship's doorway swinging open seemed unnaturally loud. Within two minutes, Sarn tensed as the door above his head opened and there was the heavy sound of someone stepping onto the walkway.

Looking up through the grid of the walkway, Sarn could see a faint light from the open door and the bulk of a man. The shoes seemed gigantic from his vantage point. They moved, and another set appeared on the walkway. A flashlight played over the *Sprint* and revealed the open port. Closing the hangar door behind him, the man with the light started down the stairs. Sarn ducked behind a drum just as the man shined the light under the walkway.

"Wait here!" he said to his companion on the walkway and strode toward the *Sprint*.

At that point in time, Sarn believed he had to do something. If the two men were friendly, they would have called out. Their manner suggested they were enemies, and they now had Toler cornered in the ship. Sam's hand found a large rivet lying on the top of the drum. In one motion he stepped from under the walkway and tossed the piece of metal high and to his left. It bounced off a wall in the next pad and skittered across the concrete.

A powerful light came on above Sam, its beam scanning the adjacent pad area. The other man backed down the *Sprint*'s ladder and called out.

"What was that?"

"I don't know. It came from over there."

"Let's look. I don't think anyone is in the ship. They must be hiding. Call Control and have them close the main doors to the bay. We don't want any slipups."

Sarn could hear the man above him talking on a radio. Within a short time, the sound of the giant doors rolling shut echoed in the cavernous hangar.

"You look from up there," the first man said, clearly in charge. He turned on his light and walked toward the next pad. The walkway spanned the length of the hangar, and the second man, light shining, made his way toward the next pad. Once his light caught the man on the ground, and Sarn saw the glint of a weapon in his hand.

Carefully Sarn stepped out from under the walkway, a second rivet in his hand, and with all his strength hurled it across the next pad into the one adjoining it. It bounced on the concrete and into a drum. The hollow metallic sound reverberated through the hangar.

One man cursed.

"Don't worry, there's no place they can go! Just don't let them get by us."

Sarn was startled by a hand on his arm. It was Toler, who pulled at Sarn to follow him. They climbed the stairs to the walkway, and Toler tried the door. It opened easily, and the two slipped out. Sarn's bag swung against the door and caused it to bang shut behind them. The excited voices of the two men could be heard clearly as they ran toward the door. Toler shined his light on the door and located a latch.

"Lock it!"

Sarn flipped the latch, and the two ran. The hallway into which they had entered was lined by doors. Toler opened one, an office, and another, which turned out to be a storage room.

"The end door—it'll take us outside!" said Toler.

It did not take long for the men to burn through the latch on the door, and they appeared in the hallway just as Toler and Sarn reached the other end. Toler put his shoulder into the outer door and turned the knob. It was locked.

Meanwhile, the two men, each with a laser gun, approached from down the hallway, surprisingly in not too great a hurry.

"We've got them now. Don't kill them."

Watching the men coming toward them, Sarn did not see Toler pull out his laser gun. He heard the shattering of the latch, and then they were tumbling through the door and onto grass. Toler got up, stood in the doorway, and fired a blast down the hallway. The two men screeched to a stop and took cover in one of the side rooms.

"Come on!" said Toler, and the two sprinted away in the darkness.

The spaceport was a huge place with numerous bays and other buildings, most of them shut down for the night. Ships dotted the pads, several bathed in strong lights as they loaded for some faraway mission. The area in which they found themselves was dark, lit only by an occasional night light. Rounding the corner of an adjacent building at full speed, they suddenly came upon a vehicle. Crouching behind it, they waited but saw no one. After several sequences of running, hiding, and waiting, there was still no sign of the pursuers. Finally they stood in the shadows of an office building with the name Colony Repairs on its front.

"Keep watch," said Toler and went to the public phone at the corner of the building. He input the number and waited.

"Is this Gen's number?" Sarn heard him ask before slamming down the receiver.

"I don't know who that was, but I don't think they're supposed to be at Gen's home at this hour of the night."

"Sarn, I don't know what is happening, but I'm scared."

Sarn turned slowly around, alert for any movement, but saw nothing. Shadows made from the variously placed lights around the field created a crazy pattern.

Toler input another number into the phone.

"Hello? Ahna? Yes, it's me. Not long ago. Listen, I can't talk now. Can you meet us? SpaceCafe. Good! And be careful that you're not followed."

"Do you think her phone is tapped?" asked Sarn. He was expecting the worst possible scenario.

"I am assuming that it is. And I am assuming that someone has just located the origin of that call and we will soon have visitors if we dally."

They had barely turned the corner of the next building when there was the sound of a vehicle arriving at Colony Repairs.

Doors slammed, and men ran across the pavement. Sarn started to run, but Toler caught his arm and pulled him into the shadows.

"Be quiet! Let's see if we can recognize any of our pursuers."

They crouched behind a stack of crates next to a building, a fairly obvious hiding place in Sarn's estimation.

"If anyone comes back here, we take him!" Sarn was surprised to hear the intense anger in Toler's voice. In fact, Toler had passed over an emotional threshold. He had been sent on a mission without proper crew or preparation, he and Sarn had been placed in danger more than once because of poor planning, and now that they were back (by a miracle!), they were directed to land in a deserted place where someone waited to ambush them. And when he called his friend and his girl, the lines were tapped. In the case of Gen, he didn't know who was at his friend's home, but they didn't sound like anyone he wanted to talk to.

It was too much! No longer was it acceptable to be treated like this!

Eight men in all exited the vehicle and began the search. Their arrival was quick, and they knew their quarry would not be far away. They spread out in pairs, covering four directions; and when a pair came to a junction, they split into singles. It was a single who came on the stacks of crates.

With laser on the ready, the man followed his light around the first stack of crates. Either he didn't expect to find anyone there or else thought that the element of surprise was his if he moved quickly. Without pausing, he went behind the crates, between them and the building, and shined his light in between each stack of crates. It was not a bad plan, for if he moved rapidly it would be harder for anyone to come up on him from behind. What he did not consider was that someone would be hiding somewhere besides behind the crates.

Toler pulled back into a doorway in the building and blended into the shadows. The pursuer was not paying attention to the building as he looked behind the large boxes. It was an easy matter for Toler to let him pass by and then stun him with the laser gun. The man went down without a sound.

"That was great!" said Sam, who appeared from behind the next stack of boxes. "I'm glad you didn't let him go any further."

"I don't think they want to hurt us. More likely they want to talk to us or rather have us talk to them. We're the only source of information about what happened on Earth."

"What are we going to do about this guy?" asked Sam. "He won't be out very long."

"Here!" Toler handed him the man's laser gun and then went through his clothing looking for identification. "Nothing! He has no name, no nothing."

"Who are these guys, anyway?"

"I suspect they're government men, working for Lybur, and he doesn't want any trace back to him. Come on, let's get out of here!"

It did not take long for them to reach the terminal's outer boundary, a high fence that had been erected years earlier.

"If we climb it, an alarm will go off and they'll know where we are," said Sarn.

"Maybe not. This is the older part of the field, and it's not kept up very well." He turned out to be right because after walking the fence for a short ways they located an unlocked gate. They slipped through and made their way to the restaurant.

Toler ate at the SpaceCafe nearly every time he came in from a trip. Like many of the other pilots, he knew the staff of the cafe by name or at least by sight. He led Sarn down a street, which brought them into sight of the front of the SpaceCafe. There they could observe the patrons through the glass walls of the establishment.

"I don't see Ahna," said Toler. "Let's just get comfortable and wait."

"How long should it take her to get here from her home?"

"She should be here anytime. If she ran into traffic or had other normal delays, it could be a little later."

The two found a natural cave in a grove of bushes where they could stand without being seen from behind. The sound of voices wafted across the park as spacemen came and went from the cafe. Occasionally there was the sound of music as the door opened to let someone in or out. A few vehicles passed, most of them carrying spacemen either home or to the terminal.

"I think that's her!" said Toler.

A woman—long hair, blue pants, and sweater—moved down the street toward the SpaceCafe. She carried herself erect and walked stiffly.

"Why does she walk that way? Is she crippled?" asked Sarn.

"She wasn't when I left. I think she is signaling us. Let's wait a while longer."

"If her phone was tapped, they know where you plan to meet her," commented Sarn.

"'I know, but she doesn't know for sure that we know."

Ahna walked into the SpaceCafe and sat at a window seat. She gave her order and was brought a cup of coffee. She poured several packs of sweetener into her cup.

"Ahna doesn't use sweetener. She's wanting us to notice that all is not right."

"Are you sure that is Ahna and not some other woman?" Sarn could not resist asking.

Toler ignored the question. He was wondering how he could communicate with her without being seen, for he was certain that she was being watched.

"Come on!" he said and made his way out of the bushes. By walking in a detour of several blocks, they were able to come up behind the SpaceCafe. It was dark except for one small light over the back door. The driveway, lined by trash cans on one side, led from the street up to the building.

"Let's scout the back. You take one side of the drive, and I'll take the other. Stay back far enough so you'll be behind anyone who is watching the driveway." Sarn checked the setting on his laser; it was still set on stun.

"Looks like they were trying to take us alive," he said. "His gun was set for stun."

"Might be better to take a lethal dose than to be captured by those guys. Lybur has a general who is called the king of torture. He'd love to meet us."

The two split up and scouted the drive. Toler found no one, but Sarn came across a man squatting behind a shrub. There was no law saying that a man couldn't squat behind a bush and watch the back of a cafe, but Sarn didn't think many people did that at night. It was a simple matter, even with his heart in his throat, to come up behind the fellow and stun him. After he and Toler met at the rear of the cafe, they securely gagged and tied the man to a tree.

"You find a hiding place and stand watch. I'm going in through the kitchen."

The hallway leading into the kitchen was dark. Toler paused in the darkness and listened. Someone was moving around, and the clang of metal and clatter of glass suggested dishes were being washed. He opened the door a crack and peered in.

There was one employee at this time of the night, and she was planted in front of the sink catching up on dishwashing. She glanced up, the movement of the door catching her eye. Sam stuck his head in and smiled, hoping she would recognize him.

"Hi! Don't I know you? Farz?"

The cook cocked her head and squinted at Toler. Her face lit up. "Toler! Isn't that your name? Where have you been?"

Toler eased his way in. "I've been on a mission, but I've been hungry for your cooking."

"Sure you are," she said sarcastically. "What can I get for you? You do look hungry like you've been living off space chow for a while."

"In a minute. First I have something I have to do. Will you help me?" Toler asked without doubting that her answer would be affirmative. Farz liked pilots because they were a rebellious, independent group who took time to share their stories with her. Farz was a vicarious pilot. She didn't like anyone who didn't like pilots.

Her face lit up. "Sure! What do you need?"

Toler moved to the door leading to the dining area, Farz following him. Ahna was still at the window seat, staring straight ahead, her coffee untouched.

"See that woman at the window? That's Ahna."

"Yeah? I think I remember her."

"I want to get her back here to the kitchen. What's the best way to do that so that if someone outside the building was watching, he wouldn't get suspicious?"

Farz thought a minute. "That's easy. I'll have the waitress take her a note telling her to go to the restroom. At the end of the hall leading to the restroom is another door. It goes to a storeroom, which is right through that door." She pointed to a door at her left. "You wait for her in the storeroom, and when she comes down the hall, you just open that other door and say, 'Hi, honey, your man is here!' That sound all right?"

"Great!"

Ahna didn't look up as the waitress brought her another cup of coffee. When her gaze went to the table, she saw a note by her cup, which simply read, "Go to the restroom."

She crumpled the note in her lap, glanced around, and casually walked to the restroom just as anyone eventually would if they sat around drinking coffee in a cafe. The door at the end of the hall opened just as she turned to go in the ladies' room. Toler leaned against the door frame, smiling.

"Are you free tonight?"

Ahna froze, eyes wide in surprise. A smile crossed her face and disappeared. She ran the two steps to him and threw her arms around his waist, sobbing into his chest.

Toler held her, surprised that their reunion was not more joyous and then not surprised as he understood the amount of pressure she must have been under—for how long?

"Let's get out of here!" Toler pulled her through the door. As they headed for the rear door, Farz asked if there was anything more she could do.

"Maybe there is. If someone comes asking where Ahna disappeared to, tell them she got sick and went home the back way or anything you think of. Just don't mention that anyone met her." It occurred to him that they would know she had been met by someone after they discovered their man tied to a tree.

"Farz, tell them something that will cover you. I don't want you getting into trouble over this. It won't matter much with us."

"You sure you'll be all right? I'll take care of myself. You two be careful!" She ushered them out the door.

Sarn stepped out of the darkness to meet them. "Everything all right?"

Sarn nodded. "Is this Ahna?"

"Yes, Ahna, this is Sarn. Now let's get out of here." Toler led them down the drive and off the street into the shrubs of the park, which surrounded most of the terminal.

"Where are we going?" asked Ahna. "We can't go to my place. I wouldn't think your place would be any better."

They shrank into the darkness as a large vehicle slowly rolled past.

"I don't know. I tried to call Gen earlier, but someone else answered. Do you know anything about that?"

"I'm not sure about anything," said Ahna. "I haven't been able to reach him at home. His office says he's taking vacation I'm afraid for his safety."

"Sarn, do you have any ideas where we can hide?"

"Why don't you call Sathel?" Sarn asked. "He's the headman and the one who sent you on the mission. Isn't this what it's all about, Star Light?"

Ahna looked at Toler. "Haven't you tried Sathel? He does seem the logical one to call."

"No. So far there has been no time. You stay here. I'll go back in the cafe and use the phone." Toler left Sarn and Ahna and made his way through the shadows.

"I'm back for a minute, Farz. Has anyone been asking for Ahna?"

Farz looked up, surprised to see him. "Come on in quick and close that door. Right after you left, two men, real slick fellows, came in the front door and asked where Ahna had gone. Of course no one knew. I finally told them she had staggered through here like she was bad sick and went out the back. They went out the back too. They were pulling out laser guns when they went."

Fear gripped Toler. That meant those two—and maybe others—were out there in the park looking for Ahna.

"Where is your phone?"

There was a phone in the kitchen. The only number he knew was Sathel's office. Never in his wildest dreams had he thought he would need Sathel's private number or an emergency number! Toler was able to get past the first secretary. He was told by the second that he should call back the next day, that the government was closed for the night. Toler screamed at her not to hang up, that it was an emergency.

She continued to speak in her singsong inane voice and said, well, if it was a real emergency she would have her supervisor call him if he would only leave his name and number.

Toler gave her his name and the number of the cafe, hung up, and waited.

It seemed an eternity before the phone rang. Toler grabbed it.

"Yes?"

"Is this Captain Toler?"

"Yes, this is Toler. Who is this?"

"I am calling for Sathel's office."

"Let me speak to him! This is an emergency!"

"I'm sorry, but you can't speak to him tonight. If you will call back tomorrow, I'm sure we can get you an appointment."

"Listen, does Sathel know I've called?"

"He is not able to talk with you tonight. Good-bye." The anonymous voice hung up.

"Damn!" He didn't like the sound of things. One thing he was convinced of, he had better leave the phone and get the others away as soon as possible. Toler had an idea that the bad guys would be back real soon.

When he rejoined Sarn and Ahna, they told him that at least one man had been looking around through the park but had not seen them. Toler told them that

Sathel was not available at the moment and he didn't know what that meant: either Sathel had disowned Toler and responsibility for the mission or the other side was intercepting his calls.

"I've thought of where we can go," said Sarn. "It's not much, but at least it's a place where I think we can be safe for a while. And it's not too far from here."

After several knocks the door opened, and Tull's sleepy face peered blearily at the trio.

"Tull, it's Sam! I roomed with you once. Thank goodness you're still here!"

Tull squinted at Sarn until a spark of recognition showed. The door opened wider.

"Yeah, sure, uh, come on in. Bring your friends."

Tull's reticence evaporated when he realized he was hosting the captain of a spaceship. He thought the lady was nice looking and it was good to see his old roommate, but he was still first of all a space freak.

"I don't have a roommate now, or there wouldn't be any room here at all. But you can use the other bed. I've got a pillow you can use." He looked at Toler. "If you're not ready to go to sleep, we can talk."

"No, I think we are too tired," said Toler, and the others nodded. "If you get up before we do, please don't tell anyone we're here."

Toler and Ahna snuggled together on the single mattress while Sarn slept on a blanket and pillow on the floor. Although the events of the night had been exciting, they were exhausted. Within a short time all were asleep.

It was midmorning before they woke up. Tull had gone to work and left a note inviting them to make themselves comfortable and that they were welcome to stay as long as they wanted; he thought he could get another bed somewhere. After getting themselves together as best they could, Sam made some coffee and the three surveyed the day ahead of them.

"First thing is to call Sathel," Toler said. "After that, we'll have a much better idea of the situation."

"One way or the other," said Ahna, "I didn't like the runaround you got last night when you tried to call him."

Toler called from the phone in the hallway. Fortunately everyone living on the floor had gone to work and he didn't have to be concerned about anyone overhearing his conversation. This time he was able to get through to Sathel's private secretary.

"This is Captain Toler. Would you please tell Sathel that I must see him at once?"

"Just one moment," the voice said matter-of-factly. "I'll see if he is available."

Toler waited impatiently while Sarn and Alma stood with him in the barren hallway.

"Maybe they're tracing the call," whispered Sam. Ahna paled at the thought, and Toler grimaced. It was hard to think as a fugitive must when you are an innocent, hardworking man minding your own business, he thought.

The voice came back. "Sathel will see you. Tell me where you are and he'll send a car."

"No, tell him we'll come to his office." Toler didn't like the idea of getting into one of those government vehicles, not knowing for sure who was waiting in it.

"I will tell him what you said. Hold on." In less than a minute she was back. "Sathel insists that he send a car. You'll be safer that way."

Ahna, with her head close to the phone, had overheard the conversation. She nodded her head to Toler. He gave the address to the secretary and hung up.

"Still the untrusting one, aren't you?" she asked, smiling.

"Aren't you a little suspicious? I may be paranoid, but I'd rather be that way and alive than trusting and dead."

"You may be right," conceded Ahna. "Let's cross the street and watch the car, see what they do. We don't have to get in."

They left the building and crossed the street to a small run-down cafe. It was not crowded yet, and they sat several tables back from the front windows where they had a clear view of the street and would not be easily seen themselves. They had hardly sat down when a large gray vehicle with dark windows drove up to the opposite curb.

"That was fast! They must have traced the call!"

"Don't jump to conclusions," said Ahna. "They probably just radioed a vehicle in this vicinity and asked them to pick us up."

It was impossible to see the occupants through the dark glass. The vehicle waited patiently while someone inside waited for Toler to come out of the building.

"Maybe they think you don't know they're here yet, and you're still in the building. Maybe in the bathroom," offered Sarn.

"We'll see how long they wait," Toler said.

Five minutes passed before the door on the other side of the vehicle opened. Someone walked up the steps to the door of the building and entered. Several more minutes passed before the front door opened again and the figure returned to the car. His face was square, hair neatly cut, and clothes nicely fitting. He did not smile.

"Looks like a typical government man," said Ahna. "They all look like that."

The vehicle pulled away from the curb and then suddenly lurched to a stop. Doors on both sides opened, and several men hit the street running toward the cafe.

"They've seen us!" exclaimed Ahna.

"Run out the back!" Toler said. He sprinted past the surprised waiter and slammed the front door shut, throwing the lock. Then he ran toward the back of the cafe where Ahna and Sarn waited for him. The waiter retreated behind the counter and disappeared. The few customers hid under their tables.

"They've split up and gone around to the back!" Ahna had watched the men leave the front of the cafe on the run after they saw the door locked in their face and their quarry head for the rear entrance.

"They've all gone around back," said Sarn. "While they're gone, why don't we see if there is anyone in the vehicle?"

Ahna and Toler looked at each other. "Good idea," said Toler. "Let's go see."

While the confused waiter watched over the top of the counter, the three hurried back to the front door, unlocked it, and ran to the vehicle, which was still idling. Laser in hand, Toler opened the door and jumped in. When Sarn stepped into the vehicle behind Ahna and closed the door, Toler was beside the driver's seat facing the rear and holding his gun on someone. His expression was both anger and amazement.

Ahna had taken the driver's seat, which was located in the middle. She was studying the console, apparently attempting to figure out how to operate the vehicle.

"Here they come," said Sarn. Several of the men emerged from the cafe, lasers in hand, and were looking at the vehicle, apparently waiting for orders. Someone barked something, and the men charged the car.

"Let's go!" yelled Sarn.

The first of the pursuers reached for the door handle just as Ahna located the accelerator and the vehicle roared off. The men stood in the street staring after them.

"I'm surprised they didn't fire at us," said Sarn. Turning his attention to Toler, he peered around the panel and into the back of the vehicle. Sitting in a chair, scowling at Toler, was a short fat man with a balding head. His eyes flashed angrily at Sarn and then back at Toler.

Sarn recoiled. "Squirb! How did you get here?"

Chapter 54

FINAL SCENE

"Who's Squirb?" asked Ahna as she guided the large rather formidable government vehicle down the street.

"One of Lybur's men. We met him on Earth when he was Derxter's henchman."

"Derxter?"

"Derxter was sent by Lybur to sabotage the messiah project."

"He almost killed us several times," Toler said grimly.

Ahna threw a quick glance at Toler. She bit her lip and frowned. Toler's adventures or misadventures on Earth would have to wait until later. She didn't have time to get upset at that moment.

"Where to, fellows?" she asked. "I want to hear all about Derxter and Squirb, but right now I want to know where to go with this crate."

"Take us to Sathel's office."

"We could call ahead," suggested Sarn. "Let him know we're coming."

"No thanks! That didn't work so well last time we tried it." Toler turned to Squirb. "Your people intercepted our calls, didn't they?"

Squirb turned his face away and muttered something obscene.

Toler moved to the back of the vehicle and grabbed the fat little man by the throat. He pushed him up against the wall and jammed the gun into his stomach. Squirb made a muffled squeal, and his eyes bulged.

"Answer my question!" Toler demanded. Sarn watched with fascination; he had never imagined his mentor capable of such aggression. Inwardly he cheered, and Ahna's expression hinted that she too was both surprised and pleased.

Squirb didn't have much stomach for violence of any kind and quickly squeaked a yes in answer. Toler loosened his grip, allowing the man to rub his throat.

"Now tell me what this is all about! Why did Lybur want to sabotage the Earth messiah?"

Squirb's lips trembled. "I don't know. I really don't. Not even Derxter knew."

Toler believed him. It didn't seem likely that Lybur would trust much information to his hirelings.

"There's a vehicle behind us," said Ahna. "It just pulled onto our street."

"Who are they? How do we tell who is on our side?" asked Sarn.

"We don't assume anyone is on our side," said Toler.

About a hundred yards behind them, the other gray vehicle was narrowing the distance between them.

"Watch Squirb," he said to Sarn. Toler moved to the front and examined the console. Its arrangement of switch function was basically like that found on a spaceship. He flipped a few toggles and spoke into a microphone, "This is Toler. I'm trying to communicate with the vehicle chasing us. Can you hear me?"

There was a pause. Then a puzzled voice answered, "Where are you, Toler? I repeat, give us your location."

"That's not the car behind us!" said Sarn. "That's somebody else!"

Another voice came in. "This is the car behind you. Pull over so that we may take you to Sathel immediately!"

Toler again identified himself and gave their location. Then he said, "We will not pull over. We will drive to the government offices ourselves. We welcome you to follow us and cover our rear."

A long pause, and then the voice from the second vehicle, "Let us pass you, and we will lead you to the government offices. We can travel faster that way."

"Come ahead," said Toler over the microphone. To Ahna he said, "Move to the side of the road but maintain speed. Be ready to stop suddenly and turn around if anything goes wrong."

The following vehicle moved up and to the left as it prepared to pass. Toler grabbed Squirb by the scruff of the neck and pulled him to a window on the left side.

"Get that window down, Sarn. If those guys are Lybur's men, maybe they'll hold back if they see we've got Squirb prisoner."

The car pulled alongside; its occupants could see Squirb framed in the window, a laser gun pointed at his head.

The voice from the other car came over the radio. "Take the man from the window and present yourself to us! We must make visual confirmation of your identity!"

"Hand me the microphone," said Toler. Sarn gave it to him; and in that instant, when Toler's hand was taken off him, Squirb threw himself to the floor. When the window of the other vehicle opened, Toler dove to the floor and yelled, "Turn it around, Ahna!"

Before Toler had the words completely out of his mouth, a burst from a laser in the other car cut through the open window and burned off the top of a seat. In the next instant Ahna braked and spun the vehicle around. This caused the second laser burst to miss the vehicle entirely. By the time the pursuers had slowed enough to turn around, Ahna had gained a sizable lead.

"Now we know," said Sarn. "Those are the bad guys." He looked at the burned seat. "I don't think they're trying to just stun us now."

Toler, kneeling on top of Squirb, spoke into the microphone, "This is Toler. The other car just fired on us. If there's anybody out there who can help, do it." Again he gave their location and direction of flight, realizing he was helping both friend and foe find them—If there was a friend listening.

Another vehicle appeared in front of them, blocking the street.

"Should I stop?" asked Ahna.

"No!"

"All right, boys, here we go!" and she swung the speeding car around to the right of the blockade, chasing several pedestrians off the walkway bordering the street. No sooner had she swerved back onto the street than still another vehicle appeared ahead of them. It lurched to a stop, and four men got out. Armed with shoulder lasers, they crouched beside their vehicle on the left side of the street. Their intent was apparently to fire directly at the driver as the vehicle tried to pass in the lane they occupied. They were not prepared when Ahna simply jumped back onto the walkway and zoomed past them on the other side of their vehicle.

"Nice going. Where did you learn to drive like that?"

"I'm just now learning," she said, "and I'm scared to death!"

"Don't stop now!" said Sarn.

Toler spoke into the microphone again, "This is Toler calling Sathel. We are proceeding to your office and will be arriving by the back door. Please be ready for us. We are being pursued by hostile forces."

To Ahna he said, "Ignore what I just said. Get on the main avenue that runs up to the government offices."

"It will be terribly crowded," Ahna said.

"Good."

At the next intersection she wheeled to the left and within a few minutes was on the main avenue, a very wide street able to accommodate twenty large vehicles abreast. It was usually crowded with business, pleasure, and government vehicles coming and going to the myriad of government offices, which housed the workings of an entire galaxy. The avenue led straight to the rather majestic capitol building. To either side of the capitol were administrative buildings, one of which housed Sathel, head of Xerxes Galaxy.

"Put on your siren and lights," said Sarn.

"No, don't," said Toler. "Not yet. That may serve only to cause people to stop. We need to flow with the traffic."

Flow was exactly what Ahna did, and it did not bother her in the least when she sideswiped other vehicles. She weaved through the traffic like she had been doing it all her life. The pursuers had been unable to close the distance between them.

"What do I do now?" she asked.

"That's Sathel's office ahead, the big building to the right of the capitol. Drive up to the front door!"

"What?" She looked at the tall fence, rows of shrubs, fountains, and streams of people between the avenue and the government building. "All right, but I think I'll turn on the siren and lights now. How do you do that?"

Sarn flipped the switches, which he had already identified; and the gray vehicle leaped the curb, lights flashing and siren screaming. As it bulled over the fence, people looked up to see the metal monster bearing down on them across the well-manicured grounds. No encouragement was required to send them leaping and sprawling out of the way. By the time Ahna pulled up in front of the offices of the head of Xerxes Galaxy, armed guards had swarmed out of the building and surrounded them.

"Whew!" Ahna sighed and slumped in her seat.

"That was terrific!" exclaimed Sarn.

"I think I must change my clothes!" said Squirb, lying on the floor. "I have never been so frightened!"

"I hope we're at the right place," said Toler. "I don't want to do any more riding today!"

Within a short time, Toler, Ahna, and Sarn were sitting in Sathel's office waiting for him to speak. He stood at his window watching the ducks, which were making a good deal of noise as they strutted down the lawn toward the pond. They seemed more nettled today than usual, he thought. But then today had been a more exciting day than usual. He turned to his visitors. "I hear you've had a rather rousing day. Did it go well?"

"First I want to know about Gen. Is he all right?" Toler asked.

"Yes, although a little worn, I'm afraid. He was kidnapped after Squirb returned. Lybur thought Gen would know what had happened on Earth. He figured if anyone had any information that might be useful to him, it would be that newshound, Gen. He probably thought a hostage might be handy to have just in case." Sathel smiled. "But we upset his game and got Gen out. We bribed his head henchman, Vashmil, paid him more than Lybur did." Sathel chuckled smugly. "I enjoyed that a great deal. Oh, Gen can't be with us right now, but he did say something about a drink at Dak's later tonight."

Toler visibly relaxed and cleared his throat. "Now I can say that the day is ending well!"

"I must apologize to you—to all of you—for the inhospitable reception given to you upon your return. You see, I just didn't receive your communications because they were intercepted by others. I didn't know you had returned."

"Like the attempts to contact you once we were here?"

"Yes, precisely. Now I suppose you are wanting an explanation of all this?"

"That, sir, is the most profound understatement of the century." Toler's mouth twitched, betraying his anger.

Sathel sat on the edge of his desk. His gray hair seemed white in the light from the window. The creases in his face were deeper, and he looked older than his public pictures portrayed him. His eyes, however, sparkled with vivacity, evidence of his vigorous interest in life.

"For many years I have been fascinated by the messiah phenomenon. As a young man, I collected everything I could on the subject. Finally it came to me that, as a serious student, I should be able to predict such an event. If I could do that, then I was well on my way to understanding the ways in which the power works.

"My first clue came about twenty-five years ago. An explorer, one of those wild, devil-may-care adventurers, happened to stop off at Earth. One of the things he brought back with him was a copy of a diary. He had made a copy of it—lucky he did. It was stolen by a native the same night."

Toler's eyes brightened. "I know what you are going to tell us. The diary was written by an officer of one of our ships, which crash-landed on Earth a thousand years ago. The captain and his crew settled in and interbred with the natives."

"And how did you know that?" Sathel's brows were raised.

"We have a friend on Earth who has the original diary. At one time Derxter had it, but Sarn managed to get it away."

"Thanks to Aleah."

"Your trip sounds like fascinating telling. Some evening soon I want you to come to the house where I can sit back and leisurely hear your tales."

"Pardon me, sir. Please go on."

"Yes, well, when I discovered that bit of knowledge, my curiosity really heated up. You may recall what was in the diary. Essentially its author complained about the presence of evil on Earth. That in itself was of little import as it could have been written by a chronic malcontent. But when you consider that the awareness of an evil presence had been consistently reported before on planets that subsequently had messiahs, then you can understand my excitement.

"So I went to the archives and checked out the crew list of that ship and discovered, as I had hoped, that the unhappy author was a sensitive."

Sathel smiled at his guests, letting this bit of knowledge sink in.

"Chances were he really did sense the presence of evil," said Sarn. "I know that feeling," he said, unsmiling.

"Earth is going to have a messiah someday, I concluded," continued Sathel with a satisfied smile. "Besides, I was desperate for a lead and was ready to try anything!

"And then"—he raised a finger for emphasis—"I discovered another piece of information, and this was the clincher. In a report put out by the Science people, there was a short documentation on an unusual star spotted over Earth several years before. The report was one of those little fillers they put in journals, the kind that pricks your interest and then you forget it."

Sathel now paced as he talked. This was his favorite of all subjects, and his face flushed as he spoke, "When I researched the exact time of the star's appearance, it was a simple matter to calculate the date of the messiah's projected appearance."

"Oh?" Ahna was puzzled. "How so?"

"In the other cases of recorded messiahs, they always appeared thirty years after the star's visit."

"Sounds like the star fertilizes a planet and the gestation period is thirty years," Ahna reflected.

"I've not heard it put just that way before," mused Sathel. "I must remember that."

Sathel continued, "The next thing I had to do was find out where on Earth this messiah was likely to appear. So I sent an undercover expedition to Earth with the ostensible purpose of cataloguing species development or some such thing but whose real goal was to gather evidence relevant to the messiah prelude. After all, if I didn't know where it would take place, it would be difficult to send an expedition to confirm its existence when it did happen. Well, lucky me!

"My team located a people who believed that they had been chosen to receive this messiah." Sathel raised his brow in question. "Now that he has finally come, are they satisfied with him?"

Toler shrugged. "Some were. Some weren't. Most didn't care. Messiahs come and go, and life goes on."

"As you well know, your job, Toler, was to observe this man and confirm that it did, in fact, happen like I thought it would. Ideally you would have filmed and taped the events, but as you know, we can't ethically do that sort of thing. I do look forward to reading your report."

"It's longer than intended. But there wasn't much else to do on the return trip," Toler offered.

"Splendid! I shall enjoy it even more. But we are here now to enlighten you. I shall be enlightened later."

"Excuse me, sir, but how come was I chosen for the crew?" asked Sarn. "Toler wasn't too happy about me at first because of my inexperience. Was there a reason you chose me?"

Sathel smiled. "I wondered how that choice went over with you, Toler. Not too well, I suspected." Toler made a wry grin. "This may sound silly, Sarn, but I wanted someone who was not known. Remember, I wanted to get this off the ground with a minimum of notice. Also, I wanted someone with a fresh outlook, and somehow it just seemed like a good idea to pick someone from the OBA steps. What caused me to choose you was one of your references on file. It said something about an interest in religion, and I thought that might make you a more motivated observer." Sathel grinned. "Now that I explain it, the choice sounds like a silly whim, doesn't it?" He shrugged and looked puzzled. "I really don't know why I chose you, Sarn, other than what I just explained."

"Why did Lybur want to sabotage the Messiah?" asked Toler. "That is the one question that has bothered me the most even before we landed on Earth."

"Good question. I knew we would get around to Lybur." Sathel's expression lost its pleasant cast and became hard and the facial lines indelible. He tensed, and his voice almost trembled. "Lybur!" He walked across the room before speaking again, taking time to regain control of his feelings.

"I wondered the same thing. At first he tried to dissuade me from sending anyone to Earth. It disturbed him greatly that I might have sent someone there, and this was puzzling. Then when I discovered he had already launched his own team—before you left, as you know—I began to suspect he was up to foul play and didn't want any witnesses to whatever he intended to do on Earth."

Anger crossed Sathel's face as he talked. "He threatened me if I sent an expedition. He said he would reveal the whole thing and I would be publicly embarrassed."

"How would that be embarrassing?" asked Ahna.

"Because some important people in the galaxy would be offended that their chosen leader was dabbling in theological gobbledygook and sending missions to disrupt life on developing planets. The ethics are strong on that point. If I influence the life on Earth today, then who knows, maybe next week I'll be meddling in someone's business here in Xerxes. My motives could have been easily misconstrued," Sathel said, "especially if his plot was successful. Lybur planned a messianic abortion—the messier the better—which he could blame on me."

"Didn't he know they always get killed anyway?" asked Sarn.

"I suppose he knew it but probably didn't really believe it. And even if he did, he didn't want to take a chance that this would be the first time a messiah lived to a ripe old age.

"But then the more I was around Lybur—we had some terrible disagreements—the more I became aware of my own feelings toward him. At first I thought I intensely disliked him simply because he is a noxious personality. Then I began to see that it was more than that. There was something about him, a presence, if you will, that pushed my uneasy button. It was like he was exuding evil vibrations."

Sarn spoke up, "I never heard the word evil very much until this trip, and now it's hard to talk without using it."

"After I was with Lybur, I would be reminded of the old diary, the author's description of a presence of evil. I wondered if Lybur was the carrier for such a presence."

"If so, and if Derxter was also a carrier, then they were merely symptoms or the material manifestations of a larger evil presence. Does that make sense?" Toler asked.

Sarn and Sathel nodded; Ahna rolled her eyes to the ceiling.

"But knowing that he was being used by an evil force didn't help me to like him any better."

"You said something a while ago," said Ahna, "which raises a question with me. If history tells us that messiahs appear on planets that have prior evil tenants, does that mean that Bigor is due to get a messiah?"

"I would think that one man, Lybur, would hardly constitute a sick planet," said Toler.

Sathel continued, "It came to me one night after I had argued with Lybur that if messiahs were delivered—or conceived—on 'sick' planets, then there must be a power opposite evil, a good, if you will. The purpose of a messiah must be to serve as an antidote for an ill planet. Not as a magical cure but as an antibody, a source by which a race can overcome evil, if they will.

"And if all that was true, then maybe Lybur was being used by this evil force to wreck the messianic inoculation on Earth. Perhaps this was a trial run for a new strategy. Or perhaps this occurs every time there is a messiah."

Ahna was fascinated by the conversation. "So there is something to the ageless conflict between good and evil."

"So it seems."

"What happened to Lybur?" asked Sam.

"Lybur, like all his hired hands, is in custody. Since you came in a while ago, inelegant and unannounced, we rounded up the lot of them. We were poised to do it anyway, and the events of the day gave us our imperative." He shook his head. "I had no idea they had spread their tentacles so far and deep. And I am embarrassed that my phone calls were being intercepted. After discovering that Lybur had learned of the Messiah's appointment on Earth through his spies in my office, I made some adjustments but obviously didn't go far enough."

"Pardon me for saying so," said Ahna, "but as interesting as all this sounds, doesn't it come down to superstition and extrasensory theory flying around in the wind? It's an intriguing discussion, but I'm a scientist, and I'm beginning to feel embarrassed for you."

Toler cringed as she spoke to Sathel in her high-handed manner. *Ah, but that was Ahna,* he thought. *She has to tell it like she sees it.*

Unexpectedly Sarn came to the defense. "It's hard to explain about this good and evil conflict unless you've been there on the frontlines. If you could have been there, seen things happen between the Messiah and evil powers, you couldn't have helped but believe it. In a way, Earth was the frontline in this conflict, and everything was clearer, stood out better where you could see it." He looked at Toler, and Toler met his eyes. They had shared events that could never be adequately explained to others.

"Consider this," said Sathel. "Consider that each of us is a battleground of this good-evil conflict. There are times when we are good people and other days when we are rotten. Temptation stalks us constantly. Do you buy that?"

Ahna shrugged. "I suppose. I might change the semantics, but the idea is one we all experience."

"If there can be a battle within each of us, does it not make sense that there can also be a larger battlefield, one which involves a whole planet? To me that is clear."

"I have read about outlaw planets, empires that were bent on conquest and destruction. Maybe they didn't get their messiah in time," Toler pondered.

Anna asked, "Just for the sake of discussion—not that I believe any of this—if messiahs are being placed on planets as an antibody against an evil virus, then who is doing it? Who is putting the messiahs there? That's what I want somebody to tell me!"

Sathel smiled gently. "The power."

"Are you saying you think there is a god behind all this?" Anna asked incredulously. She glanced at Toler for support of her doubt, for the two of them had always scoffed at anything having to do with the supernatural. He caught her eye and slowly nodded.

"I would much rather have an alternative explanation," said Sathel, "one that is more scientific. This one about a supernatural power is really too vague and hard to get hold of. Who do you think is doing it?"

Ahna grunted. That was her acknowledgment that she had no answer and would have to think about the matter.

"Hey! I've got a great idea!" Sarn exclaimed. "The next time one of those stars pops up, you, Ahna, can pack your bag and go with Toler and me to investigate. There are some questions you have that can be answered only by being there."

"And now," said Sathel, "I think you must be tired and need your rest. I have things to do what with these mass arrests and all that entails. I will notify you about getting together again. Very soon."

"One more question, please," said Ahna. "Do you have any information about where the next messiah will materialize?" She reached for Toler's hand. "I might be persuaded to go."

"Yes, as a matter of fact, I do. A strange star happened to appear for a short time above our own planet."

Three mouths dropped open in unison. "Bigor?"

"Yes. It caused a stir for a while. Lots of discussion about it, nobody able to come up with a good explanation of it. And then one day it was gone. Don't you remember that?"

"When was that?" asked Toler. "Seems like I recall something about that."

"Just over twenty years ago," said Sathel.

"Where on Bigor?" asked Ahna.

Sathel smiled enigmatically. "That, my friends, I am not prepared to say. You will know soon enough in roughly ten years."

Ahna's eyes brightened. "Thank you, but I think I'll research the placement of that star. There'll be something in the library about it. I recall the flap but didn't pay too much attention to it."

"This is exciting!" said Toler. "Bigor gets its own messiah. But tell me, fellows, what do you do while you're waiting for a messiah to come?"

"Regular stuff?" asked Sarn.

Toler took the arms of Ahna and Sarn and ushered them to the door. "Sounds like a question in need of discussion with Gen at Dak's Bar."

Printed in the United States
By Bookmasters